Ralph Waldo Emerson

The Best of Ralph Waldo Emerson

Essays • Poems • Addresses

Published for the Classics Club® by

WALTER J. BLACK, INC. · ROSLYN, N. Y.

PRINTED IN THE UNITED STATES OF AMERICA

Contents

Introduction

We have heard a good deal lately about the American way of life and its concern for the individual. Simply stated, the momentous question of our time is whether a man shall control his own affairs or obey the orders of some central authority. Since the Declaration of Independence asserted that all men are created equal, no one has spoken more eloquently in defense of the individual than Ralph Waldo Emerson. His *Essays*, published just one hundred years ago, emphatically urge the "man in the street"—the phrase is Emerson's—to know his own worth: a true man is the very center of the universe. Government, society, and nature itself revolve about him.

The state may follow how it can,
As Olympus follows Jove.

"Trust thyself: every heart vibrates to that iron string."

Emerson was born in 1803 in Boston, where his father, the Reverend William Emerson, was pastor of the First Church. Although there were seven ministers among his ancestors, this side of his inheritance must not be over-estimated, for his maternal grandfather was a "cooper and distiller," and the first of the Emersons, who came to America in 1635, was a baker. There were five other children, and when the father died, in 1811, life was far from easy for the family. Nevertheless, Ralph (or Waldo, as he preferred to be called) managed to attend the Boston Latin School and work his way through Harvard by running errands and waiting on table. After graduating in 1820 he taught in a girls' school for a few years before entering the

Harvard Divinity School to study for the ministry. Licensed to preach in 1826, he was invited three years later to become pastor of the Second Church in Boston. He also followed his father's footsteps as chaplain of the Massachusetts Senate.

In New England the Church had gone very far since the days of its Puritan founders. The Calvinist doctrine of the Trinity had gradually given way to a Unitarian concept of God in One Person. This was the faith in which Emerson was brought up and which he held for twenty-nine years. But he had not been long in his pastorate before even the Unitarian theology seemed too limited. He began to think of God as a completely impersonal moral force pervading the world, the "law for man," a spiritual truth transcending natural law or "law for thing." God, he believed, was perceived directly by an intuition that transcended the power of the senses or of reason. From this Emerson and his friends were soon being called Transcendentalists. It was impossible to reconcile these new beliefs with the more precise dogmas of the Unitarians. In 1832, with sincere regret on both sides, Emerson resigned the charge of his congregation.

After a trip abroad, during which he met Thomas Carlyle, he settled down at Concord. Here he wrote his first book, *Nature* (1836), which contains the clearest statement of his philosophy. "Our age is retrospective," he began. While the foregoing generations beheld the world face to face, we see it only through their eyes. "Why should not we also enjoy an original relation to the universe? . . . The sun shines today also. There is more wool and flax in the fields. There are new lands, new men, new thoughts. Let us demand our own works and laws and worship."

The universe, according to Emerson, consists of the Soul and Nature—the *Me* and the *Not-Me*; by submitting himself to Nature's influence man can sometimes enter into a kind of mystical communion with the divine spirit. "Standing on the bare ground—my head bathed by the blithe air, and uplifted into infinite space—all mean egotism vanishes. I become a transparent eyeball; I am nothing; I see all; the currents of the Universal

Being circulate through me; I am part or parcel of God." This Universal Being, which Emerson usually calls the Over-Soul, permeates everything. It is the only reality; and the total experience of life brings the thoughtful person to realize that it underlies all the varying appearances of the world. "To this one end of Discipline all parts of nature conspire."

Self-reliance is the first lesson Emerson drew from this philosophy. Man need go no longer skulking through the world like a trespasser in Eden; he is "part or parcel of God." "The world exists for you," Emerson told him. "All that Adam had, all that Caesar could, you have and can do. . . . Build therefore your own world."

This new world was not to follow the old crude model; an imitation would be unworthy in one whose inspiration comes from the very Source. The new world could be founded only on the self-reliant man's intuitive perception of life. In *The American Scholar*, an address he delivered before the Phi Beta Kappa Society at Harvard in 1837, Emerson called for complete intellectual independence. "We have listened too long to the courtly muses of Europe," he declared. American literature must turn from the great, the remote, the romantic. "I embrace the common, I explore and sit at the feet of the familiar, the low. Give me insight into today, and you may have the antique and future worlds. What would we really know the meaning of? The meal in the firkin; the milk in the pan; the ballad in the street; the news of the boat; the glance of the eye; the form and the gait of the body." The scholar who understands the simplest matter, who sees deep into the center of it, realizes that the Over-Soul is there as everywhere else.

> *"Who telleth one of my meanings,*
> *Is master of all I am."*

Although Emerson himself was an omnivorous reader of ancient, modern, and even the oriental literatures, the scholar he portrays will not rely primarily upon books for knowledge. Their influence is that of the past. Colleges, in the same way, he will use only for learning the rudiments; real education begins where they leave off. The true scholar is no cloistered bookworm; he takes an active part in the affairs of the world. Experience is his language, Life, his dictionary. He is the world's eye, the world's heart, perceiving the truth that lies behind appearances and discovering in his own mind the secrets of all minds.

Nor is his way an easy one. Poverty, neglect, even the hostility of society are the common penalty for those who dare to be themselves. He must therefore not wonder that he seems to stand alone. All men aspire to the highest, and most of them spend their lives seeking money and power only because they see nothing higher. There lies the scholar's duty: "Wake them and they shall quit the false good and leap to the true." "If the single man plant himself indomitably on his instincts and there abide, the huge world will come round to him."

In 1838, when the seniors of the Harvard Divinity School invited him to address them, Emerson applied these same principles to religion. Truth, he said, is known by intuition, not revelation. Without denying the divinity of Christ, he insisted upon the divinity in all men. Without disputing the miracles of the saints, he declared the blossoming of clover and the falling of rain equally miraculous. "It is the office of the true teacher to show that God is, not was; that He speaketh, not spake."

Such heterodoxy caused consternation in the Faculty. Some of the "stern old war-gods" merely shook their heads; others openly attacked Emerson's radical philosophy. It was nearly thirty years before he was invited to speak at Harvard again. He took no part in the controversy that ensued. Exclusion from pulpits where he used to be welcome gave him time to work on his *Essays*, the first series of which appeared in 1841; it was a fine example of his theory of compensation.

Still, he had to support his family somehow. His books, even at the height of his fame, brought him no more than $600 a year.

To supplement his income he turned to lecturing. It was the age of the lyceum, when every community had its lecture courses. For these Emerson was in great demand; the ideas that were so shocking from the pulpit proved to be very inspiring from the platform. His tours were extended farther and farther as new railways were built. New York, Philadelphia, and Washington were followed in time by Pittsburgh and Cincinnati, Chicago and Milwaukee, and, in 1855, across the Mississippi into Iowa. In 1871, two years after the Union Pacific was finished, he was lecturing in California.

Except for the occasional adventures of travel in those days, his life passed with little incident. His first wife, Ellen Tucker, died in 1831, before he resigned his pastorate. In 1835 he married Lydia Jackson, by whom he had four children. Waldo, the eldest son, died at the age of six; Emerson's grief is reflected in the poem "Threnody." In 1847 he went again to England, where he renewed his acquaintance with Carlyle and lectured to enthusiastic audiences.

Success abroad increased his reputation at home, both as lecturer and author. The *Essays*, of which the first series appeared in 1841, the second, in 1844, were followed by *Poems* in 1847, *Representative Men* in 1850, and *English Traits* in 1856. Half a dozen other volumes were issued during his lifetime, but after 1860 he wrote little that was new. His fame was then secure. The prophet was honored in his own country. Earnest young disciples made pilgrimages to Concord. Wild-eyed cranks strove in vain to enlist his support for their projects. Firmly, but without offense, he held himself aloof; he had taken his stand, and the world had at length come round. Harvard, in 1866, gave him the LL.D. degree and soon after made him a member of the Board of Overseers.

In 1872, when his house was partially destroyed by fire, his friends made it possible for him to take a trip to Egypt while it was rebuilt. His mind was sinking slowly into senescence. Within a few years he was forced to give up writing altogether, because his "pen refused to spell." He suffered from a curious aphasia that made him unable to recall the names of the simplest objects or of his oldest friends. However, he remained perfectly serene until his death, which occurred in 1882, just a month before his eightieth birthday.

To many readers of the *Essays* Emerson seems cold. The atmosphere he inhabits is too lofty for ordinary mortals; they recoil from a man who can suggest treating his friends like his books: "I would have them where I can find them, but I seldom use them." Other readers, disturbed by his undeviating optimism, feel that he ignores the problem of evil in the world. Carlyle tried to open Emerson's eyes by taking him through the London slums. As they walked along, each street more miserable than the one before, Carlyle would ask: "Do ye believe in the divil noo?"

But Emerson's idealism, though it forms the core of his philosophy, must not be overemphasized. His practical side—sound Yankee shrewdness—was also strongly developed. His praise of the man who hitched his wagon to a star was not a transcendental fancy; it was genuine admiration of a tide-mill on the seashore, which "engages the assistance of the moon like a hired hand to grind and wind and pump and saw and split stone and roll iron." Self-reliance was no idle advice from one who had earned his way through college. He knew from experience the penalty for being oneself. He knew better than to count on a stroke of luck to raise his spirits. "Nothing can bring you peace but yourself. Nothing can bring you peace but the triumph of principles."

In counseling independence Emerson was urging, not indifference to social obligations, but a more serious conception of them. "Solitude is impracticable," he wrote, "and society fatal. We must keep our head in the one and our hands in the other." While he took an active part in the affairs of Concord, except for the anti-slavery movement he held aloof from the many reforms—vegetarianism, woman's rights, temperance, and so forth

—that were springing up like mushrooms. "They are partial," he said in his lecture on New England reformers. "They lose their way; in the assault on the kingdom of darkness they expend all their energy on some accidental evil and lose their sanity and power of benefit. It is of little moment that one or two or twenty errors of our social system be corrected, but of much that the man be in his senses."

Emerson's political theory challenges the modern reader's attention as clearly as it did a century ago. It is not fair to call it impractical simply because it is still unrealized; on that ground one might dismiss the Sermon on the Mount. Emerson thought of government and law as growing things. "Government has been a fossil; it should be a plant. I conceive that the office of statute law should be to express and not to impede the mind of mankind. New thoughts, new things." Distinguishing carefully between personal rights, which are equal for all, and property rights, which are very unequal, Emerson sees something stronger than a majority of votes. There is another law, a law of things, a moral force that will not be set aside. "The wise know that foolish legislation is a rope of sand which perishes in the twisting; that the State must follow and not lead the character and progress of the citizen; the strongest usurper is quickly got rid of; and they only who build on Ideas build for eternity; and that the form of government which prevails is the expression of what cultivation exists in the population which permits it. The law is only a memorandum."

Tracing the history of governments from the patriarchal, despotic, and feudal to the republican, Emerson finds that trade has been the principle of liberty; trade planted America and destroyed feudalism. But that change is not completed. "In consequence of the revolution in the state of society wrought by trade, Government in our times is beginning to wear a clumsy and cumbrous appearance," he told the Young American in 1844. In the scramble of parties for the public purse, the main duties of the State have been omitted: "the duty to instruct the ignorant, to supply the poor with work and with good guidance." Emerson thought he saw a hopeful sign in the cooperative experiments like Fruitlands and Brook Farm, which had recently been organized. But the strength of any union is derived from the character of the Individual. "The wise and just man will always feel that he stands on his own feet; that he imparts strength to the State, not receives security from it; and that if all went down, he and such as he would quite easily combine in a new and better constitution."

The older generation of Emerson's day mistrusted him as a radical, tearing the foundations from under their lives. They used *transcendental* as a term of derision applied to anything fantastic or contrary to common sense. But their children understood what he meant. James Russell Lowell described the walk back to Cambridge on a crisp winter night, after listening to "that thrilling voice of his, so charged with subtle meaning and subtle music." "Did they say he was disconnected? So were the stars, that seemed larger to our eyes, still keen with that excitement, as we walked homeward with prouder stride over the creaking snow. And were *they* not knit together by a higher logic than our mere sense could master?"

In Brooklyn a carpenter named Walt Whitman looked at the world in a new light after reading Emerson and set out to embrace the common, to explore and sit at the feet of the familiar, the low. Strong and content, he traveled the open road.

I inhale great draughts of space,
The east and the west are mine, and the
north and the south are mine.
I am larger, better than I thought,
I did not know I held so much goodness.

In Amherst a lively young girl named Emily Dickinson read Emerson and withdrew from society to sit in her room writing down the thoughts that came to her—"telegrams from God."

The Soul selects her own society,
Then shuts the door.

Imperceptibly Emerson's ideas passed into general currency. His phrases became familiar quotations. Today his influence has spread so wide that, like atmospheric pressure, we are unaware of it. But it has played a vast part in shaping the American way of life.

Ralph Waldo Emerson

Edited and Arranged

BY GORDON S. HAIGHT, PH.D.

Concord Hymn

SUNG AT THE COMPLETION OF THE BATTLE MONUMENT

JULY 4, 1837

BY THE rude bridge that arched the flood,
  Their flag to April's breeze unfurled,
Here once the embattled farmers stood
  And fired the shot heard round the world.

The foe long since in silence slept;
  Alike the conqueror silent sleeps;
And Time the ruined bridge has swept
  Down the dark stream which seaward creeps.

On this green bank, by this soft stream,
  We set today a votive stone;
That memory may their deed redeem,
  When, like our sires, our sons are gone.

Spirit, that made those heroes dare
  To die, and leave their children free,
Bid Time and Nature gently spare
  The shaft we raise to them and thee.

1837

The American Scholar

AN ORATION DELIVERED BEFORE THE PHI BETA KAPPA SOCIETY, AT CAMBRIDGE, AUGUST 31, 1837.

MR. PRESIDENT AND GENTLEMEN:

I greet you on the recommencement of our literary year. Our anniversary is one of hope and, perhaps, not enough of labor. We do not meet for games of strength or skill, for the recitation of histories, tragedies, and odes, like the ancient Greeks; for parliaments of love and poesy, like the Troubadours; nor for the advancement of science, like our contemporaries in the British and European capitals. Thus far, our holiday has been simply a friendly sign of the survival of the love of letters amongst a people too busy to give to letters any more. As such it is precious as the sign of an indestructible instinct. Perhaps the time is already come when it ought to be, and will be, something else; when the sluggard intellect of this continent will look from under its iron lids and fill the postponed expectation of the world with something better than the exertions of mechanical skill. Our day of dependence, our long apprenticeship to the learning of other lands, draws to a close. The millions that around us are rushing into life cannot always be fed on the sere remains of foreign harvests. Events, actions arise that must be sung, that will sing themselves. Who can doubt that poetry will revive and lead in a new age, as the star in the constellation Harp, which now flames in our zenith, astronomers announce, shall one day be the polestar for a thousand years?

In this hope I accept the topic which not only usage but the nature of our association seem to prescribe to this day—the AMERICAN SCHOLAR. Year by year we come up hither to read one more chapter of his biography. Let us inquire what light new days and events have thrown on his character and his hopes.

It is one of those fables which out of an unknown antiquity convey an unlooked-for wisdom, that the gods, in the beginning, divided Man into men, that he might be more helpful to himself; just as the hand was divided into fingers, the better to answer its end.

The old fable covers a doctrine ever new and sublime; that there is One Man—present to all particular men only partially, or through one faculty; and that you must take the whole society to find the whole man. Man is not a farmer or a professor or an engineer, but he is all. Man is priest and scholar and statesman and producer and soldier. In the *divided* or social state these functions are parceled out to individuals, each of whom aims to do his stint of the joint work, whilst each other performs his. The fable implies that the individual, to possess himself, must sometimes return from his own labor to embrace all the other laborers. But, unfortunately, this original unit, this fountain of power, has been so distributed to multitudes, has been so minutely subdivided and peddled out, that it is spilled into drops and cannot be gathered. The state of society is one in which the members have suffered amputation from the trunk, and strut about, so many walking monsters—a good finger, a neck, a stomach, an elbow, but never a man.

Man is thus metamorphosed into a thing, into many things. The planter, who is Man sent out into the field to gather food, is seldom cheered by any idea of the true dignity of his ministry. He sees his bushel and his cart and nothing beyond, and sinks into the farmer, instead of Man on the farm. The tradesman scarcely ever gives an ideal worth to his work, but is ridden by the routine of his craft, and the soul is subject to dollars. The priest becomes a form; the attorney, a statute book; the mechanic, a machine; the sailor, a rope of the ship.

In this distribution of functions the scholar is the delegated intellect. In the right state he is *Man Thinking*. In the degenerate state, when the victim of society, he tends to become a mere thinker, or still worse, the parrot of other men's thinking.

In this view of him, as Man Thinking, the theory of his office is contained. Him Nature solicits with all her placid, all her monitory pictures; him the past instructs; him the future invites. Is not indeed every man a student, and do not all things exist for the student's behoof? And, finally, is not the true scholar the only true master? But the old oracle said, "All things have two handles: beware of the wrong one." In life, too often, the scholar errs with mankind and forfeits his privilege. Let us see him in his school, and consider him in reference to the main influences he receives.

I. The first in time and the first in importance of the influences upon the mind is that of nature. Every day, the sun; and, after sunset, Night and her stars. Ever the winds blow; ever the grass grows. Every day, men and women, conversing—beholding and beholden. The scholar is he of all men whom this spectacle most engages. He must settle its value in his mind. What is nature to him? There is never a beginning, there is never an end, to the inexplicable continuity of this web of God, but always circular power returning into itself. Therein it resembles his own spirit, whose beginning, whose ending, he never can find—so entire, so boundless. Far too as her splendors shine, system on system shooting like rays, upward, downward, without center, without circumference—in the mass and in the particle, Nature hastens to render account of herself to the mind. Classification begins. To the young mind everything is individual, stands by itself. By and by, it finds how to join two things and see in them one nature; then three, then three thousand; and so, tyrannized over by its own unifying instinct, it goes on tying things together, diminishing anomalies, discovering roots running under ground whereby contrary and remote things cohere and flower out from one stem. It presently learns that since the dawn of history there has been a constant accumulation and classifying of facts. But what is classification but the perceiving that these objects are not chaotic and are not foreign, but have a law which is also a law of the human mind? The astronomer discovers that geometry, a pure abstraction of the human mind, is the measure of planetary motion. The chemist finds proportions and intelligible method throughout matter; and science is nothing but the finding of analogy, identity, in the most remote parts. The ambitious soul sits down before each refractory fact; one after another reduces all strange constitutions, all new powers, to their class and their law and goes on forever to animate the last fiber of organization, the outskirts of nature, by insight.

Thus to him, to this schoolboy under the bending dome of day, is suggested that he and it proceed from one root; one is leaf and one is flower; relation, sympathy, stirring in every vein. And what is that root? Is not that the soul of his soul? A thought too bold; a dream too wild. Yet when this spiritual light shall have revealed the law of more earthly natures—when he has learned to worship the soul and to see that the natural philosophy that now is, is only the first gropings of its gigantic hand—he shall look forward to an ever-expanding knowledge as to a becoming creator. He shall see that nature is the opposite of the soul, answering to it part for part. One is seal and one is print. Its beauty is the beauty of his own mind. Its laws are the laws of his own mind. Nature then becomes to him the measure of his attainments. So much of nature as he is ignorant of, so much of his own mind does he not yet possess. And, in fine, the ancient precept, "Know thyself" and the modern precept, "Study nature," become at last one maxim.

II. The next great influence into the spirit of the scholar is the mind of the Past, in whatever form, whether of literature, of art, of institutions, that mind is inscribed. Books are the best type of the influence of the past, and perhaps we shall get at the truth—learn the amount of this influence more conveniently—by considering their value alone.

The theory of books is noble. The scholar of the first age received into him the world around; brooded thereon; gave it the new arrangement of his own mind and uttered it again. It came into him life; it went out from him truth. It came to him short-lived actions; it went out from him immortal thoughts. It came to him business; it went from him poetry. It was dead fact; now, it is quick thought. It can stand and it can go. It now endures, it now flies, it now inspires. Precisely in proportion to the depth of mind from which it issued, so high does it soar, so long does it sing.

Or, I might say, it depends on how far the process had gone, of transmuting life into truth. In proportion to the completeness of the distillation, so will the purity and imperishableness of the product be. But none is quite perfect. As no air-pump can by any means make a perfect vacuum, so neither can any artist entirely exclude the conventional, the local, the perishable from his book, or write a book of pure thought that shall be as efficient, in all respects, to a remote posterity as to contemporaries, or rather to the second age. Each age, it is found, must write its own books; or rather, each generation for the next succeeding. The books of an older period will not fit this.

Yet hence arises a grave mischief. The sacredness which attaches to the act of creation, the act of thought, is transferred to the record. The poet chanting was felt to be a divine man: henceforth the chant is divine also. The writer was a just and wise spirit: henceforward it is settled the book is perfect; as love of the hero corrupts into worship of his statue. Instantly the book becomes noxious: the guide is a tyrant. The sluggish and perverted mind of the multitude, slow to open to the incursions of Reason, having once so opened, having once received this book, stands upon it and makes an outcry if it is disparaged. Colleges are built on it. Books are written on it by thinkers, not by Man Thinking; by men of talent, that is, who start wrong, who set out from accepted dogmas, not from their own sight of principles. Meek young men grow up in libraries, believing it their duty to accept the views which Cicero, which Locke, which Bacon, have given; forgetful that Cicero, Locke, and Bacon were only young men in libraries when they wrote these books.

Hence, instead of Man Thinking, we have the bookworm. Hence the book-learned class, who value books, as such; not as related to nature and the human constitution but as making a sort of Third Estate with the world and the soul. Hence the restorers of readings, the emendators, the bibliomaniacs of all degrees.

Books are the best of things, well used; abused, among the worst. What is the right use? What is the one end which all means go to effect? They are for nothing but to inspire. I had better never see a book than to be warped by its attraction clean out of my own orbit and made a satellite instead of a system. The one thing in the world of value is the active soul. This every man is entitled to; this every man contains within him, although in almost all men obstructed and as yet unborn. The soul active sees absolute truth and utters truth, or creates. In this action it is genius; not the privilege of here and there a favorite, but the sound estate of every man. In its essence it is progressive. The book, the college, the school of art, the institution of any kind, stop with some past utterance of genius. This is good, say they—let us hold by this. They pin me down. They look backward and not forward. But genius looks forward; the eyes of man are set in his forehead, not in his hindhead; man hopes; genius creates. Whatever talents may be, if the man create not, the pure efflux of the Deity is not his; cinders and smoke there may be, but not yet flame. There are creative manners, there are creative actions and creative words; manners, actions, words, that is, indicative of no custom or authority but springing spontaneous from the mind's own sense of good and fair.

On the other part, instead of being its own seer, let it receive from another mind its truth, though it were in torrents of light, without periods of solitude, inquest, and self-recovery, and a fatal disservice is done. Genius is always sufficiently the enemy of genius by over-influence. The literature of every nation bears me witness. The English dramatic poets have Shakspearized now for two hundred years.

Undoubtedly there is a right way of reading, so it be sternly subordinated. Man Thinking must not be subdued by his instruments. Books are for the scholar's idle times. When he can read God directly, the hour is too precious to be wasted in other men's transcripts of their readings. But when the intervals of darkness come, as come they must—when the sun is hid and the stars withdraw their shining—we repair to the lamps which were kindled by their ray, to guide our steps to the East again, where the dawn is. We hear, that we may speak. The Arabian proverb says, "A fig tree, looking on a fig tree, becometh fruitful."

It is remarkable, the character of the pleasure we derive from the best books. They impress us with the conviction that one nature wrote and the same reads. We read the verses of one of the great English poets, of Chaucer, of Marvell, of Dryden, with the most modern joy—with a pleasure, I mean, which is in great part caused by the abstraction of all *time* from their verses. There is some awe mixed with the joy of our surprise, when this poet, who lived in some past world, two or three hundred years ago, says that which lies close to my own soul, that which I also had well-nigh thought and said. But for the evidence thence afforded to the philosophical doctrine of the identity of all minds, we should suppose some pre-established harmony, some foresight of souls that were to be, and some preparation of stores for their future wants, like the fact observed in insects, who lay up food before death for the young grub they shall never see.

I would not be hurried by any love of system, by any exaggeration of instincts, to underrate the Book. We all know that as the human body can be nourished on any food, though it were boiled grass and the broth of shoes, so the human mind can be fed by any knowledge. And great and heroic men have existed who had almost no other information than by the printed page. I only would say that it needs a strong head to bear that diet. One must be an inventor to read well. As the proverb says, "He that would bring home the wealth of the Indies must carry out the wealth of the Indies." There is then creative reading as well as creative writing. When the mind is braced by labor and invention, the page of whatever book we read becomes luminous with manifold allusion. Every sentence is doubly significant, and the sense of our author is as broad as the world. We then see, what is always true, that as the seer's hour of vision is short and rare among heavy days and months, so is its record, perchance, the least part of his volume. The discerning will read, in his Plato or Shakspeare, only that least part—only the authentic utterances of the oracle; all the rest he rejects, were it never so many times Plato's and Shakspeare's.

Of course there is a portion of reading quite indispensable to a wise man. History and exact science he must learn by laborious reading. Colleges, in like manner, have their indispensable office—to teach elements. But they can only highly serve us when they aim not to drill, but to create; when they gather from far every ray of various genius to their hospitable halls and by the concentrated fires set the hearts of their youth on flame. Thought and knowledge are natures in which apparatus and pretension avail nothing. Gowns and pecuniary foundations, though of towns of gold, can never countervail the least sentence or syllable of wit. Forget this, and our American colleges will recede in their public importance, whilst they grow richer every year.

III. There goes in the world a notion that the scholar should be a recluse, a valetudinarian—as unfit for any handiwork or public labor as a penknife for an axe. The so-called "practical men" sneer at speculative men as if, because they speculate or *see*, they could do nothing. I have heard it said that the clergy—who are always, more universally than any other class, the scholars of their day—are addressed as women; that the rough, spontaneous conversation of men they do not hear but only a mincing and diluted speech. They are often virtually disfranchised; and indeed there are advocates for their celibacy. As far as this is true of the studious classes, it is not just and wise. Action is with the scholar subordinate, but it is essential. Without it he is not yet man. Without it thought can never ripen into truth. Whilst the world hangs before the eye as a cloud of beauty, we cannot even see its beauty. Inaction is cowardice, but there can be no scholar without the heroic mind. The preamble of thought, the transition through which it passes from the unconscious to the conscious, is action. Only so much do I know as I have lived. Instantly we know whose words are loaded with life and whose not.

The world—this shadow of the soul, or *other me*—lies wide around. Its attractions are the keys which unlock my thoughts and make me acquainted with myself. I run eagerly into this resounding tumult. I grasp the hands of those next me, and take my place in the ring to suffer and to work, taught by an instinct that so shall the dumb abyss be vocal with speech. I pierce its order; I dissipate its fear; I dispose of it within the circuit of my expanding life. So much only of life as I know by experience, so much of the wilderness have I vanquished and planted, or so far have I extended my being, my dominion. I do not see how any man can afford, for the sake of his nerves and his nap, to spare any action in which he can partake. It is pearls and rubies to his discourse. Drudgery, calamity, exasperation, want, are instructors in eloquence and wisdom. The true scholar grudges every opportunity of action passed by as a loss of power. It is the raw material out of which the intellect molds her splendid products. A strange process too, this, by which experience is converted into thought as a mulberry leaf is converted into satin. The manufacture goes forward at all hours.

The actions and events of our childhood and youth are now matters of calmest observation. They lie like fair pictures in the air. Not so with our recent actions, with the business which we now have in hand. On this we are quite unable to speculate. Our affections as yet circulate through it. We no more feel or know it than we feel the feet, or the hand, or the brain of our body. The new deed is yet a part of life—remains for a time immersed in our unconscious life. In some contemplative hour it detaches itself from the life like a ripe fruit to become a thought of the mind. Instantly it is raised, transfigured; the corruptible has put on incorruption. Henceforth it is an object of beauty, however base its origin and neighborhood. Observe too the impossibility of antedating this act. In its grub state, it cannot fly, it cannot shine, it is a dull grub. But suddenly, without observation, the selfsame thing unfurls beautiful wings and is an angel of wisdom. So is there no fact, no event, in our private history, which shall not, sooner or later, lose its adhesive, inert form and astonish us by soaring from our body into the empyrean. Cradle and infancy, school and playground, the fear of boys, and dogs, and ferules, the love of little maids and berries, and many another fact that once filled the whole sky, are gone already; friend and relative, profession and party, town and country, nation and world, must also soar and sing.

Of course, he who has put forth his total strength in fit actions has the richest return of wisdom. I will not shut myself out of this globe of action, and transplant an oak into a flowerpot, there to hunger and pine; nor trust the revenue of some single faculty and exhaust one vein of thought, much like those Savoyards, who, getting their livelihood by carving shepherds, shepherdesses, and smoking Dutchmen for all Europe, went out one day to the mountain to find stock and discovered that they had whittled up the last of their pine trees. Authors we have, in numbers, who have written out their vein and who, moved by a commendable prudence, sail for Greece or Palestine, follow the trapper into the prairie, or ramble around Algiers, to replenish their merchantable stock.

If it were only for a vocabulary, the scholar would be covetous of action. Life is our dictionary. Years are well spent in country labors; in town; in the insight into trades and manufactures; in frank intercourse with many men and women; in science; in art; to the one end of mastering in all their facts a language by which to illustrate and embody our perceptions. I learn immediately from any speaker how much he has already lived, through the poverty or the splendor of his speech. Life lies behind us as the quarry from whence we get tiles and copestones for the masonry of today. This is the way to learn grammar. Colleges and books only copy the language which the field and the work-yard made.

But the final value of action, like that of books, and better than books, is that it is a resource. That great principle of Undulation in nature that shows itself in the inspiring and expiring of the breath; in desire and satiety; in the ebb and flow of the sea; in day and night; in heat and cold; and, as yet more deeply ingrained in every atom and every fluid, is known to us under the name of Polarity—these "fits of easy transmission and reflection," as Newton called them, are the law of nature because they are the law of spirit.

The mind now thinks, now acts, and each fit reproduces the other. When the artist has exhausted his materials, when the fancy no longer paints, when thoughts are no longer apprehended and books are a weariness—he has always the resource *to live*. Character is higher than intellect. Thinking is the function. Living is the functionary. The stream retreats to its source. A great soul will be strong to live, as well as strong to think. Does he lack organ or medium to impart his truths? He can still fall back on this elemental force of living them. This is a total act. Thinking is a partial act. Let the grandeur of justice shine in his affairs. Let the beauty of affection cheer his lowly roof. Those "far from fame," who dwell and act with him, will feel the force of his constitution in the doings and passages of the day better than it can be measured by any public and designed display. Time shall teach him that the scholar loses no hour which the man lives. Herein he unfolds the sacred germ of his instinct, screened from influence. What is lost in seemliness is gained in strength. Not out of those on whom systems of education have exhausted their culture comes the helpful giant to destroy the old or to build the new, but out of unhandseled [1] savage nature; out of terrible Druids and Berserkers come at last Alfred and Shakspeare.

I hear therefore with joy whatever is beginning to be said of the dignity and necessity of labor to every citizen. There is virtue yet in the hoe and the spade for learned as well as for unlearned hands. And labor is everywhere welcome; always we are invited to work; only be this limitation observed, that a man shall not for the sake of wider activity sacrifice any opinion to the popular judgments and modes of action.

I have now spoken of the education of the scholar by nature, by books, and by action. It remains to say somewhat of his duties.

They are such as become Man Thinking. They may all be comprised in self-trust. The office of the scholar is to cheer, to raise, and to guide men by showing them facts amidst appearances. He plies the slow, unhonored, and unpaid task of observation. Flamsteed and Herschel, in their glazed observatories, may catalogue the stars with the praise of all men, and the results being splendid and useful, honor is sure. But he, in his private observatory, cataloguing obscure and nebulous stars of the human mind, which as yet no man has thought of as such—watching days and months sometimes for a few facts, correcting

[1] Untried.

still his old records—must relinquish display and immediate fame. In the long period of his preparation he must betray often an ignorance and shiftlessness in popular arts, incurring the disdain of the able who shoulder him aside. Long he must stammer in his speech; often forego the living for the dead. Worse yet, he must accept—how often!—poverty and solitude. For the ease and pleasure of treading the old road, accepting the fashions, the education, the religion of society, he takes the cross of making his own, and, of course, the self-accusation, the faint heart, the frequent uncertainty and loss of time, which are the nettles and tangling vines in the way of the self-relying and self-directed; and the state of virtual hostility in which he seems to stand to society, and especially to educated society. For all this loss and scorn, what offset? He is to find consolation in exercising the highest functions of human nature. He is one who raises himself from private considerations and breathes and lives on public and illustrious thoughts. He is the world's eye. He is the world's heart. He is to resist the vulgar prosperity that retrogrades ever to barbarism, by preserving and communicating heroic sentiments, noble biographies, melodious verse, and the conclusions of history. Whatsoever oracles the human heart, in all emergencies, in all solemn hours, has uttered as its commentary on the world of actions—these he shall receive and impart. And whatsoever new verdict Reason from her inviolable seat pronounces on the passing men and events of today—this he shall hear and promulgate.

These being his functions, it becomes him to feel all confidence in himself and to defer never to the popular cry. He and he only knows the world. The world of any moment is the merest appearance. Some great decorum, some fetish of a government, some ephemeral trade, or war, or man, is cried up by half mankind and cried down by the other half, as if all depended on this particular up or down. The odds are that the whole question is not worth the poorest thought which the scholar has lost in listening to the controversy. Let him not quit his belief that a popgun is a popgun, though the ancient and honorable of the earth affirm it to be the crack of doom. In silence, in steadiness, in severe abstraction, let him hold by himself; add observation to observation, patient of neglect, patient of reproach, and bide his own time—happy enough if he can satisfy himself alone that this day he has seen something truly. Success treads on every right step. For the instinct is sure that prompts him to tell his brother what he thinks. He then learns that in going down into the secrets of his own mind he has descended into the secrets of all minds. He learns that he who has mastered any law in his private thoughts is master to that extent of all men whose language he speaks and of all into whose language his own can be translated. The poet, in utter solitude remembering his spontaneous thoughts and recording them, is found to have recorded that which men in crowded cities find true for them also. The orator distrusts at first the fitness of his frank confessions, his want of knowledge of the persons he addresses, until he finds that he is the complement of his hearers; that they drink his words because he fulfills for them their own nature; the deeper he dives into his privatest, secretest presentiment, to his wonder he finds this is the most acceptable, most public, and universally true. The people delight in it; the better part of every man feels, 'This is my music; this is myself.'

In self-trust all the virtues are comprehended. Free should the scholar be—free and brave. Free even to the definition of freedom, "without any hindrance that does not arise out of his own constitution." Brave; for fear is a thing which a scholar by his very function puts behind him. Fear always springs from ignorance. It is a shame to him if his tranquillity, amid dangerous times, arise from the presumption that, like children and women, his is a protected class; or if he seek a temporary peace by the diversion of his thoughts from politics or vexed questions, hiding his head like an ostrich in the flowering bushes, peeping into microscopes, and turning rhymes, as a boy whistles to keep his courage up. So is the danger a danger still; so is the fear worse.

Manlike let him turn and face it. Let him look into its eye and search its nature, inspect its origin—see the whelping of this lion —which lies no great way back; he will then find in himself a perfect comprehension of its nature and extent; he will have made his hands meet on the other side and can henceforth defy it and pass on superior. The world is his who can see through its pretension. What deafness, what stone-blind custom, what overgrown error you behold is there only by sufferance—by your sufferance. See it to be a lie, and you have already dealt it its mortal blow.

Yes, we are the cowed—we the trustless. It is a mischievous notion that we are come late into nature; that the world was finished a long time ago. As the world was plastic and fluid in the hands of God, so it is ever to so much of his attributes as we bring to it. To ignorance and sin it is flint. They adapt themselves to it as they may; but in proportion as a man has anything in him divine, the firmament flows before him and takes his signet and form. Not he is great who can alter matter, but he who can alter my state of mind. They are the kings of the world who give the color of their present thought to all nature and all art and persuade men by the cheerful serenity of their carrying the matter that this thing which they do is the apple which the ages have desired to pluck, now at last ripe and inviting nations to the harvest. The great man makes the great thing. Wherever Macdonald sits, there is the head of the table. Linnæus makes botany the most alluring of studies, and wins it from the farmer and the herbwoman; Davy, chemistry; and Cuvier, fossils. The day is always his who works in it with serenity and great aims. The unstable estimates of men crowd to him whose mind is filled with a truth, as the heaped waves of the Atlantic follow the moon.

For this self-trust, the reason is deeper than can be fathomed —darker than can be enlightened. I might not carry with me the feeling of my audience in stating my own belief. But I have already shown the ground of my hope, in adverting to the doctrine that man is one. I believe man has been wronged; he has wronged himself. He has almost lost the light that can lead him back to his prerogatives. Men are become of no account. Men in history, men in the world of today, are bugs, are spawn, and are called "the mass" and "the herd." In a century, in a millennium, one or two men; that is to say, one or two approximations to the right state of every man. All the rest behold in the hero or the poet their own green and crude being—ripened; yes, and are content to be less, so *that* may attain to its full stature. What a testimony, full of grandeur, full of pity, is borne to the demands of his own nature by the poor clansman, the poor partisan, who rejoices in the glory of his chief. The poor and the low find some amends to their immense moral capacity for their acquiescence in a political and social inferiority. They are content to be brushed like flies from the path of a great person, so that justice shall be done by him to that common nature which it is the dearest desire of all to see enlarged and glorified. They sun themselves in the great man's light and feel it to be their own element. They cast the dignity of man from their downtrod selves upon the shoulders of a hero, and will perish to add one drop of blood to make that great heart beat, those giant sinews combat and conquer. He lives for us, and we live in him.

Men, such as they are, very naturally seek money or power; and power because it is as good as money—the "spoils," so called, "of office." And why not? for they aspire to the highest, and this, in their sleepwalking, they dream is highest. Wake them and they shall quit the false good and leap to the true, and leave governments to clerks and desks. This revolution is to be wrought by the gradual domestication of the idea of Culture. The main enterprise of the world for splendor, for extent, is the upbuilding of a man. Here are the materials strewn along the ground. The private life of one man shall be a more illustrious monarchy, more formidable to its enemy, more sweet and serene in its influence to its friend, than any kingdom in history. For a man, rightly viewed, comprehendeth the particular natures of all men. Each philosopher, each bard, each actor, has only done for me, as by a delegate, what one day I can do for myself. The books which once we valued more than the apple of the eye we have quite exhausted. What is that but saying that we have come up with the point of view which the universal mind took through the eyes of one scribe; we have been that man and have passed on. First one, then another, we drain all cisterns and, waxing greater by all these supplies, we crave a better and more abundant food. The man has never lived that can feed us ever. The human mind cannot be enshrined in a person who shall set a barrier on any one side to this unbounded, unboundable empire. It is one central fire, which, flaming now out of the lips of Etna, lightens the capes of Sicily, and now out of the throat of Vesuvius, illuminates the towers and vineyards of Naples. It is one light which beams out of a thousand stars. It is one soul which animates all men.

But I have dwelt perhaps tediously upon this abstraction of the Scholar. I ought not to delay longer to add what I have to say of nearer reference to the time and to this country.

Historically, there is thought to be a difference in the ideas which predominate over successive epochs, and there are data for marking the genius of the Classic, of the Romantic, and now of the Reflective or Philosophical age. With the views I have intimated of the oneness or the identity of the mind through all individuals, I do not much dwell on these differences. In fact, I believe each individual passes through all three. The boy is a Greek; the youth, romantic; the adult, reflective. I deny not, however, that a revolution in the leading idea may be distinctly enough traced.

Our age is bewailed as the age of Introversion. Must that needs be evil? We, it seems, are critical; we are embarrassed with second thoughts; we cannot enjoy anything for hankering to know whereof the pleasure consists; we are lined with eyes; we see with our feet; the time is infected with Hamlet's unhappiness—

"Sicklied o'er with the pale cast of thought." It is so bad then? Sight is the last thing to be pitied. Would we be blind? Do we fear lest we should outsee nature and God, and drink truth dry? I look upon the discontent of the literary class as a mere announcement of the fact that they find themselves not in the state of mind of their fathers, and regret the coming state as untried; as a boy dreads the water before he has learned that he can swim. If there is any period one would desire to be born in, is it not the age of Revolution; when the old and the new stand side by side and admit of being compared; when the energies of all men are searched by fear and by hope; when the historic glories of the old can be compensated by the rich possibilities of the new era? This time, like all times, is a very good one, if we but know what to do with it.

I read with some joy of the auspicious signs of the coming days, as they glimmer already through poetry and art, through philosophy and science, through church and state.

One of these signs is the fact that the same movement which effected the elevation of what was called the lowest class in the state assumed in literature a very marked and as benign an aspect. Instead of the sublime and beautiful, the near, the low, the common, was explored and poetized. That which had been negligently trodden under foot by those who were harnessing and provisioning themselves for long journeys into far countries is suddenly found to be richer than all foreign parts. The literature of the poor, the feelings of the child, the philosophy of the street, the meaning of household life, are the topics of the time. It is a great stride. It is a sign—is it not?—of new vigor when the extremities are made active, when currents of warm life run into the hands and the feet. I ask not for the great, the remote, the romantic; what is doing in Italy or Arabia; what is Greek art, or Provençal minstrelsy; I embrace the common, I explore and sit at the feet of the familiar, the low. Give me insight into today, and you may have the antique and future worlds. What would we really know the meaning of? The meal in the firkin; the milk in the pan; the ballad in the street; the news of the boat; the glance of the eye; the form and the gait of the body—show me the ultimate reason of these matters; show me the sublime presence of the highest spiritual cause lurking, as always it does lurk, in these suburbs and extremities of nature; let me see every trifle bristling with the polarity that ranges it instantly on an eternal law; and the shop, the plough, and the ledger referred to the like cause by which light undulates and poets sing—and the world lies no longer a dull miscellany and lumber-room, but has form and order; there is no trifle, there is no puzzle, but one design unites and animates the farthest pinnacle and the lowest trench.

This idea has inspired the genius of Goldsmith, Burns, Cowper, and, in a newer time, of Goethe, Wordsworth, and Carlyle. This idea they have differently followed and with various success. In contrast with their writing, the style of Pope, of Johnson, of Gibbon, looks cold and pedantic. This writing is blood-warm. Man is surprised to find that things near are not less beautiful and wondrous than things remote. The near explains the far. The drop is a small ocean. A man is related to all nature. This perception of the worth of the vulgar is fruitful in discoveries. Goethe, in this very thing the most modern of the moderns, has shown us, as none ever did, the genius of the ancients.

There is one man of genius who has done much for this philosophy of life, whose literary value has never yet been rightly estimated—I mean Emanuel Swedenborg. The most imaginative of men, yet writing with the precision of a mathematician, he endeavored to engraft a purely philosophical Ethics on the popular Christianity of his time. Such an attempt, of course, must have difficulty which no genius could surmount. But he saw and showed the connection between nature and the affections of the soul. He pierced the emblematic or spiritual character of the visible, audible, tangible world. Especially did his shade-loving muse hover over and interpret the lower parts of nature; he showed the mysterious bond that allies moral evil to the foul material forms, and has given in epical parables a theory of insanity, of beasts, of unclean and fearful things.

Another sign of our times, also marked by an analogous political movement, is the new importance given to the single person. Everything that tends to insulate the individual—to surround him with barriers of natural respect, so that each man shall feel the world is his, and man shall treat with man as a sovereign state with a sovereign state—tends to true union as well as greatness. "I learned," said the melancholy Pestalozzi, "that no man in God's wide earth is either willing or able to help any other man." Help must come from the bosom alone. The scholar is that man who must take up into himself all the ability of the time, all the contributions of the past, all the hopes of the future. He must be a university of knowledges. If there be one lesson more than another which should pierce his ear, it is, The world is nothing, the man is all; in yourself is the law of all nature, and you know not yet how a globule of sap ascends; in yourself slumbers the whole of Reason; it is for you to know all; it is for you to dare all. Mr. President and Gentlemen, this confidence in the unsearched might of man belongs, by all motives, by all prophecy, by all preparation, to the American Scholar. We have listened too long to the courtly muses of Europe. The spirit of the American freeman is already suspected to be timid, imitative, tame. Public and private avarice make the air we breathe thick and fat. The scholar is decent, indolent, complaisant. See already the tragic consequence. The mind of this country, taught to aim at low objects, eats upon itself. There is no work for any but the decorous and the complaisant. Young men of the fairest promise, who begin life upon our shores, inflated by the mountain winds, shined upon by all the stars of God, find the earth below not in unison with these, but are hindered from action by the disgust which the principles on which business is managed inspire, and turn drudges, or die of disgust, some of them suicides. What is the remedy? They did not yet see, and thousands of young men as hopeful now crowding to the barriers for the career do not yet see that if the single man plant himself indomitably on his instincts and there abide, the huge world will come round to him. Patience, patience; with the shades of all the good and great for company; and for solace the perspective of your own infinite life; and for work the study and the communication of principles, the making those instincts prevalent, the conversion of the world. Is it not the chief disgrace in the world, not to be a unit—not to be reckoned one character—not to yield that peculiar fruit which each man was created to bear, but to be reckoned in the gross, in the hundred, or the thousand, of the party, the section, to which we belong; and our opinion predicted geographically, as the north, or the south? Not so, brothers and friends—please God, ours shall not be so. We will walk on our own feet; we will work with our own hands; we will speak our own minds. The study of letters shall be no longer a name for pity, for doubt, and for sensual indulgence. The dread of man and the love of man shall be a wall of defense and a wreath of joy around all. A nation of men will for the first time exist, because each believes himself inspired by the Divine Soul which also inspires all men.

1837

Uriel[1]

IT FELL in the ancient periods
Which the brooding soul surveys,
Or ever the wild Time coined itself
Into calendar months and days.

This was the lapse of Uriel,
Which in Paradise befell.
Once, among the Pleiads walking,
Seyd overheard the young gods talking;
And the treason, too long pent,
To his ears was evident.
The young deities discussed
Laws of form, and metre just,
Orb, quintessence, and sunbeams,
What subsisteth, and what seems.
One, with low tones that decide,
And doubt and reverend use defied,
With a look that solved the sphere,
And stirred the devils everywhere,
Gave his sentiment divine
Against the being of a line.
"Line in nature is not found;
Unit and universe are round;
In vain produced, all rays return;

1 This is a poetic fable of the sequel to Emerson's Divinity School Address. Seyd, the poet, overhears Uriel telling the other young gods that everything in the universe, both good and evil, is part of the divine plan. Like Uriel, Emerson was frowned on and attacked by the stern old war-gods of the Harvard Faculty.

Evil will bless, and ice will burn."
As Uriel spoke with piercing eye,
A shudder ran around the sky;
The stern old war-gods shook their heads;
The seraphs frowned from myrtle-beds;
Seemed to the holy festival
The rash word boded ill to all;
The balance-beam of Fate was bent;
The bounds of good and ill were rent;
Strong Hades could not keep his own,
But all slid to confusion.

A sad self-knowledge, withering, fell
On the beauty of Uriel;
In heaven once eminent, the god
Withdrew, that hour, into his cloud;
Whether doomed to long gyration
In the sea of generation,
Or by knowledge grown too bright
To hit the nerve of feebler sight.
Straightway, a forgetting wind
Stole over the celestial kind,
And their lips the secret kept,
If in ashes the fire-seed slept.
But now and then, truth-speaking things
Shamed the angels' veiling wings;
And, shrilling from the solar course,
Or from fruit of chemic force,
Procession of a soul in matter,
Or the speeding change of water,
Or out of the good of evil born,
Came Uriel's voice of cherub scorn,
And a blush tinged the upper sky,
And the gods shook, they knew not why.

1847

Divinity School Address

DELIVERED BEFORE THE SENIOR CLASS IN DIVINITY COLLEGE,

CAMBRIDGE, SUNDAY EVENING, JULY 15, 1838.

IN THIS refulgent summer, it has been a luxury to draw the breath of life. The grass grows, the buds burst, the meadow is spotted with fire and gold in the tint of flowers. The air is full of birds, and sweet with the breath of the pine, the balm-of-Gilead, and the new hay. Night brings no gloom to the heart with its welcome shade. Through the transparent darkness the stars pour their almost spiritual rays. Man under them seems a young child and his huge globe, a toy. The cool night bathes the world as with a river and prepares his eyes again for the crimson dawn. The mystery of nature was never displayed more happily. The corn and the wine have been freely dealt to all creatures, and the never-broken silence with which the old bounty goes forward has not yielded yet one word of explanation. One is constrained to respect the perfection of this world in which our senses converse. How wide; how rich; what invitation from every property it gives to every faculty of man! In its fruitful soils; in its navigable sea; in its mountains of metal and stone; in its forests of all woods; in its animals; in its chemical ingredients; in the powers and path of light, heat, attraction and life, it is well worth the pith and heart of great men to subdue and enjoy it. The planters, the mechanics, the inventors, the astronomers, the builders of cities, and the captains, history delights to honor.

But when the mind opens and reveals the laws which traverse the universe and make things what they are, then shrinks the great world at once into a mere illustration and fable of this mind. What am I? and What is? asks the human spirit with a curiosity new-kindled, but never to be quenched. Behold these outrunning laws, which our imperfect apprehension can see tend this way and that, but not come full circle. Behold these infinite relations, so like, so unlike; many, yet one. I would study, I would know, I would admire forever. These works of thought have been the entertainments of the human spirit in all ages.

A more secret, sweet, and overpowering beauty appears to man when his heart and mind open to the sentiment of virtue. Then he is instructed in what is above him. He learns that his being is without bound; that to the good, to the perfect, he is born, low as he now lies in evil and weakness. That which he venerates is still his own, though he has not realized it yet. *He ought*. He knows the sense of that grand word, though his analysis fails to render account of it. When in innocency or when by intellectual perception he attains to say, "I love the Right; Truth is beautiful within and without forevermore. Virtue, I am thine; save me; use me; thee will I serve, day and night, in great, in small, that I may be not virtuous but virtue"; then is the end of the creation answered, and God is well pleased.

The sentiment of virtue is a reverence and delight in the presence of certain divine laws. It perceives that this homely game of life we play, covers, under what seem foolish details, principles that astonish. The child amidst his baubles is learning the action of light, motion, gravity, muscular force; and in the game of human life, love, fear, justice, appetite, man, and God, interact. These laws refuse to be adequately stated. They will not be written out on paper, or spoken by the tongue. They elude our persevering thought; yet we read them hourly in each other's faces, in each other's actions, in our own remorse. The moral traits which are all globed into every virtuous act and thought, in speech we must sever, and describe or suggest by painful enumeration of many particulars. Yet, as this sentiment is the essence of all religion, let me guide your eye to the precise objects of the sentiment, by an enumeration of some of those classes of facts in which this element is conspicuous.

The intuition of the moral sentiment is an insight of the perfection of the laws of the soul. These laws execute themselves. They are out of time, out of space, and not subject to circumstance. Thus in the soul of man there is a justice whose retributions are instant and entire. He who does a good deed is instantly ennobled. He who does a mean deed is by the action itself contracted. He who puts off impurity thereby puts on purity. If a man is at heart just, then in so far is he God; the safety of God, the immortality of God, the majesty of God, do enter into that man with justice. If a man dissemble, deceive, he deceives himself and goes out of acquaintance with his own being. A man in the view of absolute goodness adores with total humility. Every step so downward is a step upward. The man who renounces himself comes to himself.

See how this rapid intrinsic energy worketh everywhere, righting wrongs, correcting appearances, and bringing up facts to a harmony with thoughts. Its operation in life, though slow to the senses, is at last as sure as in the soul. By it a man is made the Providence to himself, dispensing good to his goodness and evil to his sin. Character is always known. Thefts never enrich; alms never impoverish; murder will speak out of stone walls. The least admixture of a lie—for example, the taint of vanity, any attempt to make a good impression, a favorable appearance —will instantly vitiate the effect. But speak the truth, and all nature and all spirits help you with unexpected furtherance. Speak the truth, and all things alive or brute are vouchers, and the very roots of the grass underground there do seem to stir and move to bear you witness. See again the perfection of the Law as it applies itself to the affections and becomes the law of society. As we are, so we associate. The good, by affinity, seek the good; the vile, by affinity, the vile. Thus of their own volition, souls proceed into heaven, into hell.

These facts have always suggested to man the sublime creed that the world is not the product of manifold power but of one will, of one mind; and that one mind is everywhere active, in each ray of the star, in each wavelet of the pool; and whatever opposes that will is everywhere balked and baffled, because things are made so and not otherwise. Good is positive. Evil is merely privative, not absolute: it is like cold, which is the privation of heat. All evil is so much death or nonentity. Benevolence is absolute and real. So much benevolence as a man hath, so much life hath he. For all things proceed out of this same spirit, which is differently named love, justice, temperance, in its different applications, just as the ocean receives different names on the several shores which it washes. All things proceed out of the same spirit, and all things conspire with it. Whilst a man seeks good ends, he is strong by the whole strength of nature. In so far as he roves from these ends, he bereaves himself of power, or auxiliaries; his being shrinks out of all remote channels, he becomes less and less, a mote, a point, until absolute badness is absolute death.

The perception of this law of laws awakens in the mind a sentiment which we call the religious sentiment and which makes our highest happiness. Wonderful is its power to charm and to command. It is a mountain air. It is the embalmer of the world. It is myrrh and storax,[1] and chlorine and rosemary. It makes the sky and the hills sublime, and the silent song of the stars is it. By it is the universe made safe and habitable, not by science or power. Thought may work cold and intransitive in things and find no end or unity; but the dawn of the sentiment of virtue on the heart gives, and is, the assurance that Law is sovereign over all natures; and the worlds, time, space, eternity, do seem to break out into joy.

[1] Resin.

This sentiment is divine and deifying. It is the beatitude of man. It makes him illimitable. Through it, the soul first knows itself. It corrects the capital mistake of the infant man, who seeks to be great by following the great and hopes to derive advantages *from another*—by showing the fountain of all good to be in himself, and that he, equally with every man, is an inlet into the deeps of Reason. When he says, "I ought"; when love warms him; when he chooses, warned from on high, the good and great deed; then deep melodies wander through his soul from Supreme Wisdom. Then he can worship and be enlarged by his worship; for he can never go behind this sentiment. In the sublimest flights of the soul, rectitude is never surmounted, love is never outgrown.

This sentiment lies at the foundation of society and successively creates all forms of worship. The principle of veneration never dies out. Man fallen into superstition, into sensuality, is never quite without the visions of the moral sentiment. In like manner, all the expressions of this sentiment are sacred and permanent in proportion to their purity. The expressions of this sentiment affect us more than all other compositions. The sentences of the oldest time, which ejaculate this piety, are still fresh and fragrant. This thought dwelled always deepest in the minds of men in the devout and contemplative East; not alone in Palestine, where it reached its purest expression, but in Egypt, in Persia, in India, in China. Europe has always owed to oriental genius its divine impulses. What these holy bards said, all sane men found agreeable and true. And the unique impression of Jesus upon mankind, whose name is not so much written as ploughed into the history of this world, is proof of the subtle virtue of this infusion.

Meantime, whilst the doors of the temple stand open, night and day, before every man, and the oracles of this truth cease never, it is guarded by one stern condition; this, namely: it is an intuition. It cannot be received at second hand. Truly speaking, it is not instruction but provocation that I can receive from another soul. What he announces, I must find true in me, or reject; and on his word or as his second, be he who he may, I can accept nothing. On the contrary, the absence of this primary faith is the presence of degradation. As is the flood, so is the ebb. Let this faith depart, and the very words it spake and the things it made become false and hurtful. Then falls the church, the state, art, letters, life. The doctrine of the divine nature being forgotten, a sickness infects and dwarfs the constitution. Once man was all; now he is an appendage, a nuisance. And because the indwelling Supreme Spirit cannot wholly be got rid of, the doctrine of it suffers this perversion, that the divine nature is attributed to one or two persons and denied to all the rest, and denied with fury. The doctrine of inspiration is lost; the base doctrine of the majority of voices usurps the place of the doctrine of the soul. Miracles, prophecy, poetry, the ideal life, the holy life, exist as ancient history merely; they are not in the belief, nor in the aspiration of society; but, when suggested, seem ridiculous. Life is comic or pitiful as soon as the high ends of being fade out of sight, and man becomes near-sighted and can only attend to what addresses the senses.

These general views, which, whilst they are general, none will contest, find abundant illustration in the history of religion, and especially in the history of the Christian church. In that, all of us have had our birth and nurture. The truth contained in that, you, my young friends, are now setting forth to teach. As the Cultus, or established worship of the civilized world, it has great historical interest for us. Of its blessed words, which have been the consolation of humanity, you need not that I should speak. I shall endeavor to discharge my duty to you on this occasion by pointing out two errors in its administration which daily appear more gross from the point of view we have just now taken.

Jesus Christ belonged to the true race of prophets. He saw with open eye the mystery of the soul. Drawn by its severe harmony, ravished with its beauty, he lived in it and had his being there. Alone in all history he estimated the greatness of man. One man was true to what is in you and me. He saw that God incarnates Himself in man and evermore goes forth anew to take possession of His World. He said, in this jubilee of sublime emotion, 'I am divine. Through me, God acts; through me, speaks. Would you see God, see me; or see thee, when thou also thinkest as I now think.' But what a distortion did his doctrine and memory suffer in the same, in the next, and the following ages! There is no doctrine of the Reason which will bear to be taught by the Understanding. The understanding caught this high chant from the poet's lips and said, in the next age, 'This was Jehovah come down out of heaven. I will kill you, if you say he was a man.' The idioms of his language and the figures of his rhetoric have usurped the place of his truth; and churches are not built on his principles, but on his tropes. Christianity became a Mythus, as the poetic teaching of Greece and of Egypt, before. He spoke of miracles; for he felt that man's life was a miracle, and all that man doth, and he knew that this daily miracle shines as the character ascends. But the word Miracle, as pronounced by Christian churches, gives a false impression; it is Monster. It is not one with the blowing clover and the falling rain.

He felt respect for Moses and the prophets, but no unfit tenderness at postponing their initial revelations to the hour and the man that now is; to the eternal revelation in the heart. Thus was he a true man. Having seen that the law in us is commanding, he would not suffer it to be commanded. Boldly, with hand, and heart, and life, he declared it was God. Thus is he, as I think, the only soul in history who has appreciated the worth of man.

1. In this point of view we become sensible of the first defect of historical Christianity. Historical Christianity has fallen into the error that corrupts all attempts to communicate religion. As it appears to us, and as it has appeared for ages, it is not the doctrine of the soul, but an exaggeration of the personal,

the positive, the ritual. It has dwelt, it dwells, with noxious exaggeration about the *person* of Jesus. The soul knows no persons. It invites every man to expand to the full circle of the universe, and will have no preferences but those of spontaneous love. But by this eastern monarchy of a Christianity which indolence and fear have built, the friend of man is made the injurer of man. The manner in which his name is surrounded with expressions which were once sallies of admiration and love, but are now petrified into official titles, kills all generous sympathy and liking. All who hear me feel that the language that describes Christ to Europe and America is not the style of friendship and enthusiasm to a good and noble heart but is appropriated and formal—paints a demigod, as the Orientals or the Greeks would describe Osiris or Apollo. Accept the injurious impositions of our early catechetical instruction, and even honesty and self-denial were but splendid sins, if they did not wear the Christian name. One would rather be "A pagan, suckled in a creed outworn" [1] than to be defrauded of his manly right in coming into nature and finding not names and places, not land and professions, but even virtue and truth foreclosed and monopolized. You shall not be a man even. You shall not own the world; you shall not dare and live after the infinite Law that is in you, and in company with the infinite Beauty which heaven and earth reflect to you in all lovely forms; but you must subordinate your nature to Christ's nature; you must accept our interpretations and take his portrait as the vulgar draw it.

That is always best which gives me to myself. The sublime is excited in me by the great stoical doctrine, Obey thyself. That which shows God in me fortifies me. That which shows God out of me makes me a wart and a wen. There is no longer a necessary reason for my being. Already the long shadows of untimely oblivion creep over me, and I shall decease forever.

The divine bards are the friends of my virtue, of my intellect,

[1] Wordsworth, "The World Is Too Much With Us."

of my strength. They admonish me that the gleams which flash across my mind are not mine, but God's; that they had the like and were not disobedient to the heavenly vision. So I love them. Noble provocations go out from them, inviting me to resist evil; to subdue the world; and to Be. And thus, by his holy thoughts, Jesus serves us, and thus only. To aim to convert a man by miracles is a profanation of the soul. A true conversion, a true Christ, is now, as always, to be made by the reception of beautiful sentiments. It is true that a great and rich soul, like his, falling among the simple, does so preponderate that, as his did, it names the world. The world seems to them to exist for him, and they have not yet drunk so deeply of his sense as to see that only by coming again to themselves, or to God in themselves, can they grow forevermore. It is a low benefit to give me something; it is a high benefit to enable me to do somewhat of myself. The time is coming when all men will see that the gift of God to the soul is not a vaunting, overpowering, excluding sanctity but a sweet, natural goodness, a goodness like thine and mine, and that so invites thine and mine to be and to grow.

The injustice of the vulgar tone of preaching is not less flagrant to Jesus than to the souls which it profanes. The preachers do not see that they make his gospel not glad and shear him of the locks of beauty and the attributes of heaven. When I see a majestic Epaminondas, or Washington; when I see among my contemporaries a true orator, an upright judge, a dear friend; when I vibrate to the melody and fancy of a poem; I see beauty that is to be desired. And so lovely, and with yet more entire consent of my human being, sounds in my ear the severe music of the bards that have sung of the true God in all ages. Now do not degrade the life and dialogues of Christ out of the circle of this charm, by insulation and peculiarity. Let them lie as they befell, alive and warm, part of human life and of the landscape and of the cheerful day.

2. The second defect of the traditionary and limited way of using the mind of Christ is a consequence of the first; this, namely: that the Moral Nature, that Law of laws whose revelations introduce greatness—yea, God himself—into the open soul, is not explored as the fountain of the established teaching in society. Men have come to speak of the revelation as somewhat long ago given and done, as if God were dead. The injury to faith throttles the preacher; and the goodliest of institutions becomes an uncertain and inarticulate voice.

It is very certain that it is the effect of conversation with the beauty of the soul to beget a desire and need to impart to others the same knowledge and love. If utterance is denied, the thought lies like a burden on the man. Always the seer is a sayer. Somehow his dream is told; somehow he publishes it with solemn joy; sometimes with pencil on canvas, sometimes with chisel on stone, sometimes in towers and aisles of granite, his soul's worship is builded; sometimes in anthems of indefinite music; but clearest and most permanent, in words.

The man enamored of this excellency becomes its priest or poet. The office is coeval with the world. But observe the condition, the spiritual limitation of the office. The spirit only can teach. Not any profane man, not any sensual, not any liar, not any slave can teach, but only he can give who has; he only can create who is. The man on whom the soul descends, through whom the soul speaks, alone can teach. Courage, piety, love, wisdom, can teach; and every man can open his door to these angels, and they shall bring him the gift of tongues. But the man who aims to speak as books enable, as synods use, as the fashion guides, and as interest commands, babbles. Let him hush.

To this holy office you propose to devote yourselves. I wish you may feel your call in throbs of desire and hope. The office is the first in the world. It is of that reality that it cannot suffer the deduction of any falsehood. And it is my duty to say to you that the need was never greater of new revelation than now. From the views I have already expressed you will infer the sad conviction, which I share, I believe, with numbers, of the universal decay and now almost death of faith in society. The soul is not preached. The Church seems to totter to its fall, almost all life extinct. On this occasion, any complaisance would be criminal which told you, whose hope and commission it is to preach the faith of Christ, that the faith of Christ is preached.

It is time that this ill-suppressed murmur of all thoughtful men against the famine of our churches—this moaning of the heart because it is bereaved of the consolation, the hope, the grandeur that come alone out of the culture of the moral nature—should be heard through the sleep of indolence and over the din of routine. This great and perpetual office of the preacher is not discharged. Preaching is the expression of the moral sentiment in application to the duties of life. In how many churches, by how many prophets, tell me, is man made sensible that he is an infinite Soul; that the earth and heavens are passing into his mind; that he is drinking forever the soul of God? Where now sounds the persuasion that by its very melody imparadises my heart, and so affirms its own origin in heaven? Where shall I hear words such as in elder ages drew men to leave all and follow—father and mother, house and land, wife and child? Where shall I hear these august laws of moral being so pronounced as to fill my ear, and I feel ennobled by the offer of my uttermost action and passion? The test of the true faith, certainly, should be its power to charm and command the soul, as the laws of nature control the activity of the hands—so commanding that we find pleasure and honor in obeying. The faith should blend with the light of rising and of setting suns, with the flying cloud, the singing bird, and the breath of flowers. But now the priest's Sabbath has lost the splendor of nature; it is unlovely; we are glad when it is done; we can make, we do make, even sitting in our pews, a far better, holier, sweeter, for ourselves.

Whenever the pulpit is usurped by a formalist, then is the worshiper defrauded and disconsolate. We shrink as soon as the prayers begin which do not uplift, but smite and offend us. We are fain to wrap our cloaks about us and secure, as best we can, a solitude that hears not. I once heard a preacher who sorely tempted me to say I would go to church no more. Men go, thought I, where they are wont to go, else had no soul entered the temple in the afternoon. A snowstorm was falling around us. The snowstorm was real, the preacher merely spectral, and the eye felt the sad contrast in looking at him, and then out of the window behind him into the beautiful meteor of the snow. He had lived in vain. He had no one word intimating that he had laughed or wept, was married or in love, had been commended, or cheated, or chagrined. If he had ever lived and acted, we were none the wiser for it. The capital secret of his profession, namely, to convert life into truth, he had not learned. Not one fact in all his experience had he yet imported into his doctrine. This man had ploughed and planted and talked and bought and sold; he had read books; he had eaten and drunken; his head aches, his heart throbs; he smiles and suffers; yet was there not a surmise, a hint, in all the discourse that he had ever lived at all. Not a line did he draw out of real history. The true preacher can be known by this, that he deals out to the people his life—life passed through the fire of thought. But of the bad preacher, it could not be told from his sermon what age of the world he fell in; whether he had a father or a child; whether he was a freeholder or a pauper; whether he was a citizen or a countryman; or any other fact of his biography. It seemed strange that the people should come to church. It seemed as if their houses were very unentertaining, that they should prefer this thoughtless clamor. It shows that there is a commanding attraction in the moral sentiment that can lend a faint tint of light to dullness and ignorance coming in its name and place. The good hearer is sure he has been touched sometimes; is sure there is somewhat to be reached, and some word that can reach it. When he listens to these vain words, he comforts himself by their relation to his remembrance of better hours, and so they clatter and echo unchallenged.

I am not ignorant that when we preach unworthily it is not always quite in vain. There is a good ear, in some men, that draws supplies to virtue out of very indifferent nutriment. There is poetic truth concealed in all the commonplaces of prayer and of sermons, and though foolishly spoken, they may be wisely heard; for each is some select expression that broke out in a moment of piety from some stricken or jubilant soul, and its excellency made it remembered. The prayers and even the dogmas of our church are like the zodiac of Denderah [1] and the astronomical monuments of the Hindoos, wholly insulated from anything now extant in the life and business of the people. They mark the height to which the waters once rose. But this docility is a check upon the mischief from the good and devout. In a large portion of the community, the religious service gives rise to quite other thoughts and emotions. We need not chide the negligent servant. We are struck with pity, rather, at the swift retribution of his sloth. Alas for the unhappy man that is called to stand in the pulpit and *not* give bread of life. Everything that befalls accuses him. Would he ask contributions for the missions, foreign or domestic? Instantly his face is suffused with shame, to propose to his parish that they should send money a hundred or a thousand miles, to furnish such poor fare as they have at home and would do well to go the hundred or the thousand miles to escape. Would he urge people to a godly way of living; and can he ask a fellow-creature to come to Sabbath meetings, when he and they all know what is the poor uttermost they can hope for therein? Will he invite them privately to the Lord's Supper? He dares not. If no heart warm this rite, the hollow, dry, creaking for-

[1] On the ceiling of the temple of Hathor at Dendera, Egypt, the signs of the zodiac are sculptured in primitive forms.

mality is too plain than that he can face a man of wit and energy and put the invitation without terror. In the street, what has he to say to the bold village blasphemer? The village blasphemer sees fear in the face, form, and gait of the minister.

Let me not taint the sincerity of this plea by any oversight of the claims of good men. I know and honor the purity and strict conscience of numbers of the clergy. What life the public worship retains, it owes to the scattered company of pious men, who minister here and there in the churches and who, sometimes accepting with too great tenderness the tenet of the elders, have not accepted from others but from their own heart the genuine impulses of virtue, and so still command our love and awe, to the sanctity of character. Moreover, the exceptions are not so much to be found in a few eminent preachers as in the better hours, the truer inspirations of all—nay, in the sincere moments of every man. But, with whatever exception, it is still true that tradition characterizes the preaching of this country; that it comes out of the memory and not out of the soul; that it aims at what is usual and not at what is necessary and eternal; that thus historical Christianity destroys the power of preaching, by withdrawing it from the exploration of the moral nature of man, where the sublime is, where are the resources of astonishment and power. What a cruel injustice it is to that Law, the joy of the whole earth, which alone can make thought dear and rich—that Law whose fatal sureness the astronomical orbits poorly emulate—that it is travestied and depreciated, that it is behooted and behowled, and not a trait, not a word of it articulated. The pulpit, in losing sight of this Law, loses its reason and gropes after it knows not what. And for want of this culture the soul of the community is sick and faithless. It wants nothing so much as a stern, high, stoical, Christian discipline to make it know itself and the divinity that speaks through it. Now man is ashamed of himself; he skulks and sneaks through the world, to be tolerated, to be pitied, and scarcely in a thousand years does any man dare to be wise and good, and so draw after him the tears and blessings of his kind.

Certainly there have been periods when, from the inactivity of the intellect on certain truths, a greater faith was possible in names and persons. The Puritans in England and America found in the Christ of the Catholic Church and in the dogmas inherited from Rome scope for their austere piety and their longings for civil freedom. But their creed is passing away, and none arises in its room. I think no man can go with his thoughts about him into one of our churches without feeling that what hold the public worship had on men is gone or going. It has lost its grasp on the affection of the good and the fear of the bad. In the country, neighborhoods, half parishes are *signing off*, to use the local term. It is already beginning to indicate character and religion to withdraw from the religious meetings. I have heard a devout person, who prized the Sabbath, say in bitterness of heart, "On Sundays it seems wicked to go to church." And the motive that holds the best there is now only a hope and a waiting. What was once a mere circumstance, that the best and the worst men in the parish, the poor and the rich, the learned and the ignorant, young and old, should meet one day as fellows in one house, in sign of an equal right in the soul, has come to be a paramount motive for going thither.

My friends, in these two errors, I think, I find the causes of a decaying church and a wasting unbelief. And what greater calamity can fall upon a nation than the loss of worship? Then all things go to decay. Genius leaves the temple to haunt the senate or the market. Literature becomes frivolous. Science is cold. The eye of youth is not lighted by the hope of other worlds, and age is without honor. Society lives to trifles, and when men die we do not mention them.

And now, my brothers, you will ask, What in these desponding days can be done by us? The remedy is already declared in the ground of our complaint of the Church. We have contrasted the Church with the Soul. In the soul then let the redemption be sought. Wherever a man comes, there comes revolution. The old is for slaves. When a man comes, all books are legible, all things transparent, all religions are forms. He is religious. Man is the wonderworker. He is seen amid miracles. All men bless and curse. He saith yea and nay only. The stationariness of religion; the assumption that the age of inspiration is past, that the Bible is closed; the fear of degrading the character of Jesus by representing him as a man—indicate with sufficient clearness the falsehood of our theology. It is the office of a true teacher to show us that God is, not was; that He speaketh, not spake. The true Christianity—a faith like Christ's in the infinitude of man—is lost. None believeth in the soul of man but only in some man or person old and departed. Ah me! no man goeth alone. All men go in flocks to this saint or that poet, avoiding the God who seeth in secret. They cannot see in secret; they love to be blind in public. They think society wiser than their soul and know not that one soul, and their soul, is wiser than the whole world. See how nations and races flit by on the sea of time and leave no ripple to tell where they floated or sunk, and one good soul shall make the name of Moses, or of Zeno, or of Zoroaster, reverend forever. None assayeth the stern ambition to be the Self of the nation and of nature, but each would be an easy secondary to some Christian scheme, or sectarian connection, or some eminent man. Once leave your own knowledge of God, your own sentiment, and take secondary knowledge, as St. Paul's, or George Fox's, or Swedenborg's, and you get wide from God with every year this secondary form lasts, and if, as now, for centuries, the chasm yawns to that breadth that men can scarcely be convinced there is in them anything divine.

Let me admonish you, first of all, to go alone; to refuse the good models, even those which are sacred in the imagination of men, and dare to love God without mediator or veil.

Friends enough you shall find who will hold up to your emulation Wesleys and Oberlins, Saints and Prophets. Thank God for these good men, but say, 'I also am a man.' Imitation cannot go above its model. The imitator dooms himself to hopeless mediocrity. The inventor did it because it was natural to him, and so in him it has a charm. In the imitator something else is natural, and he bereaves himself of his own beauty, to come short of another man's.

Yourself a newborn bard of the Holy Ghost, cast behind you all conformity and acquaint men at first hand with Deity. Look to it first and only, that fashion, custom, authority, pleasure, and money, are nothing to you—are not bandages over your eyes, that you cannot see—but live with the privilege of the immeasurable mind. Not too anxious to visit periodically all families and each family in your parish connection, when you meet one of these men or women, be to them a divine man; be to them thought and virtue; let their timid aspirations find in you a friend; let their trampled instincts be genially tempted out in your atmosphere; let their doubts know that you have doubted and their wonder feel that you have wondered. By trusting your own heart, you shall gain more confidence in other men. For all our penny-wisdom, for all our soul-destroying slavery to habit, it is not to be doubted that all men have sublime thoughts; that all men value the few real hours of life; they love to be heard; they love to be caught up into the vision of principles. We mark with light in the memory the few interviews we have had, in the dreary years of routine and of sin, with souls that made our souls wiser; that spoke what we thought; that told us what we knew; that gave us leave to be what we inly were. Discharge to men the priestly office, and, present or absent, you shall be followed with their love as by an angel.

And, to this end, let us not aim at common degrees of merit. Can we not leave, to such as love it, the virtue that glitters for the commendation of society, and ourselves pierce the deep solitudes of absolute ability and worth? We easily come up to the standard of goodness in society. Society's praise can be cheaply secured, and almost all men are content with those easy merits; but the instant effect of conversing with God will be to put them away. There are persons who are not actors, not speakers, but influences; persons too great for fame, for display; who disdain eloquence; to whom all we call art and artist seems too nearly allied to show and by-ends, to the exaggeration of the finite and selfish and loss of the universal. The orators, the poets, the commanders encroach on us only as fair women do, by our allowance and homage. Slight them by preoccupation of mind, slight them, as you can well afford to do, by high and universal aims, and they instantly feel that you have right and that it is in lower places that they must shine. They also feel your right; for they with you are open to the influx of the all-knowing Spirit, which annihilates before its broad noon the little shades and gradations of intelligence in the compositions we call wiser and wisest.

In such high communion let us study the grand strokes of rectitude: a bold benevolence, and independence of friends, so that not the unjust wishes of those who love us shall impair our freedom, but we shall resist for truth's sake the freest flow of kindness and appeal to sympathies far in advance; and —what is the highest form in which we know this beautiful element—a certain solidity of merit that has nothing to do with opinion, and which is so essentially and manifestly virtue that it is taken for granted that the right, the brave, the generous step will be taken by it, and nobody thinks of commending it. You would compliment a coxcomb doing a good act, but you would not praise an angel. The silence that accepts merit as the most natural thing in the world is the highest applause. Such souls, when they appear, are the Imperial Guard of Virture, the perpetual reserve, the dictators of fortune. One needs not praise their courage—they are the heart and soul of nature. O my friends, there are resources in us on which we have not drawn. There are men who rise refreshed on hearing a threat; men to whom a crisis which intimidates and paralyzes the majority—demanding not the faculties of prudence and thrift, but comprehension, immovableness, the readiness of sacrifice—comes graceful and beloved as a bride. Napoleon said of Massena that he was not himself until the battle began to go against him; then, when the dead began to fall in ranks around him, awoke his powers of combination, and he put on terror and victory as a robe. So it is in rugged crises, in unweariable endurance, and in aims which put sympathy out of question, that the angel is shown. But these are heights that we can scarce remember and look up to without contrition and shame. Let us thank God that such things exist.

And now let us do what we can to rekindle the smoldering, nigh-quenched fire on the altar. The evils of the church that now is are manifest. The question returns, What shall we do? I confess, all attempts to project and establish a Cultus with new rites and forms seem to me vain. Faith makes us, and not we it, and faith makes its own forms. All attempts to contrive a system are as cold as the new worship introduced by the French to the goddess of Reason—today pasteboard and filigree, and ending tomorrow in madness and murder. Rather let the breath of new life be breathed by you through the forms already existing. For if once you are alive, you shall find they shall become plastic and new. The remedy to their deformity is first, soul, and second, soul, and evermore, soul. A whole popedom of forms one pulsation of virtue can uplift and vivify. Two inestimable advantages Christianity has given us; first the Sabbath, the jubilee of the whole world, whose light dawns welcome alike into the closet of the philosopher, into the garret of toil, and into prison-cells and everywhere suggests, even to the vile, the dignity of spiritual being. Let it stand forevermore, a temple which new love, new faith, new sight shall restore to more than its first splendor to mankind. And secondly, the institution of preaching—the speech of man to men—essentially the most flexible of all organs, of all forms. What hinders that now, everywhere, in pulpits, in lecture rooms, in houses, in fields, wherever the invitation of men or your own occasions lead you, you speak the very truth, as your life and conscience teach it, and cheer the waiting, fainting hearts of men with new hope and new revelation?

I look for the hour when that supreme Beauty which ravished the souls of those Eastern men, and chiefly of those Hebrews, and through their lips spoke oracles to all time shall speak in the West also. The Hebrew and Greek Scriptures contain immortal sentences that have been bread of life to millions. But they have no epical integrity; are fragmentary; are not shown in their order to the intellect. I look for the new Teacher that shall follow so far those shining laws that he shall see them come full circle; shall see their rounding complete grace; shall see the world to be the mirror of the soul; shall see the identity of the law of gravitation with purity of heart; and shall show that the Ought, that Duty, is one thing with Science, with Beauty, and with Joy.

1838

Hamatreya[1]

BULKELEY, Hunt, Willard, Hosmer, Meriam, Flint,
Possessed the land which rendered to their toil
Hay, corn, roots, hemp, flax, apples, wool, and wood.
Each of these landlords walked amidst his farm,
Saying, " 'Tis mine, my children's, and my name's.
How sweet the west wind sounds in my own trees!
How graceful climb those shadows on my hill!
I fancy these pure waters and the flags
Know me, as does my dog; we sympathize;
And, I affirm, my actions smack of the soil."

Where are these men? Asleep beneath their grounds;
And strangers, fond as they, their furrows plough.
Earth laughs in flowers, to see her boastful boys
Earth-proud, proud of the earth which is not theirs;
Who steer the plough, but cannot steer their feet
Clear of the grave.
They added ridge to valley, brook to pond,
And sighed for all that bounded their domain.
"This suits me for a pasture; that's my park;
We must have clay, lime, gravel, granite-ledge,
And misty lowland, where to go for peat.
The land is well,—lies fairly to the south.

[1] Hamatreya is the name of one of the disciples of the Sage in the *Vishnu Purana* (Book IV), who repeats the Song of the Earth to teach him the futility of material ambition.

'Tis good, when you have crossed the sea and back,
To find the sitfast acres where you left them."
Ah! the hot owner sees not Death, who adds
Him to his land, a lump of mould the more.
Hear what the Earth says:—

EARTH-SONG

"Mine and yours;
Mine, not yours.
Earth endures;
Stars abide—
Shine down in the old sea;
Old are the shores;
But where are old men?
I who have seen much,
Such have I never seen.

"The lawyer's deed
Ran sure,
In tail,
To them, and to their heirs
Who shall succeed,
Without fail,
Forevermore.

"Here is the land,
Shaggy with wood.
With its old valley,
Mound and flood.
But the heritors?—
Fled like the flood's foam.—
The lawyer, and the laws,
And the kingdom,
Clean swept herefrom.

"They called me theirs,
Who so controlled me;
Yet every one
Wished to stay, and is gone.
How am I theirs,
If they cannot hold me,
But I hold them?"

When I heard the Earth-song,
I was no longer brave;
My avarice cooled
Like lust in the chill of the grave.

1847

Voluntaries

III

In an age of fops and toys,
Wanting wisdom, void of right,
Who shall nerve heroic boys
To hazard all in Freedom's fight,–
Break sharply off their jolly games,
Forsake their comrades gay
And quit proud homes and youthful dames
For famine, toil and fray?
Yet on the nimble air benign
Speed nimbler messages,
That waft the breath of grace divine
To hearts in sloth and ease.
So nigh is grandeur to our dust,
So near is God to man,
When Duty whispers low, *Thou must*,
The youth replies, *I can*.

1863

The Young American

A LECTURE READ BEFORE THE MERCANTILE LIBRARY ASSOCIATION, BOSTON, FEBRUARY 7, 1844

GENTLEMEN:

It is remarkable that our people have their intellectual culture from one country and their duties from another. This false state of things is newly in a way to be corrected. America is beginning to assert herself to the senses and to the imagination of her children, and Europe is receding in the same degree. This, their reaction on education, gives a new importance to the internal improvements and to the politics of the country. Who has not been stimulated to reflection by the facilities now in progress of construction for travel and the transportation of goods in the United States?

This rage of road building is beneficent for America, where vast distance is so main a consideration in our domestic politics and trade, inasmuch as the great political promise of the invention is to hold the Union staunch, whose days seemed already numbered by the mere inconvenience of transporting representatives, judges, and officers across such tedious distances of land and water. Not only is distance annihilated, but when, as now, the locomotive and the steamboat, like enormous shuttles, shoot every day across the thousand various threads of national descent and employment and bind them fast in one web, an hourly assimilation goes forward, and there is no danger that local peculiarities and hostilities should be preserved.

1. But I hasten to speak of the utility of these improvements in creating an American sentiment. An unlooked-for consequence of the railroad is the increased acquaintance it has given the American people with the boundless resources of their own soil. If this invention has reduced England to a third of its size, by bringing people so much nearer, in this country it has given a new celerity to *time*, or anticipated by fifty years the planting of tracts of land, the choice of water privileges, the working of mines, and other natural advantages. Railroad iron is a magician's rod in its power to evoke the sleeping energies of land and water.

The railroad is but one arrow in our quiver, though it has great value as a sort of yardstick and surveyor's line. The bountiful continent is ours, state on state, and territory on territory, to the waves of the Pacific sea;

> *Our garden is the immeasurable earth,*
> *The heaven's blue pillars are Medea's house.*[1]

The task of surveying, planting, and building upon this immense tract requires an education and a sentiment commensurate thereto. A consciousness of this fact is beginning to take the place of the purely trading spirit and education which sprang up whilst all the population lived on the fringe of seacoast. And even on the coast, prudent men have begun to see that every American should be educated with a view to the values of land. The arts of engineering and of architecture are studied; scientific agriculture is an object of growing attention; the mineral riches are explored; limestone, coal, slate, and iron; and the value of timberlands is enhanced.

Columbus alleged as a reason for seeking a continent in the West that the harmony of nature required a great tract of land in the western hemisphere to balance the known extent of land in the eastern; and it now appears that we must esti-

[1] Euripides, *Medea.*

mate the native values of this broad region to redress the balance of our own judgments and appreciate the advantages opened to the human race in this country which is our fortunate home. The land is the appointed remedy for whatever is false and fantastic in our culture. The continent we inhabit is to be physic and food for our mind as well as our body. The land, with its tranquilizing, sanative influences, is to repair the errors of a scholastic and traditional education, and bring us into just relations with men and things.

The habit of living in the presence of these invitations of natural wealth is not inoperative; and this habit, combined with the moral sentiment which, in the recent years, has interrogated every institution, usage, and law, has naturally given a strong direction to the wishes and aims of active young men to withdraw from cities and cultivate the soil. This inclination has appeared in the most unlooked-for quarters, in men supposed to be absorbed in business and in those connected with the liberal professions. And since the walks of trade were crowded, whilst that of agriculture cannot easily be, inasmuch as the farmer who is not wanted by others can yet grow his own bread, whilst the manufacturer, or the trader, who is not wanted, cannot, this seemed a happy tendency. For beside all the moral benefit which we may expect from the farmer's profession, when a man enters it considerately, this promised the conquering of the soil, plenty, and beyond this the adorning of the country with every advantage and ornament which labor, ingenuity, and affection for a man's home could suggest.

Meantime, with cheap land and the pacific disposition of the people, everything invites to the arts of agriculture, of gardening, and domestic architecture. Public gardens, on the scale of such plantations in Europe and Asia, are now unknown to us. There is no feature of the old countries that strikes an American with more agreeable surprise than the beautiful gardens of Europe; such as the Boboli in Florence, the Villa Borghese in Rome, the Villa d'Este in Tivoli, the gardens at Munich, and at

Frankfort on the Main—works easily imitated here, and which might well make the land dear to the citizen, and inflame patriotism. It is the fine art which is left for us, now that sculpture, painting, and religious and civil architecture have become effete and have passed into second childhood. We have twenty degrees of latitude wherein to choose a seat, and the new modes of traveling enlarge the opportunity of selection, by making it easy to cultivate very distant tracts and yet remain in strict intercourse with the centers of trade and population. And the whole force of all the arts goes to facilitate the decoration of lands and dwellings. A garden has this advantage, that it makes it indifferent where you live. A well-laid garden makes the face of the country of no account; let that be low or high, grand or mean, you have made a beautiful abode worthy of man. If the landscape is pleasing, the garden shows it; if tame, it excludes it. A little grove, which any farmer can find or cause to grow near his house, will in a few years make cataracts and chains of mountains quite unnecessary to his scenery; and he is so contented with his alleys, woodlands, orchards, and river, that Niagara, and the Notch of the White Hills, and Nantasket Beach, are superfluities. And yet the selection of a fit house lot has the same advantage over an indifferent one as the selection to a given employment of a man who has a genius for that work. In the last case the culture of years will never make the most painstaking apprentice his equal: no more will gardening give the advantage of a happy site to a house in a hole or on a pinnacle. In America we have hitherto little to boast in this kind. The cities drain the country of the best part of its population: the flower of the youth, of both sexes, goes into the towns, and the country is cultivated by a so much inferior class. The land—travel a whole day together—looks poverty-stricken, and the buildings plain and poor. In Europe, where society has an aristocratic structure, the land is full of men of the best stock and the best culture, whose interest and pride it is to remain half the year on their estates and to fill them with every convenience and ornament. Of course, these make model farms and model architecture, and are a constant education to the eye of the surrounding population. Whatever events in progress shall go to disgust men with cities and infuse into them the passion for country life and country pleasures will render a service to the whole face of this continent and will further the most poetic of all the occupations of real life, the bringing out by art the native but hidden graces of the landscape.

I look on such improvements also as directly tending to endear the land to the inhabitant. Any relation to the land, the habit of tilling it, or mining it, or even hunting on it, generates the feeling of patriotism. He who keeps shop on it, or he who merely uses it as a support to his desk and ledger, or to his manufactory, values it less. The vast majority of the people of this country live by the land, and carry its quality in their manners and opinions. We in the Atlantic states, by position, have been commercial and have, as I said, imbibed easily an European culture. Luckily for us, now that steam has narrowed the Atlantic to a strait, the nervous, rocky West is intruding a new and continental element into the national mind, and we shall yet have an American genius. How much better when the whole land is a garden and the people have grown up in the bowers of a paradise. Without looking then to those extraordinary social influences which are now acting in precisely this direction, but only at what is inevitably doing around us, I think we must regard the *land* as a commanding and increasing power on the citizen, the sanative and Americanizing influence, which promises to disclose new virtues for ages to come.

2. In the second place, the uprise and culmination of the new and anti-feudal power of Commerce is the political fact of most significance to the American at this hour.

We cannot look on the freedom of this country, in connection with its youth, without a presentiment that here shall laws and institutions exist on some scale of proportion to the majesty of nature. To men legislating for the area betwixt the two oceans, betwixt the snows and the tropics, somewhat of the gravity of nature will infuse itself into the code. A heterogeneous population crowding on all ships from all corners of the world to the great gates of North America, namely Boston, New York, and New Orleans, and thence proceeding inward to the prairie and the mountains, and quickly contributing their private thought to the public opinion, their toll to the treasury, and their vote to the election, it cannot be doubted that the legislation of this country should become more catholic and cosmopolitan than that of any other. It seems so easy for America to inspire and express the most expansive and humane spirit; newborn, free, healthful, strong, the land of the laborer, of the democrat, of the philanthropist, of the believer, of the saint, she should speak for the human race. It is the country of the Future. From Washington, proverbially "the city of magnificent distances," through all its cities, states, and territories, it is a country of beginnings, of projects, of designs, of expectations.

Gentlemen, there is a sublime and friendly Destiny by which the human race is guided—the race never dying, the individual never spared—to results affecting masses and ages. Men are narrow and selfish, but the Genius or Destiny is not narrow but beneficent. It is not discovered in their calculated and voluntary activity but in what befalls, with or without their design. Only what is inevitable interests us, and it turns out that love and good are inevitable and in the course of things. That Genius has infused itself into nature. It indicates itself by a small excess of good, a small balance in brute facts always favorable to the side of reason. All the facts in any part of nature shall be tabulated and the results shall indicate the same security and benefit; so slight as to be hardly observable, and yet it is there. The sphere is flattened at the poles and swelled at the equator; a form flowing necessarily from the fluid state, yet *the* form, the mathematician assures us, required to prevent the protuberances of the continent, or even of lesser mountains cast up at any time by earthquakes, from continually deranging the axis of the earth. The census of the population is found to keep an invariable equality in the sexes, with a trifling predominance in favor of the male, as if to counterbalance the necessarily increased exposure of male life in war, navigation, and other accidents. Remark the unceasing effort throughout nature at somewhat better than the actual creatures: *amelioration in nature*, which alone permits and authorizes amelioration in mankind. The population of the world is a conditional population; these are not the best, but the best that could live in the existing state of soils, gases, animals, and morals: the best that could *yet* live; there shall be a better, please God. This Genius or Destiny is of the sternest administration, though rumors exist of its secret tenderness. It may be styled a cruel kindness, serving the whole even to the ruin of the member; a terrible communist, reserving all profits to the community, without dividend to individuals. Its law is, you shall have everything as a member, nothing to yourself. For Nature is the noblest engineer, yet uses a grinding economy, working up all that is wasted today into tomorrow's creation; not a superfluous grain of sand, for all the ostentation she makes of expense and public works. It is because Nature thus saves and uses, laboring for the general, that we poor particulars are so crushed and straitened and find it so hard to live. She flung us out in her plenty, but we cannot shed a hair or a paring of a nail but instantly she snatches at the shred and appropriates it to the general stock. Our condition is like that of the poor wolves: if one of the flock wound himself or so much as limp, the rest eat him up incontinently.

That serene Power interposes the check upon the caprices and officiousness of our wills. Its charity is not our charity. One of its agents is our will, but that which expresses itself in our will is stronger than our will. We are very forward to help it, but it will not be accelerated. It resists our meddling, eleemosynary contrivances. We devise sumptuary and relief laws, but the principle of population is always reducing wages to the lowest pittance on which human life can be sustained. We legislate against forestalling and monopoly; we would have a common granary for the poor; but the selfishness which hoards the corn for high prices is the preventive of famine; and the law of self-preservation is surer policy than any legislation can be. We concoct eleemosynary systems, and it turns out that our charity increases pauperism. We inflate our paper currency, we repair commerce with unlimited credit, and are presently visited with unlimited bankruptcy.

It is easy to see that the existing generation are conspiring with a beneficence which in its working for coming generations sacrifices the passing one; which infatuates the most selfish men to act against their private interest for the public welfare. We build railroads, we know not for what or for whom; but one thing is certain, that we who build will receive the very smallest share of benefit. Benefit will accrue, they are essential to the country, but that will be felt not until we are no longer countrymen. We do the like in all matters:

Man's heart the Almighty to the Future set
By secret and inviolable springs.

We plant trees, we build stone houses, we redeem the waste, we make prospective laws, we found colleges and hospitals, for remote generations. We should be mortified to learn that the little benefit we chanced in our own persons to receive was the utmost they would yield.

The history of commerce is the record of this beneficent tendency. The patriarchal form of government readily becomes despotic, as each person may see in his own family. Fathers wish to be fathers of the minds of their children and behold with impatience a new character and way of thinking presuming to show itself in their own son or daughter. This feeling, which all their love and pride in the powers of their children cannot subdue, becomes petulance and tyranny when the head of the clan, the emperor of an empire, deals with the same difference of opinion in his subjects. Difference of opinion is the one crime which kings never forgive. An empire is an immense egotism. "I am the State," said the French Louis. When a French ambassador mentioned to Paul of Russia that a man of consequence in St. Petersburg was interesting himself in some matter, the Czar interrupted him, "There is no man of consequence in this empire but he with whom I am actually speaking; and so long only as I am speaking to him is he of any consequence." And the Emperor Nicholas is reported to have said to his council, "The age is embarrassed with new opinions; rely on me, gentlemen, I shall oppose an iron will to the progress of liberal opinions."

It is easy to see that this patriarchal or family management gets to be rather troublesome to all but the papa; the scepter comes to be a crowbar. And this unpleasant egotism Feudalism opposes and finally destroys. The king is compelled to call in the aid of his brothers and cousins and remote relations to help him keep his overgrown house in order; and this club of noblemen always come at last to have a will of their own; they combine to brave the sovereign, and call in the aid of the people. Each chief attaches as many followers as he can, by kindness, maintenance, and gifts; and as long as war lasts, the nobles, who must be soldiers, rule very well. But when peace comes, the nobles prove very whimsical and uncomfortable masters; their frolics turn out to be insulting and degrading to the commoner. Feudalism grew to be a bandit and brigand.

Meantime Trade had begun to appear: Trade, a plant which grows wherever there is peace, as soon as there is peace, and as long as there is peace. The luxury and necessity of the noble fostered it. And as quickly as men go to foreign parts in ships or caravans, a new order of things springs up; new command takes place, new servants and new masters. Their information, their wealth, their correspondence, have made them quite other men than left their native shore. *They* are nobles now, and by another patent than the king's. Feudalism had been good, had broken the power of the kings, and had some good traits of its own; but it had grown mischievous, it was time for it to die, and as they say of dying people, all its faults came out. Trade was the strong man that broke it down and raised a new and unknown power in its place. It is a new agent in the world, and one of great function; it is a very intellectual force. This displaces physical strength, and installs computation, combination, information, science, in its room. It calls out all force of a certain kind that slumbered in the former dynasties. It is now in the midst of its career. Feudalism is not ended yet. Our governments still partake largely of that element. Trade goes to make the governments insignificant and to bring every kind of faculty of every individual that can in any manner serve any person *on sale*. Instead of a huge Army and Navy and Executive Departments, it converts Government into an Intelligence Office, where every man may find what he wishes to buy and expose what he has to sell; not only produce and manufactures, but art, skill, and intellectual and moral values. This is the good and this the evil of trade, that it would put everything into market; talent, beauty, virtue, and man himself.

The philosopher and lover of man have much harm to say of trade; but the historian will see that trade was the principle of Liberty; that trade planted America and destroyed Feudalism; that it makes peace and keeps peace, and it will abolish slavery. We complain of its oppression of the poor and of its building up a new aristocracy on the ruins of the aristocracy it destroyed. But the aristocracy of trade has no permanence, is not entailed, was the result of toil and talent, the result of merit of some kind, and is continually falling, like the waves of the sea, before new claims of the same sort. Trade is an instrument in the hands of that friendly Power which works for us in our own despite. We design it thus and thus; it turns out otherwise and far better. This beneficent tendency, omnipotent without violence, exists and works. Every line of history inspires a confidence that we shall not go far wrong; that things mend. That is the moral of all we learn, that it warrants Hope, the prolific mother of reforms. Our part is plainly not to throw ourselves across the track, to block improvement and sit till we are stone, but to watch the uprise of successive mornings and to conspire with the new works of new days. Government has been a fossil; it should be a plant. I conceive that the office of statute law should be to express and not to impede the mind of mankind. New thoughts, new things. Trade was one instrument, but Trade is also but for a time, and must give way to somewhat broader and better, whose signs are already dawning in the sky.

3. I pass to speak of the signs of that which is the sequel of trade.

In consequence of the revolution in the state of society wrought by trade, Government in our times is beginning to wear a clumsy and cumbrous appearance. We have already seen our way to shorter methods. The time is full of good signs. Some of them shall ripen to fruit. All this beneficent socialism is a friendly omen, and the swelling cry of voices for the education of the people indicates that Government has other offices than those of banker and executioner. Witness the new movements in the civilized world, the Communism of France, Germany, and Switzerland; the Trades' Unions, the English League against the Corn Laws; and the whole *Industrial Statistics*, so called. In Paris, the blouse, the badge of the operative, has begun to make its appearance in the salons. Witness too the spectacle of three Communities[1] which have within a very short time sprung up within this Commonwealth, besides several others undertaken by citizens of Massachusetts within the territory of other States. These proceeded from a variety of motives, from an impatience of many usages in com-

[1] Emerson here refers to Brook Farm, Fruitlands, and Hopedale, three communities recently founded as self-sufficient, cooperative organizations.

mon life, from a wish for greater freedom than the manners and opinions of society permitted, but in great part from a feeling that the true offices of the State, the State had let fall to the ground; that in the scramble of parties for the public purse, the main duties of government were omitted—the duty to instruct the ignorant, to supply the poor with work and with good guidance. These communists preferred the agricultural life as the most favorable condition for human culture; but they thought that the farm, as we manage it, did not satisfy the right ambition of man. The farmer, after sacrificing pleasure, taste, freedom, thought, love, to his work, turns out often a bankrupt, like the merchant. This result might well seem astounding. All this drudgery, from cock-crowing to starlight, for all these years, to end in mortgages and the auctioneer's flag, and removing from bad to worse. It is time to have the thing looked into, and with a sifting criticism ascertained who is the fool. It seemed a great deal worse, because the farmer is living in the same town with men who pretend to know exactly what he wants. On one side is agricultural chemistry, coolly exposing the nonsense of our spendthrift agriculture and ruinous expense of manures, and offering, by means of a teaspoonful of artificial guano, to turn a sandbank into corn; and on the other, the farmer, not only eager for the information, but with bad crops and in debt and bankruptcy, for want of it. Here are Etzlers and mechanical projectors, who, with the Fourierists, undoubtingly affirm that the smallest union would make every man rich; and, on the other side, a multitude of poor men and women seeking work, and who cannot find enough to pay their board. The science is confident, and surely the poverty is real. If any means could be found to bring these two together!

This was one design of the projectors of the Associations which are now making their first feeble experiments. They were founded in love and in labor. They proposed, as you know, that all men should take a part in the manual toil and proposed to amend the condition of men by substituting harmonious for hostile industry. It was a noble thought of Fourier, which gives a favorable idea of his system, to distinguish in his Phalanx a class as the Sacred Band, by whom whatever duties were disagreeable and likely to be omitted were to be assumed.

At least an economical success seemed certain for the enterprise, and that agricultural association must, sooner or later, fix the price of bread, and drive single farmers into association in self-defense; as the great commercial and manufacturing companies had already done. The Community is only the continuation of the same movement which made the joint-stock companies for manufactures, mining, insurance, banking, and so forth. It has turned out cheaper to make calico by companies; and it is proposed to plant corn and to bake bread by companies.

Undoubtedly, abundant mistakes will be made by these first adventures, which will draw ridicule on their schemes. I think, for example, that they exaggerate the importance of a favorite project of theirs, that of paying talent and labor at one rate, paying all sorts of service at one rate, say ten cents the hour. They have paid it so; but not an instant would a dime remain a dime. In one hand it became an eagle as it fell and in another hand, a copper cent. For the whole value of the dime is in knowing what to do with it. One man buys with it a land-title of an Indian, and makes his posterity princes; or buys corn enough to feed the world; or pen, ink, and paper, or a painter's brush, by which he can communicate himself to the human race as if he were fire; and the other buys barley candy. Money is of no value; it cannot spend itself. All depends on the skill of the spender. Whether too the objection almost universally felt by such women in the Community as were mothers to an associate life, to a common table, and a common nursery, etc., setting a higher value on the private family, with poverty, than on an association, with wealth, will not prove insuperable, remains to be determined.

But the Communities aimed at a higher success in securing to all their members an equal and thorough education. And on the whole one may say that aims so generous and so forced on them by the times will not be relinquished, even if these attempts fail, but will be prosecuted until they succeed.

This is the value of the Communities: not what they have done, but the revolution which they indicate as on the way. Yes, Government must educate the poor man. Look across the country from any hillside around us and the landscape seems to crave Government. The actual differences of men must be acknowledged and met with love and wisdom. These rising grounds which command the champaign below, seem to ask for lords, true lords, *land*lords, who understand the land and its uses and the applicabilities of men and whose government would be what it should, namely, mediation between want and supply. How gladly would each citizen pay a commission for the support and continuation of good guidance. None should be a governor who has not a talent for governing. Now many people have a native skill for carving out business for many hands; a genius for the disposition of affairs; and are never happier than when difficult practical questions, which embarrass other men, are to be solved. All lies in light before them; they are in their element. Could any means be contrived to appoint only these! There really seems a progress towards such a state of things in which this work shall be done by these natural workmen; and this, not certainly through any increased discretion shown by the citizens at elections, but by the gradual contempt into which official government falls, and the increasing disposition of private adventurers to assume its fallen functions. Thus the national Post Office is likely to go into disuse before the private telegraph and the express companies. The currency threatens to fall entirely into private hands. Justice is continually administered more and more by private reference and not by litigation. We have feudal governments in a commercial age. It would be but an easy extension of our commercial system, to pay a private emperor a fee for services, as we pay an architect, an engineer, or a lawyer. If any man has a talent for righting wrong, for administering difficult affairs, for counseling poor farmers how to turn their estates to good husbandry, for combining a hundred private enterprises to a general benefit, let him in the county town or in Court Street put up his signboard, Mr. Smith, *Governor*, Mr. Johnson, *Working king*.

How can our young men complain of the poverty of things in New England and not feel that poverty as a demand on their charity to make New England rich? Where is he who seeing a thousand men useless and unhappy and making the whole region forlorn by their inaction, and conscious himself of possessing the faculty they want, does not hear his call to go and be their king?

We must have kings, and we must have nobles. Nature provides such in every society—only let us have the real instead of the titular. Let us have our leading and our inspiration from the best. In every society some men are born to rule and some to advise. Let the powers be well directed, directed by love, and they would everywhere be greeted with joy and honor. The chief is the chief all the world over, only not his cap and his plume. It is only their dislike of the pretender which makes men sometimes unjust to the accomplished man. If society were transparent, the noble would everywhere be gladly received and accredited and would not be asked for his day's work but would be felt as benefit, inasmuch as he was noble. That were his duty and stint—to keep himself pure and purifying, the leaven of his nation. I think I see place and duties for a nobleman in every society; but it is not to drink wine and ride in a fine coach, but to guide and adorn life for the multitude by forethought, by elegant studies, by perseverance, self-devotion, and the remembrance of the humble old friend, by making his life secretly beautiful.

I call upon you, young men, to obey your heart and be the nobility of this land. In every age of the world there has been a leading nation, one of a more generous sentiment, whose eminent citizens were willing to stand for the interests of general justice and humanity at the risk of being called, by the men of the moment, chimerical and fantastic. Which should be that nation but these States? Which should lead that movement if not New England? Who should lead the leaders but the Young American? The people and the world are now suffering from the want of religion and honor in its public mind. In America, out-of-doors all seems a market; indoors an air-tight stove of conventionalism. Everybody who comes into our houses savors of these habits; the men, of the market; the women, of the custom. I find no expression in our state papers or legislative debate, in our lyceums or churches, especially in our newspapers, of a high national feeling, no lofty counsels that rightfully stir the blood. I speak of those organs which can be presumed to speak a popular sense. They recommend conventional virtues, whatever will earn and preserve property; always the capitalist; the college, the church, the hospital, the theater, the hotel, the road, the ship of the capitalist—whatever goes to secure, adorn, enlarge these is good; what jeopardizes any of these is damnable. The "opposition" papers, so called, are on the same side. They attack the great capitalist, but with the aim to make a capitalist of the poor man. The opposition is against those who have money, from those who wish to have money. But who announces to us in journal, or in pulpit, or in the street, the secret of heroism?

> *Man alone*
> *Can perform the impossible.*

I shall not need to go into an enumeration of our national defects and vices which require this Order of Censors in the State. I might not set down our most proclaimed offenses as the worst. It is not often the worst trait that occasions the loudest outcry. Men complain of their suffering and not of the crime. I fear little from the bad effect of Repudiation;[1] I do not fear that it will spread. Stealing is a suicidal business; you cannot repudiate but once. But the bold face and tardy repentance permitted to this local mischief reveal a public mind so preoccupied with the love of gain that the common sentiment of indignation at fraud does not act with its natural force. The more need of a withdrawal from the crowd, and a resort to the fountain of right, by the brave. The timidity of our public opinion is our disease, or, shall I say, the publicness of opinion, the absence of private opinion. Good nature is plentiful, but we want justice, with heart of steel, to fight down the proud. The private mind has the access to the totality of goodness and truth that it may be a balance to a corrupt society; and to stand for the private verdict against popular clamor is the office of the noble. If a humane measure is propounded in behalf of the slave, or of the Irishman, or the Catholic, or for the succor of the poor, that sentiment, that project, will have the homage of the hero. That is his nobility, his oath of knighthood, to succor the helpless and oppressed; always to throw himself on the side of weakness, of youth, of hope; on the liberal, on the expansive side, never on the defensive, the conserving, the timorous, the lock-and-bolt system. More than our good will we may not be able to give. We have our own affairs, our own genius, which chains each to his proper work. We cannot give our life to the cause of the debtor, of the slave, or the pauper, as another is doing; but to one thing we are bound, not to blaspheme the sentiment and the work of that man, not to throw stumbling-blocks in the way of the abolitionist, the philanthropist, as the organs of influence and opinion are swift to do. It is for us to confide in the beneficent Supreme Power and not to rely on our money and on the State because it is the guard of money. At this moment, the terror of old people and of vicious people is lest the Union of

[1] During the panic of 1837 some of the State governments repudiated obligations that they found themselves unable to pay. Investors were helpless, because at that time a State could not be sued without its consent.

these states be destroyed: as if the Union had any other real basis than the good pleasure of a majority of the citizens to be united. But the wise and just man will always feel that he stands on his own feet; that he imparts strength to the State, not receives security from it; and that if all went down, he and such as he would quite easily combine in a new and better constitution. Every great and memorable community has consisted of formidable individuals, who, like the Roman or the Spartan, lent his own spirit to the State and made it great. Yet only by the supernatural is a man strong; nothing is so weak as an egotist. Nothing is mightier than we when we are vehicles of a truth before which the State and the individual are alike ephemeral.

Gentlemen, the development of our American internal resources, the extension to the utmost of the commercial system, and the appearance of new moral causes which are to modify the State are giving an aspect of greatness to the future, which the imagination fears to open. One thing is plain for all men of common sense and common conscience, that here, here in America, is the home of man. After all the deductions which are to be made for our pitiful politics, which stake every gravest national question on the silly die whether James or whether Robert shall sit in the chair and hold the purse; after all the deduction is made for our frivolities and insanities, there still remains an organic simplicity and liberty, which, when it loses its balance, redresses itself presently, which offers opportunity to the human mind not known in any other region.

It is true, the public mind wants self-respect. We are full of vanity, of which the most signal proof is our sensitiveness to foreign and especially English censure. One cause of this is our immense reading, and that reading chiefly confined to the productions of the English press. It is also true that to imaginative persons in this country there is somewhat bare and bald in our short history and unsettled wilderness. They ask, 'Who would live in a new country that can live in an old?' and it is not strange that our youths and maidens should burn to see the picturesque extremes of an antiquated country. But it is one thing to visit the Pyramids and another to wish to live there. Would they like tithes to the clergy, and sevenths to the government, and Horse-Guards, and licensed press, and grief when a child is born, and threatening, starved weavers, and a pauperism now constituting one thirteenth of the population? Instead of the open future expanding here before the eye of every boy to vastness, would they like the closing in of the future to a narrow slit of sky, and that fast contracting to be no future? One thing for instance, the beauties of aristocracy, we commend to the study of the traveling American. The English, the most conservative people this side of India, are not sensible of the restraint, but an American would seriously resent it. The aristocracy, incorporated by law and education, degrades life for the unprivileged classes. It is a questionable compensation to the embittered feeling of a proud commoner, the reflection that a fop, who, by the magic of title, paralyzes his arm and plucks from him half the graces and rights of a man, is himself also an aspirant excluded with the same ruthlessness from higher circles, since there is no end to the wheels within wheels of this spiral heaven. Something may be pardoned to the spirit of loyalty when it becomes fantastic; and something to the imagination, for the baldest life is symbolic. Philip II of Spain rated his ambassador for neglecting serious affairs in Italy, whilst he debated some point of honor with the French ambassador: "You have left a business of importance for a ceremony." The ambassador replied, "Your Majesty's self is but a ceremony." In the East, where the religious sentiment comes in to the support of the aristocracy, and in the Romish church also, there is a grain of sweetness in the tyranny; but in England, the fact seems to me intolerable, what is commonly affirmed, that such is the transcendent honor accorded to wealth and birth, that no man of letters, be his eminence what it may, is received into the best society except as a lion and a show. The English have many virtues, many advantages, and the proudest history of the world;

but they need all and more than all the resources of the past to indemnify a heroic gentleman in that country for the mortifications prepared for him by the system of society, and which seem to impose the alternative to resist or to avoid it. That there are mitigations and practical alleviations to this rigor is not an excuse for the rule. Commanding worth and personal power must sit crowned in all companies, nor will extraordinary persons be slighted or affronted in any company of civilized men. But the system is an invasion of the sentiment of justice and the native rights of men, which, however decorated, must lessen the value of English citizenship. It is for Englishmen to consider, not for us; we only say, Let us live in America, too thankful for our want of feudal institutions. Our houses and towns are like mosses and lichens, so slight and new; but youth is a fault of which we shall daily mend. This land too is as old as the Flood, and wants no ornament or privilege which nature could bestow. Here stars, here woods, here hills, here animals, here men abound, and the vast tendencies concur of a new order. If only the men are employed in conspiring with the designs of the Spirit who led us hither and is leading us still, we shall quickly enough advance out of all hearing of others' censures, out of all regrets of our own, into a new and more excellent social state than history has recorded.

1844

The Rhodora:[1]

ON BEING ASKED, WHENCE IS THE FLOWER?

In May, when sea-winds pierced our solitudes,
I found the fresh Rhodora in the woods,
Spreading its leafless blooms in a damp nook,
To please the desert and the sluggish brook.
The purple petals, fallen in the pool,
Made the black water with their beauty gay;
Here might the red-bird come his plumes to cool,
And court the flower that cheapens his array.
Rhodora! if the sages ask thee why
This charm is wasted on the earth and sky,
Tell them, dear, that if eyes were made for seeing,
Then Beauty is its own excuse for being:
Why thou wert there, O rival of the rose!
I never thought to ask, I never knew:
But, in my simple ignorance, suppose
The self-same Power that brought me there brought you.

1839

[1] A shrub of the same family as the pink azalea, which it closely resembles

Nature

INTRODUCTION

Our age is retrospective. It builds the sepulchers of the fathers. It writes biographies, histories, and criticism. The foregoing generations beheld God and nature face to face; we, through their eyes. Why should not we also enjoy an original relation to the universe? Why should not we have a poetry and philosophy of insight and not of tradition, and a religion by revelation to us and not the history of theirs? Embosomed for a season in nature, whose floods of life stream around and through us and invite us by the powers they supply to action proportioned to nature, why should we grope among the dry bones of the past or put the living generation into masquerade out of its faded wardrobe? The sun shines today also. There is more wool and flax in the fields. There are new lands, new men, new thoughts. Let us demand our own works and laws and worship.

Undoubtedly we have no questions to ask which are unanswerable. We must trust the perfection of the creation so far as to believe that whatever curiosity the order of things has awakened in our minds, the order of things can satisfy. Every man's condition is a solution in hieroglyphic to those inquiries he would put. He acts it as life before he apprehends it as truth. In like manner, nature is already in its forms and tendencies describing its own design. Let us interrogate the great apparition that shines so peacefully around us. Let us inquire, to what end is nature?

All science has one aim, namely, to find a theory of nature. We have theories of races and of functions, but scarcely yet a remote approach to an idea of creation. We are now so far from the road to truth that religious teachers dispute and hate each other, and speculative men are esteemed unsound and frivolous. But to a sound judgment, the most abstract truth is the most practical. Whenever a true theory appears, it will be its own evidence. Its test is that it will explain all phenomena. Now many are thought not only unexplained but inexplicable; as language, sleep, madness, dreams, beasts, sex.

Philosophically considered, the universe is composed of Nature and the Soul. Strictly speaking, therefore, all that is separate from us, all which Philosophy distinguishes as the NOT ME, that is, both nature and art, all other men and my own body, must be ranked under this name, NATURE. In enumerating the values of nature and casting up their sum, I shall use the word in both senses—in its common and in its philosophical import. In inquiries so general as our present one, the inaccuracy is not material; no confusion of thought will occur. *Nature*, in the common sense, refers to essences unchanged by man: space, the air, the river, the leaf. *Art* is applied to the mixture of his will with the same things, as in a house, a canal, a statue, a picture. But his operations taken together are so insignificant, a little chipping, baking, patching, and washing, that in an impression so grand as that of the world on the human mind, they do not vary the result.

I. NATURE

To GO into solitude, a man needs to retire as much from his chamber as from society. I am not solitary whilst I read and write, though nobody is with me. But if a man would be alone, let him look at the stars. The rays that come from those heavenly worlds will separate between him and what he touches. One might think the atmosphere was made transparent with this design, to give man, in the heavenly bodies, the perpetual presence of the sublime. Seen in the streets of cities, how great they are! If the stars should appear one night in a thousand years, how would men believe and adore; and preserve for many generations the remembrance of the city of God which had been shown! But every night come out these envoys of beauty and light the universe with their admonishing smile.

The stars awaken a certain reverence because, though always present, they are inaccessible; but all natural objects make a kindred impression, when the mind is open to their influence. Nature never wears a mean appearance. Neither does the wisest man extort her secret and lose his curiosity by finding out all her perfection. Nature never became a toy to a wise spirit. The flowers, the animals, the mountains reflected the wisdom of his best hour as much as they had delighted the simplicity of his childhood.

When we speak of nature in this manner, we have a distinct but most poetical sense in the mind. We mean the integrity of impression made by manifold natural objects. It is this which distinguishes the stick of timber of the woodcutter from the tree of the poet. The charming landscape which I saw this morning is indubitably made up of some twenty or thirty farms. Miller owns this field, Locke that, and Manning the woodland beyond. But none of them owns the landscape. There is a property in the horizon which no man has but he whose eye can integrate all the parts, that is, the poet. This is the best part of these men's farms, yet to this their warranty-deeds give no title.

To speak truly, few adult persons can see nature. Most persons do not see the sun. At least they have a very superficial seeing. The sun illuminates only the eye of the man, but shines into the eye and the heart of the child. The lover of nature is he whose inward and outward senses are still truly adjusted to each other, who has retained the spirit of infancy even into the era of manhood. His intercourse with heaven and earth becomes part of his daily food. In the presence of nature a wild delight runs through the man, in spite of real sorrows. Nature says, He is my creature, and, maugre [1] all his impertinent griefs, he shall be glad with me. Not the sun or the summer alone but every hour and season yields its tribute of delight; for every hour and change corresponds to and authorizes a different state of the mind from breathless noon to grimmest midnight. Nature is a setting that fits equally well a comic or a mourning piece. In good health, the air is a cordial of incredible virtue. Crossing a bare common in snow puddles at twilight under a clouded sky, without having in my thoughts any occurrence of special good fortune, I have enjoyed a perfect exhilaration. I am glad to the brink of fear. In the woods, too, a man casts off his years as the snake his slough, and at what period soever of life is always a child. In the woods is perpetual youth. Within these plantations of God a decorum and sanctity reign, a perennial festival is dressed, and the guest sees not how he should tire of them in a thousand years. In the woods we return to reason and faith. There I feel that nothing can befall me in life—no disgrace, no calamity (leaving me my eyes) which nature cannot repair. Standing on the bare ground—my head bathed by the blithe air and uplifted into infinite space—all mean egotism vanishes. I become a transparent eyeball; I am nothing; I see all; the currents of the Universal Being circulate through me; I am part or parcel of God. The name of the nearest friend sounds then foreign and accidental: to be brothers, to be acquaintances, master or servant, is then a trifle and a disturbance. I am the lover of uncontained and immortal beauty. In the wilderness I find something more dear and connate than in streets or villages. In the tranquil landscape, and especially in the distant line of the horizon, man beholds somewhat as beautiful as his own nature.

The greatest delight which the fields and woods minister is the suggestion of an occult relation between man and the vegetable. I am not alone and unacknowledged. They nod to me, and I to them. The waving of the boughs in the storm is new to me and

[1] In spite of.

old. It takes me by surprise and yet is not unknown. Its effect is like that of a higher thought or a better emotion coming over me when I deemed I was thinking justly or doing right.

Yet it is certain that the power to produce this delight does not reside in nature but in man, or in a harmony of both. It is necessary to use these pleasures with great temperance. For nature is not always tricked in holiday attire, but the same scene which yesterday breathed perfume and glittered as for the frolic of the nymphs is overspread with melancholy today. Nature always wears the colors of the spirit. To a man laboring under calamity, the heat of his own fire hath sadness in it. Then there is a kind of contempt of the landscape felt by him who has just lost by death a dear friend. The sky is less grand as it shuts down over less worth in the population.

II. COMMODITY

Whoever considers the final cause of the world will discern a multitude of uses that enter as parts into that result. They all admit of being thrown into one of the following classes: Commodity; Beauty; Language; and Discipline.

Under the general name of commodity I rank all those advantages which our senses owe to nature. This, of course, is a benefit which is temporary and mediate, not ultimate, like its service to the soul. Yet although low, it is perfect in its kind and is the only use of nature which all men apprehend. The misery of man appears like childish petulance when we explore the steady and prodigal provision that has been made for his support and delight on this green ball which floats him through the heavens. What angels invented these splendid ornaments, these rich conveniences, this ocean of air above, this ocean of water beneath, this firmament of earth between? this zodiac of lights, this tent of dropping clouds, this striped coat of climates, this fourfold year? Beasts, fire, water, stones and corn serve him. The field is at once his floor, his work-yard, his play-ground, his garden, and his bed.

> *More servants wait on man*
> *Than he'll take notice of.*[1]

Nature, in its ministry to man, is not only the material but is also the process and the result. All the parts incessantly work into each other's hands for the profit of man. The wind sows the seed; the sun evaporates the sea; the wind blows the vapor to the field; the ice on the other side of the planet condenses rain on this; the rain feeds the plant; the plant feeds the animal; and thus the endless circulations of the divine charity nourish man.

The useful arts are reproductions or new combinations by the wit of man of the same natural benefactors. He no longer waits for favoring gales, but by means of steam he realizes the fable of Æolus's bag and carries the two and thirty winds in the boiler of his boat. To diminish friction, he paves the road with iron bars and, mounting a coach with a shipload of men, animals and merchandise behind him, he darts through the country, from town to town, like an eagle or a swallow through the air. By the aggregate of these aids, how is the face of the world changed, from the era of Noah to that of Napoleon! The private poor man hath cities, ships, canals, bridges built for him. He goes to the post office, and the human race run on his errands; to the bookshop, and the human race read and write of all that happens, for him; to the courthouse, and nations repair his wrongs. He sets his house upon the road, and the human race go forth every morning and shovel out the snow and cut a path for him.

But there is no need of specifying particulars in this class of uses. The catalogue is endless, and the examples so obvious that I shall leave them to the reader's reflection, with the general remark that this mercenary benefit is one which has respect to a

[1] From George Herbert's poem "Man," five stanzas of which are quoted in the last chapter of *Nature*.

farther good. A man is fed, not that he may be fed, but that he may work.

III. BEAUTY

A NOBLER want of man is served by nature, namely, the love of Beauty.

The ancient Greeks called the world κόσμος, beauty. Such is the constitution of all things, or such the plastic power of the human eye, that the primary forms, as the sky, the mountain, the tree, the animal, give us a delight *in and for themselves;* a pleasure arising from outline, color, motion, and grouping. This seems partly owing to the eye itself. The eye is the best of artists. By the mutual action of its structure and of the laws of light, perspective is produced which integrates every mass of objects, of what character soever, into a well colored and shaded globe, so that where the particular objects are mean and unaffecting, the landscape which they compose is round and symmetrical. And as the eye is the best composer, so light is the first of painters. There is no object so foul that intense light will not make beautiful. And the stimulus it affords to the sense and a sort of infinitude which it hath, like space and time, make all matter gay. Even the corpse has its own beauty. But besides this general grace diffused over nature, almost all the individual forms are agreeable to the eye, as is proved by our endless imitations of some of them, as the acorn, the grape, the pine-cone, the wheat-ear, the egg, the wings and forms of most birds, the lion's claw, the serpent, the butterfly, sea shells, flames, clouds, buds, leaves, and the forms of many trees, as the palm.

For better consideration, we may distribute the aspects of Beauty in a threefold manner.

1. First, the simple perception of natural forms is a delight. The influence of the forms and actions in nature is so needful to man that, in its lowest functions, it seems to lie on the con-

fines of commodity and beauty. To the body and mind which have been cramped by noxious work or company, nature is medicinal and restores their tone. The tradesman, the attorney, comes out of the din and craft of the street and sees the sky and the woods and is a man again. In their eternal calm he finds himself. The health of the eye seems to demand a horizon. We are never tired so long as we can see far enough.

But in other hours Nature satisfies by its loveliness, and without any mixture of corporeal benefit. I see the spectacle of morning from the hilltop over against my house, from daybreak to sunrise, with emotions which an angel might share. The long slender bars of cloud float like fishes in the sea of crimson light. From the earth, as a shore, I look out into that silent sea. I seem to partake its rapid transformations; the active enchantment reaches my dust, and I dilate and conspire with the morning wind. How does Nature deify us with a few and cheap elements! Give me health and a day, and I will make the pomp of emperors ridiculous. The dawn is my Assyria, the sunset and moonrise my Paphos and unimaginable realms of faerie; broad noon shall be my England of the senses and the understanding; the night shall be my Germany of mystic philosophy and dreams.

Not less excellent, except for our less susceptibility in the afternoon, was the charm, last evening, of a January sunset. The western clouds divided and subdivided themselves into pink flakes, modulated with tints of unspeakable softness, and the air had so much life and sweetness that it was a pain to come within doors. What was it that nature would say? Was there no meaning in the live repose of the valley behind the mill, and which Homer or Shakspeare could not re-form for me in words? The leafless trees become spires of flame in the sunset, with the blue east for their background, and the stars of the dead calices of flowers and every withered stem and stubble rimed with frost contribute something to the mute music.

The inhabitants of cities suppose that the country landscape is pleasant only half the year. I please myself with the graces of the winter scenery and believe that we are as much touched by it as by the genial influences of summer. To the attentive eye, each moment of the year has its own beauty, and in the same field it beholds every hour a picture which was never seen before and which shall never be seen again. The heavens change every moment and reflect their glory or gloom on the plains beneath. The state of the crop in the surrounding farms alters the expression of the earth from week to week. The succession of native plants in the pastures and roadsides, which makes the silent clock by which time tells the summer hours, will make even the divisions of the day sensible to a keen observer. The tribes of birds and insects, like the plants punctual to their time, follow each other, and the year has room for all. By water-courses, the variety is greater. In July the blue pontederia or pickerel-weed blooms in large beds in the shallow parts of our pleasant river and swarms with yellow butterflies in continual motion. Art cannot rival this pomp of purple and gold. Indeed the river is a perpetual gala and boasts each month a new ornament.

But this beauty of Nature which is seen and felt as beauty is the least part. The shows of day, the dewy morning, the rainbow, mountains, orchards in blossom, stars, moonlight, shadows in still water, and the like, if too eagerly hunted, become shows merely, and mock us with their unreality. Go out of the house to see the moon, and 'tis mere tinsel; it will not please as when its light shines upon your necessary journey. The beauty that shimmers in the yellow afternoons of October, who ever could clutch it? Go forth to find it, and it is gone; 'tis only a mirage as you look from the windows of diligence.

2. The presence of a higher, namely, of the spiritual element is essential to its perfection. The high and divine beauty which can be loved without effeminacy is that which is found in combination with the human will. Beauty is the mark God sets

upon virtue. Every natural action is graceful. Every heroic act is also decent and causes the place and the bystanders to shine. We are taught by great actions that the universe is the property of every individual in it. Every rational creature has all nature for his dowry and estate. It is his, if he will. He may divest himself of it; he may creep into a corner and abdicate his kingdom as most men do; but he is entitled to the world by his constitution. In proportion to the energy of his thought and will, he takes up the world into himself. "All those things for which men plough, build, or sail, obey virtue," said Sallust. "The winds and waves," said Gibbon, "are always on the side of the ablest navigators." So are the sun and moon and all the stars of heaven. When a noble act is done—perchance in a scene of great natural beauty: when Leonidas and his three hundred martyrs consume one day in dying, and the sun and moon come each and look at them once in the steep defile of Thermopylæ; when Arnold Winkelried, in the high Alps under the shadow of the avalanche, gathers in his side a sheaf of Austrian spears to break the line for his comrades—are not these heroes entitled to add the beauty of the scene to the beauty of the deed? When the bark of Columbus nears the shore of America—before it the beach lined with savages fleeing out of all their huts of cane; the sea behind; and the purple mountains of the Indian Archipelago around—can we separate the man from the living picture? Does not the New World clothe his form with her palm-groves and savannahs as fit drapery? Ever does natural beauty steal in like air and envelope great actions. When Sir Harry Vane was dragged up the Tower hill, sitting on a sled, to suffer death as the champion of the English laws, one of the multitude cried out to him, "You never sate on so glorious a seat!" Charles II, to intimidate the citizens of London, caused the patriot Lord Russell to be drawn in an open coach through the principal streets of the city on his way to the scaffold. "But," his biographer says, "the multitude imagined they saw liberty and virtue sitting by his side." In private places, among sordid objects, an act of truth or heroism seems at once to draw to itself the sky as its temple, the sun as its candle. Nature stretches out her arms to embrace man, only let his thoughts be of equal greatness. Willingly does she follow his steps with the rose and the violet and bend her lines of grandeur and grace to the decoration of her darling child. Only let his thoughts be of equal scope and the frame will suit the picture. A virtuous man is in unison with her works and makes the central figure of the visible sphere. Homer, Pindar, Socrates, Phocion, associate themselves fitly in our memory with the geography and climate of Greece. The visible heavens and earth sympathize with Jesus. And in common life whosoever has seen a person of powerful character and happy genius will have remarked how easily he took all things along with him—the persons, the opinions, and the day, and nature became ancillary to a man.

3. There is still another aspect under which the beauty of the world may be viewed, namely, as it becomes an object of the intellect. Beside the relation of things to virtue, they have a relation to thought. The intellect searches out the absolute order of things as they stand in the mind of God and without the colors of affection. The intellectual and the active powers seem to succeed each other, and the exclusive activity of the one generates the exclusive activity of the other. There is something unfriendly in each to the other, but they are like the alternate periods of feeding and working in animals; each prepares and will be followed by the other. Therefore does beauty, which, in relation to actions, as we have seen, comes unsought, and comes because it is unsought, remain for the apprehension and pursuit of the intellect; and then again, in its turn, of the active power. Nothing divine dies. All good is eternally reproductive. The beauty of nature re-forms itself in the mind, and not for barren contemplation but for new creation.

All men are in some degree impressed by the face of the world, some men even to delight. This love of beauty is Taste. Others have the same love in such excess that, not content with admiring, they seek to embody it in new forms. The creation of beauty is Art.

The production of a work of art throws a light upon the mystery of humanity. A work of art is an abstract or epitome of the world. It is the result or expression of nature in miniature. For although the works of nature are innumerable and all different, the result or the expression of them all is similar and single. Nature is a sea of forms radically alike and even unique. A leaf, a sunbeam, a landscape, the ocean, make an analogous impression on the mind. What is common to them all—that perfectness and harmony—is beauty. The standard of beauty is the entire circuit of natural forms, the totality of nature, which the Italians expressed by defining beauty "*il più nell' uno*." [1] Nothing is quite beautiful alone, nothing but is beautiful in the whole. A single object is only so far beautiful as it suggests this universal grace. The poet, the painter, the sculptor, the musician, the architect, seek each to concentrate this radiance of the world on one point, and each in his several work to satisfy the love of beauty which stimulates him to produce. Thus is Art a nature passed through the alembic of man. Thus in art does Nature work through the will of a man filled with the beauty of her first works.

The world thus exists to the soul to satisfy the desire of beauty. This element I call an ultimate end. No reason can be asked or given why the soul seeks beauty. Beauty, in its largest and profoundest sense, is one expression for the universe. God is the all-fair. Truth and goodness and beauty are but different faces of the same All. But beauty in nature is not ultimate. It is the herald of inward and eternal beauty and is not alone a solid and satisfactory good. It must stand as a part, and not as yet the last or highest expression of the final cause of Nature.

[1] Many in one.

IV. LANGUAGE

LANGUAGE is a third use which Nature subserves to man. Nature is the vehicle of thought, and in a simple, double and threefold degree.

1. Words are signs of natural facts.
2. Particular natural facts are symbols of particular spiritual facts.
3. Nature is the symbol of spirit.

1. Words are signs of natural facts. The use of natural history is to give us aid in supernatural history; the use of the outer creation, to give us language for the beings and changes of the inward creation. Every word which is used to express a moral or intellectual fact, if traced to its root, is found to be borrowed from some material appearance. *Right* means *straight; wrong* means *twisted. Spirit* primarily means *wind; transgression*, the crossing of a *line; supercilious*, the *raising of the eyebrow.* We say the *heart* to express emotion, the *head* to denote thought; and *thought* and *emotion* are words borrowed from sensible things and now appropriated to spiritual nature. Most of the process by which this transformation is made is hidden from us in the remote time when language was framed; but the same tendency may be daily observed in children. Children and savages use only nouns or names of things which they convert into verbs and apply to analogous mental acts.

2. But this origin of all words that convey a spiritual import—so conspicuous a fact in the history of language—is our least debt to nature. It is not words only that are emblematic; it is things which are emblematic. Every natural fact is a symbol of some spiritual fact. Every appearance in nature corresponds to some state of the mind; and that state of the mind can only be described by presenting that natural appearance as

its picture. An enraged man is a lion, a cunning man is a fox, a firm man is a rock, a learned man is a torch. A lamb is innocence; a snake is subtle spite; flowers express to us the delicate affections. Light and darkness are our familiar expression for knowledge and ignorance, and heat for love. Visible distance behind and before us is respectively our image of memory and hope.

Who looks upon a river in a meditative hour and is not reminded of the flux of all things? Throw a stone into the stream, and the circles that propagate themselves are the beautiful type of all influence. Man is conscious of a universal soul within or behind his individual life, wherein, as in a firmament, the natures of Justice, Truth, Love, Freedom arise and shine. This universal soul he calls Reason: it is not mine, or thine or his, but we are its; we are its property and men. And the blue sky in which the private earth is buried, the sky with its eternal calm, and full of everlasting orbs, is the type of Reason. That which intellectually considered we call Reason, considered in relation to nature, we call Spirit. Spirit is the Creator. Spirit hath life in itself. And man in all ages and countries embodies it in his language as the FATHER.

It is easily seen that there is nothing lucky or capricious in these analogies, but that they are constant and pervade nature. These are not the dreams of a few poets, here and there, but man is an analogist and studies relations in all objects. He is placed in the center of beings, and a ray of relation passes from every other being to him. And neither can man be understood without these objects, nor these objects without man. All the facts in natural history taken by themselves have no value, but are barren, like a single sex. But marry it to human history, and it is full of life. Whole floras, all Linnæus's and Buffon's volumes, are dry catalogues of facts; but the most trivial of these facts, the habit of a plant, the organs or work or noise of an insect, applied to the illustration of a fact in intellectual philosophy or in any way associated to human nature, affects us in the most lively and agreeable manner. The seed of a plant—to what affecting analogies in the nature of man is that little fruit made use of, in all discourse, up to the voice of Paul who calls the human corpse a seed: "It is sown a natural body; it is raised a spiritual body."[1] The motion of the earth round its axis and round the sun makes the day and the year. These are certain amounts of brute light and heat. But is there no intent of an analogy between man's life and the seasons? And do the seasons gain no grandeur or pathos from that analogy? The instincts of the ant are very unimportant considered as the ant's; but the moment a ray of relation is seen to extend from it to man, and the little drudge is seen to be a monitor, a little body with a mighty heart, then all its habits, even that said to be recently observed, that it never sleeps, become sublime.

Because of this radical correspondence between visible things and human thoughts, savages, who have only what is necessary, converse in figures. As we go back in history, language becomes more picturesque, until its infancy, when it is all poetry; or all spiritual facts are represented by natural symbols. The same symbols are found to make the original elements of all languages. It has moreover been observed that the idioms of all languages approach each other in passages of the greatest eloquence and power. And as this is the first language, so is it the last. This immediate dependence of language upon nature, this conversion of an outward phenomenon into a type of somewhat in human life, never loses its power to affect us. It is this which gives that piquancy to the conversation of a strong-natured farmer or backwoodsman, which all men relish.

A man's power to connect his thought with its proper symbol, and so to utter it, depends on the simplicity of his character, that is, upon his love of truth and his desire to communicate it without loss. The corruption of man is followed by the corruption of language. When simplicity of character and the sov-

[1] I Corinthians, 15:42.

ereignty of ideas is broken up by the prevalence of secondary desires—the desire of riches, of pleasure, of power, and of praise—and duplicity and falsehood take place of simplicity and truth, the power over nature as an interpreter of the will is in a degree lost; new imagery ceases to be created, and old words are perverted to stand for things which are not; a paper currency is employed when there is no bullion in the vaults. In due time the fraud is manifest, and words lose all power to stimulate the understanding or the affections. Hundreds of writers may be found in every long-civilized nation who for a short time believe and make others believe that they see and utter truths, who do not of themselves clothe one thought in its natural garment, but who feed unconsciously on the language created by the primary writers of the country, those, namely, who hold primarily on nature.

But wise men pierce this rotten diction and fasten words again to visible things; so that picturesque language is at once a commanding certificate that he who employs it is a man in alliance with truth and God. The moment our discourse rises above the ground line of familiar facts and is inflamed with passion or exalted by thought, it clothes itself in images. A man conversing in earnest, if he watch his intellectual processes, will find that a material image more or less luminous arises in his mind, contemporaneous with every thought, which furnishes the vestment of the thought. Hence, good writing and brilliant discourse are perpetual allegories. This imagery is spontaneous. It is the blending of experience with the present action of the mind. It is proper creation. It is the working of the Original Cause through the instruments he has already made.

These facts may suggest the advantage which the country life possesses for a powerful mind, over the artificial and curtailed life of cities. We know more from nature than we can at will communicate. Its light flows into the mind evermore, and we forget its presence. The poet, the orator, bred in the woods, whose senses have been nourished by their fair and appeasing changes year after year, without design and without heed, shall not lose their lesson altogether in the roar of cities or the broil of politics. Long hereafter, amidst agitation and terror in national councils—in the hour of revolution—these solemn images shall reappear in their morning luster as fit symbols and words of the thoughts which the passing events shall awaken. At the call of a noble sentiment, again the woods wave, the pines murmur, the river rolls and shines, and the cattle low upon the mountains, as he saw and heard them in his infancy. And with these forms, the spells of persuasion, the keys of power are put into his hands.

3. We are thus assisted by natural objects in the expression of particular meanings. But how great a language to convey such peppercorn informations! Did it need such noble races of creatures, this profusion of forms, this host of orbs in heaven, to furnish man with the dictionary and grammar of his municipal speech? Whilst we use this grand cipher to expedite the affairs of our pot and kettle, we feel that we have not yet put it to its use, neither are able. We are like travelers using the cinders of a volcano to roast their eggs. Whilst we see that it always stands ready to clothe what we would say, we cannot avoid the question whether the characters are not significant of themselves. Have mountains and waves and skies no significance but what we consciously give them when we employ them as emblems of our thoughts? The world is emblematic. Parts of speech are metaphors because the whole of nature is a metaphor of the human mind. The laws of moral nature answer to those of matter as face to face in a glass. "The visible world and the relation of its parts is the dial plate of the invisible." The axioms of physics translate the laws of ethics. Thus: "The whole is greater than its part"; "Reaction is equal to action"; "The smallest weight may be made to lift the greatest, the difference of weight being compensated by time"; and many the like propositions which have an ethical as well as physical sense. These

propositions have a much more extensive and universal sense when applied to human life than when confined to technical use.

In like manner, the memorable words of history and the proverbs of nations consist usually of a natural fact, selected as a picture or parable of a moral truth. Thus: "A rolling stone gathers no moss"; "A bird in the hand is worth two in the bush"; "A cripple in the right way will beat a racer in the wrong"; "Make hay while the sun shines"; " 'Tis hard to carry a full cup even"; "Vinegar is the son of wine"; "The last ounce broke the camel's back"; "Long-lived trees make roots first"; and the like. In their primary sense these are trivial facts, but we repeat them for the value of their analogical import. What is true of proverbs is true of all fables, parables, and allegories.

This relation between the mind and matter is not fancied by some poet, but stands in the will of God and so is free to be known by all men. It appears to men or it does not appear. When in fortunate hours we ponder this miracle, the wise man doubts if at all other times he is not blind and deaf:

> *Can such things be,*
> *And overcome us like a summer's cloud,*
> *Without our special wonder?* [1]

for the universe becomes transparent, and the light of higher laws than its own shines through it. It is the standing problem which has exercised the wonder and the study of every fine genius since the world began, from the era of the Egyptians and the Brahmins to that of Pythagoras, of Plato, of Bacon, of Leibnitz, of Swedenborg. There sits the Sphinx at the roadside, and from age to age, as each prophet comes by, he tries his fortune at reading her riddle. There seems to be a necessity in spirit to manifest itself in material forms; and day and night,

[1] Shakespeare, Macbeth, III, iv.

river and storm, beast and bird, acid and alkali, pre-exist in necessary Ideas in the mind of God, and are what they are by virtue of preceding affections in the world of spirit. A Fact is the end or last issue of spirit. The visible creation is the terminus or the circumference of the invisible world. "Material objects," said a French philosopher, "are necessarily kinds of scoriae of the substantial thoughts of the Creator, which must always preserve an exact relation to their first origin; in other words, visible nature must have a spiritual and moral side."

This doctrine is abstruse, and though the images of "garment," "scoriae," "mirror," etc., may stimulate the fancy, we must summon the aid of subtler and more vital expositors to make it plain. "Every scripture is to be interpreted by the same spirit which gave it forth," is the fundamental law of criticism. A life in harmony with Nature, the love of truth and of virtue, will purge the eyes to understand her text. By degrees we may come to know the primitive sense of the permanent objects of nature, so that the world shall be to us an open book and every form significant of its hidden life and final cause.

A new interest surprises us whilst, under the view now suggested, we contemplate the fearful extent and multitude of objects; since "every object rightly seen unlocks a new faculty of the soul." That which was unconscious truth becomes, when interpreted and defined in an object, a part of the domain of knowledge—a new weapon in the magazine of power.

V. DISCIPLINE

In view of the significance of nature, we arrive at once at a new fact, that nature is a discipline. This use of the world includes the preceding uses as parts of itself.

Space, time, society, labor, climate, food, locomotion, the animals, the mechanical forces give us sincerest lessons, day by day, whose meaning is unlimited. They educate both the Understanding and the Reason. Every property of matter is a school for the understanding—its solidity or resistance, its inertia, its extension, its figure, its divisibility. The understanding adds, divides, combines, measures, and finds nutriment and room for its activity in this worthy scene. Meantime, Reason transfers all these lessons into its own world of thought by perceiving the analogy that marries Matter and Mind.

1. Nature is a discipline of the understanding in intellectual truths. Our dealing with sensible objects is a constant exercise in the necessary lessons of difference, of likeness, of order, of being and seeming, of progressive arrangement; of ascent from particular to general; of combination to one end of manifold forces. Proportioned to the importance of the organ to be formed is the extreme care with which its tuition is provided—a care pretermitted [1] in no single case. What tedious training, day after day, year after year, never ending, to form the common sense; what continual reproduction of annoyances, inconveniences, dilemmas; what rejoicing over us of little men; what disputing of prices; what reckonings of interest—and all to form the Hand of the mind, to instruct us that "good thoughts are no better than good dreams, unless they be executed!"

The same good office is performed by Property and its filial systems of debt and credit. Debt, grinding debt, whose iron face the widow, the orphan, and the sons of genius fear and hate; debt, which consumes so much time, which so cripples and disheartens a great spirit with cares that seem so base, is a preceptor whose lessons cannot be foregone and is needed most by those who suffer from it most. Moreover, property, which has been well compared to snow—"if it fall level today, it will be blown into drifts tomorrow"—is the surface action of internal machinery, like the index on the face of a clock. Whilst now it is the gymnastics of the understanding, it is hiving, in the foresight of the spirit, experience in profounder laws.

The whole character and fortune of the individual are af-

[1] Omitted.

fected by the least inequalities in the culture of the understanding; for example, in the perception of differences. Therefore is Space, and therefore Time, that man may know that things are not huddled and lumped, but sundered and individual. A bell and a plough have each their use, and neither can do the office of the other. Water is good to drink, coal to burn, wool to wear; but wool cannot be drunk, nor water spun, nor coal eaten. The wise man shows his wisdom in separation, in gradation, and his scale of creatures and of merits is as wide as nature. The foolish have no range in their scale but suppose every man is as every other man. What is not good they call the worst, and what is not hateful they call the best.

In like manner, what good heed Nature forms in us! She pardons no mistakes. Her yea is yea, and her nay, nay.

The first steps in agriculture, astronomy, zoölogy (those first steps which the farmer, the hunter, and the sailor take) teach that Nature's dice are always loaded, that in her heaps and rubbish are concealed sure and useful results.

How calmly and genially the mind apprehends one after another the laws of physics! What noble emotions dilate the mortal as he enters into the councils of the creation and feels by knowledge the privilege to BE! His insight refines him. The beauty of nature shines in his own breast. Man is greater that he can see this, and the universe less, because Time and Space relations vanish as laws are known.

Here again we are impressed and even daunted by the immense Universe to be explored. "What we know is a point to what we do not know." Open any recent journal of science and weigh the problems suggested concerning light, heat, electricity, magnetism, physiology, geology, and judge whether the interest of natural science is likely to be soon exhausted.

Passing by many particulars of the discipline of nature, we must not omit to specify two.

The exercise of the Will, or the lesson of power, is taught in every event. From the child's successive possession of his several senses up to the hour when he saith, "Thy will be done!" he is learning the secret that he can reduce under his will not only particular events but great classes, nay, the whole series of events, and so conform all facts to his character. Nature is thoroughly mediate. It is made to serve. It receives the dominion of man as meekly as the ass on which the Saviour rode. It offers all its kingdoms to man as the raw material which he may mold into what is useful. Man is never weary of working it up. He forges the subtile and delicate air into wise and melodious words and gives them wing as angels of persuasion and command. One after another his victorious thought comes up with and reduces all things, until the world becomes at last only a realized will—the double of the man.

2. Sensible objects conform to the premonitions of Reason and reflect the conscience. All things are moral, and in their boundless changes have an unceasing reference to spiritual nature. Therefore is nature glorious with form, color, and motion; that every globe in the remotest heaven, every chemical change from the rudest crystal up to the laws of life, every change of vegetation from the first principle of growth in the eye of a leaf, to the tropical forest and antediluvian coal-mine, every animal function from the sponge up to Hercules, shall hint or thunder to man the laws of right and wrong and echo the Ten Commandments. Therefore is Nature ever the ally of Religion: lends all her pomp and riches to the religious sentiment. Prophet and priest, David, Isaiah, Jesus, have drawn deeply from this source. This ethical character so penetrates the bone and marrow of nature as to seem the end for which it was made. Whatever private purpose is answered by any member or part, this is its public and universal function and is never omitted. Nothing in nature is exhausted in its first use. When a thing has served an end to the uttermost, it is wholly new for an ulterior service. In God, every end is converted into a new means. Thus the use of commodity, regarded by itself, is mean

and squalid. But it is to the mind an education in the doctrine of Use, namely, that a thing is good only so far as it serves; that a conspiring of parts and efforts to the production of an end is essential to any being. The first and gross manifestation of this truth is our inevitable and hated training in values and wants, in corn and meat.

It has already been illustrated that every natural process is a version of a moral sentence. The moral law lies at the center of nature and radiates to the circumference. It is the pith and marrow of every substance, every relation, and every process. All things with which we deal preach to us. What is a farm but a mute gospel? The chaff and the wheat, weeds and plants, blight, rain, insects, sun—it is a sacred emblem from the first furrow of spring to the last stack which the snow of winter overtakes in the fields. But the sailor, the shepherd, the miner, the merchant, in their several resorts, have each an experience precisely parallel and leading to the same conclusion: because all organizations are radically alike. Nor can it be doubted that this moral sentiment, which thus scents the air, grows in the grain and impregnates the waters of the world, is caught by man and sinks into his soul. The moral influence of nature upon every individual is that amount of truth which it illustrates to him. Who can estimate this? Who can guess how much firmness the sea-beaten rock has taught the fisherman? how much tranquillity has been reflected to man from the azure sky, over whose unspotted deeps the winds forevermore drive flocks of stormy clouds and leave no wrinkle or stain? how much industry and providence and affection we have caught from the pantomime of brutes? What a searching preacher of self-command is the varying phenomenon of Health!

Herein is especially apprehended the unity of Nature—the unity in variety—which meets us everywhere. All the endless variety of things make an identical impression. Xenophanes complained in his old age that, look where he would, all things hastened back to Unity. He was weary of seeing the same entity in the tedious variety of forms. The fable of Proteus has a cordial truth. A leaf, a drop, a crystal, a moment of time, is related to the whole and partakes of the perfection of the whole. Each particle is a microcosm and faithfully renders the likeness of the world.

Not only resemblances exist in things whose analogy is obvious, as when we detect the type of the human hand in the flipper of the fossil saurus, but also in objects wherein there is great superficial unlikeness. Thus architecture is called "frozen music," by De Staël and Goethe. Vitruvius thought an architect should be a musician. "A Gothic church," said Coleridge, "is a petrified religion." Michelangelo maintained that to an architect a knowledge of anatomy is essential. In Haydn's oratorios, the notes present to the imagination not only motions, as of the snake, the stag, and the elephant, but colors also, as the green grass. The law of harmonic sounds reappears in the harmonic colors. The granite is differenced in its laws only by the more or less of heat from the river that wears it away. The river, as it flows, resembles the air that flows over it; the air resembles the light which traverses it with more subtile currents; the light resembles the heat which rides with it through Space. Each creature is only a modification of the other; the likeness in them is more than the difference, and their radical law is one and the same. A rule of one art, or a law of one organization, holds true throughout nature. So intimate is this Unity that it is easily seen, it lies under the undermost garment of Nature and betrays its source in Universal Spirit. For it pervades Thought also. Every universal truth which we express in words implies or supposes every other truth. *Omne verum vero consonat.*[1] It is like a great circle on a sphere, comprising all possible circles; which, however, may be drawn and comprise it in like manner. Every such truth is the absolute Ens[2] seen from one side. But it has innumerable sides.

[1] Every truth agrees with the true.

[2] Being; having existence.

The central Unity is still more conspicuous in actions. Words are finite organs of the infinite mind. They cannot cover the dimensions of what is in truth. They break, chop, and impoverish it. And action is the perfection and publication of thought. A right action seems to fill the eye and to be related to all nature. "The wise man, in doing one thing, does all; or, in the one thing he does rightly, he sees the likeness of all which is done rightly."

Words and actions are not the attributes of brute nature. They introduce us to the human form, of which all other organizations appear to be degradations. When this appears among so many that surround it, the spirit prefers it to all others. It says, "From such as this have I drawn joy and knowledge; in such as this have I found and beheld myself; I will speak to it; it can speak again; it can yield me thought already formed and alive." In fact, the eye—the mind—is always accompanied by these forms, male and female; and these are incomparably the richest informations of the power and order that lie at the heart of things. Unfortunately every one of them bears the marks as of some injury, is marred and superficially defective. Nevertheless, far different from the deaf and dumb nature around them, these all rest like fountain-pipes on the unfathomed sea of thought and virtue whereto they alone, of all organizations, are the entrances.

It were a pleasant inquiry to follow into detail their ministry to our education, but where would it stop? We are associated in adolescent and adult life with some friends who, like skies and waters, are coextensive with our idea; who, answering each to a certain affection of the soul, satisfy our desire on that side; whom we lack power to put at such focal distance from us that we can mend or even analyze them. We cannot choose but love them. When much intercourse with a friend has supplied us with a standard of excellence and has increased our respect for the resources of God who thus sends a real person to outgo our ideal; when he has, moreover, become an object of thought and, whilst his character retains all its unconscious effect, is converted in the mind into solid and sweet wisdom—is a sign to us that his office is closing, and he is commonly withdrawn from our sight in a short time.

VI. IDEALISM

Thus is the unspeakable but intelligible and practicable meaning of the world conveyed to man, the immortal pupil, in every object of sense. To this one end of Discipline all parts of nature conspire.

A noble doubt perpetually suggests itself—whether this end be not the Final Cause of the Universe; and whether nature outwardly exists. It is a sufficient account of that Appearance we call the World that God will teach a human mind, and so makes it the receiver of a certain number of congruent sensations which we call sun and moon, man and woman, house and trade. In my utter impotence to test the authenticity of the report of my senses, to know whether the impressions they make on me correspond with outlying objects, what difference does it make whether Orion is up there in heaven, or some god paints the image in the firmament of the soul? The relations of parts and the end of the whole remaining the same, what is the difference, whether land and sea interact and worlds revolve and intermingle without number or end—deep yawning under deep, and galaxy balancing galaxy throughout absolute space—or whether, without relations of time and space, the same appearances are inscribed in the constant faith of man? Whether nature enjoy a substantial existence without or is only in the apocalypse of the mind, it is alike useful and alike venerable to me. Be it what it may, it is ideal to me so long as I cannot try the accuracy of my senses.

The frivolous make themselves merry with the Ideal theory, as if its consequences were burlesque, as if it affected the stability of nature. It surely does not. God never jests with us and will not compromise the end of nature by permitting any inconsequence in its procession. Any distrust of the permanence of laws would paralyze the faculties of man. Their permanence is sacredly respected, and his faith therein is perfect. The wheels and springs of man are all set to the hypothesis of the permanence of nature. We are not built like a ship to be tossed, but like a house to stand. It is a natural consequence of this structure that so long as the active powers predominate over the reflective, we resist with indignation any hint that nature is more short-lived or mutable than spirit. The broker, the wheelwright, the carpenter, the tollman, are much displeased at the intimation.

But whilst we acquiesce entirely in the permanence of natural laws, the question of the absolute existence of nature still remains open. It is the uniform effect of culture on the human mind not to shake our faith in the stability of particular phenomena, as of heat, water, azote, [1] but to lead us to regard nature as phenomenon, not a substance, to attribute necessary existence to spirit, to esteem nature as an accident and an effect.

To the senses and the unrenewed understanding belongs a sort of instinctive belief in the absolute existence of nature. In their view man and nature are indissolubly joined. Things are ultimates and they never look beyond their sphere. The presence of Reason mars this faith. The first effort of thought tends to relax this despotism of the senses which binds us to nature as if we were a part of it, and shows us nature aloof and, as it were, afloat. Until this higher agency intervened, the animal eye sees, with wonderful accuracy, sharp outlines and colored surfaces. When the eye of Reason opens, to outline and surface are at once added grace and expression. These proceed from imagination and affection, and abate somewhat of the angular distinctness of objects. If the Reason be stimulated to more earnest vision, outlines and surfaces become transparent and are no longer seen; causes and spirits are seen through them.

[1] Nitrogen.

The best moments of life are these delicious awakenings of the higher powers and the reverential withdrawing of nature before its God.

Let us proceed to indicate the effects of culture.

1. Our first institution in the Ideal philosophy is a hint from Nature herself.

Nature is made to conspire with spirit to emancipate us. Certain mechanical changes, a small alteration in our local position apprises us of a dualism. We are strangely affected by seeing the shore from a moving ship, from a balloon, or through the tints of an unusual sky. The least change in our point of view gives the whole world a pictorial air. A man who seldom rides needs only to get into a coach and traverse his own town to turn the street into a puppet-show. The men, the women—talking, running, bartering, fighting—the earnest mechanic, the lounger, the beggar, the boys, the dogs, are unrealized at once, or, at least, wholly detached from all relation to the observer and seen as apparent, not substantial beings. What new thoughts are suggested by seeing a face of country quite familiar, in the rapid movement of the railroad car! Nay, the most wonted objects (make a very slight change in the point of vision,) please us most. In a camera obscura, the butcher's cart and the figure of one of our own family amuse us. So a portrait of a well-known face gratifies us. Turn the eyes upside down, by looking at the landscape through your legs, and how agreeable is the picture, though you have seen it any time these twenty years!

In these cases, by mechanical means, is suggested the difference between the observer and the spectacle—between man and nature. Hence arises a pleasure mixed with awe; I may say, a low degree of the sublime is felt, from the fact, probably, that man is hereby apprised that whilst the world is a spectacle, something in himself is stable.

2. In a higher manner the poet communicates the same pleas-

ure. By a few strokes he delineates, as on air, the sun, the mountain, the camp, the city, the hero, the maiden, not different from what we know them, but only lifted from the ground and afloat before the eye. He unfixes the land and the sea, makes them revolve around the axis of his primary thought and disposes them anew. Possessed himself by a heroic passion, he uses matter as symbols of it. The sensual man conforms thoughts to things; the poet conforms things to his thoughts. The one esteems nature as rooted and fast; the other, as fluid, and impresses his being thereon. To him, the refractory world is ductile and flexible; he invests dust and stones with humanity and makes them the words of the Reason. The Imagination may be defined to be the use which the Reason makes of the material world. Shakspeare possesses the power of subordinating nature for the purposes of expression, beyond all poets. His imperial muse tosses the creation like a bauble from hand to hand and uses it to embody any caprice of thought that is uppermost in his mind. The remotest spaces of nature are visited, and the farthest sundered things are brought together, by a subtile spiritual connection. We are made aware that magnitude of material things is relative, and all objects shrink and expand to serve the passion of the poet. Thus in his sonnets, the lays of birds, the scents and dyes of flowers he finds to be the *shadow* of his beloved; time, which keeps her from him, is his *chest;* the suspicion she has awakened, is her *ornament;*

> *The ornament of beauty is Suspect,*
> *A crow which flies in heaven's sweetest air.*[1]

His passion is not the fruit of chance; it swells, as he speaks, to a city, or a state.

> *No, it was builded far from accident;*
> *It suffers not in smiling pomp, nor falls*
> *Under the brow of thralling discontent;*
> *It fears not policy, that heretic,*

[1] Sonnet 70.

That works on leases of short numbered hours,
But all alone stands hugely politic.[1]

In the strength of his constancy, the Pyramids seem to him recent and transitory. The freshness of youth and love dazzles him with its resemblance to morning:

Take those lips away
Which so sweetly were forsworn;
And those eyes,—the break of day,
Lights that do mislead the morn.[2]

The wild beauty of this hyperbole, I may say in passing, it would not be easy to match in literature.

This transfiguration which all material objects undergo through the passion of the poet—this power which he exerts to dwarf the great, to magnify the small—might be illustrated by a thousand examples from his plays. I have before me *The Tempest,* and will cite only these few lines.

PROSPERO. *The strong based promontory*
Have I made shake, and by the spurs plucked up
The pine and cedar.

Prospero calls for music to soothe the frantic Alonzo, and his companions:

A solemn air, and the best comforter
To an unsettled fancy, cure thy brains
Now useless, boiled within thy skull.

Again:

The charm dissolves apace,
And, as the morning steals upon the night,
Melting the darkness, so their rising senses
Begin to chase the ignorant fumes that mantle
Their clearer reason.

[1] Sonnet 124.
[2] *Measure for Measure,* IV. i.

Their understanding
Begins to swell: and the approaching tide
Will shortly fill the reasonable shores
That now lie foul and muddy.

The perception of real affinities between events (that is to say, of *ideal* affinities, for those only are real), enables the poet thus to make free with the most imposing forms and phenomena of the world and to assert the predominance of the soul.

3. While thus the poet animates nature with his own thoughts, he differs from the philosopher only herein, that the one proposes Beauty as his main end; the other Truth. But the philosopher, not less than the poet, postpones the apparent order and relations of things to the empire of thought. "The problem of philosophy," according to Plato, "is, for all that exists conditionally, to find a ground unconditioned and absolute." It proceeds on the faith that a law determines all phenomena, which being known, the phenomena can be predicted. That law, when in the mind, is an idea. Its beauty is infinite. The true philosopher and the true poet are one, and a beauty, which is truth, and a truth, which is beauty, is the aim of both. Is not the charm of one of Plato's or Aristotle's definitions strictly like that of the Antigone of Sophocles? It is, in both cases, that a spiritual life has been imparted to nature; that the solid seeming block of matter has been pervaded and dissolved by a thought; that this feeble human being has penetrated the vast masses of nature with an informing soul and recognized itself in their harmony, that is, seized their law. In physics, when this is attained, the memory disburdens itself of its cumbrous catalogues of particulars and carries centuries of observation in a single formula.

Thus even in physics, the material is degraded before the spiritual. The astronomer, the geometer rely on their irrefragable analysis and disdain the results of observation. The sublime remark of Euler on his law of arches, "This will be found contrary to all experience, yet is true," had already transferred nature into the mind, and left matter like an outcast corpse.

4. Intellectual science has been observed to beget invariably a doubt of the existence of matter. Turgot said, "He that has never doubted the existence of matter may be assured he has no aptitude for metaphysical inquiries." It fastens the attention upon immortal, necessary, uncreated natures, that is, upon Ideas; and in their presence we feel that the outward circumstance is a dream and a shade. Whilst we wait in this Olympus of gods, we think of nature as an appendix to the soul. We ascend into their region and know that these are the thoughts of the Supreme Being. "These are they who were set up from everlasting, from the beginning, or ever the earth was. When he prepared the heavens, they were there; when he established the clouds above, when he strengthened the fountains of the deep. Then they were by him, as one brought up with him. Of them took he counsel." [1]

Their influence is proportionate. As objects of science they are accessible to few men. Yet all men are capable of being raised by piety or by passion into their region. And no man touches these divine natures without becoming, in some degree, himself divine. Like a new soul, they renew the body. We become physically nimble and lightsome; we tread on air; life is no longer irksome, and we think it will never be so. No man fears age or misfortune or death in their serene company, for he is transported out of the district of change. Whilst we behold unveiled the nature of Justice and Truth, we learn the difference between the absolute and the conditional or relative. We apprehend the absolute. As it were, for the first time, *we exist.* We become immortal, for we learn that time and space are relations of matter; that with a perception of truth or a virtuous will they have no affinity.

5. Finally, religion and ethics, which may be fitly called the practice of ideas, or the introduction of ideas into life, have an

[1] Paraphrased from Proverbs, 8:23-30.

analogous effect with all lower culture, in degrading nature and suggesting its dependence on spirit. Ethics and religion differ herein: that the one is the system of human duties commencing from man; the other, from God. Religion includes the personality of God; ethics does not. They are one to our present design. They both put nature underfoot. The first and last lesson of religion is, "The things that are seen are temporal; the things that are unseen are eternal." It puts an affront upon nature. It does that for the unschooled which philosophy does for Berkeley and Viasa. The uniform language that may be heard in the churches of the most ignorant sects is, "Contemn the unsubstantial shows of the world; they are vanities, dreams, shadows, unrealities; seek the realities of religion." The devotee flouts nature. Some theosophists have arrived at a certain hostility and indignation towards matter, as the Manichean and Plotinus. They distrusted in themselves any looking back to these fleshpots of Egypt. Plotinus was ashamed of his body. In short, they might all say of matter, what Michelangelo said of external beauty, "It is the frail and weary weed in which God dresses the soul which he has called into time."

It appears that motion, poetry, physical and intellectual science, and religion, all tend to affect our convictions of the reality of the external world. But I own there is something ungrateful in expanding too curiously the particulars of the general proposition, that all culture tends to imbue us with idealism. I have no hostility to nature, but a child's love to it. I expand and live in the warm day like corn and melons. Let us speak her fair. I do not wish to fling stones at my beautiful mother, nor soil my gentle nest. I only wish to indicate the true position of nature in regard to man, wherein to establish man all right education tends; as the ground which to attain is the object of human life, that is, of man's connection with nature. Culture inverts the vulgar views of nature and brings the mind to call that apparent which it uses to call real, and that real which it uses to call visionary. Children, it is true, believe in the external world.

The belief that it appears only is an afterthought, but with culture this faith will as surely arise on the mind as did the first.

The advantage of the ideal theory over the popular faith is this, that it presents the world in precisely that view which is most desirable to the mind. It is, in fact, the view which Reason, both speculative and practical, that is, philosophy and virtue, take. For seen in the light of thought, the world always is phenomenal; and virtue subordinates it to the mind. Idealism sees the world in God. It beholds the whole circle of persons and things, of actions and events, of country and religion, not as painfully accumulated, atom after atom, act after act, in an aged creeping Past, but as one vast picture which God paints on the instant eternity for the contemplation of the soul. Therefore the soul holds itself off from a too trivial and microscopic study of the universal tablet. It respects the end too much to immerse itself in the means. It sees something more important in Christianity than the scandals of ecclesiastical history or the niceties of criticism; and, very incurious concerning persons or miracles and not at all disturbed by chasms of historical evidence, it accepts from God the phenomenon, as it finds it, as the pure and awful form of religion in the world. It is not hot and passionate at the appearance of what it calls its own good or bad fortune, at the union or opposition of other persons. No man is its enemy. It accepts whatsoever befalls, as part of its lesson. It is a watcher more than a doer, and it is a doer, only that it may the better watch.

VII. SPIRIT

It is essential to a true theory of nature and of man that it should contain somewhat progressive. Uses that are exhausted or that may be, and facts that end in the statement, cannot be all that is true of this brave lodging wherein man is harbored and wherein all his faculties find appropriate and endless exercise. And all the uses of nature admit of being summed in one, which yields the activity of man an infinite scope. Through all its kingdoms, to the suburbs and outskirts of things, it is faithful to the cause whence it had its origin. It always speaks of Spirit. It suggests the absolute. It is a perpetual effect. It is a great shadow pointing always to the sun behind us.

The aspect of Nature is devout. Like the figure of Jesus, she stands with bended head and hands folded upon the breast. The happiest man is he who learns from nature the lesson of worship.

Of that ineffable essence which we call Spirit, he that thinks most, will say least. We can foresee God in the coarse and, as it were, distant phenomena of matter; but when we try to define and describe himself, both language and thought desert us, and we are as helpless as fools and savages. That essence refuses to be recorded in propositions, but when man has worshiped him intellectually, the noblest ministry of nature is to stand as the apparition of God. It is the organ through which the universal spirit speaks to the individual, and strives to lead back the individual to it.

When we consider Spirit, we see that the views already presented do not include the whole circumference of man. We must add some related thoughts.

Three problems are put by nature to the mind: What is matter? Whence is it? and Whereto? The first of these questions only, the ideal theory answers. Idealism saith: matter is a phenomenon, not a substance. Idealism acquaints us with the total disparity between the evidence of our own being and the evidence of the world's being. The one is perfect; the other, incapable of any assurance; the mind is a part of the nature of things; the world is a divine dream, from which we may presently awake to the glories and certainties of day. Idealism is a hypothesis to account for nature by other principles than those of carpentry and chemistry. Yet, if it only deny the existence of matter, it does not satisfy the demands of the spirit. It leaves

God out of me. It leaves me in the splendid labyrinth of my perceptions, to wander without end. Then the heart resists it because it balks the affections in denying substantive being to men and women. Nature is so pervaded with human life that there is something of humanity in all and in every particular. But this theory makes nature foreign to me and does not account for that consanguinity which we acknowledge to it.

Let it stand then, in the present state of our knowledge, merely as a useful introductory hypothesis, serving to apprise us of the eternal distinction between the soul and the world.

But when, following the invisible steps of thought, we come to inquire, Whence is matter? and Whereto? many truths arise to us out of the recesses of consciousness. We learn that the highest is present to the soul of man; that the dread universal essence, which is not wisdom or love or beauty or power, but all in one, and each entirely, is that for which all things exist and that by which they are; that spirit creates; that behind nature, throughout nature, spirit is present; one and not compound, it does not act upon us from without, that is, in space and time, but spiritually, or through ourselves: therefore, that spirit, that is, the Supreme Being, does not build up nature around us, but puts it forth through us, as the life of the tree puts forth new branches and leaves through the pores of the old. As a plant upon the earth, so a man rests upon the bosom of God; he is nourished by unfailing fountains and draws at his need inexhaustible power. Who can set bounds to the possibilities of man? Once inhale the upper air, being admitted to behold the absolute natures of justice and truth, and we learn that man has access to the entire mind of the Creator, is himself the creator in the finite. This view, which admonishes me where the sources of wisdom and power lie and points to virtue as to

The golden key
Which opes the palace of eternity,[1]

[1] Milton, *Comus*, lines 13-14.

carries upon its face the highest certificate of truth, because it animates me to create my own world through the purification of my soul.

The world proceeds from the same spirit as the body of man. It is a remoter and inferior incarnation of God, a projection of God in the unconscious. But it differs from the body in one important respect. It is not, like that, now subjected to the human will. Its serene order is inviolable by us. It is, therefore, to us, the present expositor of the divine mind. It is a fixed point whereby we may measure our departure. As we degenerate, the contrast between us and our house is more evident. We are as much strangers in nature as we are aliens from God. We do not understand the notes of birds. The fox and the deer run away from us; the bear and tiger rend us. We do not know the uses of more than a few plants, as corn and the apple, the potato and the vine. Is not the landscape, every glimpse of which hath a grandeur, a face of him? Yet this may show us what discord is between man and nature, for you cannot freely admire a noble landscape if laborers are digging in the field hard by. The poet finds something ridiculous in his delight until he is out of the sight of men.

VIII. PROSPECTS

In inquiries respecting the laws of the world and the frame of things, the highest reason is always the truest. That which seems faintly possible, it is so refined, is often faint and dim because it is deepest seated in the mind among the eternal verities. Empirical science is apt to cloud the sight and by the very knowledge of functions and processes to bereave the student of the manly contemplation of the whole. The savant becomes unpoetic. But the best-read naturalist who lends an entire and devout attention to truth will see that there remains much to learn of his relation to the world, and that it is not to be learned by any addition or subtraction or other comparison of known quantities, but is arrived at by untaught sallies of the spirit, by a continual self-recovery, and by entire humility. He will perceive that there are far more excellent qualities in the student than preciseness and infallibility; that a guess is often more fruitful than an indisputable affirmation, and that a dream may let us deeper into the secret of nature than a hundred concerted experiments.

For the problems to be solved are precisely those which the physiologist and the naturalist omit to state. It is not so pertinent to man to know all the individuals of the animal kingdom as it is to know whence and whereto is this tyrannizing unity in his constitution, which evermore separates and classifies things, endeavoring to reduce the most diverse to one form. When I behold a rich landscape, it is less to my purpose to recite correctly the order and superposition of the strata than to know why all thought of multitude is lost in a tranquil sense of unity. I cannot greatly honor minuteness in details, so long as there is no hint to explain the relation between things and thoughts; no ray upon the *metaphysics* of conchology, of botany, of the arts, to show the relation of the forms of flowers, shells, animals, architecture, to the mind, and build science upon ideas. In a cabinet of natural history, we become sensible of a certain occult recognition and sympathy in regard to the most unwieldy and eccentric forms of beast, fish, and insect. The American who has been confined, in his own country, to the sight of buildings designed after foreign models is surprised on entering York Minster or St. Peter's at Rome by the feeling that these structures are imitations also—faint copies of an invisible archetype. Nor has science sufficient humanity, so long as the naturalist overlooks that wonderful congruity which subsists between man and the world; of which he is lord, not because he is the most subtle inhabitant, but because he is its head and heart and finds something of himself in every great and small thing, in every mountain stratum, in every new law of color, fact of astronomy, or atmospheric influence which observation or analysis lays open. A perception of this mystery inspires the muse of George Herbert, the beautiful psalmist of the seventeenth century. The following lines are part of his little poem on Man.

Man is all symmetry,
Full of proportions, one limb to another,
And all to all the world besides.
Each part may call the farthest, brother;
For head with foot hath private amity,
And both with moons and tides.

Nothing hath got so far
But man hath caught and kept it as his prey;
His eyes dismount the highest star:
He is in little all the sphere.
Herbs gladly cure our flesh, because that they
Find their acquaintance there.

For us, the winds do blow,
The earth doth rest, heaven move, and fountains flow;
Nothing we see, but means our good,
As our delight, or as our treasure;
The whole is either our cupboard of food,
Or cabinet of pleasure.

The stars have us to bed:
Night draws the curtain; which the sun withdraws.
Music and light attend our head.
All things unto our flesh are kind,
In their descent and being; to our mind,
In their ascent and cause.

More servants wait on man
Than he'll take notice of. In every path,
He treads down that which doth befriend him
When sickness makes him pale and wan.
Oh mighty love! Man is one world, and hath
Another to attend him.

The perception of this class of truths makes the attraction which draws men to science, but the end is lost sight of in attention to the means. In view of this half-sight of science, we accept the sentence of Plato, that "poetry comes nearer to vital truth than history." Every surmise and vaticination[1] of the mind is entitled to a certain respect, and we learn to prefer imperfect theories and sentences which contain glimpses of truth to digested systems which have no one valuable suggestion. A wise writer will feel that the ends of study and composition are best answered by announcing undiscovered regions of thought, and so communicating, through hope, new activity to the torpid spirit.

I shall therefore conclude this essay with some traditions of man and nature, which a certain poet sang to me; and which, as they have always been in the world, and perhaps reappear to every bard, may be both history and prophecy.

'The foundations of man are not in matter but in spirit. But the element of spirit is eternity. To it, therefore, the longest series of events, the oldest chronologies are young and recent. In the cycle of the universal man, from whom the known individuals proceed, centuries are points, and all history is but the epoch of one degradation.

'We distrust and deny inwardly our sympathy with nature. We own and disown our relation to it, by turns. We are like Nebuchadnezzar, dethroned, bereft of reason, and eating grass like an ox. But who can set limits to the remedial force of spirit?

'A man is a god in ruins. When men are innocent, life shall

[1] Prophecy.

be longer and shall pass into the immortal as gently as we awake from dreams. Now, the world would be insane and rabid, if these disorganizations should last for hundreds of years. It is kept in check by death and infancy. Infancy is the perpetual Messiah, which comes into the arms of fallen men and pleads with them to return to paradise.

'Man is the dwarf of himself. Once he was permeated and dissolved by spirit. He filled nature with his overflowing currents. Out from him sprang the sun and moon; from man the sun, from woman the moon. The laws of his mind, the periods of his actions externized themselves into day and night, into the year and the seasons. But, having made for himself this huge shell, his waters retired; he no longer fills the veins and veinlets; he is shrunk to a drop. He sees that the structure still fits him, but fits him colossally. Say, rather, once it fitted him, now it corresponds to him from far and on high. He adores timidly his own work. Now is man the follower of the sun, and woman the follower of the moon. Yet sometimes he starts in his slumber and wonders at himself and his house and muses strangely at the resemblance betwixt him and it. He perceives that if his law is still paramount, if still he have elemental power, if his word is sterling yet in nature, it is not conscious power, it is not inferior but superior to his will. It is instinct.' Thus my Orphic poet sang.

At present, man applies to nature but half his force. He works on the world with his understanding alone. He lives in it and masters it by a penny-wisdom; and he that works most in it is but a half-man, and whilst his arms are strong and his digestion good, his mind is imbruted, and he is a selfish savage. His relation to nature, his power over it, is through the understanding, as by manure; the economic use of fire, wind, water, and the mariner's needle; steam, coal, chemical agriculture; the repairs of the human body by the dentist and the surgeon. This is such a resumption of power as if a banished king should buy his territories inch by inch, instead of vaulting at once into his throne. Meantime, in the thick darkness, there are not wanting gleams of a better light—occasional examples of the action of man upon nature with his entire force—with reason as well as understanding. Such examples are, the traditions of miracles in the earliest antiquity of all nations; the history of Jesus Christ; the achievements of a principle, as in religious and political revolutions, and in the abolition of the slave trade; the miracles of enthusiasm, as those reported of Swedenborg, Hohenlohe, and the Shakers; many obscure and yet contested facts, now arranged under the name of Animal Magnetism; prayer; eloquence; self-healing; and the wisdom of children. These are examples of Reason's momentary grasp of the scepter; the exertions of a power which exists not in time or space, but an instantaneous in-streaming causing power. The difference between the actual and the ideal force of man is happily figured by the schoolmen, in saying, that the knowledge of man is an evening knowledge, *vespertina cognitio*, but that of God is a morning knowledge, *matutina cognitio*.

The problem of restoring to the world original and eternal beauty is solved by the redemption of the soul. The ruin, or the blank, that we see when we look at nature is in our own eye. The axis of vision is not coincident with the axis of things, and so they appear not transparent but opaque. The reason why the world lacks unity and lies broken and in heaps is because man is disunited with himself. He cannot be a naturalist until he satisfies all the demands of the spirit. Love is as much its demand as perception. Indeed, neither can be perfect without the other. In the uttermost meaning of the words, thought is devout, and devotion is thought. Deep calls unto deep. But in actual life, the marriage is not celebrated. There are innocent men who worship God after the tradition of their fathers, but their sense of duty has not yet extended to the use of all their faculties. And there are patient naturalists, but they freeze their subject under the wintry light of the understanding. Is not prayer also a study of truth—a sally of the soul into the unfound infinite? No man ever prayed heartily without learning something. But when a faithful thinker, resolute to detach every object from personal relations and see it in the light of thought, shall, at the same time, kindle science with the fire of the holiest affections, then will God go forth anew into the creation.

It will not need, when the mind is prepared for study, to search for objects. The invariable mark of wisdom is to see the miraculous in the common. What is a day? What is a year? What is summer? What is woman? What is a child? What is sleep? To our blindness, these things seem unaffecting. We make fables to hide the baldness of the fact and conform it, as we say, to the higher law of the mind. But when the fact is seen under the light of an idea, the gaudy fable fades and shrivels. We behold the real higher law. To the wise, therefore, a fact is true poetry and the most beautiful of fables. These wonders are brought to our own door. You also are a man. Man and woman and their social life, poverty, labor, sleep, fear, fortune, are known to you. Learn that none of these things is superficial but that each phenomenon has its roots in the faculties and affections of the mind. Whilst the abstract question occupies your intellect, nature brings it in the concrete to be solved by your hands. It were a wise inquiry for the closet, to compare, point by point, especially at remarkable crises in life, our daily history with the rise and progress of ideas in the mind.

So shall we come to look at the world with new eyes. It shall answer the endless inquiry of the intellect, What is truth? and of the affections, What is good?—by yielding itself passive to the educated Will. Then shall come to pass what my poet said: 'Nature is not fixed but fluid. Spirit alters, molds, makes it. The immobility or bruteness of nature is the absence of spirit; to pure spirit it is fluid, it is volatile, it is obedient. Every spirit builds itself a house, and beyond its house a world, and beyond its world a heaven. Know then that the world exists for you.

For you is the phenomenon perfect. What we are, that only can we see. All that Adam had, all that Cæsar could, you have and can do. Adam called his house heaven and earth; Cæsar called his house Rome; you perhaps call yours a cobbler's trade; a hundred acres of ploughed land; or a scholar's garret. Yet line for line and point for point your dominion is as great as theirs, though without fine names. Build therefore your own world. As fast as you conform your life to the pure idea in your mind, that will unfold its great proportions. A correspondent revolution in things will attend the influx of the spirit. So fast will disagreeable appearances, swine, spiders, snakes, pests, mad-houses, prisons, enemies, vanish; they are temporary and shall be no more seen. The sordor [1] and filths of nature, the sun shall dry up and the wind exhale. As when the summer comes from the south the snow banks melt and the face of the earth becomes green before it, so shall the advancing spirit create its ornaments along its path and carry with it the beauty it visits and the song which enchants it; it shall draw beautiful faces, warm hearts, wise discourse, and heroic acts around its way, until evil is no more seen. The kingdom of man over nature, which cometh not with observation—a dominion such as now is beyond his dream of God—he shall enter without more wonder than the blind man feels who is gradually restored to perfect sight.'

1836

[1] Refuse, filth.

Fable

THE mountain and the squirrel
Had a quarrel,
And the former called the latter "Little Prig";
Bun replied,
"You are doubtless very big;
But all sorts of things and weather
Must be taken in together,
To make up a year
And a sphere.
And I think it no disgrace
To occupy my place.
If I'm not so large as you,
You are not so small as I,
And not half so spry.
I'll not deny you make
A very pretty squirrel track;
Talents differ; all is well and wisely put;
If I cannot carry forests on my back,
Neither can you crack a nut."

1847

Self-Reliance

"Ne te quæsiveris extra."

MAN is his own star; and the soul that can
Render an honest and a perfect man,
Commands all light, all influence, all fate;
Nothing to him falls early or too late.
Our acts our angels are, or good or ill,
Our fatal shadows that walk by us still.

Epilogue to Beaumont and Fletcher's
Honest Man's Fortune

Cast the bantling on the rocks,
Suckle him with the she-wolf's teat,
Wintered with the hawk and fox,
Power and speed be hands and feet.

I READ the other day some verses written by an eminent painter which were original and not conventional. The soul always hears an admonition in such lines, let the subject be what it may. The sentiment they instill is of more value than any thought they may contain. To believe your own thought, to believe that what is true for you in your private heart is true for all men—that is genius. Speak your latent conviction, and it shall be the universal sense; for the inmost in due time becomes the outmost, and our first thought is rendered back to us by the trumpets of the Last Judgment. Familiar as the voice of the mind is to each, the highest merit we ascribe to Moses, Plato, and Milton is that they set at naught books and traditions and spoke not what men, but what *they* thought. A man should learn to detect and watch that gleam of light which flashes across his mind from within more than the luster of the firmament of bards and sages. Yet he dismisses without notice his thought, because it is his. In every work of genius we recognize our own rejected thoughts; they come back to us with a certain alienated majesty. Great works of art have no more affecting lesson for us than this. They teach us to abide by our spontaneous impression with good-humored inflexibility then most when the whole cry of voices is on the other side. Else tomorrow a stranger will say with masterly good sense precisely what we have thought and felt all the time, and we shall be forced to take with shame our own opinion from another.

There is a time in every man's education when he arrives at the conviction that envy is ignorance; that imitation is suicide; that he must take himself for better for worse as his portion; that though the wide universe is full of good, no kernel of nourishing corn can come to him but through his toil bestowed on that plot of ground which is given to him to till. The power which resides in him is new in nature, and none but he knows what that is which he can do, nor does he know until he has tried. Not for nothing one face, one character, one fact, makes much impression on him, and another none. This sculpture in the memory is not without pre-established harmony. The eye was placed where one ray should fall, that it might testify of that particular ray. We but half express ourselves and are ashamed of that divine idea which each of us represents. It may be safely trusted as proportionate and of good issues, so it be faithfully imparted, but God will not have his work made manifest by cowards. A man is relieved and gay when he has put his heart into his work and done his best; but what he has said or done otherwise shall give him no peace. It is a deliverance which does not deliver. In the attempt his genius deserts him; no muse befriends; no invention, no hope.

Trust thyself: every heart vibrates to that iron string. Accept the place the Divine Providence has found for you, the society of your contemporaries, the connection of events. Great men have always done so, and confided themselves childlike to the genius of their age, betraying their perception that the absolutely trustworthy was seated at their heart, working through their hands, predominating in all their being. And we are now men and must accept in the highest mind the same transcendent destiny; and not minors and invalids in a protected corner, not cowards fleeing before a revolution, but guides, redeemers, and benefactors, obeying the Almighty effort and advancing on Chaos and the Dark.

What pretty oracles nature yields us on this text in the face and behavior of children, babes, and even brutes! That divided and rebel mind, that distrust of a sentiment because our arithmetic has computed the strength and means opposed to our purpose, these have not. Their mind being whole, their eye is as yet unconquered, and when we look in their faces we are disconcerted. Infancy conforms to nobody; all conform to it; so that one babe commonly makes four or five out of the adults who prattle and play to it. So God has armed youth and puberty and manhood no less with its own piquancy and charm, and made it enviable and gracious and its claims not to be put by, if it will stand by itself. Do not think the youth has no force, because he cannot speak to you and me. Hark! in the next room his voice is sufficiently clear and emphatic. It seems he knows how to speak to his contemporaries. Bashful or bold then, he will know how to make us seniors very unnecessary.

The nonchalance of boys who are sure of a dinner, and would disdain as much as a lord to do or say aught to conciliate one, is the healthy attitude of human nature. A boy is in the parlor what the pit is in the playhouse; independent, irresponsible, looking out from his corner on such people and facts as pass by, he tries and sentences them on their merits, in the swift, summary way of boys, as good, bad, interesting, silly, eloquent, troublesome. He cumbers himself never about consequences, about interests; he gives an independent, genuine verdict. You must court him; he does not court you. But the man is as it were clapped into jail by his consciousness. As soon as he has once acted or spoken with *éclat* he is a committed person, watched by the sympathy or the hatred of hundreds whose affections must now enter into his account. There is no Lethe for this. Ah, that he could pass again into his neutrality! Who can thus avoid all pledges and, having observed, observe again from the same unaffected, unbiased, unbribable, unaffrighted innocence, must always be formidable. He would utter opinions on all passing affairs which, being seen to be not private but necessary, would sink like darts into the ear of men and put them in fear.

These are the voices which we hear in solitude, but they grow faint and inaudible as we enter into the world. Society everywhere is in conspiracy against the manhood of every one of its members. Society is a joint-stock company in which the members agree, for the better securing of his bread to each shareholder, to surrender the liberty and culture of the eater. The virtue in most request is conformity. Self-reliance is its aversion. It loves not realities and creators, but names and customs.

Whoso would be a man must be a nonconformist. He who would gather immortal palms must not be hindered by the name of goodness, but must explore if it be goodness. Nothing is at last sacred but the integrity of your own mind. Absolve you to yourself, and you shall have the suffrage of the world. I remember an answer which when quite young I was prompted to make to a valued adviser who was wont to importune me with the dear old doctrines of the church. On my saying, "What have I to do with the sacredness of traditions, if I live wholly from within?" my friend suggested, "But these impulses may be from below, not from above." I replied, "They do not seem to me to be such; but if I am the Devil's child, I will live then from the Devil." No law can be sacred to me but that of my nature. Good and bad are but names very readily transferable to that or this; the only right is what is after my constitution; the only wrong, what is against it. A man is to carry himself in the presence of all opposition as if everything were titular and ephemeral but he. I am ashamed to think how easily we capitulate to badges and names, to large societies and dead institutions. Every decent and well-spoken individual affects and sways me more than is right. I ought to go upright and vital, and speak the rude truth in all ways. If malice and vanity wear the coat of philanthropy, shall that pass? If an angry bigot assumes this bountiful cause of Abolition and comes to me with his last news from Barbados, why should I not say to him, 'Go love thy infant; love thy wood-chopper; be good-natured and modest; have that grace; and never varnish your hard, uncharitable ambition with this incredible tenderness for black folk a thousand miles off. Thy love afar is spite at home.' Rough and graceless would be such greeting, but truth is handsomer than the affectation of love. Your goodness must have some edge to it, else it is none. The doctrine of hatred must be preached, as the counteraction of the doctrine of love, when that pules and whines. I shun father and mother and wife and brother when my genius calls me. I would write on the lintels of the door-post, *Whim*. I hope it is somewhat better than whim at last, but we cannot spend the day in explanation. Expect me not to show cause why I seek or why I exclude company. Then again, do not tell me, as a good man did today, of my obligation to put all poor men in good situations. Are they *my* poor? I tell thee, thou foolish philanthropist, that I grudge the dollar, the dime, the cent I give to such men as do not belong to me and to whom I do not belong. There is a class of persons to whom by all spiritual affinity I am bought and sold; for them I will go to prison if need be; but your miscellaneous popular charities; the education at college of fools; the building of meeting-houses to the vain end to which many now stand; alms to sots, and the thousandfold Relief Societies—though I confess with shame I sometimes succumb and give the dollar, it is a wicked dollar, which by and by I shall have the manhood to withhold.

Virtues are, in the popular estimate, rather the exception than the rule. There is the man *and* his virtues. Men do what is called a good action, as some piece of courage or charity, much as they would pay a fine in expiation of daily nonappearance on parade. Their works are done as an apology or extenuation of their living in the world—as invalids and the insane pay a high board. Their virtues are penances. I do not wish to expiate but to live. My life is for itself and not for a spectacle. I much prefer that it should be of a lower strain, so it be genuine and equal, than that it should be glittering and unsteady. I wish it to be sound and sweet and not to need diet and bleeding. I ask primary evidence that you are a man, and refuse this appeal from the man to his actions. I know that for myself it makes no difference whether I do or forbear those actions which are reckoned excellent. I cannot consent to pay for a privilege where I have intrinsic right. Few and mean as my gifts may be, I actually am, and do not need for my own assurance or the assurance of my fellows any secondary testimony.

What I must do is all that concerns me, not what the people think. This rule, equally arduous in actual and in intellectual life, may serve for the whole distinction between greatness and meanness. It is the harder because you will always find those who think they know what is your duty better than you know it. It is easy in the world to live after the world's opinion; it is easy in solitude to live after our own; but the great man is he who in the midst of the crowd keeps with perfect sweetness the independence of solitude.

The objection to conforming to usages that have become dead to you is that it scatters your force. It loses your time and blurs the impression of your character. If you maintain a dead church, contribute to a dead Bible society, vote with a great party either for the government or against it, spread your table like base housekeepers—under all these screens I have difficulty to detect the precise man you are; and, of course, so much force is withdrawn from your proper life. But do your work, and I shall know you. Do your work, and you shall reinforce yourself. A man must consider what a blindman's-buff is this game of conformity. If I know your sect I anticipate your argument. I hear a preacher announce for his text and topic the expediency of one of the institutions of his church. Do I not know beforehand that not possibly can he say a new and spontaneous word? Do I not know that with all this ostentation of examining the grounds of the institution he will do no such thing? Do I not know that he is pledged to himself not to look but at one side, the permitted side, not as a man but as a parish minister? He is a retained attorney, and these airs of the bench are the emptiest affectation. Well, most men have bound their eyes with one or another handkerchief and attached themselves to some one of these communities of opinion. This conformity makes them not false in a few particulars, authors of a few lies, but false in all particulars. Their every truth is not quite true. Their two is not the real two, their four not the real four;

so that every word they say chagrins us and we know not where to begin to set them right. Meantime nature is not slow to equip us in the prison uniform of the party to which we adhere. We come to wear one cut of face and figure, and acquire by degrees the gentlest asinine expression. There is a mortifying experience in particular, which does not fail to wreak itself also in the general history; I mean "the foolish face of praise," the forced smile which we put on in company where we do not feel at ease, in answer to conversation which does not interest us. The muscles, not spontaneously moved but moved by a low usurping wilfulness, grow tight about the outline of the face, with the most disagreeable sensation.

For nonconformity the world whips you with its displeasure. And therefore a man must know how to estimate a sour face. The bystanders look askance on him in the public street or in the friend's parlor. If this aversion had its origin in contempt and resistance like his own he might well go home with a sad countenance; but the sour faces of the multitude, like their sweet faces, have no deep cause, but are put on and off as the wind blows and a newspaper directs. Yet is the discontent of the multitude more formidable than that of the senate and the college. It is easy enough for a firm man who knows the world to brook the rage of the cultivated classes. Their rage is decorous and prudent, for they are timid, as being very vulnerable themselves. But when to their feminine rage the indignation of the people is added, when the ignorant and the poor are aroused, when the unintelligent brute force that lies at the bottom of society is made to growl and mow, it needs the habit of magnanimity and religion to treat it godlike as a trifle of no concernment.

The other terror that scares us from self-trust is our consistency; a reverence for our past act or word because the eyes of others have no other data for computing our orbit than our past acts, and we are loth to disappoint them.

But why should you keep your head over your shoulder?

Why drag about this corpse of your memory, lest you contradict somewhat you have stated in this or that public place? Suppose you should contradict yourself; what then? It seems to be a rule of wisdom never to rely on your memory alone, scarcely even in acts of pure memory, but to bring the past for judgment into the thousand-eyed present and live ever in a new day. In your metaphysics you have denied personality to the Deity, yet when the devout motions of the soul come, yield to them heart and life, though they should clothe God with shape and color. Leave your theory, as Joseph his coat in the hand of the harlot, and flee.

A foolish consistency is the hobgoblin of little minds, adored by little statesmen and philosophers and divines. With consistency a great soul has simply nothing to do. He may as well concern himself with his shadow on the wall. Speak what you think now in hard words and tomorrow speak what tomorrow thinks in hard words again, though it contradict everything you said today.—'Ah, so you shall be sure to be misunderstood.'—Is it so bad then to be misunderstood? Pythagoras was misunderstood, and Socrates, and Jesus, and Luther, and Copernicus, and Galileo, and Newton, and every pure and wise spirit that ever took flesh. To be great is to be misunderstood.

I suppose no man can violate his nature. All the sallies of his will are rounded in by the law of his being, as the inequalities of Andes and Himmaleh are insignificant in the curve of the sphere. Nor does it matter how you gauge and try him. A character is like an acrostic or Alexandrian stanza—read it forward, backward, or across, it still spells the same thing. In this pleasing contrite wood-life which God allows me, let me record day by day my honest thought without prospect or retrospect, and, I cannot doubt, it will be found symmetrical, though I mean it not and see it not. My book should smell of pines and resound with the hum of insects. The swallow over my window should interweave that thread or straw he carries in his bill into my web also. We pass for what we are. Character teaches above our wills. Men imagine that they communicate their virtue or vice only by overt actions, and do not see that virtue or vice emit a breath every moment.

There will be an agreement in whatever variety of actions, so they be each honest and natural in their hour. For of one will, the actions will be harmonious, however unlike they seem. These varieties are lost sight of at a little distance, at a little height of thought. One tendency unites them all. The voyage of the best ship is a zigzag line of a hundred tacks. See the line from a sufficient distance, and it straightens itself to the average tendency. Your genuine action will explain itself and will explain your other genuine actions. Your conformity explains nothing. Act singly, and what you have already done singly will justify you now. Greatness appeals to the future. If I can be firm enough today to do right and scorn eyes, I must have done so much right before as to defend me now. Be it how it will, do right now. Always scorn appearances and you always may. The force of character is cumulative. All the foregone days of virtue work their health into this. What makes the majesty of the heroes of the senate and the field, which so fills the imagination? The consciousness of a train of great days and victories behind. They shed a united light on the advancing actor. He is attended as by a visible escort of angels. That is it which throws thunder into Chatham's voice, and dignity into Washington's port, and America into Adams's eye. Honor is venerable to us because it is no ephemera. It is always ancient virtue. We worship it today because it is not of today. We love it and pay it homage because it is not a trap for our love and homage, but is self-dependent, self-derived, and therefore of an old immaculate pedigree, even if shown in a young person.

I hope in these days we have heard the last of conformity and consistency. Let the words be gazetted and ridiculous henceforward. Instead of the gong for dinner, let us hear a whistle from the Spartan fife. Let us never bow and apologize more. A great man is coming to eat at my house. I do not wish to please him; I wish that he should wish to please me. I will stand here for humanity, and though I would make it kind, I would make it true. Let us affront and reprimand the smooth mediocrity and squalid contentment of the times, and hurl in the face of custom and trade and office the fact which is the upshot of all history, that there is a great responsible Thinker and Actor working wherever a man works; that a true man belongs to no other time or place, but is the center of things. Where he is, there is nature. He measures you and all men and all events. Ordinarily, everybody in society reminds us of somewhat else, or of some other person. Character, reality, reminds you of nothing else; it takes place of the whole creation. The man must be so much that he must make all circumstances indifferent. Every true man is a cause, a country, and an age; requires infinite spaces and numbers and time fully to accomplish his design; and posterity seem to follow his steps as a train of clients. A man Cæsar is born, and for ages after we have a Roman Empire. Christ is born, and millions of minds so grow and cleave to his genius that he is confounded with virtue and the possible of man. An institution is the lengthened shadow of one man; as Monachism, of the Hermit Antony;[1] the Reformation, of Luther; Quakerism, of Fox; Methodism, of Wesley; Abolition, of Clarkson.[2] Scipio, Milton called "the height of Rome"; and all history resolves itself very easily into the biography of a few stout and earnest persons.

Let a man then know his worth, and keep things under his feet. Let him not peep or steal, or skulk up and down with the air of a charity-boy, a bastard, or an interloper in the world which exists for him. But the man in the street, finding no worth in himself which corresponds to the force which built a tower

[1] St. Anthony of Egypt founded the first order of Christian monks about 300 A.D.

[2] Thomas Clarkson (1760-1846), a Quaker, wrote *A History of the Abolition of the Slave Trade*, 1808.

or sculptured a marble god, feels poor when he looks on these. To him a palace, a statue, or a costly book have an alien and forbidding air, much like a gay equipage, and seem to say like that, "Who are you, sir?" Yet they all are his, suitors for his notice, petitioners to his faculties that they will come out and take possession. The picture waits for my verdict; it is not to command me, but I am to settle its claims to praise. That popular fable of the sot who was picked up dead-drunk in the street, carried to the duke's house, washed and dressed and laid in the duke's bed, and, on his waking, treated with all obsequious ceremony like the duke, and assured that he had been insane, owes its popularity to the fact that it symbolizes so well the state of man, who is in the world a sort of sot, but now and then wakes up, exercises his reason and finds himself a true prince.

Our reading is mendicant and sycophantic. In history our imagination plays us false. Kingdom and lordship, power and estate, are a gaudier vocabulary than private John and Edward in a small house and common day's work; but the things of life are the same to both; the sum total of both is the same. Why all this deference to Alfred and Scanderbeg and Gustavus? Suppose they were virtuous; did they wear out virtue? As great a stake depends on your private act today as followed their public and renowned steps. When private men shall act with original views, the luster will be transferred from the actions of kings to those of gentlemen.

The world has been instructed by its kings, who have so magnetized the eyes of nations. It has been taught by this colossal symbol the mutual reverence that is due from man to man. The joyful loyalty with which men have everywhere suffered the king, the noble, or the great proprietor to walk among them by a law of his own, make his own scale of men and things and reverse theirs, pay for benefits not with money but with honor, and represent the law in his person, was the hieroglyphic by which they obscurely signified their consciousness of their own right and comeliness, the right of every man.

The magnetism which all original action exerts is explained when we inquire the reason of self-trust. Who is the Trustee? What is the aboriginal Self, on which a universal reliance may be grounded? What is the nature and power of that science-baffling star, without parallax,[1] without calculable elements, which shoots a ray of beauty even into trivial and impure actions if the least mark of independence appear? The inquiry leads us to that source, at once the essence of genius, of virtue, and of life, which we call Spontaneity or Instinct. We denote this primary wisdom as Intuition, whilst all later teachings are tuitions. In that deep force, the last fact behind which analysis cannot go, all things find their common origin. For the sense of being which in calm hours rises, we know not how, in the soul, is not diverse from things, from space, from light, from time, from man, but one with them and proceeds obviously from the same source whence their life and being also proceed. We first share the life by which things exist and afterwards see them as appearances in nature and forget that we have shared their cause. Here is the fountain of action and of thought. Here are the lungs of that inspiration which giveth man wisdom and which cannot be denied without impiety and atheism. We lie in the lap of immense intelligence which makes us receivers of its truth and organs of its activity. When we discern justice, when we discern truth, we do nothing of ourselves, but allow a passage to its beams. If we ask whence this comes, if we seek to pry into the soul that causes, all philosophy is at fault. Its presence or its absence is all we can affirm. Every man discriminates between the voluntary acts of his mind and his involuntary perceptions, and knows that to his involuntary perceptions a perfect faith is due. He may err in the expression of them, but he knows that these things are so, like day and night, not to be

[1] The apparent difference in the position of an object when seen from different points.

disputed. My wilful actions and acquisitions are but roving; the idlest reverie, the faintest native emotion, command my curiosity and respect. Thoughtless people contradict as readily the statement of perceptions as of opinions, or rather much more readily; for they do not distinguish between perception and notion. They fancy that I choose to see this or that thing. But perception is not whimsical but fatal. If I see a trait, my children will see it after me, and in course of time all mankind, although it may chance that no one has seen it before me. For my perception of it is as much a fact as the sun.

The relations of the soul to the divine spirit are so pure that it is profane to seek to interpose helps. It must be that when God speaketh He should communicate, not one thing, but all things; should fill the world with His voice; should scatter forth light, nature, time, souls, from the center of the present thought; and new date and new create the whole. Whenever a mind is simple and receives a divine wisdom, old things pass away—means, teachers, texts, temples fall; it lives now and absorbs past and future into the present hour. All things are made sacred by relation to it, one as much as another. All things are dissolved to their center by their cause, and in the universal miracle petty and particular miracles disappear. If therefore a man claims to know and speak of God and carries you backward to the phraseology of some old moldered nation in another country, in another world, believe him not. Is the acorn better than the oak which is its fullness and completion? Is the parent better than the child into whom he has cast his ripened being? Whence then this worship of the past? The centuries are conspirators against the sanity and authority of the soul. Time and space are but physiological colors which the eye makes, but the soul is light: where it is, is day; where it was, is night; and history is an impertinence and an injury if it be anything more than a cheerful apologue or parable of my being and becoming.

Man is timid and apologetic; he is no longer upright; he dares not say 'I think,' 'I am,' but quotes some saint or sage. He is ashamed before the blade of grass or the blowing rose. These roses under my window make no reference to former roses or to better ones; they are for what they are; they exist with God today. There is no time to them. There is simply the rose; it is perfect in every moment of its existence. Before a leaf-bud has burst, its whole life acts; in the full-blown flower there is no more; in the leafless root there is no less. Its nature is satisfied and it satisfies nature in all moments alike. But man postpones or remembers; he does not live in the present, but with reverted eye laments the past, or, heedless of the riches that surround him, stands on tiptoe to foresee the future. He cannot be happy and strong until he too lives with nature in the present, above time.

This should be plain enough. Yet see what strong intellects dare not yet hear God himself unless he speak the phraseology of I know not what David or Jeremiah or Paul. We shall not always set so great a price on a few texts, on a few lives. We are like children who repeat by rote the sentences of grandames and tutors, and, as they grow older, of the men of talents and character they chance to see, painfully recollecting the exact words they spoke; afterwards, when they come into the point of view which those had who uttered these sayings, they understand them and are willing to let the words go; for at any time they can use words as good when occasion comes. If we live truly, we shall see truly. It is as easy for the strong man to be strong as it is for the weak to be weak. When we have new perception, we shall gladly disburden the memory of its hoarded treasures as old rubbish. When a man lives with God, his voice shall be as sweet as the murmur of the brook and the rustle of the corn.

And now at last the highest truth on this subject remains unsaid; probably cannot be said; for all that we say is the far-off remembering of the intuition. That thought by what I can now nearest approach to say it, is this. When good is near you, when you have life in yourself, it is not by any known or accustomed way; you shall not discern the footprints of any other; you shall not see the face of man; you shall not hear any name; the way, the thought, the good shall be wholly strange and new. It shall exclude example and experience. You take the way from man, not to man. All persons that ever existed are its forgotten ministers. Fear and hope are alike beneath it. There is somewhat low even in hope. In the hour of vision there is nothing that can be called gratitude, nor properly joy. The soul raised over passion beholds identity and eternal causation, perceives the self-existence of Truth and Right and calms itself with knowing that all things go well. Vast spaces of nature, the Atlantic Ocean, the South Sea; long intervals of time, years, centuries, are of no account. This which I think and feel underlay every former state of life and circumstances, as it does underlie my present and what is called life and what is called death.

Life only avails, not the having lived. Power ceases in the instant of repose; it resides in the moment of transition from a past to a new state, in the shooting of the gulf, in the darting to an aim. This one fact the world hates: that the soul *becomes;* for that forever degrades the past, turns all riches to poverty, all reputation to a shame, confounds the saint with the rogue, shoves Jesus and Judas equally aside. Why then do we prate of self-reliance? Inasmuch as the soul is present there will be power not confident but agent. To talk of reliance is a poor external way of speaking. Speak rather of that which relies because it works and is. Who has more obedience than I masters me, though he should not raise his finger. Round him I must revolve by the gravitation of spirits. We fancy it rhetoric when we speak of eminent virtue. We do not yet see that virtue is Height, and that a man or a company of men, plastic and permeable to principles, by the law of nature must overpower and ride all cities, nations, kings, rich men, poets, who are not.

This is the ultimate fact which we so quickly reach on this, as on every topic, the resolution of all into the ever-blessed ONE. Self-existence is the attribute of the Supreme Cause, and it constitutes the measure of good by the degree in which it enters into all lower forms. All things real are so by so much virtue as they contain. Commerce, husbandry, hunting, whaling, war, eloquence, personal weight, are somewhat, and engage my respect as examples of its presence and impure action. I see the same law working in nature for conservation and growth. Power is, in nature, the essential measure of right. Nature suffers nothing to remain in her kingdoms which cannot help itself. The genesis and maturation of a planet, its poise and orbit, the bended tree recovering itself from the strong wind, the vital resources of every animal and vegetable, are demonstrations of the self-sufficing and therefore self-relying soul.

Thus all concentrates: let us not rove; let us sit at home with the cause. Let us stun and astonish the intruding rabble of men and books and institutions by a simple declaration of the divine fact. Bid the invaders take the shoes from off their feet, for God is here within. Let our simplicity judge them, and our docility to our own law demonstrate the poverty of nature and fortune beside our native riches.

But now we are a mob. Man does not stand in awe of man, nor is his genius admonished to stay at home, to put itself in communication with the internal ocean, but it goes abroad to beg a cup of water of the urns of other men. We must go alone. I like the silent church before the service begins better than any preaching. How far off, how cool, how chaste the persons look, begirt each one with a precinct or sanctuary! So let us always sit. Why should we assume the faults of our friend, or wife, or father, or child, because they sit around our hearth, or are said to have the same blood? All men have my blood and I all men's. Not for that will I adopt their petulance or folly, even to the extent of being ashamed of it. But your isolation must not be mechanical, but spiritual, that is, must be elevation. At times the whole world seems to be in conspiracy to importune you with emphatic trifles. Friend, client, child, sickness, fear, want, charity, all knock at once at thy closet door and say, 'Come out unto us.' But keep thy state; come not into their confusion. The power men possess to annoy me I give them by a weak curiosity. No man can come near me but through my act. "What we love that we have, but by desire we bereave ourselves of the love."

If we cannot at once rise to the sanctities of obedience and faith, let us at least resist our temptations; let us enter into the state of war and wake Thor and Woden, courage and constancy, in our Saxon breasts. This is to be done in our smooth times by speaking the truth. Check this lying hospitality and lying affection. Live no longer to the expectation of these deceived and deceiving people with whom we converse. Say to them, 'O father, O mother, O wife, O brother, O friend, I have lived with you after appearances hitherto. Henceforward I am the truth's. Be it known unto you that henceforward I obey no law less than the eternal law. I will have no covenants but proximities. I shall endeavor to nourish my parents, to support my family, to be the chaste husband of one wife, but these relations I must fill after a new and unprecedented way. I appeal from your customs. I must be myself. I cannot break myself any longer for you, or you. If you can love me for what I am, we shall be the happier. If you cannot, I will still seek to deserve that you should. I will not hide my tastes or aversions. I will so trust that what is deep is holy, that I will do strongly before the sun and moon whatever inly rejoices me and the heart appoints. If you are noble, I will love you; if you are not, I will not hurt you and myself by hypocritical attentions. If you are true, but not in the same truth with me, cleave to your companions; I will seek my own. I do this not selfishly but humbly and truly. It is alike your interest, and mine, and all men's, however long we have dwelt in lies, to live in truth. Does this sound harsh today? You will soon love what is dictated by your nature as well as mine, and if we follow the truth it will bring us out safe at last.' But so may you give these friends pain. Yes, but I cannot sell my liberty and my power to save their sensibility. Besides, all persons have their moments of reason, when they look out into the region of absolute truth; then will they justify me and do the same thing.

The populace think that your rejection of popular standards is a rejection of all standard, and mere antinomianism;[1] and the bold sensualist will use the name of philosophy to gild his crimes. But the law of consciousness abides. There are two confessionals, in one or the other of which we must be shriven. You may fulfill your round of duties by clearing yourself in the *direct* or in the *reflex* way. Consider whether you have satisfied your relations to father, mother, cousin, neighbor, town, cat and dog—whether any of these can upbraid you. But I may also neglect this reflex standard and absolve me to myself. I have my own stern claims and perfect circle. It denies the name of duty to many offices that are called duties. But if I can discharge its debts it enables me to dispense with the popular code. If anyone imagines that this law is lax, let him keep its commandment one day.

And truly it demands something godlike in him who has cast off the common motives of humanity and has ventured to trust himself for a taskmaster. High be his heart, faithful his will, clear his sight, that he may in good earnest be doctrine, society, law, to himself, that a simple purpose may be to him as strong as iron necessity is to others!

If any man consider the present aspects of what is called by distinction *society*, he will see the need of these ethics. The sinew and heart of man seem to be drawn out, and we are become timorous, desponding whimperers. We are afraid of truth, afraid of fortune, afraid of death, and afraid of each other. Our age yields no great and perfect persons. We want men and women who shall renovate life and our social state, but we see that most natures are insolvent, cannot satisfy their own wants, have an ambition out of all proportion to their practical force and do lean and beg day and night continually. Our housekeep-

[1] Contradiction.

ing is mendicant, our arts, our occupations, our marriages, our religion we have not chosen, but society has chosen for us. We are parlor soldiers. We shun the rugged battle of fate, where strength is born.

If our young men miscarry in their first enterprises, they lose all heart. If the young merchant fails, men say he is *ruined*. If the finest genius studies at one of our colleges and is not installed in an office within one year afterwards in the cities or suburbs of Boston or New York, it seems to his friends and to himself that he is right in being disheartened and in complaining the rest of his life. A sturdy lad from New Hampshire or Vermont, who in turn tries all the professions, who *teams it*, *farms it*, *peddles*, keeps a school, preaches, edits a newspaper, goes to Congress, buys a township, and so forth, in successive years, and always like a cat falls on his feet, is worth a hundred of these city dolls. He walks abreast with his days and feels no shame in not 'studying a profession,' for he does not postpone his life, but lives already. He has not one chance, but a hundred chances. Let a Stoic open the resources of man and tell men they are not leaning willows, but can and must detach themselves; that with the exercise of self-trust, new powers shall appear; that a man is the word made flesh, born to shed healing to the nations; that he should be ashamed of our compassion, and that the moment he acts from himself, tossing the laws, the books, idolatries and customs out of the window, we pity him no more but thank and revere him; and that teacher shall restore the life of man to splendor and make his name dear to all history.

It is easy to see that a greater self-reliance must work a revolution in all the offices and relations of men; in their religion; in their education; in their pursuits; their modes of living; their association; in their property; in their speculative views.

1. In what prayers do men allow themselves! That which they call a holy office is not so much as brave and manly.

Prayer looks abroad and asks for some foreign addition to come through some foreign virtue, and loses itself in endless mazes of natural and supernatural, and mediatorial and miraculous. Prayer that craves a particular commodity, anything less than all good, is vicious. Prayer is the contemplation of the facts of life from the highest point of view. It is the soliloquy of a beholding and jubilant soul. It is the spirit of God pronouncing his works good. But prayer as a means to effect a private end is meanness and theft. It supposes dualism and not unity in nature and consciousness. As soon as the man is at one with God, he will not beg. He will then see prayer in all action. The prayer of the farmer kneeling in his field to weed it, the prayer of the rower kneeling with the stroke of his oar, are true prayers heard throughout nature, though for cheap ends. Caratach, in Fletcher's *Bonduca*, when admonished to inquire the mind of the god Audate, replies,

> *His hidden meaning lies in our endeavors;*
> *Our valors are our best gods.*

Another sort of false prayers are our regrets. Discontent is the want of self-reliance: it is infirmity of will. Regret calamities if you can thereby help the sufferer; if not, attend your own work and already the evil begins to be repaired. Our sympathy is just as base. We come to them who weep foolishly and sit down and cry for company, instead of imparting to them truth and health in rough electric shocks, putting them once more in communication with their own reason. The secret of fortune is joy in our hands. Welcome evermore to gods and men is the self-helping man. For him all doors are flung wide; him all tongues greet, all honors crown, all eyes follow with desire. Our love goes out to him and embraces him because he did not need it. We solicitously and apologetically caress and celebrate him because he held on his way and scorned our disapprobation. The gods love him because men hated him. "To the persevering mortal," said Zoroaster, "the blessed Immortals are swift."

As men's prayers are a disease of the will, so are their creeds a disease of the intellect. They say with those foolish Israelites, 'Let not God speak to us, lest we die. Speak thou, speak any man with us, and we will obey.' Everywhere I am hindered of meeting God in my brother, because he has shut his own temple doors and recites fables merely of his brother's or his brother's brother's God. Every new mind is a new classification. If it prove a mind of uncommon activity and power, a Locke, a Lavoisier, a Hutton, a Bentham, a Fourier, it imposes its classification on other men, and lo! a new system. In proportion to the depth of the thought, and so to the number of the objects it touches and brings within reach of the pupil, is his complacency. But chiefly is this apparent in creeds and churches, which are also classifications of some powerful mind acting on the elemental thought of duty and man's relation to the Highest. Such is Calvinism, Quakerism, Swedenborgism. The pupil takes the same delight in subordinating everything to the new terminology as a girl who has just learned botany in seeing a new earth and new seasons thereby. It will happen for a time that the pupil will find his intellectual power has grown by the study of his master's mind. But in all unbalanced minds the classification is idolized, passes for the end and not for a speedily exhaustible means, so that the walls of the system blend to their eye in the remote horizon with the walls of the universe; the luminaries of heaven seem to them hung on the arch their master built. They cannot imagine how you aliens have any right to see, how you can see; 'It must be somehow that you stole the light from us.' They do not yet perceive that light, unsystematic, indomitable, will break into any cabin, even into theirs. Let them chirp awhile and call it their own. If they are honest and do well, presently their neat new pinfold will be too strait and low, will crack, will lean, will rot and vanish, and the immortal light, all young and joyful, million-orbed, million-colored, will beam over the universe as on the first morning.

2. It is for want of self-culture that the superstition of Traveling, whose idols are Italy, England, Egypt, retains its fascination for all educated Americans. They who made England, Italy, or Greece venerable in the imagination did so by sticking fast where they were, like an axis of the earth. In manly hours we feel that duty is our place. The soul is no traveler; the wise man stays at home, and when his necessities, his duties, on any occasion call him from his house, or into foreign lands, he is at home still and shall make men sensible by the expression of his countenance that he goes, the missionary of wisdom and virtue, and visits cities and men like a sovereign and not like an interloper or a valet.

I have no churlish objection to the circumnavigation of the globe for the purposes of art, of study, and benevolence, so that the man is first domesticated, or does not go abroad with the hope of finding somewhat greater than he knows. He who travels to be amused, or to get somewhat which he does not carry, travels away from himself, and grows old even in youth among old things. In Thebes, in Palmyra, his will and mind have become old and dilapidated as they. He carries ruins to ruins.

Traveling is a fool's paradise. Our first journeys discover to us the indifference of places. At home I dream that at Naples, at Rome, I can be intoxicated with beauty and lose my sadness. I pack my trunk, embrace my friends, embark on the sea and at last wake up in Naples, and there beside me is the stern fact, the sad self, unrelenting, identical, that I fled from. I seek the Vatican and the palaces. I affect to be intoxicated with sights and suggestions, but I am not intoxicated. My giant goes with me wherever I go.

3. But the rage of traveling is a symptom of a deeper unsoundness affecting the whole intellectual action. The intellect is vagabond, and our system of education fosters restlessness. Our minds travel when our bodies are forced to stay at home. We imitate; and what is imitation but the traveling of the

mind? Our houses are built with foreign taste; our shelves are garnished with foreign ornaments; our opinions, our tastes, our faculties, lean and follow the Past and the Distant. The soul created the arts wherever they have flourished. It was in his own mind that the artist sought his model. It was an application of his own thought to the thing to be done and the conditions to be observed. And why need we copy the Doric or the Gothic model? Beauty, convenience, grandeur of thought, and quaint expression, are as near to us as to any, and if the American artist will study with hope and love the precise thing to be done by him, considering the climate, the soil, the length of the day, the wants of the people, the habit and form of the government, he will create a house in which all these will find themselves fitted, and taste and sentiment will be satisfied also.

Insist on yourself; never imitate. Your own gift you can present every moment with the cumulative force of a whole life's cultivation; but of the adopted talent of another you have only an extemporaneous half possession. That which each can do best, none but his Maker can teach him. No man yet knows what it is, nor can, till that person has exhibited it. Where is the master who could have taught Shakspeare? Where is the master who could have instructed Franklin, or Washington, or Bacon, or Newton? Every great man is a unique. The Scipionism of Scipio is precisely that part he could not borrow. Shakspeare will never be made by the study of Shakspeare. Do that which is assigned you, and you cannot hope too much or dare too much. There is at this moment for you an utterance brave and grand as that of the colossal chisel of Phidias, or trowel of the Egyptians, or the pen of Moses or Dante, but different from all these. Not possibly will the soul, all rich, all eloquent, with thousand-cloven tongue, deign to repeat itself; but if you can hear what these patriarchs say, surely you can reply to them in the same pitch of voice; for the ear and the tongue are two organs of one nature. Abide in the simple and noble regions of thy life, obey thy heart, and thou shalt reproduce the Fore-world again.

4. As our Religion, our Education, our Art look abroad, so does our spirit of society. All men plume themselves on the improvement of society, and no man improves.

Society never advances. It recedes as fast on one side as it gains on the other. It undergoes continual changes; it is barbarous, it is civilized, it is Christianized, it is rich, it is scientific; but this change is not amelioration. For everything that is given something is taken. Society acquires new arts and loses old instincts. What a contrast between the well-clad, reading, writing, thinking American, with a watch, a pencil, and a bill of exchange in his pocket, and the naked New Zealander, whose property is a club, a spear, a mat, and an undivided twentieth of a shed to sleep under! But compare the health of the two men and you shall see that the white man has lost his aboriginal strength. If the traveler tell us truly, strike the savage with a broad-axe and in a day or two the flesh shall unite and heal as if you struck the blow into soft pitch, and the same blow shall send the white to his grave.

The civilized man has built a coach, but has lost the use of his feet. He is supported on crutches, but lacks so much support of muscle. He has a fine Geneva watch, but he fails of the skill to tell the hour by the sun. A Greenwich nautical almanac he has, and so being sure of the information when he wants it, the man in the street does not know a star in the sky. The solstice he does not observe; the equinox he knows as little; and the whole bright calendar of the year is without a dial in his mind. His notebooks impair his memory; his libraries overload his wit; the insurance office increases the number of accidents; and it may be a question whether machinery does not encumber; whether we have not lost by refinement some energy, by a Christianity, entrenched in establishments and forms, some vigor of wild virtue. For every Stoic was a Stoic; but in Christendom where is the Christian?

There is no more deviation in the moral standard than in the standard of height or bulk. No greater men are now than ever were. A singular equality may be observed between the great men of the first and of the last ages; nor can all the science, art, religion, and philosophy of the nineteenth century avail to educate greater men than Plutarch's heroes, three or four and twenty centuries ago. Not in time is the race progressive. Phocion, Socrates, Anaxagoras, Diogenes, are great men, but they leave no class. He who is really of their class will not be called by their name, but will be his own man, and in his turn the founder of a sect. The arts and inventions of each period are only its costume and do not invigorate men. The harm of the improved machinery may compensate its good. Hudson and Behring accomplished so much in their fishing boats as to astonish Parry and Franklin, whose equipment exhausted the resources of science and art. Galileo, with an opera-glass, discovered a more splendid series of celestial phenomena than anyone since. Columbus found the New World in an undecked boat. It is curious to see the periodical disuse and perishing of means and machinery which were introduced with loud laudation a few years or centuries before. The great genius returns to essential man. We reckoned the improvements of the art of war among the triumphs of science, and yet Napoleon conquered Europe by the bivouac, which consisted of falling back on naked valor and disencumbering it of all aids. The Emperor held it impossible to make a perfect army, says Las Cases, "without abolishing our arms, magazines, commissaries, and carriages, until, in imitation of the Roman custom, the soldier should receive his supply of corn, grind it in his hand-mill and bake his bread himself."

Society is a wave. The wave moves onward, but the water of which it is composed does not. The same particle does not rise from the valley to the ridge. Its unity is only phenomenal. The persons who make up a nation today next year die, and their experience dies with them.

And so the reliance on Property, including the reliance on governments which protect it, is the want of self-reliance. Men have looked away from themselves and at things so long that they have come to esteem the religious, learned, and civil institutions as guards of property, and they deprecate assaults on these, because they feel them to be assaults on property. They measure their esteem of each other by what each has and not by what each is. But a cultivated man becomes ashamed of his property, out of new respect for his nature. Especially he hates what he has if he see that it is accidental, came to him by inheritance, or gift, or crime; then he feels that it is not having; it does not belong to him, has no root in him and merely lies there because no revolution or no robber takes it away. But that which a man is, does always by necessity acquire; and what the man acquires is living property, which does not wait the beck of rulers, or mobs, or revolutions, or fire, or storm, or bankruptcies, but perpetually renews itself wherever the man breathes. "Thy lot or portion of life," said the Caliph Ali, "is seeking after thee; therefore be at rest from seeking after it." Our dependence on these foreign goods leads us to our slavish respect for numbers. The political parties meet in numerous conventions; the greater the concourse and with each new uproar of announcement, The delegation from Essex! The Democrats from New Hampshire! The Whigs of Maine! the young patriot feels himself stronger than before by a new thousand of eyes and arms. In like manner the reformers summon conventions and vote and resolve in multitude. Not so, O friends! will the God deign to enter and inhabit you but by a method precisely the reverse. It is only as a man puts off all foreign support and stands alone that I see him to be strong and to prevail. He is weaker by every recruit to his banner. Is not a man better than a town? Ask nothing of men, and, in the endless mutation, thou only firm column must presently appear the upholder of all that surrounds thee. He who knows that power is inborn, that he is weak because he has looked for good out of him and elsewhere and, so perceiving, throws himself unhesitatingly on his thought, instantly rights himself, stands in the erect position, commands his limbs, works miracles; just as a man who stands on his feet is stronger than a man who stands on his head.

So use all that is called Fortune. Most men gamble with her and gain all and lose all as her wheel rolls. But do thou leave as unlawful these winnings and deal with Cause and Effect, the chancellors of God. In the Will work and acquire, and thou hast chained the wheel of Chance and shall sit hereafter out of fear from her rotations. A political victory, a rise of rents, the recovery of your sick or the return of your absent friend, or some other favorable event raises your spirits, and you think good days are preparing for you. Do not believe it. Nothing can bring you peace but yourself. Nothing can bring you peace but the triumph of principles.

1841

Compensation

THE wings of Time are black and white,
Pied with morning and with night.
Mountain tall and ocean deep
Trembling balance duly keep.
In changing moon, in tidal wave,
Glows the feud of Want and Have.
Gauge of more and less through space
Electric star and pencil plays.
The lonely Earth amid the balls
That hurry through the eternal halls.
A makeweight flying to the void,
Supplemental asteroid,
Or compensatory spark,
Shoots across the neutral Dark.

Man's the elm, and Wealth the vine,
Stanch and strong the tendrils twine:
Though the frail ringlets thee deceive,
None from its stock that vine can reave.
Fear not, then, thou child infirm,
There's no god dare wrong a worm.
Laurel crowns cleave to deserts
And power to him who power exerts;
Hast not thy share? On wingèd feet,
Lo! it rushes thee to meet;
And all that Nature made thy own,
Floating in air or pent in stone,
Will rive the hills and swim the sea
And, like thy shadow, follow thee.

EVER since I was a boy I have wished to write a discourse on Compensation; for it seemed to me when very young that on this subject life was ahead of theology and the people knew more than the preachers taught. The documents, too, from which the doctrine is to be drawn charmed my fancy by their endless variety, and lay always before me, even in sleep; for they are the tools in our hands, the bread in our basket, the transactions of the street, the farm and the dwelling-house; greetings, relations, debts and credits, the influence of character, the nature and endowment of all men. It seemed to me also that in it might be shown men a ray of divinity, the present action of the soul of this world, clean from all vestige of tradition; and so the heart of man might be bathed by an inundation of eternal love, conversing with that which he knows was always and always must be, because it really is now. It appeared moreover that if this doctrine could be stated in terms with any resemblance to those bright intuitions in which this truth is sometimes revealed to us, it would be a star in many dark hours and crooked passages in our journey that would not suffer us to lose our way.

I was lately confirmed in these desires by hearing a sermon at church. The preacher, a man esteemed for his orthodoxy, unfolded in the ordinary manner the doctrine of the Last Judgment. He assumed that judgment is not executed in this world; that the wicked are successful; that the good are miserable; and then urged from reason and from Scripture a compensation to be made to both parties in the next life. No offense appeared to be taken by the congregation at this doctrine. As far as I could observe when the meeting broke up they separated without remark on the sermon.

Yet what was the import of this teaching? What did the preacher mean by saying that the good are miserable in the present life? Was it that houses and lands, offices, wine, horses, dress, luxury, are had by unprincipled men, whilst the saints are poor and despised; and that a compensation is to be made to these last hereafter, by giving them the like gratifications another day—bank stock and doubloons, venison and champagne? This must be the compensation intended; for what else? Is it that they are to have leave to pray and praise? to love and serve men? Why, that they can do now. The legitimate inference the disciple would draw was: 'We are to have *such* a good time as the sinners have now;' or, to push it to its extreme import, 'You sin now, we shall sin by and by; we would sin now, if we could; not being successful we expect our revenge tomorrow.'

The fallacy lay in the immense concession that the bad are successful; that justice is not done now. The blindness of the preacher consisted in deferring to the base estimate of the market of what constitutes a manly success, instead of confronting and convicting the world from the truth; announcing the presence of the soul; the omnipotence of the will; and so establishing the standard of good and ill, of success and falsehood.

I find a similar base tone in the popular religious works of the day and the same doctrines assumed by the literary men when occasionally they treat the related topics. I think that our popular theology has gained in decorum, and not in principle, over the superstitions it has displaced. But men are better than their theology. Their daily life gives it the lie. Every ingenuous and aspiring soul leaves the doctrine behind him in his own experience, and all men feel sometimes the falsehood which they cannot demonstrate. For men are wiser than they know. That which they hear in schools and pulpits without afterthought, if said in conversation would probably be questioned in silence. If a man dogmatize in a mixed company on Providence and the divine laws, he is answered by a silence which conveys well enough to an observer the dissatisfaction of the hearer, but his incapacity to make his own statement.

I shall attempt in this and the following chapter to record some facts that indicate the path of the law of Compensation; happy beyond my expectation if I shall truly draw the smallest arc of this circle.

Polarity, or action and reaction, we meet in every part of nature; in darkness and light; in heat and cold; in the ebb and flow of waters; in male and female; in the inspiration and expiration of plants and animals; in the equation of quantity and quality in the fluids of the animal body; in the systole and diastole of the heart; in the undulations of fluids and of sound; in the centrifugal and centripetal gravity; in electricity, galvanism, and chemical affinity. Superinduce magnetism at one end of a needle, the opposite magnetism takes place at the other end. If the south attracts, the north repels. To empty here, you must condense there. An inevitable dualism bisects nature, so that each thing is a half, and suggests another thing to make it whole; as, spirit, matter; man, woman; odd, even; subjective, objective; in, out; upper, under; motion, rest; yea, nay.

Whilst the world is thus dual, so is every one of its parts. The entire system of things gets represented in every particle. There is somewhat that resembles the ebb and flow of the sea, day and night, man and woman, in a single needle of the pine, in a kernel of corn, in each individual of every animal tribe. The reaction, so grand in the elements, is repeated within these small boundaries. For example, in the animal kingdom the physiologist has observed that no creatures are favorites, but a certain compensation balances every gift and every defect. A surplusage given to one part is paid out of a reduction from another part of the same creature. If the head and neck are enlarged, the trunk and extremities are cut short.

The theory of the mechanic forces is another example. What we gain in power is lost in time, and the converse. The periodic or compensating errors of the planets is another instance. The influences of climate and soil in political history is another. The cold climate invigorates. The barren soil does not breed fevers, crocodiles, tigers, or scorpions.

The same dualism underlies the nature and condition of man. Every excess causes a defect; every defect an excess. Every sweet hath its sour; every evil its good. Every faculty which is a receiver of pleasure has an equal penalty put on its abuse. It is to answer for its moderation with its life. For every grain of wit there is a grain of folly. For everything you have missed you have gained something else; and for everything you gain you lose something. If riches increase, they are increased that use them. If the gatherer gathers too much, Nature takes out of the man what she puts into his chest; swells the estate, but kills the owner. Nature hates monopolies and exceptions. The waves of the sea do not more speedily seek a level from their loftiest tossing than the varieties of condition tend to equalize themselves. There is always some leveling circumstance that puts down the overbearing, the strong, the rich, the fortunate, substantially on the same ground with all others. Is a man too strong and fierce for society and by temper and position a bad citizen—a morose ruffian with a dash of the pirate in him? Nature sends him a troop of pretty sons and daughters who are getting along in the dame's classes at the village school, and love and fear for them smooths his grim scowl to courtesy. Thus she contrives to intenerate [1] the granite and felspar, takes the boar out and puts the lamb in and keeps her balance true.

The farmer imagines power and place are fine things. But the President has paid dear for his White House. It has commonly cost him all his peace and the best of his manly attributes. To preserve for a short time so conspicuous an appearance before the world, he is content to eat dust before the real masters who stand erect behind the throne. Or do men desire the more substantial and permanent grandeur of genius? Neither has this an immunity. He who by force of will or of thought is great and overlooks thousands has the charges of that eminence.

[1] Soften.

With every influx of light comes new danger. Has he light? he must bear witness to the light, and always outrun that sympathy which gives him such keen satisfaction by his fidelity to new revelations of the incessant soul. He must hate father and mother, wife and child. Has he all that the world loves and admires and covets? he must cast behind him their admiration and afflict them by faithfulness to his truth and become a by-word and a hissing.

This law writes the laws of cities and nations. It is in vain to build or plot or combine against it. Things refuse to be mis-managed long. *Res nolunt diu male administrari.* Though no checks to a new evil appear, the checks exist and will appear. If the government is cruel, the governor's life is not safe. If you tax too high, the revenue will yield nothing. If you make the criminal code sanguinary, juries will not convict. If the law is too mild, private vengeance comes in. If the government is a terrific democracy, the pressure is resisted by an overcharge of energy in the citizen, and life glows with a fiercer flame. The true life and satisfactions of man seem to elude the utmost rigors or felicities of condition and to establish themselves with great indifferency under all varieties of circumstances. Under all governments the influence of character remains the same, in Turkey and in New England about alike. Under the primeval despots of Egypt, history honestly confesses that man must have been as free as culture could make him.

These appearances indicate the fact that the universe is represented in every one of its particles. Everything in nature contains all the powers of nature. Everything is made of one hidden stuff; as the naturalist sees one type under every metamorphosis and regards a horse as a running man, a fish as a swimming man, a bird as a flying man, a tree as a rooted man. Each new form repeats not only the main character of the type, but part for part all the details, all the aims, furtherances, hindrances, energies, and whole system of every other. Every occupation, trade, art, transaction, is a compend of the world and a correlative of every other. Each one is an entire emblem of human life; of its good and ill, its trials, its enemies, its course and its end. And each one must somehow accommodate the whole man and recite all his destiny.

The world globes itself in a drop of dew. The microscope cannot find the animalcule which is less perfect for being little. Eyes, ears, taste, smell, motion, resistance, appetite, and organs of reproduction that take hold on eternity, all find room to consist in the small creature. So do we put our life into every act. The true doctrine of omnipresence is that God reappears with all His parts in every moss and cobweb. The value of the universe contrives to throw itself into every point. If the good is there, so is the evil; if the affinity, so the repulsion; if the force, so the limitation.

Thus is the universe alive. All things are moral. That soul which within us is a sentiment, outside of us is a law. We feel its inspiration; but there in history we can see its fatal strength. "It is in the world, and the world was made by it." Justice is not postponed. A perfect equity adjusts its balance in all parts of life. *'Αεὶ γὰϱ εὖ πὶπτουσιν οἱ Διὸς κύβοι*—the dice of God are always loaded. The world looks like a multiplication table, or a mathematical equation, which, turn it how you will, balances itself. Take what figure you will, its exact value, nor more nor less, still returns to you. Every secret is told, every crime is punished, every virtue rewarded, every wrong redressed, in silence and certainty. What we call retribution is the universal necessity by which the whole appears wherever a part appears. If you see smoke, there must be fire. If you see a hand or a limb, you know that the trunk to which it belongs is there behind.

Every act rewards itself, or in other words integrates itself, in a twofold manner; first in the thing, or in real nature; and secondly in the circumstance, or in apparent nature. Men call the circumstance the retribution. The causal retribution is in the thing and is seen by the soul. The retribution in the circumstance is seen by the understanding; it is inseparable from the thing, but is often spread over a long time and so does not become distinct until after many years. The specific stripes may follow late after the offense, but they follow because they accompany it. Crime and punishment grow out of one stem. Punishment is a fruit that unsuspected ripens within the flower of the pleasure which concealed it. Cause and effect, means and ends, seed and fruit, cannot be severed; for the effect already blooms in the cause, the end pre-exists in the means, the fruit in the seed.

Whilst thus the world will be whole and refuses to be disparted, we seek to act partially, to sunder, to appropriate; for example, to gratify the senses we sever the pleasure of the senses from the needs of the character. The ingenuity of man has always been dedicated to the solution of one problem—how to detach the sensual sweet, the sensual strong, the sensual bright, etc., from the moral sweet, the moral deep, the moral fair; that is, again, to contrive to cut clean off this upper surface so thin as to leave it bottomless; to get a *one end*, without an *other end*. The soul says, 'Eat'; the body would feast. The soul says, 'The man and woman shall be one flesh and one soul'; the body would join the flesh only. The soul says, 'Have dominion over all things to the ends of virtue'; the body would have the power over things to its own ends.

The soul strives amain to live and work through all things. It would be the only fact. All things shall be added unto it—power, pleasure, knowledge, beauty. The particular man aims to be somebody; to set up for himself; to truck and higgle for a private good; and, in particulars, to ride that he may ride; to dress that he may be dressed; to eat that he may eat; and to govern that he may be seen. Men seek to be great; they would have offices, wealth, power, and fame. They think that to be great is to possess one side of nature—the sweet, without the other side, the bitter.

This dividing and detaching is steadily counteracted. Up to

this day it must be owned no projector has had the smallest success. The parted water reunites behind our hand. Pleasure is taken out of pleasant things, profit out of profitable things, power out of strong things, as soon as we seek to separate them from the whole. We can no more halve things and get the sensual good, by itself, than we can get an inside that shall have no outside, or a light without a shadow. "Drive out Nature with a fork, she comes running back." [1]

Life invests itself with inevitable conditions, which the unwise seek to dodge, which one and another brags that he does not know, that they do not touch him; but the brag is on his lips, the conditions are in his soul. If he escapes them in one part, they attack him in another more vital part. If he has escaped them in form and in the appearance, it is because he has resisted his life and fled from himself, and the retribution is so much death. So signal is the failure of all attempts to make this separation of the good from the tax that the experiment would not be tried—since to try it is to be mad—but for the circumstance that when the disease began in the will, of rebellion and separation, the intellect is at once infected, so that the man ceases to see God whole in each object, but is able to see the sensual allurement of an object and not see the sensual hurt; he sees the mermaid's head but not the dragon's tail, and thinks he can cut off that which he would have from that which he would not have. "How secret art thou who dwellest in the highest heavens in silence, O Thou only great God, sprinkling with an unwearied providence certain penal blindnesses upon such as have unbridled desires!" [2]

The human soul is true to these facts in the painting of fable, of history, of law, of proverbs, of conversation. It finds a tongue in literature unawares. Thus the Greeks called Jupiter, Supreme Mind; but having traditionally ascribed to him many base actions, they involuntarily made amends to reason by tying up

[1] Horace, *Epistles*, I, x.

[2] St. Augustine, *Confessions*, Book I.

the hands of so bad a god. He is made as helpless as a king of England. Prometheus knows one secret which Jove must bargain for; Minerva, another. He cannot get his own thunders; Minerva keeps the key of them:

> *Of all the gods, I only know the keys*
> *That ope the solid doors within whose vaults*
> *His thunders sleep.*[1]

A plain confession of the in-working of the All and of its moral aim. The Indian mythology ends in the same ethics; and it would seem impossible for any fable to be invented and get any currency which was not moral. Aurora forgot to ask youth for her lover, and though Tithonus is immortal, he is old. Achilles is not quite invulnerable; the sacred waters did not wash the heel by which Thetis held him. Siegfried, in the Nibelungen, is not quite immortal, for a leaf fell on his back whilst he was bathing in the dragon's blood, and that spot which it covered is mortal. And so it must be. There is a crack in everything God has made. It would seem there is always this vindicative circumstance stealing in at unawares even into the wild poesy in which the human fancy attempted to make bold holiday and to shake itself free of the old laws—this backstroke, this kick of the gun, certifying that the law is fatal; that in nature nothing can be given, all things are sold.

This is that ancient doctrine of Nemesis, who keeps watch in the universe and lets no offense go unchastised. The Furies, they said, are attendants on justice, and if the sun in heaven should transgress his path they would punish him. The poets related that stone walls and iron swords and leathern thongs had an occult sympathy with the wrongs of their owners; that the belt which Ajax gave Hector dragged the Trojan hero over the field at the wheels of the car of Achilles and the sword which Hector gave Ajax was that on whose point Ajax fell. They recorded that when the Thasians erected a statue to Theogenes,

[1] Aeschylus, *Prometheus Bound*.

a victor in the games, one of his rivals went to it by night and endeavored to throw it down by repeated blows, until at last he moved it from its pedestal and was crushed to death beneath its fall.

This voice of fable has in it somewhat divine. It came from thought above the will of the writer. That is the best part of each writer which has nothing private in it; that which he does not know; that which flowed out of his constitution and not from his too active invention; that which in the study of a single artist you might not easily find, but in the study of many you would abstract as the spirit of them all. Phidias it is not, but the work of man in that early Hellenic world that I would know. The name and circumstance of Phidias, however convenient for history, embarrass when we come to the highest criticism. We are to see that which man was tending to do in a given period and was hindered, or, if you will, modified in doing, by the interfering volitions of Phidias, of Dante, of Shakspeare, the organ whereby man at the moment wrought.

Still more striking is the expression of this fact in the proverbs of all nations, which are always the literature of reason, or the statements of an absolute truth without qualification. Proverbs, like the sacred books of each nation, are the sanctuary of the intuitions. That which the droning world, chained to appearances, will not allow the realist to say in his own words, it will suffer him to say in proverbs without contradiction. And this law of laws, which the pulpit, the senate, and the college deny, is hourly preached in all markets and workshops by flights of proverbs whose teaching is as true and as omnipresent as that of birds and flies.

All things are double, one against another.—Tit for tat; an eye for an eye; a tooth for a tooth; blood for blood; measure for measure; love for love.—Give, and it shall be given you.—He that watereth shall be watered himself.—What will you have? quoth God; pay for it and take it.—Nothing venture, nothing have.—Thou shalt be paid exactly for what thou hast done, no more, no less.—Who doth not work shall not eat. —Harm watch, harm catch.—Curses always recoil on the head of him who imprecates them.—If you put a chain around the neck of a slave, the other end fastens itself around your own. —Bad counsel confounds the adviser.—The Devil is an ass.

It is thus written because it is thus in life. Our action is overmastered and characterized above our will by the law of nature. We aim at a petty end quite aside from the public good, but our act arranges itself by irresistible magnetism in a line with the poles of the world.

A man cannot speak but he judges himself. With his will or against his will he draws his portrait to the eye of his companions by every word. Every opinion reacts on him who utters it. It is a thread-ball thrown at a mark, but the other end remains in the thrower's bag. Or rather it is a harpoon hurled at the whale, unwinding, as it flies, a coil of cord in the boat, and if the harpoon is not good or not well thrown, it will go nigh to cut the steersman in twain or to sink the boat.

You cannot do wrong without suffering wrong. "No man had ever a point of pride that was not injurious to him," said Burke. The exclusive in fashionable life does not see that he excludes himself from enjoyment in the attempt to appropriate it. The exclusionist in religion does not see that he shuts the door of heaven on himself in striving to shut out others. Treat men as pawns and ninepins, and you shall suffer as well as they. If you leave out their heart, you shall lose your own. The senses would make things of all persons; of women, of children, of the poor. The vulgar proverb, "I will get it from his purse or get it from his skin," is sound philosophy.

All infractions of love and equity in our social relations are speedily punished. They are punished by fear. Whilst I stand in simple relations to my fellow man, I have no displeasure in meeting him. We meet as water meets water, or as two currents of air mix, with perfect diffusion and interpenetration of nature. But as soon as there is any departure from simplicity and attempt at halfness, or good for me that is not good for him, my neighbor feels the wrong; he shrinks from me as far as I have shrunk from him; his eyes no longer seek mine; there is war between us; there is hate in him and fear in me.

All the old abuses in society, universal and particular, all unjust accumulations of property and power, are avenged in the same manner. Fear is an instructor of great sagacity and the herald of all revolutions. One thing he teaches, that there is rottenness where he appears. He is a carrion crow, and though you see not well what he hovers for, there is death somewhere. Our property is timid, our laws are timid, our cultivated classes are timid. Fear for ages has boded and mowed and gibbered over government and property. That obscene bird is not there for nothing. He indicates great wrongs which must be revised.

Of the like nature is that expectation of change which instantly follows the suspension of our voluntary activity. The terror of cloudless noon, the emerald of Polycrates, the awe of prosperity, the instinct which leads every generous soul to impose on itself tasks of a noble asceticism and vicarious virtue, are the tremblings of the balance of justice through the heart and mind of man.

Experienced men of the world know very well that it is best to pay scot and lot as they go along and that a man often pays dear for a small frugality. The borrower runs in his own debt. Has a man gained anything who has received a hundred favors and rendered none? Has he gained by borrowing, through indolence or cunning, his neighbor's wares, or horses, or money? There arises on the deed the instant acknowledgment of benefit on the one part and of debt on the other; that is, of superiority and inferiority. The transaction remains in the memory of himself and his neighbor; and every new transaction alters according to its nature their relation to each other. He may soon come to see that he had better have broken his own bones than to have ridden in his neighbor's coach, and that "the highest price he can pay for a thing is to ask for it."

A wise man will extend this lesson to all parts of life, and know that it is the part of prudence to face every claimant and pay every just demand on your time, your talents, or your heart. Always pay; for first or last you must pay your entire debt. Persons and events may stand for a time between you and justice, but it is only a postponement. You must pay at last your own debt. If you are wise you will dread a prosperity which only loads you with more. Benefit is the end of nature. But for every benefit which you receive, a tax is levied. He is great who confers the most benefits. He is base—and that is the one base thing in the universe—to receive favors and render none. In the order of nature we cannot render benefits to those from whom we receive them, or only seldom. But the benefit we receive must be rendered again, line for line, deed for deed, cent for cent, to somebody. Beware of too much good staying in your hand. It will fast corrupt and worm worms. Pay it away quickly in some sort.

Labor is watched over by the same pitiless laws. Cheapest, say the prudent, is the dearest labor. What we buy in a broom, a mat, a wagon, a knife, is some application of good sense to a common want. It is best to pay in your land a skillful gardener or to buy good sense applied to gardening; in your sailor, good sense applied to navigation; in the house, good sense applied to cooking, sewing, serving; in your agent, good sense applied to accounts and affairs. So do you multiply your presence or spread yourself throughout your estate. But because of the dual constitution of things, in labor as in life there can be no cheating. The thief steals from himself. The swindler swindles himself. For the real price of labor is knowledge and virtue, whereof wealth and credit are signs. These signs, like paper money, may be counterfeited or stolen, but that which they represent, namely, knowledge and virtue, cannot be counterfeited or stolen. These ends of labor cannot be answered but by real exertions of the mind and in obedience to pure motives. The cheat, the defaulter, the gambler, cannot extort the knowledge of material and moral nature which his honest care and pains yield to the operative. The law of nature is, Do the thing, and you shall have the power; but they who do not the thing have not the power.

Human labor, through all its forms, from the sharpening of a stake to the construction of a city or an epic, is one immense illustration of the perfect compensation of the universe. The absolute balance of Give and Take, the doctrine that every thing has its price—and if that price is not paid, not that thing but something else is obtained, and that it is impossible to get anything without its price—is not less sublime in the columns of a ledger than in the budgets of states, in the laws of light and darkness, in all the action and reaction of nature. I cannot doubt that the high laws which each man sees implicated in those processes with which he is conversant, the stern ethics which sparkle on his chisel edge, which are measured out by his plumb and foot rule, which stand as manifest in the footing of the shop bill as in the history of a state, do recommend to him his trade, and though seldom named, exalt his business to his imagination.

The league between virtue and nature engages all things to assume a hostile front to vice. The beautiful laws and substances of the world persecute and whip the traitor. He finds that things are arranged for truth and benefit, but there is no den in the wide world to hide a rogue. Commit a crime, and the earth is made of glass. Commit a crime, and it seems as if a coat of snow fell on the ground, such as reveals in the woods the track of every partridge and fox and squirrel and mole. You cannot recall the spoken word, you cannot wipe out the foot track, you cannot draw up the ladder, so as to leave no inlet or clue. Some damning circumstance always transpires. The laws and substances of nature—water, snow, wind, gravitation—become penalties to the thief.

On the other hand the law holds with equal sureness for all right action. Love, and you shall be loved. All love is mathematically just, as much as the two sides of an algebraic equation. The good man has absolute good, which like fire turns everything to its own nature, so that you cannot do him any harm; but as the royal armies sent against Napoleon when he approached cast down their colors and from enemies became friends, so disasters of all kinds, as sickness, offense, poverty, prove benefactors:

> *Winds blow and waters roll*
> *Strength to the brave and power and deity,*
> *Yet in themselves are nothing.*[1]

The good are befriended even by weakness and defect. As no man had ever a point of pride that was not injurious to him, so no man had ever a defect that was not somewhere made useful to him. The stag in the fable admired his horns and blamed his feet, but when the hunter came, his feet saved him, and afterwards, caught in the thicket, his horns destroyed him. Every man in his lifetime needs to thank his faults. As no man thoroughly understands a truth until he has contended against it, so no man has a thorough acquaintance with the hindrances or talents of men until he has suffered from the one and seen the triumph of the other over his own want of the same. Has he a defect of temper that unfits him to live in society? Thereby he is driven to entertain himself alone and acquire habits of self-help; and thus, like the wounded oyster, he mends his shell with pearl.

Our strength grows out of our weakness. The indignation which arms itself with secret forces does not awaken until we are pricked and stung and sorely assailed. A great man is always willing to be little. Whilst he sits on the cushion of advantages, he goes to sleep. When he is pushed, tormented, defeated, he has a chance to learn something; he has been put on his wits, on his manhood; he has gained facts; learns his ignorance; is cured of the insanitv of conceit; has got modera-

[1] Wordsworth, *September 1802*.

tion and real skill. The wise man throws himself on the side of his assailants. It is more his interest than it is theirs to find his weak point. The wound cicatrizes and falls off from him like a dead skin, and when they would triumph, lo! he has passed on invulnerable. Blame is safer than praise. I hate to be defended in a newspaper. As long as all that is said is said against me, I feel a certain assurance of success. But as soon as honeyed words of praise are spoken for me I feel as one that lies unprotected before his enemies. In general, every evil to which we do not succumb is a benefactor. As the Sandwich Islander believes that the strength and valor of the enemy he kills passes into himself, so we gain the strength of the temptation we resist.

The same guards which protect us from disaster, defect, and enmity defend us, if we will, from selfishness and fraud. Bolts and bars are not the best of our institutions, nor is shrewdness in trade a mark of wisdom. Men suffer all their life long under the foolish superstition that they can be cheated. But it is as impossible for a man to be cheated by anyone but himself as for a thing to be and not to be at the same time. There is a third silent party to all our bargains. The nature and soul of things takes on itself the guaranty of the fulfillment of every contract, so that honest service cannot come to loss. If you serve an ungrateful master, serve him the more. Put God in your debt. Every stroke shall be repaid. The longer the payment is withholden, the better for you; for compound interest on compound interest is the rate and usage of this exchequer.

The history of persecution is a history of endeavors to cheat nature, to make water run up hill, to twist a rope of sand. It makes no difference whether the actors be many or one, a tyrant or a mob. A mob is a society of bodies voluntarily bereaving themselves of reason and traversing its work. The mob is man voluntarily descending to the nature of the beast. Its fit hour of activity is night. Its actions are insane, like its whole constitution. It persecutes a principle; it would whip a right; it would tar and feather justice, by inflicting fire and outrage upon the houses and persons of those who have these. It resembles the prank of boys, who run with fire-engines to put out the ruddy aurora streaming to the stars. The inviolate spirit turns their spite against the wrongdoers. The martyr cannot be dishonored. Every lash inflicted is a tongue of fame; every prison a more illustrious abode; every burned book or house enlightens the world; every suppressed or expunged word reverberates through the earth from side to side. Hours of sanity and consideration are always arriving to communities, as to individuals, when the truth is seen and the martyrs are justified.

Thus do all things preach the indifferency of circumstances. The man is all. Everything has two sides, a good and an evil. Every advantage has its tax. I learn to be content. But the doctrine of compensation is not the doctrine of indifferency. The thoughtless say, on hearing these representations, 'What boots it to do well? there is one event to good and evil; if I gain any good I must pay for it; if I lose any good I gain some other; all actions are indifferent.'

There is a deeper fact in the soul than compensation, to wit, its own nature. The soul is not a compensation, but a life. The soul *is*. Under all this running sea of circumstance, whose waters ebb and flow with perfect balance, lies the aboriginal abyss of real Being. Essence, or God, is not a relation or a part, but the whole. Being is the vast affirmative, excluding negation, self-balanced, and swallowing up all relations, parts and times within itself. Nature, truth, virtue, are the influx from thence. Vice is the absence or departure of the same. Nothing, Falsehood, may indeed stand as the great Night or shade on which as a background the living universe paints itself forth, but no fact is begotten by it; it cannot work, for it is not. It cannot work any good; it cannot work any harm. It is harm inasmuch as it is worse not to be than to be.

We feel defrauded of the retribution due to evil acts, because the criminal adheres to his vice and contumacy and does not come to a crisis or judgment anywhere in visible nature. There is no stunning confutation of his nonsense before men and angels. Has he therefore outwitted the law? Inasmuch as he carries the malignity and the lie with him he so far deceases from nature. In some manner there will be a demonstration of the wrong to the understanding also; but, should we not see it, this deadly deduction makes square the eternal account.

Neither can it be said, on the other hand, that the gain of rectitude must be bought by any loss. There is no penalty to virtue; no penalty to wisdom; they are proper additions of being. In a virtuous action I properly *am;* in a virtuous act I add to the world; I plant into deserts conquered from Chaos and Nothing and see the darkness receding on the limits of the horizon. There can be no excess to love, none to knowledge, none to beauty, when these attributes are considered in the purest sense. The soul refuses limits, and always affirms an Optimism, never a Pessimism.

Man's life is a progress, and not a station. His instinct is trust. Our instinct uses "more" and "less" in application to man, of the *presence of the soul* and not of its absence; the brave man is greater than the coward; the true, the benevolent, the wise, is more a man and not less than the fool and knave. There is no tax on the good of virtue, for that is the incoming of God himself, or absolute existence, without any comparative. Material good has its tax, and if it came without desert or sweat, has no root in me, and the next wind will blow it away. But all the good of nature is the soul's and may be had if paid for in nature's lawful coin, that is, by labor which the heart and the head allow. I no longer wish to meet a good I do not earn, for example to find a pot of buried gold, knowing that it brings with it new burdens. I do not wish more external goods—neither possessions, nor honors, nor powers, nor persons. The gain is apparent; the tax is certain. But there is no tax on the knowledge that the compensation exists and that it is not desirable to dig up treasure. Herein I rejoice with a serene eternal peace. I contract the boundaries of possible mischief. I learn the wisdom of St. Bernard—"Nothing can work me damage except myself; the harm that I sustain I carry about with me, and never am a real sufferer but by my own fault."

In the nature of the soul is the compensation for the inequalities of condition. The radical tragedy of nature seems to be the distinction of More and Less. How can Less not feel the pain; how not feel indignation or malevolence towards More? Look at those who have less faculty, and one feels sad and knows not well what to make of it. He almost shuns their eye; he fears they will upbraid God. What should they do? It seems a great injustice. But see the facts nearly and these mountainous inequalities vanish. Love reduces them as the sun melts the iceberg in the sea. The heart and soul of all men being one, this bitterness of *His* and *Mine* ceases. His is mine. I am my brother and my brother is me. If I feel over-shadowed and outdone by great neighbors, I can yet love; I can still receive; and he that loveth maketh his own the grandeur he loves. Thereby I make the discovery that my brother is my guardian, acting for me with the friendliest designs, and the estate I so admired and envied is my own. It is the nature of the soul to appropriate all things. Jesus and Shakspeare are fragments of the soul, and by love I conquer and incorporate them in my own conscious domain. His virtue—is not that mine? His wit—if it cannot be made mine, it is not wit.

Such also is the natural history of calamity. The changes which break up at short intervals the prosperity of men are advertisements of a nature whose law is growth. Every soul is by this intrinsic necessity quitting its whole system of things, its friends and home and laws and faith, as the shellfish crawls out of its beautiful but stony case, because it no longer admits of its growth, and slowly forms a new house. In proportion to the vigor of the individual these revolutions are frequent, until in some happier mind they are incessant and all worldly relations hang very loosely about him, becoming as it were a transparent fluid membrane through which the living form is seen, and not, as in most men, an indurated heterogeneous fabric of many dates and of no settled character, in which the man is imprisoned. Then there can be enlargement, and the man of today scarcely recognizes the man of yesterday. And such should be the outward biography of man in time, a putting off of dead circumstances day by day, as he renews his raiment day by day. But to us, in our lapsed estate, resting, not advancing, resisting, not co-operating with the divine expansion, this growth comes by shocks.

We cannot part with our friends. We cannot let our angels go. We do not see that they only go out that archangels may come in. We are idolaters of the old. We do not believe in the riches of the soul, in its proper eternity and omnipresence. We do not believe there is any force in today to rival or recreate that beautiful yesterday. We linger in the ruins of the old tent where once we had bread and shelter and organs, nor believe that the spirit can feed, cover, and nerve us again. We cannot again find aught so dear, so sweet, so graceful. But we sit and weep in vain. The voice of the Almighty saith, 'Up and onward for evermore!' We cannot stay amid the ruins. Neither will we rely on the new; and so we walk ever with reverted eyes, like those monsters who look backwards.

And yet the compensations of calamity are made apparent to the understanding also, after long intervals of time. A fever, a mutilation, a cruel disappointment, a loss of wealth, a loss of friends, seems at the moment unpaid loss, and unpayable. But the sure years reveal the deep remedial force that underlies all facts. The death of a dear friend, wife, brother, lover, which seemed nothing but privation, somewhat later assumes the aspect of a guide or genius; for it commonly operates revolutions in our way of life, terminates an epoch of infancy or of youth which was waiting to be closed, breaks up a wonted occupation, or a household, or style of living, and allows the formation of new ones more friendly to the growth of character. It permits or constrains the formation of new acquaintances and the reception of new influences that prove of the first importance to the next years; and the man or woman who would have remained a sunny garden flower, with no room for its roots and too much sunshine for its head, by the falling of the walls and the neglect of the gardener is made the banyan of the forest, yielding shade and fruit to wide neighborhoods of men.

1841

Give All To Love

GIVE all to love;
Obey thy heart;
Friends, kindred, days,
Estate, good-fame,
Plans, credit, and the Muse,–
Nothing refuse.

'Tis a brave master;
Let it have scope:
Follow it utterly,
Hope beyond hope;
High and more high
It dives into noon,
With wing unspent,
Untold intent;
But it is a god,
Knows its own path
And the outlets of the sky.

It was not for the mean;
It requireth courage stout.
Souls above doubt,
Valor unbending,
It will reward,–
They shall return
More than they were,
And ever ascending.

Leave all for love;
Yet, hear me, yet,
One word more thy heart behoved,
One pulse more of firm endeavor,—
Keep thee today,
Tomorrow, forever,
Free as an Arab
Of thy beloved.

Cling with life to the maid;
But when the surprise,
First vague shadow of surmise
Flits across her bosom young
Of a joy apart from thee,
Free be she, fancy-free;
Nor thou detain her vesture's hem,
Nor the palest rose she flung
From her summer diadem.

Though thou loved her as thyself,
As a self of purer clay,
Though her parting dims the day,
Stealing grace from all alive;
Heartily know,
When half-gods go,
The gods arrive.

1847

Love

I WAS as a gem concealed;
Me my burning ray revealed.
Koran

EVERY promise of the soul has innumerable fulfillments; each of its joys ripens into a new want. Nature, uncontainable, flowing, forelooking, in the first sentiment of kindness anticipates already a benevolence which shall lose all particular regards in its general light. The introduction to this felicity is in a private and tender relation of one to one, which is the enchantment of human life; which, like a certain divine rage and enthusiasm, seizes on man at one period and works a revolution in his mind and body; unites him to his race, pledges him to the domestic and civic relations, carries him with new sympathy into nature, enhances the power of the senses, opens the imagination, adds to his character heroic and sacred attributes, establishes marriage, and gives permanence to human society.

The natural association of the sentiment of love with the heyday of the blood seems to require that in order to portray it in vivid tints, which every youth and maid should confess to be true to their throbbing experience, one must not be too old. The delicious fancies of youth reject the least savor of a mature philosophy, as chilling with age and pedantry their purple bloom. And therefore I know I incur the imputation of unnecessary hardness and stoicism from those who compose the Court and Parliament of Love. But from these formidable censors I shall appeal to my seniors. For it is to be considered that this passion of which we speak, though it begin with the young, yet forsakes not the old, or rather suffers no one who is its servant to grow old, but makes the aged participators of it not less than the tender maiden, though in a different and nobler sort. For it is a fire that kindling its first embers in the narrow nook of a private bosom, caught from a wandering spark out of another private heart, glows and enlarges until it warms and beams upon multitudes of men and women, upon the universal heart of all, and so lights up the whole world and all nature with its generous flames. It matters not therefore whether we attempt to describe the passion at twenty, thirty, or at eighty years. He who paints it at the first period will lose some of its later, who paints it at the last, some of its earlier traits. Only it is to be hoped that by patience and the Muses' aid we may attain to that inward view of the law which shall describe a truth ever young and beautiful, so central that it shall commend itself to the eye at whatever angle beholden.

And the first condition is that we must leave a too close and lingering adherence to facts, and study the sentiment as it appeared in hope, and not in history. For each man sees his own life defaced and disfigured, as the life of man is not to his imagination. Each man sees over his own experience a certain stain of error, whilst that of other men looks fair and ideal. Let any man go back to those delicious relations which make the beauty of his life, which have given him sincerest instruction and nourishment, he will shrink and moan. Alas! I know not why, but infinite compunctions embitter in mature life the remembrances of budding joy, and cover every beloved name. Everything is beautiful seen from the point of the intellect, or as truth. But all is sour if seen as experience. Details are melancholy; the plan is seemly and noble. In the actual world—the painful kingdom of time and place—dwell care and canker and fear. With thought, with the ideal, is immortal hilarity, the rose of joy.

Round it all the Muses sing. But grief cleaves to names and persons and the partial interests of today and yesterday.

The strong bent of nature is seen in the proportion which this topic of personal relations usurps in the conversation of society. What do we wish to know of any worthy person so much as how he has sped in the history of this sentiment? What books in the circulating library circulate? How we glow over these novels of passion, when the story is told with any spark of truth and nature! And what fastens attention, in the intercourse of life, like any passage betraying affection between two parties? Perhaps we never saw them before and never shall meet them again. But we see them exchange a glance or betray a deep emotion, and we are no longer strangers. We understand them and take the warmest interest in the development of the romance. All mankind love a lover. The earliest demonstrations of complacency and kindness are nature's most winning pictures. It is the dawn of civility and grace in the coarse and rustic. The rude village boy teases the girls about the schoolhouse door; but today he comes running into the entry and meets one fair child disposing her satchel; he holds her books to help her, and instantly it seems to him as if she removed herself from him infinitely, and was a sacred precinct. Among the throng of girls he runs rudely enough, but one alone distances him; and these two little neighbors, that were so close just now, have learned to respect each other's personality. Or who can avert his eyes from the engaging, half-artful, half-artless ways of schoolgirls who go into the country shops to buy a skein of silk or a sheet of paper, and talk half an hour about nothing with the broad-faced, good-natured shopboy. In the village they are on a perfect equality, which love delights in, and without any coquetry the happy, affectionate nature of woman flows out in this pretty gossip. The girls may have little beauty, yet plainly do they establish between them and the good boy the most agreeable, confiding relations; what with their fun and their earnest, about Edgar and Jonas and Almira, and who was invited to the party, and who danced at the dancing-school, and when the singing-school would begin, and other nothings concerning which the parties cooed. By and by that boy wants a wife, and very truly and heartily will he know where to find a sincere and sweet mate, without any risk such as Milton deplores as incident to scholars and great men.

I have been told that in some public discourses of mine my reverence for the intellect has made me unjustly cold to the personal relations. But now I almost shrink at the remembrance of such disparaging words. For persons are love's world, and the coldest philosopher cannot recount the debt of the young soul wandering here in nature to the power of love, without being tempted to unsay, as treasonable to nature, aught derogatory to the social instincts. For though the celestial rapture falling out of heaven seizes only upon those of tender age, and although a beauty overpowering all analysis or comparison and putting us quite beside ourselves we can seldom see after thirty years, yet the remembrance of these visions outlasts all other remembrances and is a wreath of flowers on the oldest brows. But here is a strange fact; it may seem to many men, in revising their experience, that they have no fairer page in their life's book than the delicious memory of some passages wherein affection contrived to give a witchcraft, surpassing the deep attraction of its own truth, to a parcel of accidental and trivial circumstances. In looking backward they may find that several things which were not the charm have more reality to this groping memory than the charm itself which embalmed them. But be our experience in particulars what it may, no man ever forgot the visitations of that power to his heart and brain which created all things anew; which was the dawn in him of music, poetry, and art; which made the face of nature radiant with purple light, the morning and the night varied enchantments; when a single tone of one voice could make the heart bound and the most trivial circumstance associated with one form is put in the amber of memory; when he became all eye when one was present and all memory when one was gone; when the youth becomes a watcher of windows and studious of a glove, a veil, a ribbon, or the wheels of a carriage; when no place is too solitary and none too silent for him who has richer company and sweeter conversation in his new thoughts than any old friends, though best and purest, can give him; for the figures, the motions, the words of the beloved object are not, like other images, written in water, but, as Plutarch said, "enameled in fire," and make the study of midnight:

> *Thou art not gone being gone, where'er thou art,*
> *Thou leav'st in him thy watchful eyes, in him thy*
> *loving heart.*[1]

In the noon and the afternoon of life we still throb at the recollection of days when happiness was not happy enough, but must be drugged with the relish of pain and fear; for he touched the secret of the matter who said of love,

> *All other pleasures are not worth its pains:*[2]

and when the day was not long enough, but the night too must be consumed in keen recollections; when the head boiled all night on the pillow with the generous deed it resolved on; when the moonlight was a pleasing fever and the stars were letters and the flowers ciphers and the air was coined into song; when all business seemed an impertinence, and all the men and women running to and fro in the streets, mere pictures.

The passion rebuilds the world for the youth. It makes all things alive and significant. Nature grows conscious. Every bird on the boughs of the tree sings now to his heart and soul. The notes are almost articulate. The clouds have faces as he looks on them. The trees of the forest, the waving grass and the peeping flowers have grown intelligent; and he almost fears to trust

[1] John Donne, "Epithalamion," ix.

[2] This line was written by an unidentified friend of Emerson.

them with the secret which they seem to invite. Yet nature soothes and sympathizes. In the green solitude he finds a dearer home than with men:

Fountain-heads and pathless groves,
Places which pale passion loves,
Moonlight walks, when all the fowls
Are safely housed, save bats and owls,
A midnight bell, a passing groan—
These are the sounds we feed upon.[1]

Behold there in the wood the fine madman! He is a palace of sweet sounds and sights; he dilates; he is twice a man; he walks with arms akimbo; he soliloquizes; he accosts the grass and the trees; he feels the blood of the violet, the clover and the lily in his veins; and he talks with the brook that wets his foot.

The heats that have opened his perceptions of natural beauty have made him love music and verse. It is a fact often observed, that men have written good verses under the inspiration of passion who cannot write well under any other circumstances.

The like force has the passion over all his nature. It expands the sentiment; it makes the clown gentle and gives the coward heart. Into the most pitiful and abject it will infuse a heart and courage to defy the world, so only it have the countenance of the beloved object. In giving him to another it still more gives him to himself. He is a new man, with new perceptions, new and keener purposes, and a religious solemnity of character and aims. He does not longer appertain to his family and society; *he* is somewhat; *he* is a person; *he* is a soul.

And here let us examine a little nearer the nature of that influence which is thus potent over the human youth. Beauty, whose revelation to man we now celebrate, welcome as the sun wherever it pleases to shine, which pleases everybody with it and with themselves, seems sufficient to itself. The lover cannot

[1] From William Strode, "A Song in Praise of Melancholy," introduced by John Fletcher into *A Nice Valour*, III, iii.

paint his maiden to his fancy poor and solitary. Like a tree in flower, so much soft, budding, informing loveliness is society for itself; and she teaches his eye why Beauty was pictured with Loves and Graces attending her steps. Her existence makes the world rich. Though she extrudes all other persons from his attention as cheap and unworthy, she indemnifies him by carrying out her own being into somewhat impersonal, large, mundane, so that the maiden stands to him for a representative of all select things and virtues. For that reason the lover never sees personal resemblances in his mistress to her kindred or to others. His friends find in her a likeness to her mother, or her sisters, or to persons not of her blood. The lover sees no resemblance except to summer evenings and diamond mornings, to rainbows and the song of birds.

The ancients called beauty the flowering of virtue. Who can analyze the nameless charm which glances from one and another face and form? We are touched with emotions of tenderness and complacency, but we cannot find whereat this dainty emotion, this wandering gleam, points. It is destroyed for the imagination by any attempt to refer it to organization. Nor does it point to any relations of friendship or love known and described in society, but, as it seems to me, to a quite other and unattainable sphere, to relations of transcendent delicacy and sweetness, to what roses and violets hint and foreshow. We cannot approach beauty. Its nature is like opaline doves'-neck lusters, hovering and evanescent. Herein it resembles the most excellent things, which all have this rainbow character, defying all attempts at appropriation and use. What else did Jean Paul Richter signify, when he said to music, "Away! away! thou speakest to me of things which in all my endless life I have not found and shall not find." The same fluency may be observed in every work of the plastic arts. The statue is then beautiful when it begins to be incomprehensible, when it is passing out of criticism and can no longer be defined by compass and measuring-wand, but demands an active imagination to go with it and to say what it is in the act of doing. The god or hero of the sculptor is always represented in a transition *from* that which is representable to the senses *to* that which is not. Then first it ceases to be a stone. The same remark holds of painting. And of poetry the success is not attained when it lulls and satisfies, but when it astonishes and fires us with new endeavors after the unattainable. Concerning it Landor inquires "whether it is not to be referred to some purer state of sensation and existence."

In like manner, personal beauty is then first charming and itself when it dissatisfies us with any end; when it becomes a story without an end; when it suggests gleams and visions and not earthly satisfactions; when it makes the beholder feel his unworthiness; when he cannot feel his right to it, though he were Cæsar; he cannot feel more right to it than to the firmament and the splendors of a sunset.

Hence arose the saying, "If I love you, what is that to you?" We say so because we feel that what we love is not in your will, but above it. It is not you, but your radiance. It is that which you know not in yourself and can never know.

This agrees well with that high philosophy of Beauty which the ancient writers delighted in; for they said that the soul of man, embodied here on earth, went roaming up and down in quest of that other world of its own out of which it came into this, but was soon stupefied by the light of the natural sun, and unable to see any other objects than those of this world, which are but shadows of real things. Therefore the Deity sends the glory of youth before the soul, that it may avail itself of beautiful bodies as aids to its recollection of the celestial good and fair; and the man beholding such a person in the female sex runs to her and finds the highest joy in contemplating the form, movement, and intelligence of this person, because it suggests to him the presence of that which indeed is within the beauty, and the cause of the beauty.

If, however, from too much conversing with material objects, the soul was gross and misplaced its satisfaction in the body, it reaped nothing but sorrow; body being unable to fulfill the promise which beauty holds out; but if, accepting the hint of these visions and suggestions which beauty makes to his mind, the soul passes through the body and falls to admire strokes of character, and the lovers contemplate one another in their discourses and their actions, then they pass to the true palace of beauty, more and more inflame their love of it and by this love extinguishing the base affection, as the sun puts out fire by shining on the hearth, they become pure and hallowed. By conversation with that which is in itself excellent, magnanimous, lowly, and just, the lover comes to a warmer love of these nobilities and a quicker apprehension of them. Then he passes from loving them in one to loving them in all, and so is the one beautiful soul only the door through which he enters to the society of all true and pure souls. In the particular society of his mate he attains a clearer sight of any spot, any taint which her beauty has contracted from this world, and is able to point it out, and this with mutual joy that they are now able, without offense, to indicate blemishes and hindrances in each other and give to each all help and comfort in curing the same. And beholding in many souls the traits of the divine beauty and separating in each soul that which is divine from the taint which it has contracted in the world, the lover ascends to the highest beauty, to the love and knowledge of the Divinity, by steps on this ladder of created souls.

Somewhat like this have the truly wise told us of love in all ages. The doctrine is not old, nor is it new. If Plato, Plutarch, and Apuleius taught it, so have Petrarch, Angelo, and Milton. It awaits a truer unfolding in opposition and rebuke to that subterranean prudence which presides at marriages with words that take hold of the upper world, whilst one eye is prowling in the cellar; so that its gravest discourse has a savor of hams and powdering-tubs. Worst, when this sensualism intrudes into the education of young women and withers the hope and affection of human nature by teaching that marriage signifies nothing but a housewife's thrift and that woman's life has no other aim.

But this dream of love, though beautiful, is only one scene in our play. In the procession of the soul from within outward, it enlarges its circles ever, like the pebble thrown into the pond, or the light proceeding from an orb. The rays of the soul alight first on things nearest, on every utensil and toy, on nurses and domestics, on the house and yard and passengers, on the circle of household acquaintance, on politics and geography and history. But things are ever grouping themselves according to higher or more interior laws. Neighborhood, size, numbers, habits, persons, lose by degrees their power over us. Cause and effect, real affinities, the longing for harmony between the soul and the circumstance, the progressive, idealizing instinct predominate later, and the step backward from the higher to the lower relations is impossible. Thus even love, which is the deification of persons, must become more impersonal every day. Of this at first it gives no hint. Little think the youth and maiden who are glancing at each other across crowded rooms with eyes so full of mutual intelligence, of the precious fruit long hereafter to proceed from this new, quite external stimulus. The work of vegetation begins first in the irritability of the bark and leaf-buds. From exchanging glances, they advance to acts of courtesy, of gallantry, then to fiery passion, to plighting troth and marriage. Passion beholds its object as a perfect unit. The soul is wholly embodied, and the body is wholly ensouled:

Her pure and eloquent blood
Spoke in her cheeks, and so distinctly wrought,
That one might almost say her body thought.[1]

Romeo, if dead, should be cut up into little stars to make the heavens fine. Life, with this pair, has no other aim, asks no

[1] John Donne, "The Second Anniversary," lines 244-246.

more, than Juliet, than Romeo. Night, day, studies, talents, kingdoms, religion, are all contained in this form full of soul, in this soul which is all form. The lovers delight in endearments, in avowals of love, in comparisons of their regards. When alone, they solace themselves with the remembered image of the other. Does that other see the same star, the same melting cloud, read the same book, feel the same emotion, that now delights me? They try and weigh their affection, and adding up costly advantages, friends, opportunities, properties, exult in discovering that willingly, joyfully, they would give all as a ransom for the beautiful, the beloved head, not one hair of which shall be harmed. But the lot of humanity is on these children. Danger, sorrow, and pain arrive to them as to all. Love prays. It makes covenants with Eternal Power in behalf of this dear mate. The union which is thus effected and which adds a new value to every atom in nature—for it transmutes every thread throughout the whole web of relation into a golden ray, and bathes the soul in a new and sweeter element—is yet a temporary state. Not always can flowers, pearls, poetry, protestations, nor even home in another heart, content the awful soul that dwells in clay. It arouses itself at last from these endearments as toys and puts on the harness and aspires to vast and universal aims. The soul which is in the soul of each, craving a perfect beatitude, detects incongruities, defects and disproportion in the behavior of the other. Hence arise surprise, expostulation and pain. Yet that which drew them to each other was signs of loveliness, signs of virtue; and these virtues are there, however eclipsed. They appear and reappear and continue to attract; but the regard changes, quits the sign and attaches to the substance. This repairs the wounded affection. Meantime, as life wears on, it proves a game of permutation and combination of all possible positions of the parties, to employ all the resources of each and acquaint each with the strength and weakness of the other. For it is the nature and end of this relation that they should represent the human race to each other. All that is in the world, which is or ought to be known, is cunningly wrought into the texture of man, of woman:

> *The person love does to us fit,*
> *Like manna, has the taste of all in it.*[1]

The world rolls; the circumstances vary every hour. The angels that inhabit this temple of the body appear at the windows, and the gnomes and vices also. By all the virtues they are united. If there be virtue, all the vices are known as such; they confess and flee. Their once flaming regard is sobered by time in either breast, and losing in violence what it gains in extent, it becomes a thorough good understanding. They resign each other without complaint to the good offices which man and woman are severally appointed to discharge in time, and exchange the passion which once could not lose sight of its object for a cheerful disengaged furtherance, whether present or absent, of each other's designs. At last they discover that all which at first drew them together—those once sacred features, that magical play of charms—was deciduous, had a prospective end, like the scaffolding by which the house was built; and the purification of the intellect and the heart from year to year is the real marriage, foreseen and prepared from the first, and wholly above their consciousness. Looking at these aims with which two persons, a man and a woman, so variously and correlatively gifted, are shut up in one house to spend in the nuptial society forty or fifty years, I do not wonder at the emphasis with which the heart prophesies this crisis from early infancy, at the profuse beauty with which the instincts deck the nuptial bower, and nature and intellect and art emulate each other in the gifts and the melody they bring to the epithalamium.

Thus are we put in training for a love which knows not sex, nor person, nor partiality, but which seeks virtue and wisdom everywhere, to the end of increasing virtue and wisdom. We

[1] Abraham Cowley, "Resolved to be Beloved."

are by nature observers and thereby learners. That is our permanent state. But we are often made to feel that our affections are but tents of a night. Though slowly and with pain, the objects of the affections change, as the objects of thought do. There are moments when the affections rule and absorb the man and make his happiness dependent on a person or persons. But in health the mind is presently seen again, its overarching vault, bright with galaxies of immutable lights, and the warm loves and fears, that swept over us as clouds, must lose their finite character and blend with God, to attain their own perfection. But we need not fear that we can lose anything by the progress of the soul. The soul may be trusted to the end. That which is so beautiful and attractive as these relations must be succeeded and supplanted only by what is more beautiful, and so on forever.

1841

Friendship

A RUDDY drop of manly blood
The surging sea outweighs;
The world uncertain comes and goes,
The lover rooted stays.
I fancied he was fled,
And, after many a year,
Glowed unexhausted kindliness
Like daily sunrise there.
My careful heart was free again,—
O friend, my bosom said,
Through thee alone the sky is arched,
Through thee the rose is red,
All things through thee take nobler form
And look beyond the earth,
The mill-round of our fate appears
A sun-path in thy worth.
Me too thy nobleness has taught
To master my despair;
The fountains of my hidden life
Are through thy friendship fair.

WE HAVE a great deal more kindness than is ever spoken. Maugre all the selfishness that chills like east winds the world, the whole human family is bathed with an element of love like a fine ether. How many persons we meet in houses, whom we scarcely speak to, whom yet we honor and who honor us! How many we see in the street, or sit with in church, whom, though silently, we warmly rejoice to be with! Read the language of these wandering eye-beams. The heart knoweth.

The effect of the indulgence of this human affection is a certain cordial exhilaration. In poetry and in common speech the emotions of benevolence and complacency which are felt towards others are likened to the material effects of fire; so swift, or much more swift, more active, more cheering, are these fine inward irradiations. From the highest degree of passionate love to the lowest degree of good will, they make the sweetness of life.

Our intellectual and active powers increase with our affection. The scholar sits down to write, and all his years of meditation do not furnish him with one good thought or happy expression; but it is necessary to write a letter to a friend—and forthwith troops of gentle thoughts invest themselves, on every hand, with chosen words. See, in any house where virtue and self-respect abide, the palpitation which the approach of a stranger causes. A commended stranger is expected and announced, and an uneasiness betwixt pleasure and pain invades all the hearts of a household. His arrival almost brings fear to the good hearts that would welcome him. The house is dusted, all things fly into their places, the old coat is exchanged for the new, and they must get up a dinner if they can. Of a commended stranger, only the good report is told by others, only the good and new is heard by us. He stands to us for humanity. He is what we wish. Having imagined and invested him, we ask how we should stand related in conversation and action with such a man, and are uneasy with fear. The same idea exalts conversation with him. We talk better than we are wont. We have the nimblest fancy, a richer memory, and our dumb devil has taken leave for the time. For long hours we can continue a series of sincere, graceful, rich communications, drawn from the oldest, secretest experience, so that they who sit by, of our own kinsfolk and acquaintance, shall feel a lively surprise at our unusual powers. But as soon as the stranger begins to intrude his partialities, his definitions, his defects into the conversation, it is all over. He has heard the first, the last, and best he will ever hear from us. He is no stranger now. Vulgarity, ignorance, misapprehension are old acquaintances. Now, when he comes, he may get the order, the dress and the dinner, but the throbbing of the heart and the communications of the soul, no more.

What is so pleasant as these jets of affection which make a young world for me again? What so delicious as a just and firm encounter of two, in a thought, in a feeling? How beautiful, on their approach to this beating heart, the steps and forms of the gifted and the true! The moment we indulge our affections, the earth is metamorphosed; there is no winter and no night; all tragedies, all ennuis vanish—all duties even; nothing fills the proceeding eternity but the forms all radiant of beloved persons. Let the soul be assured that somewhere in the universe it should rejoin its friend, and it would be content and cheerful alone for a thousand years.

I awoke this morning with devout thanksgiving for my friends, the old and the new. Shall I not call God the Beautiful, who daily showeth himself so to me in his gifts? I chide society, I embrace solitude, and yet I am not so ungrateful as not to see the wise, the lovely and the noble-minded, as from time to time they pass my gate. Who hears me, who understands me, becomes mine, a possession for all time. Nor is Nature so poor but she gives me this joy several times, and thus we weave social threads of our own, a new web of relations; and, as many thoughts in succession substantiate themselves, we shall by and by stand in a new world of our own creation, and no longer strangers and pilgrims in a traditionary globe. My friends have come to me unsought. The great God gave them to me. By oldest right, by the divine affinity of virtue with itself, I find them, or rather not I, but the Deity in me and in them derides and cancels the thick walls of individual character, relation, age, sex, circumstance, at which he usually connives, and now makes many one. High thanks I owe you, excellent lovers, who carry out the world for me to new and noble depths and enlarge the meaning of all my thoughts. These are new poetry of the first Bard—poetry without stop—hymn, ode, and epic, poetry still flowing, Apollo and the Muses chanting still. Will these too separate themselves from me again, or some of them? I know not, but I fear it not; for my relation to them is so pure that we hold by simple affinity, and the Genius of my life being thus social, the same affinity will exert its energy on whomsoever is as noble as these men and women, wherever I may be.

I confess to an extreme tenderness of nature on this point. It is almost dangerous to me to "crush the sweet poison of misused wine" [1] of the affections. A new person is to me a great event and hinders me from sleep. I have often had fine fancies about persons which have given me delicious hours; but the joy ends in the day; it yields no fruit. Thought is not born of it; my action is very little modified. I must feel pride in my friend's accomplishments as if they were mine, and a property in his virtues. I feel as warmly when he is praised as the lover when he hears applause of his engaged maiden. We overestimate the conscience of our friend. His goodness seems better than our goodness, his nature finer, his temptations less. Everything that is his, his name, his form, his dress, books and instruments, fancy

[1] Milton, *Comus,* line 47.

enhances. Our own thought sounds new and larger from his mouth.

Yet the systole and diastole of the heart are not without their analogy in the ebb and flow of love. Friendship, like the immortality of the soul, is too good to be believed. The lover, beholding his maiden, half knows that she is not verily that which he worships; and in the golden hour of friendship we are surprised with shades of suspicion and unbelief. We doubt that we bestow on our hero the virtues in which he shines and afterwards worship the form to which we have ascribed this divine inhabitation. In strictness, the soul does not respect men as it respects itself. In strict science all persons underlie the same condition of an infinite remoteness. Shall we fear to cool our love by mining for the metaphysical foundation of this Elysian temple? Shall I not be as real as the things I see? If I am, I shall not fear to know them for what they are. Their essence is not less beautiful than their appearance, though it needs finer organs for its apprehension. The root of the plant is not unsightly to science, though for chaplets and festoons we cut the stem short. And I must hazard the production of the bald fact amidst these pleasing reveries, though it should prove an Egyptian skull at our banquet. A man who stands united with his thought conceives magnificently of himself. He is conscious of a universal success, even though bought by uniform particular failures. No advantages, no powers, no gold or force, can be any match for him. I cannot choose but rely on my own poverty more than on your wealth. I cannot make your consciousness tantamount to mine. Only the star dazzles; the planet has a faint, moonlike ray. I hear what you say of the admirable parts and tried temper of the party you praise, but I see well that, for all his purple cloaks, I shall not like him unless he is at least a poor Greek like me. I cannot deny it, O friend, that the vast shadow of the Phenomenal includes thee also in its pied and painted immensity—thee also, compared with whom all else is shadow. Thou art not Being, as Truth is, as Justice is—

thou art not my soul, but a picture and effigy of that. Thou hast come to me lately and already thou are seizing thy hat and cloak. Is it not that the soul puts forth friends as the tree puts forth leaves, and presently, by the germination of new buds, extrudes the old leaf? The law of nature is alternation forevermore. Each electrical state superinduces the opposite. The soul environs itself with friends that it may enter into a grander self-acquaintance or solitude; and it goes alone for a season that it may exalt its conversation or society. This method betrays itself along the whole history of our personal relations. The instinct of affection revives the hope of union with our mates, and the returning sense of insulation recalls us from the chase. Thus every man passes his life in the search after friendship, and if he should record his true sentiment, he might write a letter like this to each new candidate for his love:

DEAR FRIEND,

If I was sure of thee, sure of thy capacity, sure to match my mood with thine, I should never think again of trifles in relation to thy comings and goings. I am not very wise; my moods are quite attainable, and I respect thy genius; it is to me as yet unfathomed; yet dare I not presume in thee a perfect intelligence of me, and so thou art to me a delicious torment. Thine ever, or never.

Yet these uneasy pleasures and fine pains are for curiosity and not for life. They are not to be indulged. This is to weave cobweb, and not cloth. Our friendships hurry to short and poor conclusions, because we have made them a texture of wine and dreams instead of the tough fiber of the human heart. The laws of friendship are austere and eternal, of one web with the laws of nature and of morals. But we have aimed at a swift and petty benefit, to suck a sudden sweetness. We snatch at the slowest fruit in the whole garden of God, which many summers and many winters must ripen. We seek our friend not sacredly, but with an adulterate passion which would appropriate him to ourselves. In vain. We are armed all over with subtle antagonisms which, as soon as we meet, begin to play, and translate all poetry into stale prose. Almost all people descend to meet. All association must be a compromise, and, what is worst, the very flower and aroma of the flower of each of the beautiful natures disappears as they approach each other. What a perpetual disappointment is actual society, even of the virtuous and gifted! After interviews have been compassed with long foresight we must be tormented presently by baffled blows, by sudden, unseasonable apathies, by epilepsies of wit and of animal spirits, in the heyday of friendship and thought. Our faculties do not play us true, and both parties are relieved by solitude.

I ought to be equal to every relation. It makes no difference how many friends I have and what content I can find in conversing with each if there be one to whom I am not equal. If I have shrunk unequal from one contest, the joy I find in all the rest becomes mean and cowardly. I should hate myself if then I made my other friends my asylum:

The valiant warrior famousèd for fight,
After a hundred victories, once foiled,
Is from the book of honor razèd quite
And all the rest forgot for which he toiled.[1]

Our impatience is thus sharply rebuked. Bashfulness and apathy are a tough husk in which a delicate organization is protected from premature ripening. It would be lost if it knew itself before any of the best souls were yet ripe enough to know and own it. Respect the *Naturlangsamkeit*[2] which hardens the ruby in a million years and works in duration in which Alps and Andes come and go as rainbows. The good spirit of our life has no heaven which is the price of rashness. Love, which is the essence of God, is not for levity, but for the total worth of

[1] Shakespeare, Sonnet 25. It reads "The *painful* warrior" and "After a *thousand* victories."

[2] Slowness or deliberateness of nature.

man. Let us not have this childish luxury in our regards but the austerest worth; let us approach our friend with an audacious trust in the truth of his heart, in the breadth, impossible to be overturned, of his foundations.

The attractions of this subject are not to be resisted, and I leave, for the time, all account of subordinate social benefit, to speak of that select and sacred relation which is a kind of absolute and which even leaves the language of love suspicious and common, so much is this purer, and nothing is so much divine.

I do not wish to treat friendships daintily, but with roughest courage. When they are real, they are not glass threads or frost-work, but the solidest thing we know. For now, after so many ages of experience, what do we know of nature or of ourselves? Not one step has man taken toward the solution of the problem of his destiny. In one condemnation of folly stand the whole universe of men. But the sweet sincerity of joy and peace which I draw from this alliance with my brother's soul is the nut itself whereof all nature and all thought is but the husk and shell. Happy is the house that shelters a friend! It might well be built, like a festal bower or arch, to entertain him a single day. Happier, if he know the solemnity of that relation and honor its law! He who offers himself a candidate for that covenant comes up, like an Olympian, to the great games where the first-born of the world are the competitors. He proposes himself for contests where Time, Want, Danger are in the lists, and he alone is victor who has truth enough in his constitution to preserve the delicacy of his beauty from the wear and tear of all these. The gifts of fortune may be present or absent, but all the speed in that contest depends on intrinsic nobleness and the contempt of trifles. There are two elements that go to the composition of friendship, each so sovereign that I can detect no superiority in either, no reason why either should be first named. One is truth. A friend is a person with whom I may be sincere. Before him I may think aloud. I am arrived at last in the presence of a man so real and equal that I may drop even those undermost garments of dissimulation, courtesy, and second thought, which men never put off, and may deal with him with the simplicity and wholeness with which one chemical atom meets another. Sincerity is the luxury allowed, like diadems and authority, only to the highest rank; *that* being permitted to speak truth, as having none above it to court or conform unto. Every man alone is sincere. At the entrance of a second person, hypocrisy begins. We parry and fend the approach of our fellow man by compliments, by gossip, by amusements, by affairs. We cover up our thought from him under a hundred folds. I knew a man who under a certain religious frenzy cast off this drapery, and omitting all compliment and commonplace, spoke to the conscience of every person he encountered, and that with great insight and beauty. At first he was resisted, and all men agreed he was mad. But persisting—as indeed he could not help doing—for some time in this course, he attained to the advantage of bringing every man of his acquaintance into true relations with him. No man would think of speaking falsely with him, or of putting him off with any chat of markets or reading-rooms. But every man was constrained by so much sincerity to the like plain dealing, and what love of nature, what poetry, what symbol of truth he had, he did certainly show him.[1] But to most of us society shows not its face and eye, but its side and its back. To stand in true relations with men in a false age is worth a fit of insanity, is it not? We can seldom go erect. Almost every man we meet requires some civility—requires to be humored; he has some fame, some talent, some whim of religion or philanthropy in his head that is not to be questioned and which spoils all conversation with him. But a friend is a sane man who exercises not my ingenuity but me.

[1] This passage alludes to Jones Very (1813-1880), poet and religious mystic, whose belief that all his actions were prompted by God led many of his friends to consider him insane.

My friend gives me entertainment without requiring any stipulation on my part. A friend therefore is a sort of paradox in nature. I who alone am, I who see nothing in nature whose existence I can affirm with equal evidence to my own, behold now the semblance of my being in all its height, variety, and curiosity, reiterated in a foreign form; so that a friend may well be reckoned the masterpiece of nature.

The other element of friendship is tenderness. We are holden to men by every sort of tie, by blood, by pride, by fear, by hope, by lucre, by lust, by hate, by admiration, by every circumstance and badge and trifle—but we can scarce believe that so much character can subsist in another as to draw us by love. Can another be so blessed and we so pure that we can offer him tenderness? When a man becomes dear to me I have touched the goal of fortune. I find very little written directly to the heart of this matter in books. And yet I have one text which I cannot choose but remember. My author [1] says, "I offer myself faintly and bluntly to those whose I effectually am, and tender myself least to him to whom I am the most devoted." I wish that friendship should have feet as well as eyes and eloquence. It must plant itself on the ground before it vaults over the moon. I wish it to be a little of a citizen before it is quite a cherub. We chide the citizen because he makes love a commodity. It is an exchange of gifts, of useful loans; it is good neighborhood; it watches with the sick; it holds the pall at the funeral; and quite loses sight of the delicacies and nobility of the relation. But though we cannot find the god under this disguise of a sutler, yet on the other hand we cannot forgive the poet if he spins his thread too fine and does not substantiate his romance by the municipal virtues of justice, punctuality, fidelity, and pity. I hate the prostitution of the name of friendship to signify modish and worldly alliances. I much prefer the company of ploughboys and tin-peddlers to the silken and perfumed amity which celebrates its days of encounter by a frivolous display, by rides

[1] Montaigne, *Essays*, I, xxxix, "A Consideration upon Cicero."

in a curricle and dinners at the best taverns. The end of friendship is a commerce the most strict and homely that can be joined; more strict than any of which we have experience. It is for aid and comfort through all the relations and passages of life and death. It is fit for serene days and graceful gifts and country rambles, but also for rough roads and hard fare, shipwreck, poverty, and persecution. It keeps company with the sallies of the wit and the trances of religion. We are to dignify to each other the daily needs and offices of man's life and embellish it by courage, wisdom, and unity. It should never fall into something usual and settled, but should be alert and inventive and add rhyme and reason to what was drudgery.

Friendship may be said to require natures so rare and costly, each so well tempered and so happily adapted, and withal so circumstanced (for even in that particular, a poet says, love demands that the parties be altogether paired), that its satisfaction can very seldom be assured. It cannot subsist in its perfection, say some of those who are learned in this warm lore of the heart, betwixt more than two. I am not quite so strict in my terms, perhaps because I have never known so high a fellowship as others. I please my imagination more with a circle of godlike men and women variously related to each other and between whom subsists a lofty intelligence. But I find this law of *one to one* peremptory for conversation, which is the practice and consummation of friendship. Do not mix waters too much. The best mix as ill as good and bad. You shall have very useful and cheering discourse at several times with two several men, but let all three of you come together and you shall not have one new and hearty word. Two may talk and one may hear, but three cannot take part in a conversation of the most sincere and searching sort. In good company there is never such discourse between two, across the table, as takes place when you leave them alone. In good company the individuals merge their egotism into a social soul exactly coextensive with the several consciousnesses there present. No partialities of friend to friend, no fondnesses of brother to sister, of wife to husband, are there pertinent, but quite otherwise. Only he may then speak who can sail on the common thought of the party and not poorly limited to his own. Now this convention, which good sense demands, destroys the high freedom of great conversation, which requires an absolute running of two souls into one.

No two men but being left alone with each other enter into simpler relations. Yet it is affinity that determines *which* two shall converse. Unrelated men give little joy to each other, will never suspect the latent powers of each. We talk sometimes of a great talent for conversation, as if it were a permanent property in some individuals. Conversation is an evanescent relation—no more. A man is reputed to have thought and eloquence; he cannot, for all that, say a word to his cousin or his uncle. They accuse his silence with as much reason as they would blame the insignificance of a dial in the shade. In the sun it will mark the hour. Among those who enjoy his thought he will regain his tongue.

Friendship requires that rare mean betwixt likeness and unlikeness that piques each with the presence of power and of consent in the other party. Let me be alone to the end of the world, rather than that my friend should overstep, by a word or a look, his real sympathy. I am equally balked by antagonism and by compliance. Let him not cease an instant to be himself. The only joy I have in his being mine is that the *not mine* is *mine*. I hate, where I looked for a manly furtherance or at least a manly resistance, to find a mush of concession. Better be a nettle in the side of your friend than his echo. The condition which high friendship demands is ability to do without it. That high office requires great and sublime parts. There must be very two before there can be very one. Let it be an alliance of two large, formidable natures, mutually beheld, mutually feared, before yet they recognize the deep identity which, beneath these disparities, unites them.

He only is fit for this society who is magnanimous; who is sure that greatness and goodness are always economy; who is not swift to intermeddle with his fortunes. Let him not intermeddle with this. Leave to the diamond its ages to grow, nor expect to accelerate the births of the eternal. Friendship demands a religious treatment. We talk of choosing our friends, but friends are self-elected. Reverence is a great part of it. Treat your friend as a spectacle. Of course he has merits that are not yours and that you cannot honor if you must needs hold him close to your person. Stand aside; give those merits room; let them mount and expand. Are you the friend of your friend's buttons or of his thought? To a great heart he will still be a stranger in a thousand particulars, that he may come near in the holiest ground. Leave it to girls and boys to regard a friend as property, and to suck a short and all-confounding pleasure instead of the noblest benefit.

Let us buy our entrance to this guild by a long probation. Why should we desecrate noble and beautiful souls by intruding on them? Why insist on rash personal relations with your friend? Why go to his house, or know his mother and brother and sisters? Why be visited by him at your own? Are these things material to our covenant? Leave this touching and clawing. Let him be to me a spirit. A message, a thought, a sincerity, a glance from him, I want, but not news, nor pottage. I can get politics and chat and neighborly conveniences from cheaper companions. Should not the society of my friend be to me poetic, pure, universal, and great as nature itself? Ought I to feel that our tie is profane in comparison with yonder bar of cloud that sleeps on the horizon or that clump of waving grass that divides the brook? Let us not vilify, but raise it to that standard. That great defying eye, that scornful beauty of his mien and action, do not pique yourself on reducing, but rather fortify and enhance. Worship his superiorities; wish him not less by a thought, but hoard and tell them all. Guard him as thy counterpart. Let him be to thee forever a sort of beautiful enemy, untamable, devoutly revered, and not a trivial conveniency to be soon outgrown and cast aside. The hues of the opal, the light of the diamond, are not to be seen if the eye is too near. To my friend I write a letter and from him I receive a letter. That seems to you a little. It suffices me. It is a spiritual gift, worthy of him to give and of me to receive. It profanes nobody. In these warm lines the heart will trust itself, as it will not to the tongue, and pour out the prophecy of a godlier existence than all the annals of heroism have yet made good.

Respect so far the holy laws of this fellowship as not to prejudice its perfect flower by your impatience for its opening. We must be our own before we can be another's. There is at least this satisfaction in crime, according to the Latin proverb—you can speak to your accomplice on even terms. *Crimen quos inquinat, æquat.*[1] To those whom we admire and love, at first we cannot. Yet the least defect of self-possession vitiates, in my judgment, the entire relation. There can never be deep peace between two spirits, never mutual respect, until in their dialogue each stands for the whole world.

What is so great as friendship, let us carry with what grandeur of spirit we can. Let us be silent—so we may hear the whisper of the gods. Let us not interfere. Who set you to cast about what you should say to the select souls or how to say anything to such? No matter how ingenious, no matter how graceful and bland. There are innumerable degrees of folly and wisdom, and for you to say aught is to be frivolous. Wait, and thy heart shall speak. Wait until the necessary and everlasting overpowers you, until day and night avail themselves of your lips. The only reward of virtue is virtue; the only way to have a friend is to be one. You shall not come nearer a man by getting into his house. If unlike, his soul only flees the faster from you, and you shall never catch a true glance of his eye. We see the noble afar off and they repel us, why should we intrude? Late, very late, we perceive that no arrangements, no intro-

[1] Crime makes equal those whom it corrupts.

ductions, no consuetudes or habits of society would be of any avail to establish us in such relations with them as we desire, but solely the uprise of nature in us to the same degree it is in them; then shall we meet as water with water; and if we should not meet them then, we shall not want them, for we are already they. In the last analysis, love is only the reflection of a man's own worthiness from other men. Men have sometimes exchanged names with their friends, as if they would signify that in their friend each loved his own soul.

The higher the style we demand of friendship, of course the less easy to establish it with flesh and blood. We walk alone in the world. Friends such as we desire are dreams and fables. But a sublime hope cheers ever the faithful heart that elsewhere, in other regions of the universal power, souls are now acting, enduring, and daring which can love us and which we can love. We may congratulate ourselves that the period of nonage, of follies, of blunders and of shame, is passed in solitude, and when we are finished men we shall grasp heroic hands in heroic hands. Only be admonished by what you already see not to strike leagues of friendship with cheap persons, where no friendship can be. Our impatience betrays us into rash and foolish alliances which no god attends. By persisting in your path, though you forfeit the little you gain the great. You demonstrate yourself, so as to put yourself out of the reach of false relations, and you draw to you the first-born of the world—those rare pilgrims whereof only one or two wander in nature at once and before whom the vulgar great show as specters and shadows merely.

It is foolish to be afraid of making our ties too spiritual, as if so we could lose any genuine love. Whatever correction of our popular views we make from insight, nature will be sure to bear us out in and, though it seem to rob us of some joy, will repay us with a greater. Let us feel if we will the absolute insulation of man. We are sure that we have all in us. We go to Europe, or we pursue persons, or we read books, in the instinctive faith that these will call it out and reveal us to ourselves. Beggars all. The persons are such as we; the Europe, an old faded garment of dead persons; the books, their ghosts. Let us drop this idolatry. Let us give over this mendicancy. Let us even bid our dearest friends farewell, and defy them, saying, 'Who are you? Unhand me: I will be dependent no more.' Ah! seest thou not, O brother, that thus we part only to meet again on a higher platform and only be more each other's because we are more our own? A friend is Janus-faced; he looks to the past and the future. He is the child of all my foregoing hours, the prophet of those to come, and the harbinger of a greater friend.

I do then with my friends as I do with my books. I would have them where I can find them, but I seldom use them. We must have society on our own terms and admit or exclude it on the slightest cause. I cannot afford to speak much with my friend. If he is great he makes me so great that I cannot descend to converse. In the great days, presentiments hover before me in the firmament. I ought then to dedicate myself to them. I go in that I may seize them, I go out that I may seize them. I fear only that I may lose them receding into the sky in which now they are only a patch of brighter light. Then, though I prize my friends, I cannot afford to talk with them and study their visions, lest I lose my own. It would indeed give me a certain household joy to quit this lofty seeking, this spiritual astronomy or search of stars, and come down to warm sympathies with you; but then I know well I shall mourn always the vanishing of my mighty gods. It is true, next week I shall have languid moods when I can well afford to occupy myself with foreign objects; then I shall regret the lost literature of your mind and wish you were by my side again. But if you come, perhaps you will fill my mind only with new visions; not with yourself but with your lusters,[1] and I shall not be able any more than now to converse with you. So I will owe to

[1] Bright-colored surfaces.

my friends this evanescent intercourse. I will receive from them not what they have but what they are. They shall give me that which properly they cannot give but which emanates from them. But they shall not hold me by any relations less subtile and pure. We will meet as though we met not, and part as though we parted not.

It has seemed to me lately more possible than I knew to carry a friendship greatly, on one side, without due correspondence on the other. Why should I cumber myself with regrets that the receiver is not capacious? It never troubles the sun that some of his rays fall wide and vain into ungrateful space and only a small part on the reflecting planet. Let your greatness educate the crude and cold companion. If he is unequal, he will presently pass away; but thou art enlarged by thy own shining and, no longer a mate for frogs and worms, dost soar and burn with the gods of the empyrean. It is thought a disgrace to love unrequited. But the great will see that true love cannot be unrequited. True love transcends the unworthy object and dwells and broods on the eternal, and when the poor interposed mask crumbles, it is not sad, but feels rid of so much earth and feels its independency the surer. Yet these things may hardly be said without a sort of treachery to the relation. The essence of friendship is entireness, a total magnanimity and trust. It must not surmise or provide for infirmity. It treats its object as a god, that it may deify both.

1841

Forbearance

HAST thou named all the birds without a gun?
Loved the wood-rose, and left it on its stalk?
At rich men's tables eaten bread and pulse?
Unarmed, faced danger with a heart of trust?
And loved so well a high behavior,
In man or maid, that thou from speech refrained,
Nobility more nobly to repay?
O, be my friend, and teach me to be thine!

1842

The Over-Soul

But souls that of his own good life partake,
He loves as his own self; dear as his eye
They are to Him: He'll never them forsake:
When they shall die, then God himself shall die:
They live, they live in blest eternity.

Henry More

Space is ample, east and west,
But two cannot go abreast,
Cannot travel in it two:
Yonder masterful cuckoo
Crowds every egg out of the nest,
Quick or dead, except its own;
A spell is laid on sod and stone,
Night and Day 've been tampered with,
Every quality and pith
Surcharged and sultry with a power
That works its will on age and hour.

THERE is a difference between one and another hour of life in their authority and subsequent effect. Our faith comes in moments; our vice is habitual. Yet there is a depth in those brief moments which constrains us to ascribe more reality to them than to all other experiences. For this reason the argument which is always forthcoming to silence those who conceive extraordinary hopes of man, namely the appeal to experience, is forever invalid and vain. We give up the past to the objector and yet we hope. He must explain this hope. We grant that human life is mean, but how did we find out that it was mean? What is the ground of this uneasiness of ours; of this old discontent? What is the universal sense of want and ignorance, but the fine innuendo by which the soul makes its enormous claim? Why do men feel that the natural history of man has never been written, but he is always leaving behind what you have said of him, and it becomes old, and books of metaphysics worthless? The philosophy of six thousand years has not searched the chambers and magazines of the soul. In its experiments there has always remained, in the last analysis, a residuum it could not resolve. Man is a stream whose source is hidden. Our being is descending into us from we know not whence. The most exact calculator has no prescience that somewhat incalculable may not balk the very next moment. I am constrained every moment to acknowledge a higher origin for events than the will I call mine.

As with events, so is it with thoughts. When I watch that flowing river which, out of regions I see not, pours for a season its streams into me, I see that I am a pensioner; not a cause but a surprised spectator of this ethereal water; that I desire and look up and put myself in the attitude of reception, but from some alien energy the visions come.

The Supreme Critic on the errors of the past and the present and the only prophet of that which must be is that great nature in which we rest as the earth lies in the soft arms of the atmosphere; that Unity, that Over-Soul, within which every man's particular being is contained and made one with all other; that common heart of which all sincere conversation is the worship, to which all right action is submission; that overpowering reality which confutes our tricks and talents and constrains everyone to pass for what he is and to speak from his character and not from his tongue, and which evermore tends to pass into our thought and hand and become wisdom and virtue and power and beauty. We live in succession, in division, in parts, in particles. Meantime within man is the soul of the whole; the wise silence; the universal beauty, to which every part and particle is equally related; the eternal ONE. And this deep power in which we exist and whose beatitude is all accessible to us is not only self-sufficing and perfect in every hour, but the act of seeing and the thing seen, the seer and the spectacle, the subject and the object, are one. We see the world piece by piece, as the sun, the moon, the animal, the tree; but the whole, of which these are the shining parts, is the soul. Only by the vision of that Wisdom can the horoscope of the ages be read, and by falling back on our better thoughts, by yielding to the spirit of prophecy which is innate in every man, we can know what it saith. Every man's words who speaks from that life must sound vain to those who do not dwell in the same thought on their own part. I dare not speak for it. My words do not carry its august sense; they fall short and cold. Only itself can inspire whom it will, and behold! their speech shall be lyrical and sweet and universal as the rising of the wind. Yet I desire, even by profane words if I may not use sacred, to indicate the heaven of this deity and to report what hints I have collected of the transcendent simplicity and energy of the Highest Law.

If we consider what happens in conversation, in reveries, in remorse, in times of passion, in surprises, in the instructions of dreams wherein often we see ourselves in masquerade—the droll disguises only magnifying and enhancing a real element and forcing it on our distant notice—we shall catch many hints that will broaden and lighten into knowledge of the secret of nature. All goes to show that the soul in man is not an organ, but animates and exercises all the organs; is not a function, like the power of memory, of calculation, of comparison, but uses these as hands and feet; is not a faculty, but a light; is not the intellect or the will but the master of the intellect and the will; is the background of our being, in which they lie—an immensity not possessed and that cannot be possessed. From within or from behind a light shines through us upon things and makes us aware that we are nothing, but the light is all. A man is the façade of a temple wherein all wisdom and all good abide. What we commonly call man, the eating, drinking, planting, counting man, does not, as we know him, represent himself, but misrepresents himself. Him we do not respect, but the soul, whose organ he is, would he let it appear through his action, would make our knees bend. When it breathes through his intellect, it is genius; when it breathes through his will, it is virtue; when it flows through his affection, it is love. And the blindness of the intellect begins when it would be something of itself. The weakness of the will begins when the individual would be something of himself. All reform aims in some one particular to let the soul have its way through us; in other words, to engage us to obey.

Of this pure nature every man is at some time sensible. Language cannot paint it with his colors. It is too subtle. It is undefinable, unmeasurable; but we know that it pervades and contains us. We know that all spiritual being is in man. A wise old proverb says, "God comes to see us without bell"; that is, as there is no screen or ceiling between our heads and the infinite heavens, so is there no bar or wall in the soul, where man, the effect, ceases and God, the cause, begins. The walls are taken away. We lie open on one side to the deeps of spiritual nature, to the attributes of God. Justice we see and know, Love, Freedom, Power. These natures no man ever got above, but they tower over us, and most in the moment when our interests tempt us to wound them.

The sovereignty of this nature whereof we speak is made known by its independency of those limitations which circumscribe us on every hand. The soul circumscribes all things. As I have said, it contradicts all experience. In like manner, it abolishes time and space. The influence of the senses has in most men overpowered the mind to that degree that the walls of time and space have come to look real and insurmountable; and to speak with levity of these limits is, in the world, the sign of insanity. Yet time and space are but inverse measures of the force of the soul. The spirit sports with time,

Can crowd eternity into an hour,
Or stretch an hour to eternity.

We are often made to feel that there is another youth and age than that which is measured from the year of our natural birth. Some thoughts always find us young and keep us so. Such a thought is the love of the universal and eternal beauty. Every man parts from that contemplation with the feeling that it rather belongs to ages than to mortal life. The least activity of the intellectual powers redeems us in a degree from the conditions of time. In sickness, in languor, give us a strain of poetry or a profound sentence, and we are refreshed; or produce a volume of Plato or Shakspeare, or remind us of their names, and instantly we come into a feeling of longevity. See how the deep divine thought reduces centuries and millenniums and makes itself present through all ages. Is the teaching of Christ less effective now than it was when first his mouth was opened? The emphasis of facts and persons in my thought has nothing to do with time. And so always the soul's scale is one, the scale of the senses and the understanding is another. Before the revelations of the soul, Time, Space, and Nature shrink away. In common speech we refer all things to time, as we habitually refer the immensely sundered stars to one concave sphere. And so we say that the Judgment is distant or near, that the Millennium approaches, that a day of certain political, moral, social reforms is at hand, and the like, when we mean that in the nature of things one of the facts we contemplate is external and fugitive and the other is permanent and connate with the soul. The things we now esteem fixed shall, one by one, detach themselves like ripe fruit from our experience and fall. The wind shall blow them none knows whither. The landscape, the figures, Boston, London, are facts as fugitive as any institution past, or any whiff of mist or smoke, and so is society, and so is the world. The soul looketh steadily forwards, creating a world before her, leaving worlds behind her. She has no dates, nor rites, nor persons, nor specialties, nor men. The soul knows only the soul; the web of events is the flowing robe in which she is clothed.

After its own law and not by arithmetic is the rate of its progress to be computed. The soul's advances are not made by gradation, such as can be represented by motion in a straight line, but rather by ascension of state, such as can be represented by metamorphosis, from the egg to the worm, from the worm to the fly. The growths of genius are of a certain *total* character that does not advance the elect individual first over John, then Adam, then Richard, and give to each the pain of discovered inferiority, but by every throe of growth the man expands there where he works, passing, at each pulsation, classes, populations, of men. With each divine impulse the mind rends the thin rinds of the visible and finite, and comes out into eternity, and inspires and expires its air. It converses with truths that have always been spoken in the world and becomes conscious of a closer sympathy with Zeno and Arrian than with persons in the house.

This is the law of moral and of mental gain. The simple rise as by specific levity not into a particular virtue, but into the region of all the virtues. They are in the spirit which contains them all. The soul requires purity, but purity is not it; requires justice, but justice is not that; requires beneficence, but is somewhat better; so that there is a kind of descent and accommodation felt when we leave speaking of moral nature to urge a virtue which it enjoins. To the wellborn child all the virtues are natural and not painfully acquired. Speak to his heart, and the man becomes suddenly virtuous.

Within the same sentiment is the germ of intellectual growth, which obeys the same law. Those who are capable of humility, of justice, of love, of aspiration, stand already on a platform that commands the sciences and arts, speech and poetry, action and grace. For whoso dwells in this moral beatitude already anticipates those special powers which men prize so highly. The lover has no talent, no skill, which passes for quite nothing with his enamored maiden, however little she may possess of related faculty; and the heart which abandons itself to the Supreme Mind finds itself related to all its works and will travel a royal road to particular knowledges and powers. In ascending to this primary and aboriginal sentiment we have come from our remote station on the circumference instantaneously to the center of the world, where, as in the closet of God, we see causes, and anticipate the universe, which is but a slow effect.

One mode of the divine teaching is the incarnation of the spirit in a form—in forms, like my own. I live in society with persons who answer to thoughts in my own mind, or express a certain obedience to the great instincts to which I live. I see its presence to them. I am certified of a common nature; and these other souls, these separated selves, draw me as nothing else can. They stir in me the new emotions we call passion; of love, hatred, fear, admiration, pity; thence come conversation, competition, persuasion, cities, and war. Persons are supplementary to the primary teaching of the soul. In youth we are mad for persons. Childhood and youth see all the world in them. But the larger experience of man discovers the identical nature appearing through them all. Persons themselves acquaint us with the impersonal. In all conversation between two persons tacit reference is made, as to a third party, to a common nature. That third party or common nature is not social; it is impersonal; is God. And so in groups where debate is earnest, and especially on high questions, the company become aware that the thought rises to an equal level in all bosoms, that all have a spiritual property in what was said, as well as the sayer. They all become wiser than they were. It arches over them like a temple, this unity of thought in which every heart beats with nobler sense of power and duty, and thinks and acts with unusual solemnity. All are conscious of attaining to a higher self-possession. It shines for all. There is a certain wisdom of humanity which is common to the greatest men with the lowest, and which our ordinary education often labors to silence and obstruct. The mind is one, and the best minds, who love truth for its own sake, think much less of property in truth. They accept it thankfully everywhere and do not label or stamp it with any man's name, for it is theirs long beforehand, and from eternity. The learned and the studious of thought have no monopoly of wisdom. Their violence of direction in some degree disqualifies them to think truly. We owe many valuable observations to people who are not very acute or profound and who say the thing without effort which we want and have long been hunting in vain. The action of the soul is oftener in that which is felt and left unsaid than in that which is said in any conversation. It broods over every society, and they unconsciously seek for it in each other. We know better than we do. We do not yet possess ourselves, and we know at the same time that we are much more. I feel the same truth how often in my trivial conversation with my neighbors, that somewhat higher in each of us overlooks this byplay and Jove nods to Jove from behind each of us.

Men descend to meet. In their habitual and mean service to the world, for which they forsake their native nobleness, they resemble those Arabian sheiks who dwell in mean houses and affect an external poverty to escape the rapacity of the Pasha and reserve all their display of wealth for their interior and guarded retirements.

As it is present in all persons, so it is in every period of life. It is adult already in the infant man. In my dealing with my child, my Latin and Greek, my accomplishments and my money stead me nothing; but as much soul as I have avails. If I am willful, he sets his will against mine, one for one, and leaves me, if I please, the degradation of beating him by my superiority of strength. But if I renounce my will and act for the soul, setting that up as umpire between us two, out of his young eyes looks the same soul; he reveres and loves with me.

The soul is the perceiver and revealer of truth. We know truth when we see it, let skeptic and scoffer say what they choose. Foolish people ask you, when you have spoken what they do not wish to hear, 'How do you know it is truth, and not an error of your own?' We know truth when we see it, from opinion, as we know when we are awake that we are awake. It was a grand sentence of Emanuel Swedenborg, which would alone indicate the greatness of that man's perception, "It is no proof of a man's understanding to be able to affirm whatever he pleases; but to be able to discern that what is true is true, and that what is false is false—this is the mark and character of intelligence." In the book I read, the good thought returns to me, as every truth will, the image of the whole soul. To the bad thought which I find in it, the same soul becomes a discerning, separating sword and lops it away. We are wiser than we know. If we will not interfere with our thought, but will act entirely, or see how the thing stands in God, we know the particular thing and everything and every man. For the Maker of all things and all persons stands behind us and casts his dread omniscience through us over things.

But beyond this recognition of its own in particular passages of the individual's experience, it also reveals truth. And here we should seek to reinforce ourselves by its very presence and to speak with a worthier, loftier strain of that advent. For the soul's communication of truth is the highest event in nature, since it then does not give somewhat from itself, but it gives itself, or passes into and becomes that man whom it enlightens; or in proportion to that truth he receives, it takes him to itself.

We distinguish the announcements of the soul, its manifestations of its own nature, by the term *Revelation*. These are always attended by the emotion of the sublime. For this communication is an influx of the Divine mind into our mind. It is an ebb of the individual rivulet before the flowing surges of the sea of life. Every distinct apprehension of this central commandment agitates men with awe and delight. A thrill passes through all men at the reception of new truth, or at the performance of a great action, which comes out of the heart of nature. In these communications the power to see is not separated from the will to do, but the insight proceeds from obedience, and the obedience proceeds from a joyful perception. Every moment when the individual feels himself invaded by it is memorable. By the necessity of our constitution a certain enthusiasm attends the individual's consciousness of that divine presence. The character and duration of this enthusiasm vary with the state of the individual, from an ecstasy and trance and prophetic inspiration—which is its rarer appearance—to the faintest glow of virtuous emotion, in which form it warms, like our household fires, all the families and associations of men, and makes society possible. A certain tendency to insanity has always attended the opening of the religious sense in men, as if they had been "blasted with excess of light." The trances of Socrates, the "union" of Plotinus, the vision of Porphyry, the conversion of Paul, the aurora of Behmen, the convulsions of George Fox and his Quakers, the illumination of Swedenborg, are of this kind. What was in the case of these remarkable persons a ravishment has, in innumerable instances in common life, been exhibited in less striking manner. Everywhere the history of religion betrays a tendency to enthusiasm. The rapture of the Moravian and Quietist, the opening of the eternal sense of the Word in the language of the New Jerusalem Church, the *revival* of the Calvinistic churches, the *experiences* of the Methodists, are varying forms of that shudder of awe and delight with which the individual soul always mingles with the universal soul.

The nature of these revelations is the same; they are perceptions of the absolute law. They are solutions of the soul's own questions. They do not answer the questions which the understanding asks. The soul answers never by words, but by the thing itself that is inquired after.

Revelation is the disclosure of the soul. The popular notion of a revelation is that it is a telling of fortunes. In past oracles of the soul the understanding seeks to find answers to sensual questions, and undertakes to tell from God how long men shall exist, what their hands shall do, and who shall be their company, adding names and dates and places. But we must pick no locks. We must check this low curiosity. An answer in words is delusive; it is really no answer to the questions you ask. Do not require a description of the countries towards which you sail. The description does not describe them to you, and tomorrow you arrive there and know them by inhabiting them. Men ask concerning the immortality of the soul, the employments of heaven, the state of the sinner, and so forth. They even dream that Jesus has left replies to precisely these interrogatories. Never a moment did that sublime spirit speak in their *patois*. To truth, justice, love, the attributes of the soul, the idea of immutableness is essentially associated. Jesus, living in these moral sentiments, heedless of sensual fortunes, heeding only the manifestations of these, never made the separation of the idea of duration from the essence of these attributes, nor uttered a syllable concerning the duration of the soul. It was left to his disciples to sever duration from the moral elements and to teach the immortality of the soul as a doctrine and maintain it by evidences. The moment the doctrine of the immortality is separately taught, man is already fallen. In the flowing of love, in the adoration of humility, there is no question of continuance. No inspired man ever asks this question or condescends to these evidences. For the soul is true to itself, and the man in whom it is shed abroad cannot wander from the present which is infinite to a future which would be finite.

These questions which we lust to ask about the future are a confession of sin. God has no answer for them. No answer in words can reply to a question of things. It is not in an arbitrary "decree of God," but in the nature of man, that a veil shuts down on the facts of tomorrow; for the soul will not have us read any other cipher than that of cause and effect. By this veil which curtains events it instructs the children of men to live in today. The only mode of obtaining an answer to these questions of the senses is to forego all low curiosity and, accepting the tide of being which floats us into the secret of nature, work and live, work and live, and all unawares the advancing soul has built and forged for itself a new condition, and the question and the answer are one.

By the same fire, vital, consecrating, celestial, which burns until it shall dissolve all things into the waves and surges of an ocean of light, we see and know each other and what spirit each is of. Who can tell the grounds of his knowledge of the character of the several individuals in his circle of friends? No man. Yet their acts and words do not disappoint him. In that man, though he knew no ill of him, he put no trust. In that other, though they had seldom met, authentic signs had yet passed to signify that he might be trusted as one who had an interest in his own character. We know each other very well—which of us has been just to himself and whether that which we teach or behold is only an aspiration or is our honest effort also.

We are all discerners of spirits. That diagnosis lies aloft in our life or unconscious power. The intercourse of society, its trade, its religion, its friendships, its quarrels, is one wide judicial investigation of character. In full court, or in small committee, or confronted face to face, accuser and accused, men offer themselves to be judged. Against their will they exhibit those decisive trifles by which character is read. But who judges? and what? Not our understanding. We do not read them by learning or craft. No; the wisdom of the wise man consists herein, that he does not judge them; he lets them judge themselves and merely reads and records their own verdict.

By virtue of this inevitable nature, private will is overpowered, and, maugre our efforts or our imperfections, your genius will speak from you, and mine from me. That which we are, we shall teach, not voluntarily but involuntarily. Thoughts come into our minds by avenues which we never left open, and thoughts go out of our minds through avenues which we never voluntarily opened. Character teaches over our head. The infallible index of true progress is found in the tone the man takes. Neither his age, nor his breeding, nor company, nor books, nor actions, nor talents, nor all together can hinder him from being deferential to a higher spirit than his own. If he have not found his home in God, his manners, his forms of speech, the turn of his sentences, the build, shall I say, of all his opinions will involuntarily confess it, let him brave it out how he will. If he have found his center, the Deity will shine through him through all the disguises of ignorance, of ungenial temperament, of unfavorable circumstance. The tone of seeking is one, and the tone of having is another.

The great distinction between teachers sacred or literary—between poets like Herbert and poets like Pope, between philosophers like Spinoza, Kant, and Coleridge, and philosophers like Locke, Paley, Mackintosh, and Stewart, between men of the world who are reckoned accomplished talkers, and here and there a fervent mystic, prophesying half insane under the infinitude of his thought—is that one class speak *from within,* or from experience, as parties and possessors of the fact; and the other class *from without,* as spectators merely, or perhaps as acquainted with the fact on the evidence of third persons. It is of no use to preach to me from without. I can do that too easily myself. Jesus speaks always from within and in a degree that transcends all others. In that is the miracle. I believe beforehand that it ought so to be. All men stand continually in the expectation of the appearance of such a teacher. But if a man do not speak from within the veil, where the word is one with that it tells of, let him lowly confess it.

The same Omniscience flows into the intellect and makes what we call genius. Much of the wisdom of the world is not wisdom, and the most illuminated class of men are no doubt superior to literary fame, and are not writers. Among the multitude of scholars and authors we feel no hallowing presence; we are sensible of a knack and skill rather than of inspiration; they have a light and know not whence it comes and call it their own; their talent is some exaggerated faculty, some overgrown member, so that their strength is a disease. In these instances the intellectual gifts do not make the impression of virtue, but almost of vice; and we feel that a man's talents stand in the way of his advancement in truth. But genius is religious. It is a larger imbibing of the common heart. It is not anomalous, but more like and not less like other men. There is in all great poets a wisdom of humanity which is superior to any talents they exercise. The author, the wit, the partisan, the fine gentleman, does not take place of the man. Humanity shines in Homer, in Chaucer, in Spenser, in Shakspeare, in Milton. They are content with truth. They use the positive degree. They seem frigid and phlegmatic to those who have been spiced with the frantic passion and violent coloring of inferior but popular writers. For they are poets by the free course which they allow to the informing soul, which through their eyes beholds again and blesses the things which it hath made. The soul is superior to its knowledge, wiser than any of its works. The great poet makes us feel our own wealth, and then we think less of his compositions. His best communication to our mind is to teach us to despise all he has done. Shakspeare carries us to such a lofty strain of intelligent activity as to suggest a wealth which beggars his own; and we then feel that the splendid works which he has created, and which in other hours we extol as a sort of self-existent poetry, take no stronger hold of real nature than the shadow of a passing traveler on the rock. The inspiration which uttered itself in Hamlet and Lear could utter things as good from day to day forever. Why then should I make account of Hamlet and Lear, as if we had not the soul from which they fell as syllables from the tongue?

This energy does not descend into individual life on any other condition than entire possession. It comes to the lowly and simple; it comes to whomsoever will put off what is foreign and proud; it comes as insight; it comes as serenity and grandeur. When we see those whom it inhabits, we are apprised of new degrees of greatness. From that inspiration the man comes back with a changed tone. He does not talk with men with an eye to their opinion. He tries them. It requires of us to be plain and true. The vain traveler attempts to embellish his life by quoting my lord and the prince and the countess, who thus said or did to *him*. The ambitious vulgar show you their spoons and brooches and rings, and preserve their cards and compliments. The more cultivated, in their account of their own experience, cull out the pleasing, poetic circumstance—the visit to Rome, the man of genius they saw, the brilliant friend they know; still further on perhaps the gorgeous landscape, the mountain lights, the mountain thoughts they enjoyed yesterday—and so seek to throw a romantic color over their life. But the soul that ascends to worship the great God is plain and true; has no rose-color, no fine friends, no chivalry, no adventures; does not want admiration; dwells in the hour that now is, in the earnest experience of the common day—by reason of the present moment and the mere trifle having become porous to thought and bibulous of the sea of light.

Converse with a mind that is grandly simple, and literature

looks like word-catching. The simplest utterances are worthiest to be written, yet are they so cheap and so things of course that in the infinite riches of the soul it is like gathering a few pebbles off the ground, or bottling a little air in a phial, when the whole earth and the whole atmosphere are ours. Nothing can pass there, or make you one of the circle, but the casting aside your trappings and dealing man to man in naked truth, plain confession, and omniscient affirmation.

Souls such as these treat you as gods would, walk as gods in the earth, accepting without any admiration your wit, your bounty, your virtue even—say rather your act of duty, for your virtue they own as their proper blood, royal as themselves and over-royal and the father of the gods. But what rebuke their plain fraternal bearing casts on the mutual flattery with which authors solace each other and wound themselves! These flatter not. I do not wonder that these men go to see Cromwell and Christina and Charles the Second and James the First and the Grand Turk. For they are, in their own elevation, the fellows of kings and must feel the servile tone of conversation in the world. They must always be a godsend to princes, for they confront them, a king to a king, without ducking or concession, and give a high nature the refreshment and satisfaction of resistance, of plain humanity, of even companionship and of new ideas. They leave them wiser and superior men. Souls like these make us feel that sincerity is more excellent than flattery. Deal so plainly with man and woman as to constrain the utmost sincerity and destroy all hope of trifling with you. It is the highest compliment you can pay. Their "highest praising," said Milton, "is not flattery, and their plainest advice is a kind of praising."

Ineffable is the union of man and God in every act of the soul. The simplest person who in his integrity worships God becomes God; yet forever and ever the influx of this better and universal self is new and unsearchable. It inspires awe and astonishment. How dear, how soothing to man, arises the idea of God, peopling the lonely place, effacing the scars of our mistakes and disappointments! When we have broken our god of tradition and ceased from our god of rhetoric, then may God fire the heart with his presence. It is the doubling of the heart itself, nay, the infinite enlargement of the heart with a power of growth to a new infinity on every side. It inspires in man an infallible trust. He has not the conviction, but the sight, that the best is the true, and may in that thought easily dismiss all particular uncertainties and fears, and adjourn to the sure revelation of time the solution of his private riddles. He is sure that his welfare is dear to the heart of being. In the presence of law to his mind he is overflowed with a reliance so universal that it sweeps away all cherished hopes and the most stable projects of mortal condition in its flood. He believes that he cannot escape from his good. The things that are really for thee gravitate to thee. You are running to seek your friend. Let your feet run, but your mind need not. If you do not find him, will you not acquiesce that it is best you should not find him? for there is a power which, as it is in you, is in him also, and could therefore very well bring you together, if it were for the best. You are preparing with eagerness to go and render a service to which your talent and your taste invite you, the love of men and the hope of fame. Has it not occurred to you that you have no right to go unless you are equally willing to be prevented from going? O, believe, as thou livest, that every sound that is spoken over the round world which thou oughtest to hear will vibrate on thine ear! Every proverb, every book, every byword that belongs to thee for aid or comfort, shall surely come home through open or winding passages. Every friend whom not thy fantastic will but the great and tender heart in thee craveth shall lock thee in his embrace. And this because the heart in thee is the heart of all; not a valve, not a wall, not an intersection is there anywhere in nature, but one blood rolls uninterruptedly an endless circulation through all men as the water of the globe is all one sea and, truly seen, its tide is one.

Let man then learn the revelation of all nature and all thought to his heart; this, namely; that the Highest dwells with him; that the sources of nature are in his own mind, if the sentiment of duty is there. But if he would know what the great God speaketh, he must 'go into his closet and shut the door,' as Jesus said. God will not make himself manifest to cowards. He must greatly listen to himself, withdrawing himself from all the accents of other men's devotion. Even their prayers are hurtful to him, until he have made his own. Our religion vulgarly stands on numbers of believers. Whenever the appeal is made—no matter how indirectly—to numbers, proclamation is then and there made that religion is not. He that finds God a sweet enveloping thought to him never counts his company. When I sit in that presence, who shall dare to come in? When I rest in perfect humility, when I burn with pure love, what can Calvin or Swedenborg say?

It makes no difference whether the appeal is to numbers or to one. The faith that stands on authority is not faith. The reliance on authority measures the decline of religion, the withdrawal of the soul. The position men have given to Jesus, now for many centuries of history, is a position of authority. It characterizes themselves. It cannot alter the eternal facts. Great is the soul, and plain. It is no flatterer, it is no follower; it never appeals from itself. It believes in itself. Before the immense possibilities of man all mere experience, all past biography, however spotless and sainted, shrinks away. Before that heaven which our presentiments foreshow us, we cannot easily praise any form of life we have seen or read of. We not only affirm that we have few great men, but, absolutely speaking, that we have none; that we have no history, no record of any character or mode of living that entirely contents us. The saints and demigods whom history worships we are constrained to accept with a grain of allowance. Though in our lonely hours we draw a new strength out of their memory, yet, pressed on our attention as they are by the thoughtless and customary, they fatigue and invade. The soul gives itself, alone, original, and pure, to the

Lonely, Original, and Pure, who, on that condition, gladly inhabits, leads, and speaks through it. Then is it glad, young, and nimble. It is not wise, but it sees through all things. It is not called religious, but it is innocent. It calls the light its own and feels that the grass grows and the stone falls by a law inferior to, and dependent on, its nature. Behold, it saith, I am born into the great, the universal mind. I, the imperfect, adore my own Perfect. I am somehow receptive of the great soul, and thereby I do overlook the sun and the stars and feel them to be the fair accidents and effects which change and pass. More and more the surges of everlasting nature enter into me, and I become public and human in my regards and actions. So come I to live in thoughts and act with energies which are immortal. Thus revering the soul, and learning, as the ancient said, that "its beauty is immense," man will come to see that the world is the perennial miracle which the soul worketh, and be less astonished at particular wonders; he will learn that there is no profane history; that all history is sacred; that the universe is represented in an atom, in a moment of time. He will weave no longer a spotted life of shreds and patches, but he will live with a divine unity. He will cease from what is base and frivolous in his life and be content with all places and with any service he can render. He will calmly front the morrow in the negligency of that trust which carries God with it and so hath already the whole future in the bottom of the heart.

1841

Brahma[1]

IF the red slayer thinks he slays,
  Or if the slain think he is slain,
They know not well the subtle ways
  I keep, and pass, and turn again.

Far or forgot to me is near;
  Shadow and sunlight are the same;
The vanished gods to me appear;
  And one to me are shame and fame.

They reckon ill who leave me out;
  When me they fly, I am the wings;
I am the doubter and the doubt,
  And I the hymn the Brahmin sings.

The strong gods pine for my abode,
  And pine in vain the sacred Seven;
But thou, meek lover of the good!
  Find me, and turn thy back on heaven.

1857

[1] The causative or creative power of the universe. This poem closely paraphrases passages in the *Vishnu Purana, Bhagavad-Gita*, and *Upanishad*, which Emerson had read and copied into his Journal.

The Poet

A MOODY child and wildly wise
Pursued the game with joyful eyes,
Which chose, like meteors, their way,
And rived the dark with private ray:
They overleapt the horizon's edge,
Searched with Apollo's privilege;
Through man, and woman, and sea, and star
Saw the dance of nature forward far;
Through worlds, and races, and terms, and times
Saw musical order, and pairing rhymes.

Olympian bards who sung
  Divine ideas below,
Which always find us young,
  And always keep us so.

THOSE who are esteemed umpires of taste are often persons who have acquired some knowledge of admired pictures or sculptures, and have an inclination for whatever is elegant; but if you inquire whether they are beautiful souls and whether their own acts are like fair pictures, you learn that they are selfish and sensual. Their cultivation is local, as if you should rub a log of dry wood in one spot to produce fire, all the rest remaining cold. Their knowledge of the fine arts is some study of rules and particulars, or some limited judgment of color or form, which is exercised for amusement or for show. It is a proof of the shallowness of the doctrine of beauty as it lies in the minds of our amateurs, that men seem to have lost the perception of the instant dependence of form upon soul. There is no doctrine of forms in our philosophy. We were put into our bodies, as fire is put into a pan to be carried about; but there is no accurate adjustment between the spirit and the organ, much less is the latter the germination of the former. So in regard to other forms, the intellectual men do not believe in any essential dependence of the material world on thought and volition. Theologians think it a pretty air-castle to talk of the spiritual meaning of a ship or a cloud, of a city or a contract, but they prefer to come again to the solid ground of historical evidence; and even the poets are contented with a civil and conformed manner of living, and to write poems from the fancy, at a safe distance from their own experience. But the highest minds of the world have never ceased to explore the double meaning, or shall I say the quadruple or the centuple or much more manifold meaning, of every sensuous fact; Orpheus, Empedocles, Heraclitus, Plato, Plutarch, Dante, Swedenborg, and the masters of sculpture, picture, and poetry. For we are not pans and barrows, nor even porters of the fire and torch-bearers, but children of the fire, made of it, and only the same divinity transmuted and at two or three removes, when we know least about it. And this hidden truth, that the fountains whence all this river of Time and its creatures floweth are intrinsically ideal and beautiful, draws us to the consideration of the nature and functions of the Poet, or the man of Beauty; to the means and materials he uses and to the general aspect of the art in the present time.

The breadth of the problem is great, for the poet is representative. He stands among partial men for the complete man, and apprises us not of his wealth, but of the common wealth. The young man reveres men of genius because, to speak truly, they are more himself than he is. They receive of the soul as he also receives, but they more. Nature enhances her beauty, to the eye of loving men, from their belief that the poet is beholding her shows at the same time. He is isolated among his contemporaries by truth and by his art, but with this consolation in his pursuits, that they will draw all men sooner or late. For all men live by truth and stand in need of expression. In love, in art, in avarice, in politics, in labor, in games, we study to utter our painful secret. The man is only half himself, the other half is his expression.

Notwithstanding this necessity to be published, adequate expression is rare. I know not how it is that we need an interpreter, but the great majority of men seem to be minors, who have not yet come into possession of their own, or mutes, who cannot report the conversation they have had with nature. There is no man who does not anticipate a supersensual utility in the sun and stars, earth and water. These stand and wait to render him a peculiar service. But there is some obstruction or some excess of phlegm in our constitution, which does not suffer them to yield the due effect. Too feeble fall the impressions of nature on us to make us artists. Every touch should thrill. Every man should be so much an artist that he could report in conversation what had befallen him. Yet, in our experience, the rays or appulses have sufficient force to arrive at the senses, but not enough to reach the quick and compel the reproduction of themselves in speech. The poet is the person in whom these powers are in balance, the man without impediment, who sees and handles that which others dream of, traverses the whole scale of experience, and is representative of man, in virtue of being the largest power to receive and to impart.

For the Universe has three children, born at one time, which reappear under different names in every system of thought, whether they be called cause, operation, and effect; or, more poetically, Jove, Pluto, Neptune; or, theologically, the Father, the Spirit, and the Son; but which we will call here the Knower, the Doer, and the Sayer. These stand respectively for the love of truth, for the love of good, and for the love of beauty. These three are equal. Each is that which he is, essentially, so that he cannot be surmounted or analyzed, and each of these three has the power of the others latent in him and his own, patent.

The poet is the sayer, the namer, and represents beauty. He is a sovereign and stands on the center. For the world is not painted or adorned, but is from the beginning beautiful; and God has not made some beautiful things, but Beauty is the creator of the universe. Therefore the poet is not any permissive potentate but is emperor in his own right. Criticism is infested with a cant of materialism, which assumes that manual skill and activity is the first merit of all men, and disparages such as say and do not, overlooking the fact that some men, namely poets, are natural sayers, sent into the world to the end of expression, and confounds them with those whose province is action but who quit it to imitate the sayers. But Homer's words are as costly and admirable to Homer as Agamemnon's victories are to Agamemnon. The poet does not wait for the hero or the sage, but, as they act and think primarily, so he writes primarily what will and must be spoken, reckoning the others, though primaries also, yet, in respect to him, secondaries and servants; as sitters or models in the studio of a painter, or as assistants who bring building materials to an architect.

For poetry was all written before time was, and whenever we are so finely organized that we can penetrate into that region where the air is music, we hear those primal warblings and attempt to write them down, but we lose ever and anon a word or a verse and substitute something of our own, and thus miswrite the poem. The men of more delicate ear write down these cadences more faithfully, and these transcripts, though imperfect, become the songs of the nations. For nature is as truly beautiful as it is good, or as it is reasonable, and must as much appear as it must be done, or be known. Words and deeds are quite indifferent modes of the divine energy. Words are also actions, and actions are a kind of words.

The sign and credentials of the poet are that he announces that which no man foretold. He is the true and only doctor; he knows and tells; he is the only teller of news, for he was present and privy to the appearance which he describes. He is a beholder of ideas and an utterer of the necessary and causal. For we do not speak now of men of poetical talents, or of industry and skill in meter, but of the true poet. I took part in a conversation the other day concerning a recent writer of lyrics, a man of subtle mind, whose head appeared to be a music-box of delicate tunes and rhythms, and whose skill and command of language we could not sufficiently praise. But when the question arose whether he was not only a lyrist but a poet, we were obliged to confess that he is plainly a contemporary, not an eternal man. He does not stand out of our low limitations, like a Chimborazo [1] under the line, running up from a torrid base through all the climates of the globe, with belts of the herbage of every latitude on its high and mottled sides; but this genius is the landscape-garden of a modern house, adorned with fountains and statues, with well-bred men and women standing and sitting in the walks and terraces. We hear through

[1] One of the highest mountains in the Andes.

all the varied music the ground-tone of conventional life. Our poets are men of talents who sing, and not the children of music. The argument is secondary, the finish of the verses is primary.

For it is not meters, but a meter-making argument that makes a poem—a thought so passionate and alive that like the spirit of a plant or an animal it has an architecture of its own, and adorns nature with a new thing. The thought and the form are equal in the order of time, but in the order of genesis the thought is prior to the form. The poet has a new thought; he has a whole new experience to unfold; he will tell us how it was with him, and all men will be the richer in his fortune. For the experience of each new age requires a new confession, and the world seems always waiting for its poet. I remember when I was young how much I was moved one morning by tidings that genius had appeared in a youth who sat near me at table. He had left his work and gone rambling none knew whither, and had written hundreds of lines, but could not tell whether that which was in him was therein told; he could tell nothing but that all was changed —man, beast, heaven, earth, and sea. How gladly we listened! how credulous! Society seemed to be compromised. We sat in the aurora of a sunrise which was to put out all the stars. Boston seemed to be at twice the distance it had the night before, or was much farther than that. Rome—what was Rome? Plutarch and Shakspeare were in the yellow leaf, and Homer no more should be heard of. It is much to know that poetry has been written this very day, under this very roof, by your side. What! that wonderful spirit has not expired! These stony moments are still sparkling and animated! I had fancied that the oracles were all silent and nature had spent her fires; and behold! all night, from every pore, these fine auroras have been streaming. Everyone has some interest in the advent of the poet, and no one knows how much it may concern him. We know that the secret of the world is profound, but who or what shall be our interpreter we know not. A mountain ramble, a new style of face, a new person, may put the key into our hands. Of course the value of genius to us is in the veracity of its report. Talent may frolic and juggle; genius realizes and adds. Mankind in good earnest have availed so far in understanding themselves and their work that the foremost watchman on the peak announces his news. It is the truest word ever spoken, and the phrase will be the fittest, most musical, and the unerring voice of the world for that time.

All that we call sacred history attests that the birth of a poet is the principal event in chronology. Man, never so often deceived, still watches for the arrival of a brother who can hold him steady to a truth until he has made it his own. With what joy I begin to read a poem which I confide in as an inspiration! And now my chains are to be broken; I shall mount above these clouds and opaque airs in which I live—opaque, though they seem transparent—and from the heaven of truth I shall see and comprehend my relations. That will reconcile me to life and renovate nature, to see trifles animated by a tendency, and to know what I am doing. Life will no more be a noise; now I shall see men and women and know the signs by which they may be discerned from fools and satans. This day shall be better than my birthday: then I became an animal; now I am invited into the science of the real. Such is the hope, but the fruition is postponed. Oftener it falls that this winged man, who will carry me into the heaven, whirls me into mists, then leaps and frisks about with me as it were from cloud to cloud, still affirming that he is bound heavenward; and I, being myself a novice, am slow in perceiving that he does not know the way into the heavens, and is merely bent that I should admire his skill to rise like a fowl or a flying fish a little way from the ground or the water; but the all-piercing, all-feeding and ocular air of heaven that man shall never inhabit. I tumble down again soon into my old nooks, and lead the life of exaggerations as before, and have lost my faith in the possibility of any guide who can lead me thither where I would be.

But leaving these victims of vanity, let us, with new hope, observe how nature, by worthier impulses, has insured the poet's fidelity to his office of announcement and affirming, namely by the beauty of things, which becomes a new and higher beauty when expressed. Nature offers all her creatures to him as a picture-language. Being used as a type, a second wonderful value appears in the object, far better than its old value; as the carpenter's stretched cord, if you hold your ear close enough, is musical in the breeze. "Things more excellent than every image," says Jamblichus,[1] "are expressed through images." Things admit of being used as symbols because nature is a symbol, in the whole and in every part. Every line we can draw in the sand has expression; and there is no body without its spirit or genius. All form is an effect of character; all condition, of the quality of the life; all harmony, of health; and for this reason a perception of beauty should be sympathetic, or proper only to the good. The beautiful rests on the foundations of the necessary. The soul makes the body, as the wise Spenser teaches:

> *So every spirit, as it is more pure,*
> *And hath in it the more of heavenly light,*
> *So it the fairer body doth procure*
> *To habit in, and it more fairly dight,*
> *With cheerful grace and amiable sight.*
> *For, of the soul, the body form doth take,*
> *For soul is form, and doth the body make.*[2]

Here we find ourselves suddenly not in a critical speculation but in a holy place, and should go very warily and reverently. We stand before the secret of the world, there where Being passes into Appearance and Unity into Variety.

The Universe is the externization of the soul. Wherever the

[1] Iamblichus, Neoplatonic philosopher of the fourth century.
[2] Edmund Spenser, "A Hymn in Honour of Beautie," stanza 19.

life is, that bursts into appearance around it. Our science is sensual, and therefore superficial. The earth and the heavenly bodies, physics and chemistry, we sensually treat, as if they were self-existent; but these are the retinue of that Being we have. "The mighty heaven," said Proclus,[1] "exhibits, in its transfigurations, clear images of the splendor of intellectual perceptions; being moved in conjunction with the unapparent periods of intellectual natures." Therefore science always goes abreast with the just elevation of the man, keeping step with religion and metaphysics; or the state of science is an index of our self-knowledge. Since everything in nature answers to a moral power, if any phenomenon remains brute and dark it is because the corresponding faculty in the observer is not yet active.

No wonder then, if these waters be so deep, that we hover over them with a religious regard. The beauty of the fable proves the importance of the sense; to the poet and to all others; or, if you please, every man is so far a poet as to be susceptible of these enchantments of nature; for all men have the thoughts whereof the universe is the celebration. I find that the fascination resides in the symbol. Who loves nature? Who does not? Is it only poets, and men of leisure and cultivation, who live with her? No; but also hunters, farmers, grooms, and butchers, though they express their affection in their choice of life and not in their choice of words. The writer wonders what the coachman or the hunter values in riding, in horses and dogs. It is not superficial qualities. When you talk with him he holds these at as slight a rate as you. His worship is sympathetic; he has no definitions, but he is commanded in nature by the living power which he feels to be there present. No imitation or playing of these things would content him; he loves the earnest of the north wind, of rain, of stone and wood and iron. A beauty not explicable is dearer than a beauty which we can see to the

[1] Proclus, or Proculus (410-485), Neoplatonic philosopher.

end of. It is nature the symbol, nature certifying the supernatural, body overflowed by life which he worships with coarse but sincere rites.

The inwardness and mystery of this attachment drive men of every class to the use of emblems. The schools of poets and philosophers are not more intoxicated with their symbols than the populace with theirs. In our political parties, compute the power of badges and emblems. See the great ball which they roll from Baltimore to Bunker Hill! In the political processions, Lowell goes in a loom, and Lynn in a shoe, and Salem in a ship. Witness the cider barrel, the log cabin, the hickory stick, the palmetto, and all the cognizances of party. See the power of national emblems. Some stars, lilies, leopards, a crescent, a lion, an eagle, or other figure which came into credit God knows how on an old rag of bunting, blowing in the wind on a fort at the ends of the earth, shall make the blood tingle under the rudest or the most conventional exterior. The people fancy they hate poetry, and they are all poets and mystics!

Beyond this universality of the symbolic language, we are apprised of the divineness of this superior use of things, whereby the world is a temple whose walls are covered with emblems, pictures, and commandments of the Deity, in this, that there is no fact in nature which does not carry the whole sense of nature; and the distinctions which we make in events and in affairs, of low and high, honest and base, disappear when nature is used as a symbol. Thought makes everything fit for use. The vocabulary of an omniscient man would embrace words and images excluded from polite conversation. What would be base, or even obscene, to the obscene, becomes illustrious, spoken in a new connection of thought. The piety of the Hebrew prophets purges their grossness. The circumcision is an example of the power of poetry to raise the low and offensive. Small and mean things serve as well as great symbols. The meaner the type by which a law is expressed, the more pungent it is, and the more lasting in the memories of men; just as we choose the smallest box or case in which any needful utensil can be carried. Bare lists of words are found suggestive to an imaginative and excited mind; as it is related of Lord Chatham that he was accustomed to read in Bailey's Dictionary when he was preparing to speak in Parliament. The poorest experience is rich enough for all the purposes of expressing thought. Why covet a knowledge of new facts? Day and night, house and garden, a few books, a few actions, serve us as well as would all trades and all spectacles. We are far from having exhausted the significance of the few symbols we use. We can come to use them yet with a terrible simplicity. It does not need that a poem should be long. Every word was once a poem. Every new relation is a new word. Also we use defects and deformities to a sacred purpose, so expressing our sense that the evils of the world are such only to the evil eye. In the old mythology, mythologists observe, defects are ascribed to divine natures, as lameness to Vulcan, blindness to Cupid, and the like, to signify exuberances.

For as it is dislocation and detachment from the life of God that makes things ugly, the poet, who re-attaches things to nature and the Whole—re-attaching even artificial things and violation of nature, to nature, by a deeper insight—disposes very easily of the most disagreeable facts. Readers of poetry see the factory village and the railway, and fancy that the poetry of the landscape is broken up by these; for these works of art are not yet consecrated in their reading; but the poet sees them fall within the great Order not less than the beehive or the spider's geometrical web. Nature adopts them very fast into her vital circles, and the gliding train of cars she loves like her own. Besides, in a centered mind, it signifies nothing how many mechanical inventions you exhibit. Though you add millions, and never so surprising, the fact of mechanics has not gained a grain's weight. The spiritual fact remains unalterable, by many or by few particulars; as no mountain is of any appreciable height to break the curve of the sphere. A shrewd country boy goes to the city for the first time, and the complacent citizen is not satisfied with his little wonder. It is not that he does not see all the fine houses and know that he never saw such before, but he disposes of them as easily as the poet finds place for the railway. The chief value of the new fact is to enhance the great and constant fact of Life, which can dwarf any and every circumstance, and to which the belt of wampum and the commerce of America are alike.

The world being thus put under the mind for verb and noun, the poet is he who can articulate it. For though life is great, and fascinates and absorbs; and though all men are intelligent of the symbols through which it is named; yet they cannot originally use them. We are symbols and inhabit symbols; workmen, work, and tools, words and things, birth and death, all are emblems; but we sympathize with the symbols, and being infatuated with the economical uses of things, we do not know that they are thoughts. The poet, by an ulterior intellectual perception, gives them a power which makes their old use forgotten, and puts eyes and a tongue into every dumb and inanimate object. He perceives the independence of the thought on the symbol, the stability of the thought, the accidency and fugacity of the symbol. As the eyes of Lyncæus were said to see through the earth, so the poet turns the world to glass, and shows us all things in their right series and procession. For through that better perception he stands one step nearer to things, and sees the flowing or metamorphosis; perceives that thought is multiform; that within the form of every creature is a force impelling it to ascend into a higher form; and following with his eyes the life, uses the forms which express that life, and so his speech flows with the flowing of nature. All the facts of the animal economy, sex, nutriment, gestation, birth, growth, are symbols of the passage of the world into the soul of man, to suffer there a change and reappear a new and higher fact. He uses forms according to the life, and not according to the form. This is true science. The poet alone knows astronomy, chemistry, vegetation, and animation, for he does not stop at these facts, but employs them as signs. He knows why the plain or meadow of space was strown with these flowers we call suns and moons and stars; why the great deep is adorned with animals, with men, and gods; for in every word he speaks he rides on them as the horses of thought.

By virtue of this science the poet is the Namer or Language-maker, naming things sometimes after their appearance, sometimes after their essence, and giving to every one its own name and not another's, thereby rejoicing the intellect, which delights in detachment or boundary. The poets made all the words, and therefore language is the archives of history and, if we must say it, a sort of tomb of the muses. For though the origin of most of our words is forgotten, each word was at first a stroke of genius, and obtained currency because for the moment it symbolized the world to the first speaker and to the hearer. The etymologist finds the deadest word to have been once a brilliant picture. Language is fossil poetry. As the limestone of the continent consists of infinite masses of the shells of animalcules, so language is made up of images or tropes, which now, in their secondary use, have long ceased to remind us of their poetic origin. But the poet names the thing because he sees it, or comes one step nearer to it than any other. This expression or naming is not art, but a second nature, grown out of the first, as a leaf out of a tree. What we call nature is a certain self-regulated motion or change; and nature does all things by her own hands, and does not leave another to baptize her but baptizes herself; and this through the metamorphosis again. I remember that a certain poet described it to me thus:

Genius is the activity which repairs the decays of things, whether wholly or partly of a material and finite kind. Nature, through all her kingdoms, insures herself. Nobody cares for planting the poor fungus; so she shakes down from the gills of one agaric countless spores, any one of which, being preserved, transmits new billions of spores tomorrow or next day. The new agaric of this hour has a chance which the old one had not. This atom of seed is thrown into a new place, not subject to the accidents which destroyed its parent two rods off. She makes a man; and having brought him to ripe age, she will no longer run the risk of losing this wonder at a blow, but she detaches from him a new self, that the kind may be safe from accidents to which the individual is exposed. So when the soul of the poet has come to ripeness of thought, she detaches and sends away from it its poems or songs—a fearless, sleepless, deathless progeny, which is not exposed to the accidents of the weary kingdom of time; a fearless, vivacious offspring, clad with wings (such was the virtue of the soul out of which they came) which carry them fast and far and infix them irrecoverably into the hearts of men. These wings are the beauty of the poet's soul. The songs, thus flying immortal from their mortal parent, are pursued by clamorous flights of censures, which swarm in far greater numbers and threaten to devour them; but these last are not winged. At the end of a very short leap they fall plump down and rot, having received from the souls out of which they came no beautiful wings. But the melodies of the poet ascend and leap and pierce into the deeps of infinite time.

So far the bard taught me, using his freer speech. But nature has a higher end, in the production of new individuals, than security, namely *ascension*, or the passage of the soul into higher forms. I knew in my younger days the sculptor who made the statue of the youth which stands in the public garden. He was, as I remember, unable to tell directly what made him happy or unhappy, but by wonderful indirections he could tell. He rose one day, according to his habit, before the dawn and saw the morning break, grand as the eternity out of which it came, and for many days after he strove to express this tranquillity, and lo! his chisel had fashioned out of marble the form of a beautiful youth, Phosphorus, whose aspect is such that it is said all persons who look on it become silent. The poet also resigns himself to his mood, and that thought which agitated him is expressed, but *alter idem,*[1] in a manner totally new. The expression is organic, or the new type which things themselves take when liberated. As, in the sun, objects paint their images on the retina of the eye, so they, sharing the aspiration of the whole universe, tend to paint a far more delicate copy of their essence in his mind. Like the metamorphosis of things into higher organic forms is their change into melodies. Over everything stands its dæmon or soul, and, as the form of the thing is reflected by the eye, so the soul of the thing is reflected by a melody. The sea, the mountain ridge, Niagara, and every flower bed, pre-exist, or super-exist, in pre-cantations, which sail like odors in the air, and when any man goes by with an ear sufficiently fine, he overhears them and endeavors to write down the notes without diluting or depraving them. And herein is the legitimation of criticism, in the mind's faith that the poems are a corrupt version of some text in nature with which they ought to be made to tally. A rhyme in one of our sonnets should not be less pleasing than the iterated nodes of a seashell or the resembling difference of a group of flowers. The pairing of the birds is an idyl, not tedious as our idyls are; a tempest is a rough ode, without falsehood or rant; a summer, with its harvest sown, reaped, and stored, is an epic song, subordinating how many admirably executed parts. Why should not the symmetry and truth that modulate these glide into our spirits, and we participate the invention of nature?

This insight, which expresses itself by what is called Imagination, is a very high sort of seeing, which does not come by study, but by the intellect being where and what it sees; by sharing the path or circuit of things through forms, and so making them translucid to others. The path of things is silent. Will they suffer a speaker to go with them? A spy they will not suffer; a lover, a poet, is the transcendency of their own nature—him they will suffer. The condition of true naming, on the poet's part, is his

[1] The same but different.

resigning himself to the divine *aura* which breathes through forms, and accompanying that.

It is a secret which every intellectual man quickly learns that beyond the energy of his possessed and conscious intellect he is capable of a new energy (as of an intellect doubled on itself) by abandonment to the nature of things; that beside his privacy of power as an individual man, there is a great public power on which he can draw, by unlocking, at all risks, his human doors and suffering the ethereal tides to roll and circulate through him; then he is caught up into the life of the Universe, his speech is thunder, his thought is law, and his words are universally intelligible as the plants and animals. The poet knows that he speaks adequately then only when he speaks somewhat wildly, or "with the flower of the mind"; not with the intellect used as an organ, but with the intellect released from all service and suffered to take its direction from its celestial life; or as the ancients were wont to express themselves, not with intellect alone but with the intellect inebriated by nectar. As the traveler who has lost his way throws his reins on his horse's neck and trusts to the instinct of the animal to find his road, so must we do with the divine animal who carries us through this world. For if in any manner we can stimulate this instinct, new passages are opened for us into nature; the mind flows into and through things hardest and highest, and the metamorphosis is possible.

This is the reason why bards love wine, mead, narcotics, coffee, tea, opium, the fumes of sandalwood and tobacco, or whatever other procurers of animal exhilaration. All men avail themselves of such means as they can, to add this extraordinary power to their normal powers; and to this end they prize conversation, music, pictures, sculpture, dancing, theaters, traveling, war, mobs, fires, gaming, politics, or love, or science, or animal intoxication—which are several coarser or finer *quasi*-mechanical substitutes for the true nectar, which is the ravishment of the intellect by coming nearer to the fact. These are auxiliaries to the centrifugal tendency of a man, to his passage out into free space, and they help him to escape the custody of that body in which he is pent up, and of that jail-yard of individual relations in which he is enclosed. Hence a great number of such as were professionally expressers of Beauty, as painters, poets, musicians, and actors, have been more than others wont to lead a life of pleasure and indulgence; all but the few who received the true nectar; and, as it was a spurious mode of attaining freedom, as it was an emancipation not into the heavens but into the freedom of baser places, they were punished for that advantage they won, by a dissipation and deterioration. But never can any advantage be taken of nature by a trick. The spirit of the world, the great calm presence of the Creator, comes not forth to the sorceries of opium or of wine. The sublime vision comes to the pure and simple soul in a clean and chaste body. That is not an inspiration which we owe to narcotics, but some counterfeit excitement and fury. Milton says that the lyric poet may drink wine and live generously, but the epic poet, he who shall sing of the gods and their descent unto men, must drink water out of a wooden bowl. For poetry is not 'Devil's wine,' but God's wine. It is with this as it is with toys. We fill the hands and nurseries of our children with all manner of dolls, drums, and horses; withdrawing their eyes from the plain face and sufficing objects of nature, the sun and moon, the animals, the water and stones, which should be their toys. So the poet's habit of living should be set on a key so low that the common influences should delight him. His cheerfulness should be the gift of the sunlight; the air should suffice for his inspiration, and he should be tipsy with water. That spirit which suffices quiet hearts, which seems to come forth to such from every dry knoll of sere grass, from every pine stump and half-imbedded stone on which the dull March sun shines, comes forth to the poor and hungry, and such as are of simple taste. If thou fill thy brain with Boston and New York, with fashion and covetousness, and wilt stimulate thy jaded senses with wine and French coffee, thou shalt find no radiance of wisdom in the lonely waste of the pine woods.

If the imagination intoxicates the poet, it is not inactive in other men. The metamorphosis excites in the beholder an emotion of joy. The use of symbols has a certain power of emancipation and exhilaration for all men. We seem to be touched by a wand which makes us dance and run about happily like children. We are like persons who come out of a cave or cellar into the open air. This is the effect on us of tropes, fables, oracles, and all poetic forms. Poets are thus liberating gods. Men have really got a new sense and found within their world another world, or nest of worlds; for, the metamorphosis once seen, we divine that it does not stop. I will not now consider how much this makes the charm of algebra and the mathematics, which also have their tropes, but it is felt in every definition; as when Aristotle defines *space* to be an immovable vessel in which things are contained; or when Plato defines a *line* to be a flowing point; or *figure* to be a bound of solid; and many the like. What a joyful sense of freedom we have when Vitruvius announces the old opinion of artists that no architect can build any house well who does not know something of anatomy. When Socrates, in *Charmides*, tells us that the soul is cured of its maladies by certain incantations, and that these incantations are beautiful reasons, from which temperance is generated in souls; when Plato calls the world an animal, and Timæus affirms that the plants also are animal; or affirms a man to be a heavenly tree, growing with his root, which is his head, upward; and, as George Chapman, following him, writes,

> *So in our tree of man, whose nervie root*
> *Springs in his top;*[1]

when Orpheus speaks of hoariness as "that white flower which marks extreme old age"; when Proclus calls the universe the statue of the intellect; when Chaucer, in his praise of Gentilesse, compares good blood in mean condition to fire, which, though carried to the darkest house betwixt this and the mount of

[1] In the dedication of his translation of Homer.

Caucasus, will yet hold its natural office and burn as bright as if twenty thousand men did it behold; when John saw, in the Apocalypse, the ruin of the world through evil and the stars fall from heaven as the fig tree casteth her untimely fruit; when Æsop reports the whole catalogue of common daily relations through the masquerade of birds and beasts; we take the cheerful hint of the immortality of our essence and its versatile habit and escapes, as when the gypsies say of themselves, 'It is in vain to hang them, they cannot die.'

The poets are thus liberating gods. The ancient British bards had for the title of their order, "Those who are free throughout the world." They are free, and they make free. An imaginative book renders us much more service at first, by stimulating us through its tropes, than afterward when we arrive at the precise sense of the author. I think nothing is of any value in books excepting the transcendental and extraordinary. If a man is inflamed and carried away by his thought, to that degree that he forgets the authors and the public and heeds only this one dream which holds him like an insanity, let me read his paper, and you may have all the arguments and histories and criticism. All the value which attaches to Pythagoras, Paracelsus, Cornelius Agrippa, Cardan, Kepler, Swedenborg, Schelling, Oken, or any other who introduces questionable facts into his cosmogony, as angels, devils, magic, astrology, palmistry, mesmerism, and so on, is the certificate we have of departure from routine, and that here is a new witness. That also is the best success in conversation, the magic of liberty, which puts the world like a ball in our hands. How cheap even the liberty then seems; how mean to study, when an emotion communicates to the intellect the power to sap and upheave nature; how great the perspective! nations, times, systems, enter and disappear like threads in tapestry of large figure and many colors; dream delivers us to dream, and while the drunkenness lasts we will sell our bed, our philosophy, our religion, in our opulence.

There is good reason why we should prize this liberation. The fate of the poor shepherd, who, blinded and lost in the snowstorm, perishes in a drift within a few feet of his cottage door, is an emblem of the state of man. On the brink of the waters of life and truth, we are miserably dying. The inaccessibleness of every thought but that we are in is wonderful. What if you come near to it; you are as remote when you are nearest as when you are farthest. Every thought is also a prison; every heaven is also a prison. Therefore we love the poet, the inventor, who in any form, whether in an ode or in an action or in looks and behavior, has yielded us a new thought. He unlocks our chains and admits us to a new scene.

This emancipation is dear to all men, and the power to impart it, as it must come from greater depth and scope of thought, is a measure of intellect. Therefore all books of the imagination endure, all which ascend to that truth that the writer sees nature beneath him, and uses it as his exponent. Every verse or sentence possessing this virtue will take care of its own immortality. The religions of the world are the ejaculations of a few imaginative men.

But the quality of the imagination is to flow, and not to freeze. The poet did not stop at the color or the form, but read their meaning; neither may he rest in this meaning, but he makes the same objects exponents of his new thought. Here is the difference betwixt the poet and the mystic, that the last nails a symbol to one sense, which was a true sense for a moment, but soon becomes old and false. For all symbols are fluxional; all language is vehicular and transitive, and is good, as ferries and horses are, for conveyance, not, as farms and houses are, for homestead. Mysticism consists in the mistake of an accidental and individual symbol for an universal one. The morning-redness happens to be the favorite meteor to the eyes of Jacob Behmen, and comes to stand to him for truth and faith; and, he believes, should stand for the same realities to every reader. But the first reader prefers as naturally the symbol of a mother and child or a gardener and his bulb or a jeweler polishing a gem. Either of these, or of a myriad more, are equally good to the person to whom they are significant. Only they must be held lightly and be very willingly translated into the equivalent terms which others use. And the mystic must be steadily told: All that you say is just as true without the tedious use of that symbol as with it. Let us have a little algebra, instead of this trite rhetoric—universal signs, instead of these village symbols—and we shall both be gainers. The history of hierarchies seems to show that all religious error consisted in making the symbol too stark and solid and was at last nothing but an excess of the organ of language.

Swedenborg, of all men in the recent ages, stands eminently for the translator of nature into thought. I do not know the man in history to whom things stood so uniformly for words. Before him the metamorphosis continually plays. Everything on which his eye rests obeys the impulses of moral nature. The figs become grapes whilst he eats them. When some of his angels affirmed a truth, the laurel twig which they held blossomed in their hands. The noise which at a distance appeared like gnashing and thumping on coming nearer was found to be the voice of disputants. The men in one of his visions, seen in heavenly light, appeared like dragons and seemed in darkness; but to each other they appeared as men, and when the light from heaven shone into their cabin, they complained of the darkness, and were compelled to shut the window that they might see.

There was this perception in him which makes the poet or seer an object of awe and terror, namely that the same man or society of men may wear one aspect to themselves and their companions, and a different aspect to higher intelligences. Certain priests, whom he describes as conversing very learnedly together, appeared to the children who were at some distance like dead horses; and many the like misappearances. And instantly the mind inquires whether these fishes under the bridge, yonder oxen in the pasture, those dogs in the yard are immutably fishes, oxen and dogs or only so appear to me, and perchance to themselves appear upright men; and whether I appear as a man to all eyes. The Brahmins and Pythagoras propounded the same question, and if any poet has witnessed the transformation he doubtless found it in harmony with various experiences. We have all seen changes as considerable in wheat and caterpillars. He is the poet and shall draw us with love and terror, who sees through the flowing vest the firm nature, and can declare it.

I look in vain for the poet whom I describe. We do not with sufficient plainness or sufficient profoundness address ourselves to life, nor dare we chaunt our own times and social circumstance. If we filled the day with bravery, we should not shrink from celebrating it. Time and nature yield us many gifts, but not yet the timely man, the new religion, the reconciler, whom all things await. Dante's praise is that he dared to write his autobiography in colossal cipher, or into universality. We have yet had no genius in America, with tyrannous eye, which knew the value of our incomparable materials and saw in the barbarism and materialism of the times another carnival of the same gods whose picture he so much admires in Homer; then in the Middle Ages; then in Calvinism. Banks and tariffs, the newspaper and caucus, Methodism and Unitarianism, are flat and dull to dull people, but rest on the same foundations of wonder as the town of Troy and the temple of Delphi, and are as swiftly passing away. Our log-rolling, our stumps and their politics, our fisheries, our Negroes and Indians, our boats, and our Repudiations, the wrath of rogues and the pusillanimity of honest men, the northern trade, the southern planting, the western clearing, Oregon and Texas, are yet unsung. Yet America is a poem in our eyes; its ample geography dazzles the imagination, and it will not wait long for meters. If I have not found that excellent combination of gifts in my countrymen which I seek, neither could I aid myself to fix the idea of the poet by reading now and then in Chalmers's collection of five centuries of English poets. These are wits more than poets, though there have been poets among them. But when we adhere to the ideal of the poet, we have our difficulties even with Milton and Homer. Milton is too literary, and Homer too literal and historical.

But I am not wise enough for a national criticism, and must use the old largeness a little longer, to discharge my errand from the muse to the poet concerning his art.

Art is the path of the creator to his work. The paths or methods are ideal and eternal, though few men ever see them; not the artist himself for years, or for a lifetime, unless he come into the conditions. The painter, the sculptor, the composer, the epic rhapsodist, the orator, all partake one desire, namely to express themselves symmetrically and abundantly, not dwarfishly and fragmentarily. They found or put themselves in certain conditions, as, the painter and sculptor before some impressive human figures; the orator into the assembly of the people; and the others in such scenes as each has found exciting to his intellect; and each presently feels the new desire. He hears a voice, he sees a beckoning. Then he is apprised, with wonder, what herds of dæmons hem him in. He can no more rest; he says, with the old painter, "By God it is in me and must go forth of me." He pursues a beauty, half seen, which flies before him. The poet pours out verses in every solitude. Most of the things he says are conventional, no doubt; but by and by he says something which is original and beautiful. That charms him. He would say nothing else but such things. In our way of talking we say, 'That is yours, this is mine'; but the poet knows well that it is not his; that it is as strange and beautiful to him as to you; he would fain hear the like eloquence at length. Once having tasted this immortal ichor, he cannot have enough of it, and as an admirable creative power exists in these intellections, it is of the last importance that these things get spoken. What a little of all we know is said! What drops of all the sea of our science are baled up! and by what accident it is that these are exposed, when so many secrets sleep in nature! Hence the necessity of speech and song; hence these throbs and heart-beatings in the orator, at the door of the assembly, to the end namely that thought may be ejaculated as Logos, or Word.

Doubt not, O poet, but persist. Say, "It is in me, and shall out." Stand there, balked and dumb, stuttering and stammering, hissed and hooted, stand and strive, until at last rage draw out of thee that *dream*-power which every night shows thee is thine own; a power transcending all limit and privacy, and by virtue of which a man is the conductor of the whole river of electricity. Nothing walks, or creeps, or grows, or exists, which must not in turn arise and walk before him as exponent of his meaning. Comes he to that power, his genius is no longer exhaustible. All the creatures by pairs and by tribes pour into his mind as into a Noah's ark, to come forth again to people a new world. This is like the stock of air for our respiration or for the combustion of our fireplace; not a measure of gallons, but the entire atmosphere if wanted. And therefore, the rich poets, as Homer, Chaucer, Shakspeare, and Raphael, have obviously no limits to their works except the limits of their lifetime, and resemble a mirror carried through the street, ready to render an image of every created thing.

O poet! a new nobility is conferred in groves and pastures, and not in castles or by the sword blade any longer. The conditions are hard but equal. Thou shalt leave the world and know the muse only. Thou shalt not know any longer the times, customs, graces, politics, or opinions of men, but shalt take all from the muse. For the time of towns is tolled from the world by funereal chimes, but in nature the universal hours are counted by succeeding tribes of animals and plants, and by growth of joy on joy. God wills also that thou abdicate a manifold and duplex life and that thou be content that others speak for thee. Others shall be thy gentlemen and shall represent all courtesy and worldly life for thee; others shall do the great and resounding actions also. Thou shalt lie close hid with nature, and canst not be afforded to the Capitol or the Exchange. The world is full of renunciations and apprenticeships, and this is thine; thou must pass for a fool and a churl for a long season. This is the screen and sheath in which Pan has protected his well-beloved flower, and thou shalt be known only to thine own, and they shall console thee with tenderest love. And thou shalt not be able to rehearse the names of thy friends in thy verse, for an old shame before the holy ideal. And this is the reward: that the ideal shall be real to thee, and the impressions of the actual world shall fall like summer rain, copious, but not troublesome to thy invulnerable essence. Thou shalt have the whole land for thy park and manor, the sea for thy bath and navigation, without tax and without envy; the woods and the rivers thou shalt own, and thou shalt possess that wherein others are only tenants and boarders. Thou true land-lord! sea-lord! air-lord! Wherever snow falls or water flows or birds fly, wherever day and night meet in twilight, wherever the blue heaven is hung by clouds or sown with stars, wherever are forms with transparent boundaries, wherever are outlets into celestial space, wherever is danger, and awe, and love—there is Beauty, plenteous as rain, shed for thee, and though thou shouldst walk the world over, thou shalt not be able to find a condition inopportune or ignoble.

1844

Days

DAUGHTERS of Time, the hypocritic Days,
Muffled and dumb like barefoot dervishes,
And marching single in an endless file,
Bring diadems and fagots in their hands.
To each they offer gifts after his will,
Bread, kingdoms, stars, and sky that holds them all.
I, in my pleached garden, watched the pomp,
Forgot my morning wishes, hastily
Took a few herbs and apples, and the Day
Turned and departed silent. I, too late,
Under her solemn fillet saw the scorn.

1857

Politics

Gold and iron are good
To buy iron and gold;
All earth's fleece and food
For their like are sold.
Boded Merlin wise,
Proved Napoleon great,—
Nor kind nor coinage buys
Aught above its rate.
Fear, Craft and Avarice
Cannot rear a State.
Out of dust to build
What is more than dust,—
Walls Amphion piled
Phœbus stablish must.
When the Muses nine
With the Virtues meet,
Find to their design
An Atlantic seat,
By green orchard boughs
Fended from the heat,
Where the statesman ploughs
Furrow for the wheat;
When the Church is social worth,
When the state-house is the hearth,
Then the perfect State is come,
The republican at home.

IN DEALING with the State we ought to remember that its institutions are not aboriginal, though they existed before we were born; that they are not superior to the citizen; that every one of them was once the act of a single man; every law and usage was a man's expedient to meet a particular case; that they all are imitable, all alterable; we may make as good, we may make better. Society is an illusion to the young citizen. It lies before him in rigid repose, with certain names, men, and institutions rooted like oak trees to the center, round which all arrange themselves the best they can. But the old statesman knows that society is fluid; there are no such roots and centers, but any particle may suddenly become the center of the movement and compel the system to gyrate round it; as every man of strong will, like Pisistratus or Cromwell, does for a time, and every man of truth, like Plato or Paul, does forever. But politics rest on necessary foundations, and cannot be treated with levity. Republics abound in young civilians who believe that the laws make the city, that grave modifications of the policy and modes of living and employments of the population, that commerce, education, and religion may be voted in or out; and that any measure, though it were absurd, may be imposed on a people if only you can get sufficient voices to make it a law. But the wise know that foolish legislation is a rope of sand which perishes in the twisting; that the State must follow and not lead the character and progress of the citizen; the strongest usurper is quickly got rid of; and they only who build on Ideas, build for eternity; and that the form of government which prevails is the expression of what cultivation exists in the population which permits it. The law is only a memorandum. We are superstitious and esteem the statute somewhat: so much life as it has in the character of living men is its force. The statute stands there to say, Yesterday we agreed so and so, but how feel ye this article today? Our statute is a currency which we stamp with our own portrait: it soon becomes unrecognizable, and in process of time will return to the mint. Nature is not democratic nor limited-monarchical, but despotic, and will not be fooled or abated of any jot of her authority by the pertest of her sons; and as fast as the public mind is opened to more intelligence, the code is seen to be brute and stammering. It speaks not articulately and must be made to. Meantime the education of the general mind never stops. The reveries of the true and simple are prophetic. What the tender poetic youth dreams and prays and paints today, but shuns the ridicule of saying aloud, shall presently be the resolutions of public bodies; then shall be carried as grievance and bill of rights through conflict and war, and then shall be triumphant law and establishment for a hundred years, until it gives place in turn to new prayers and pictures. The history of the State sketches in coarse outline the progress of thought, and follows at a distance the delicacy of culture and of aspiration.

The theory of politics which has possessed the mind of men, and which they have expressed the best they could in their laws and in their revolutions, considers persons and property as the two objects for whose protection government exists. Of persons, all have equal rights, in virtue of being identical in nature. This interest of course with its whole power demands a democracy. Whilst the rights of all as persons are equal, in virtue of their access to reason, their rights in property are very unequal. One man owns his clothes, and another owns a county. This accident, depending primarily on the skill and virtue of the parties, of which there is every degree, and secondarily on patrimony, falls unequally, and its rights of course are unequal. Personal rights, universally the same, demand a government framed on the ratio of the census; property demands a government framed on the ratio of owners and of owning. Laban, who has flocks and herds, wishes them looked after by an officer on the frontiers, lest the Midianites shall drive them off; and pays a tax to that end. Jacob has no flocks or herds and no fear of the Midianites, and pays no tax to the officer. It seemed fit that Laban and Jacob should have equal rights to elect the officer who is to defend their persons, but that Laban and not Jacob should elect the officer who is to guard the sheep and cattle. And if question arise whether additional officers or watchtowers should be provided, must not Laban and Isaac and those who must sell part of their herds to buy protection for the rest judge better of this, and with more right, than Jacob, who, because he is a youth and a traveler, eats their bread and not his own?

In the earliest society the proprietors made their own wealth, and so long as it comes to the owners in the direct way, no other opinion would arise in any equitable community than that property should make the law for property and persons the law for persons.

But property passes through donation or inheritance to those who do not create it. Gift, in one case, makes it as really the new owner's, as labor made it the first owner's: in the other case, of patrimony, the law makes an ownership which will be valid in each man's view according to the estimate which he sets on the public tranquillity.

It was not, however, found easy to embody the readily admitted principle that property should make law for property and persons for persons; since persons and property mixed themselves in every transaction. At last it seemed settled that the rightful distinction was that the proprietors should have more elective franchise than non-proprietors, on the Spartan principle of "calling that which is just, equal; not that which is equal, just."

That principle no longer looks so self-evident as it appeared in former times, partly because doubts have arisen whether too much weight had not been allowed in the laws to property, and such a structure given to our usages as allowed the rich to encroach on the poor, and to keep them poor; but mainly because there is an instinctive sense, however obscure and yet inarticulate, that the whole constitution of property on its present tenures is injurious, and its influence on persons deteriorating and degrading; that truly the only interest for the consideration of the State is persons; that property will always follow persons; that the highest end of government is the culture of men; and that if men can be educated, the institutions will share their improvement and the moral sentiment will write the law of the land.

If it be not easy to settle the equity of this question, the peril is less when we take note of our natural defenses. We are kept by better guards than the vigilance of such magistrates as we commonly elect. Society always consists in greatest part of young and foolish persons. The old, who have seen through the hypocrisy of courts and statesmen, die and leave no wisdom to their sons. They believe their own newspaper, as their fathers did at their age. With such an ignorant and deceivable majority, States would soon run to ruin, but that there are limitations beyond which the folly and ambition of governors cannot go. Things have their laws as well as men; and things refuse to be trifled with. Property will be protected. Corn will not grow unless it is planted and manured; but the farmer will not plant or hoe it unless the chances are a hundred to one that he will cut and harvest it. Under any forms, persons and property must and will have their just sway. They exert their power, as steadily as matter its attraction. Cover up a pound of earth never so cunningly, divide and subdivide it; melt it to liquid, convert it to gas; it will always weigh a pound; it will always attract and resist other matter by the full virtue of one pound weight: and the attributes of a person, his wit and his moral energy, will exercise, under any law or extinguishing tyranny, their proper force, if not overtly, then covertly; if not for the law, then against it; if not wholesomely, then poisonously; with right or by might.

The boundaries of personal influence it is impossible to fix, as persons are organs of moral or supernatural force. Under the dominion of an idea which possesses the minds of multitudes, as civil freedom or the religious sentiment, the powers of persons are no longer subjects of calculation. A nation of men unanimously bent on freedom or conquest can easily confound the arithmetic of statists, and achieve extravagant actions, out of all proportion to their means; as the Greeks, the Saracens, the Swiss, the Americans, and the French have done.

In like manner to every particle of property belongs its own attraction. A cent is the representative of a certain quantity of corn or other commodity. Its value is in the necessities of the animal man. It is so much warmth, so much bread, so much water, so much land. The law may do what it will with the owner of property; its just power will still attach to the cent. The law may in a mad freak say that all shall have power except the owners of property; they shall have no vote. Nevertheless, by a higher law, the property will year after year write every statute that respects property. The non-proprietor will be the scribe of the proprietor. What the owners wish to do, the whole power of property will do, either through the law or else in defiance of it. Of course I speak of all the property, not merely of the great estates. When the rich are outvoted, as frequently happens, it is the joint treasury of the poor which exceeds their accumulations. Every man owns something, if it is only a cow or a wheelbarrow or his arms, and so has that property to dispose of.

The same necessity which secures the rights of person and property against the malignity or folly of the magistrate determines the form and methods of governing which are proper to each nation and to its habit of thought and nowise transferable to other states of society. In this country we are very vain of our political institutions, which are singular in this, that they sprung, within the memory of living men, from the character and condition of the people, which they still express with sufficient fidelity—and we ostentatiously prefer them to any other in history. They are not better but only fitter for us. We may be wise in asserting the advantage in modern times of the democratic form, but to other states of society, in which religion consecrated the monarchical, that and not this was expedient. Democracy is better for us because the religious sentiment of the present time accords better with it. Born democrats, we are nowise qualified to judge of monarchy, which, to our fathers living in the monarchical idea, was also relatively right. But our institutions, though in coincidence with the spirit of the age, have not any exemption from the practical defects which have discredited other forms. Every actual State is corrupt. Good men must not obey the laws too well. What satire on government can equal the severity of censure conveyed in the word *politic*, which now for ages has signified *cunning*, intimating that the State is a trick?

The same benign necessity and the same practical abuse appear in the parties, into which each State divides itself, of opponents and defenders of the administration of the government. Parties are also founded on instincts and have better guides to their own humble aims than the sagacity of their leaders. They have nothing perverse in their origin, but rudely mark some real and lasting relation. We might as wisely reprove the east wind or the frost as a political party whose members, for the most part, could give no account of their position, but stand for the defense of those interests in which they find themselves. Our quarrel with them begins when they quit this deep natural ground at the bidding of some leader and, obeying personal considerations, throw themselves into the maintenance and defense of points nowise belonging to their system. A party is perpetually corrupted by personality. Whilst we absolve the association from dishonesty, we cannot extend the same charity to their leaders. They reap the rewards of the docility and zeal of the masses which they direct. Ordinarily our parties are parties of circumstance and not of principle; as the planting interest in conflict with the commercial; the party of capitalists and that of operatives: parties which are identical in their moral character and which can easily change ground with each other in the support of many of their measures. Parties of principle, as religious sects, or the party of free trade, of universal suffrage, of abolition of slavery, of abolition of capital punishment, degenerate into personalities or would inspire enthusiasm. The vice of our leading parties in this country (which may be cited as a fair specimen of these societies of opinion) is that they do not plant themselves on the deep and necessary grounds to which they are respectively entitled, but lash themselves to fury in the carrying of some local and momentary measure, nowise useful to the commonwealth. Of the two great parties which at this hour almost share the nation between them, I should say that one was the best cause, and the other contains the best men. The philosopher, the poet, or the religious man, will of course wish to cast his vote with the democrat, for free trade, for wide suffrage, for the abolition of legal cruelties in the penal code, and for facilitating in every manner the access of the young and the poor to the sources of wealth and power. But he can rarely accept the persons whom the so-called popular party propose to him as representatives of these liberalities. They have not at heart the ends which give to the name of democracy what hope and virtue are in it. The spirit of our American radicalism is destructive and aimless: it is not loving; it has no ulterior and divine ends, but is destructive only out of hatred and selfishness. On the other side, the conservative party, composed of the most moderate, able, and cultivated part of the population, is timid and merely defensive of property. It vindicates no right, it aspires to no real good, it brands no crime, it proposes no generous policy; it does not build, nor write, nor cherish the arts, nor foster religion, nor establish schools, nor encourage science, nor emancipate the slave, nor befriend the poor, or the Indian, or the immigrant. From neither party, when in power, has the world any benefit to expect in science, art, or humanity, at all commensurate with the resources of the nation.

I do not for these defects despair of our republic. We are not at the mercy of any waves of chance. In the strife of ferocious parties, human nature always finds itself cherished; as the children of the convicts at Botany Bay are found to have as healthy a moral sentiment as other children. Citizens of feudal states are alarmed at our democratic institutions lapsing into anarchy, and the older and more cautious among ourselves are learning from Europeans to look with some terror at our turbulent freedom. It is said that in our license of construing the Constitution and in the despotism of public opinion we have no anchor; and one foreign observer thinks he has found the safeguard in the sanctity of Marriage among us; and another thinks he has found it in our Calvinism. Fisher Ames expressed the popular security more wisely, when he compared a monarchy and a republic, saying that a monarchy is a merchantman which sails well, but will sometimes strike on a rock and go to the bottom; whilst a republic is a raft which would never sink, but then your feet are always in water. No forms can have any dangerous importance whilst we are befriended by the laws of things. It makes no difference how many tons' weight of atmosphere presses on our heads, so long as the same pressure resists it within the lungs. Augment the mass a thousandfold, it cannot begin to crush us, as long as reaction is equal to action. The fact of two poles, of two forces, centripetal and centrifugal, is universal, and each force by its own activity develops the other. Wild liberty develops iron conscience. Want of liberty, by strengthening law and decorum, stupefies conscience. 'Lynch-law' prevails only where there is greater hardihood and self-subsistency in the leaders. A mob cannot be a permanency; everybody's interest requires that it should not exist, and only justice satisfies all.

We must trust infinitely to the beneficent necessity which shines through all laws. Human nature expresses itself in them as characteristically as in statues, or songs, or railroads; and an abstract of the codes of nations would be a transcript of the common conscience. Governments have their origin in the moral identity of men. Reason for one is seen to be reason for another, and for every other. There is a middle measure which satisfies all parties, be they never so many or so resolute for their own. Every man finds a sanction for his simplest claims and deeds, in decisions of his own mind, which he calls Truth and Holiness. In these decisions all the citizens find a perfect agreement, and only in these; not in what is good to eat, good to wear, good use of time, or what amount of land or of public aid each is entitled to claim. This truth and justice men presently endeavor to make application of to the measuring of land, the apportionment of service, the protection of life and property. Their first endeavors, no doubt, are very awkward. Yet absolute right is the first governor; or, every government is an impure theocracy. The idea after which each community is aiming to make and mend its law is the will of the wise man. The wise man it cannot find in nature, and it makes awkward but earnest efforts to secure his government by contrivance; as by causing the entire people to give their voices on every measure; or by a double choice to get the representation of the whole; or by a selection of the best citizens; or to secure the advantages of efficiency and internal peace by confiding the government to one, who may himself select his agents. All forms of government symbolize an immortal government, common to all dynasties and independent of numbers, perfect where two men exist, perfect where there is only one man.

Every man's nature is a sufficient advertisement to him of the character of his fellows. My right and my wrong is their right and their wrong. Whilst I do what is fit for me and abstain from what is unfit, my neighbor and I shall often agree in our means, and work together for a time to one end. But whenever I find my dominion over myself not sufficient for me and undertake the direction of him also, I overstep the truth and come into false relations to him. I may have so much more skill or strength than he that he cannot express adequately his sense of wrong, but it is a lie and hurts like a lie both him and me. Love and nature cannot maintain the assumption; it must be executed by a practical lie, namely by force. This undertaking for another is the blunder which stands in colossal ugliness in the governments of the world. It is the same thing in numbers as in a pair, only not quite so intelligible. I can see well enough a great difference between my setting myself down to a self-control and my going to make somebody else act after my views; but when a quarter of the human race assume to tell me what I must do, I may be too much disturbed by the circumstances to see so clearly the absurdity of their command. Therefore all public ends look vague and quixotic beside private ones. For any laws but those which men make for themselves are laughable. If I put myself in the place of my child, and we stand in one thought and see that things are thus or thus, that perception is law for him and me. We are both there, both act. But if, without carrying him into the thought, I look over into his plot and, guessing how it is with him, ordain this or that, he will never obey me. This is the history of governments—one man does something which is to bind another. A man who cannot be acquainted with me taxes me; looking from afar at me ordains that a part of my labor shall go to this or that whimsical end—not as I, but as he happens to fancy. Behold the consequence. Of all debts men are least willing to pay the taxes. What a satire is this on government! Everywhere they think they get their money's worth, except for these.

Hence the less government we have the better—the fewer laws, and the less confided power. The antidote to this abuse of formal government is the influence of private character, the growth of the Individual; the appearance of the principal to supersede the proxy; the appearance of the wise man; of whom the existing government is, it must be owned, but a shabby imitation. That which all things tend to educe; which freedom, cultivation, intercourse, revolutions, go to form and deliver, is character; that is the end of Nature, to reach unto this coronation of her king. To educate the wise man the State exists, and with the appearance of the wise man the State expires. The appearance of character makes the State unnecessary. The wise man is the State. He needs no army, fort, or navy—he loves men too well; no bribe, or feast, or palace, to draw friends to him; no vantage ground, no favorable circumstance. He needs no library, for he has not done thinking; no church, for he is a prophet; no statute book, for he has the lawgiver; no money, for he is value; no road, for he is at home where he is; no experience, for the life of the creator shoots through him and looks from his eyes. He has no personal friends, for he who has the spell to draw the prayer and piety of all men unto him needs not husband and educate a few to share with him a select and poetic life. His relation to men is angelic; his memory is myrrh to them, his presence, frankincense and flowers.

We think our civilization near its meridian, but we are yet only at the cock-crowing and the morning star. In our barbarous society the influence of character is in its infancy. As a political power, as the rightful lord who is to tumble all rulers from their chairs, its presence is hardly yet suspected. Malthus and Ricardo quite omit it; the *Annual Register* is silent; in the *Conversations' Lexicon* it is not set down; the President's Message, the Queen's Speech, have not mentioned it; and yet it is never nothing. Every thought which genius and piety throw into the world alters the world. The gladiators in the lists of power feel, through all their frocks of force and simulation, the presence of worth. I think the very strife of trade and ambition is confession of this divinity; and successes in those fields are the poor amends, the fig-leaf with which the shamed soul attempts to hide its nakedness. I find the like unwilling homage in all quarters. It is because we know how much is due from us that we are impatient to show some petty talent as a substitute for worth. We are haunted by a conscience of this right to grandeur of character and are false to it. But each of us has some talent, can do somewhat useful, or graceful, or formidable, or amusing, or lucrative. That we do, as an apology to others and to ourselves for not reaching the mark of a good and equal life. But it does not satisfy *us*, whilst we thrust it on the notice of our companions. It may throw dust in their eyes, but does not smooth our own brow or give us the tranquillity of the strong when we walk abroad. We do penance as we go. Our talent is a sort of expiation, and we are constrained to reflect on our splendid moment with a certain humiliation, as somewhat too fine and not as one act of many acts, a fair expression of our permanent energy. Most persons of ability meet in society with a kind of tacit appeal. Each seems to say, 'I am not all here.' Senators and presidents have climbed so high with pain enough, not because they think the place specially agreeable, but as an apology for real worth, and to vindicate their manhood in our eyes. This conspicuous chair is their compensation to themselves for being of a poor, cold, hard nature. They must do what they can. Like one class of forest animals, they have nothing but a prehensile tail; climb they must or crawl. If a man found himself so rich-natured that he could enter into strict relations with the best persons and make life serene around him by the dignity and sweetness of his behavior, could he afford to circumvent the favor of the caucus and the press and covet relations so hollow and pompous as those of a politician? Surely nobody would be a charlatan who could afford to be sincere.

The tendencies of the times favor the idea of self-government and leave the individual, for all code, to the rewards and penalties of his own constitution; which work with more energy than we believe whilst we depend on artificial restraints. The movement in this direction has been very marked in modern history. Much has been blind and discreditable, but the nature of the revolution is not affected by the vices of the revolters; for this is a purely moral force. It was never adopted by any party in history, neither can be. It separates the individual from all party and unites him at the same time to the race. It promises a recognition of higher rights than those of personal freedom or the security of property. A man has a right to be employed, to be trusted, to be loved, to be revered. The power of love as the basis of a State has never been tried. We must not imagine that all things are lapsing into confusion if every tender protestant be not compelled to bear his part in certain social conventions; nor doubt that roads can be built, letters carried, and the fruit of labor secured, when the government of force is at an end. Are our methods now so excellent that all competition is hopeless? Could not a nation of friends even devise better ways? On the other hand, let not the most conservative and timid fear anything from a premature surrender of the bayonet and the system of force. For according to the order of nature, which is quite superior to our will, it stands thus: there will always be a government of force where men are selfish; and when they are pure enough to abjure the code of force they will be wise enough to see how these public ends of the post office, of the highway, of commerce and the exchange of property, of museums and libraries, of institutions of art and science, can be answered.

We live in a very low state of the world and pay unwilling tribute to governments founded on force. There is not, among the most religious and instructed men of the most religious and civil nations, a reliance on the moral sentiment and a sufficient belief in the unity of things, to persuade them that society can be maintained without artificial restraints, as well as the solar system; or that the private citizen might be reasonable and a good neighbor, without the hint of a jail or a confiscation. What is strange too, there never was in any man sufficient faith in the power of rectitude to inspire him with the broad design of renovating the State on the principle of right and love. All those who have pretended this design have been partial reformers, and have admitted in some manner the supremacy of the bad State. I do not call to mind a single human being who has steadily denied the authority of the laws, on the simple ground of his own moral nature. Such designs, full of genius and full of faith as they are, are not entertained except avowedly as air-pictures. If the individual who exhibits them dare to think them practicable, he disgusts scholars and churchmen; and men of talent and women of superior sentiments cannot hide their contempt. Not the less does nature continue to fill the heart of youth with suggestions of this enthusiasm, and there are now men—if indeed I can speak in the plural number—more exactly, I will say, I have just been conversing with one man, to whom no weight of adverse experience will make it for a moment appear impossible that thousands of human beings might exercise towards each other the grandest and simplest sentiments, as well as a knot of friends, or a pair of lovers.

1844

Each and All

LITTLE thinks, in the field, yon red-cloaked clown,
Of thee from the hilltop looking down;
The heifer that lows in the upland farm,
Far-heard, lows not thine ear to charm;
The sexton, tolling his bell at noon,
Deems not that great Napoleon
Stops his horse, and lists with delight,
Whilst his files sweep round yon Alpine height;
Nor knowest thou what argument
Thy life to thy neighbor's creed has lent.
All are needed by each one;
Nothing is fair or good alone.
I thought the sparrow's note from heaven,
Singing at dawn on the alder bough;
I brought him home, in his nest, at even;
He sings the song, but it cheers not now,
For I did not bring home the river and sky;–
He sang to my ear,–they sang to my eye.
The delicate shells lay on the shore;
The bubbles of the latest wave
Fresh pearls to their enamel gave,
And the bellowing of the savage sea
Greeted their safe escape to me.
I wiped away the weeds and foam,
I fetched my sea-born treasures home;
But the poor, unsightly, noisome things

Had left their beauty on the shore
With the sun and the sand and the wild uproar.
The lover watched his graceful maid,
As 'mid the virgin train she strayed,
Nor knew her beauty's best attire
Was woven still by the snow-white choir.
At last she came to his hermitage,
Like the bird from the woodlands to the cage;–
The gay enchantment was undone,
A gentle wife, but fairy none.
Then I said, "I covet truth;
Beauty is unripe childhood's cheat;
I leave it behind with the games of youth":–
As I spoke, beneath my feet
The ground-pine curled its pretty wreath,
Running over the club-moss burrs;
I inhaled the violet's breath;
Around me stood the oaks and firs;
Pine-cones and acorns lay on the ground;
Over me soared the eternal sky,
Full of light and of deity;
Again I saw, again I heard,
The rolling river, the morning bird;–
Beauty through my senses stole;
I yielded myself to the perfect whole.

1839

Illusions

Flow, flow the waves hated,
Accursed, adored,
The waves of mutation;
No anchorage is.
Sleep is not, death is not;
Who seem to die live.
House you were born in,
Friends of your spring-time,
Old man and young maid,
Day's toil and its guerdon,
They are all vanishing,
Fleeing to fables,
Cannot be moored.
See the stars through them,
Through treacherous marbles.
Know the stars yonder,
The stars everlasting,
Are fugitive also,
And emulate, vaulted,
The lambent heat lightning
And fire-fly's flight.

When thou dost return
On the wave's circulation,
Behold the shimmer,
The wild dissipation,
And, out of endeavor
To change and to flow,
The gas become solid,
And phantoms and nothings
Return to be things,
And endless imbroglio
Is law and the world,—
Then first shalt thou know,
That in the wild turmoil,
Horsed on the Proteus,
Thou ridest to power,
And to endurance.

SOME years ago, in company with an agreeable party, I spent a long summer day in exploring the Mammoth Cave in Kentucky. We traversed, through spacious galleries affording a solid masonry foundation for the town and county overhead, the six or eight black miles from the mouth of the cavern to the innermost recess which tourists visit—a niche or grotto made of one seamless stalactite, and called, I believe, "Serena's Bower." I lost the light of one day. I saw high domes and bottomless pits; heard the voice of unseen waterfalls; paddled three quarters of a mile in the deep Echo River, whose waters are peopled with the blind fish; crossed the streams "Lethe" and "Styx"; plied with music and guns the echoes in these alarming galleries; saw every form of stalagmite and stalactite in the sculptured and fretted chambers—icicle, orange-flower, acanthus, grapes, and snowball. We shot Bengal lights into the vaults and groins of the sparry cathedrals and examined all the masterpieces which the four combined engineers, water, limestone, gravitation, and time, could make in the dark.

The mysteries and scenery of the cave had the same dignity that belongs to all natural objects, and which shames the fine things to which we foppishly compare them. I remarked especially the mimetic habit with which nature, on new instruments, hums her old tunes, making night to mimic day, and chemistry to ape vegetation. But I then took notice and still chiefly remember that the best thing which the cave had to offer was an illusion. On arriving at what is called the "Star-Chamber," our lamps were taken from us by the guide and extinguished or put aside, and, on looking upwards, I saw or seemed to see the night heaven thick with stars glimmering more or less brightly over our heads, and even what seemed a comet flaming among them. All the party were touched with astonishment and pleasure. Our musical friends sung with much feeling a pretty song, "The stars are in the quiet sky," etc., and I sat down on the rocky floor to enjoy the serene picture. Some crystal specks in the black ceiling high overhead, reflecting the light of a half-hid lamp, yielded this magnificent effect.

I own I did not like the cave so well for eking out its sublimities with this theatrical trick. But I have had many experiences like it, before and since; and we must be content to be pleased without too curiously analyzing the occasions. Our conversation with nature is not just what it seems. The cloud-rack, the sunrise and sunset glories, rainbows and Northern Lights are not quite so spheral as our childhood thought them, and the part our organization plays in them is too large. The senses interfere everywhere and mix their own structure with all they report of. Once we fancied the earth a plane, and stationary. In admiring the sunset we do not yet deduct the rounding, coordinating, pictorial powers of the eye.

The same interference from our organization creates the most of our pleasure and pain. Our first mistake is the belief that the circumstance gives the joy which we give to the circumstance. Life is an ecstasy. Life is sweet as nitrous oxide; and the fisherman dripping all day over a cold pond, the switchman at the railway intersection, the farmer in the field, the Negro in the rice-swamp, the fop in the street, the hunter in the woods, the barrister with the jury, the belle at the ball, all ascribe a certain pleasure to their employment, which they themselves give it. Health and appetite impart the sweetness to sugar, bread, and meat. We fancy that our civilization has got on far, but we still come back to our primers.

We live by our imaginations, by our admirations, by our sentiments. The child walks amid heaps of illusions which he does not like to have disturbed. The boy, how sweet to him is his fancy! how dear the story of barons and battles! What a hero he is, whilst he feeds on his heroes! What a debt is his to imaginative books! He has no better friend or influence than Scott, Shakspeare, Plutarch, and Homer. The man lives to other objects, but who dare affirm that they are more real? Even the prose of the streets is full of refractions. In the life of the dreariest alderman, fancy enters into all details and colors them with rosy hue. He imitates the air and actions of people whom he admires, and is raised in his own eyes. He pays a debt quicker to a rich man than to a poor man. He wishes the bow and compliment of some leader in the state or in society; weighs what he says; perhaps he never comes nearer to him for that, but dies at last better contented for this amusement of his eyes and his fancy.

The world rolls, the din of life is never hushed. In London, in Paris, in Boston, in San Francisco, the carnival, the masquerade is at its height. Nobody drops his domino. The unities, the fictions of the piece it would be an impertinence to break. The chapter of fascinations is very long. Great is paint; nay, God is the painter; and we rightly accuse the critic who destroys too many illusions. Society does not love its unmaskers. It was wittily if somewhat bitterly said by D'Alembert, "*qu'un état de vapeur était un état très fâcheux, parce-qu'il nous faisait voir les choses comme elles sont.*" [1] I find men victims of illusion in all parts of life. Children, youths, adults and old men, all are led by one bauble or another. Yoganindra, the goddess of illusion, Proteus, or Momus, or Gylfi's Mocking [2]—for the Power has many names—is stronger than the Titans, stronger than

[1] Emerson usually quoted from memory and very inaccurately. Translated literally this passage means: "that a misty state is a very troublesome one, because it makes us see things as they are." But such a statement is neither witty, nor bitter, nor true. No one sees things clearer in a fog. Mrs. F. M. Loving suggests that, instead of *vapeur*, Emerson may have meant *nature*; the sense of the passage would then be: "that a state of nature is a very troublesome one, because it makes us see things as they are."

[2] Yoganindra is the Hindu personification of illusion. Proteus, the old man of the sea in Greek myth, could change his shape at will. Momus, the god of mockery, ridiculed everything that the gods did. The *Gylfaginning* or *Delusion of Gylfi*, in the *Prose Edda* describes how the Norse king Gylfi was deceived by the gods at Asgard.

Apollo. Few have overheard the gods or surprised their secret. Life is a succession of lessons which must be lived to be understood. All is riddle, and the key to a riddle is another riddle. There are as many pillows of illusion as flakes in a snowstorm. We wake from one dream into another dream. The toys to be sure are various, and are graduated in refinement to the quality of the dupe. The intellectual man requires a fine bait; the sots are easily amused. But everybody is drugged with his own frenzy, and the pageant marches at all hours, with music and banner and badge.

Amid the joyous troop who give in to the charivari, comes now and then a sad-eyed boy whose eyes lack the requisite refractions to clothe the show in due glory, and who is afflicted with a tendency to trace home the glittering miscellany of fruits and flowers to one root. Science is a search after identity, and the scientific whim is lurking in all corners. At the State Fair a friend of mine complained that all the varieties of fancy pears in our orchards seem to have been selected by somebody who had a whim for a particular kind of pear, and only cultivated such as had that perfume; they were all alike. And I remember the quarrel of another youth with the confectioners, that when he racked his wit to choose the best confits in the shops, in all the endless varieties of sweetmeat he could find only three flavors, or two. What then? Pears and cakes are good for something; and because you unluckily have an eye or nose too keen, why need you spoil the comfort which the rest of us find in them? I knew a humorist who in a good deal of rattle had a grain or two of sense. He shocked the company by maintaining that the attributes of God were two—power and risibility, and that it was the duty of every pious man to keep up the comedy. And I have known gentlemen of great stake in the community, but whose sympathies were cold—presidents of colleges and governors and senators—who held themselves bound to sign every temperance pledge, and act with Bible societies and missions and peace-makers, and cry *Hist-a-boy!* to every good dog. We must not carry comity too far, but we all have kind impulses in this direction. When the boys come into my yard for leave to gather horse-chestnuts, I own I enter into nature's game, and effect to grant the permission reluctantly, fearing that any moment they will find out the imposture of that showy chaff. But this tenderness is quite unnecessary; the enchantments are laid on very thick. Their young life is thatched with them. Bare and grim to tears is the lot of the children in the hovel I saw yesterday; yet not the less they hung it round with frippery romance, like the children of the happiest fortune, and talked of "the dear cottage where so many joyful hours had flown." Well, this thatching of hovels is the custom of the country. Women, more than all, are the element and kingdom of illusion. Being fascinated, they fascinate. They see through Claude-Lorraines. And how dare anyone, if he could, pluck away the *coulisses,* stage effects and ceremonies, by which they live? Too pathetic, too pitiable, is the region of affection and its atmosphere always liable to *mirage.*

We are not very much to blame for our bad marriages. We live amid hallucinations; and this especial trap is laid to trip up our feet with, and all are tripped up first or last. But the mighty Mother who had been so sly with us, as if she felt that she owed us some indemnity, insinuates into the Pandora-box of marriage some deep and serious benefits and some great joys. We find a delight in the beauty and happiness of children that makes the heart too big for the body. In the worst-assorted connections there is ever some mixture of true marriage. Teague and his jade get some just relations of mutual respect, kindly observation, and fostering of each other; learn something, and would carry themselves wiselier if they were now to begin.

'Tis fine for us to point at one or another fine madman, as if there were any exempts. The scholar in his library is none. I, who have all my life heard any number of orations and debates, read poems and miscellaneous books, conversed with many geniuses, am still the victim of any new page; and if Marmaduke, or Hugh, or Moosehead, or any other, invent a new style or mythology, I fancy that the world will be all brave and right if dressed in these colors, which I had not thought of. Then at once I will daub with this new paint; but it will not stick. 'Tis like the cement which the peddler sells at the door; he makes broken crockery hold with it, but you can never buy of him a bit of the cement which will make it hold when he is gone.

Men who make themselves felt in the world avail themselves of a certain fate in their constitution which they know how to use. But they never deeply interest us unless they lift a corner of the curtain, or betray, never so slightly, their penetration of what is behind it. 'Tis the charm of practical men that outside of their practicality are a certain poetry and play, as if they led the good horse Power by the bridle, and preferred to walk, though they can ride so fiercely. Bonaparte is intellectual, as well as Cæsar; and the best soldiers, sea-captains, and railway men have a gentleness when off duty, a good-natured admission that there are illusions, and who shall say that he is not their sport? We stigmatize the cast-iron fellows who cannot so detach themselves, as "dragon-ridden," "thunder-stricken," and fools of fate, with whatever powers endowed.

Since our tuition is through emblems and indirections, it is well to know that there is method in it, a fixed scale and rank above rank in the phantasms. We begin low with coarse masks and rise to the most subtle and beautiful. The red men told Columbus "they had an herb which took away fatigue"; but he found the illusion of "arriving from the east at the Indies" more composing to his lofty spirit than any tobacco. Is not our faith in the impenetrability of matter more sedative than narcotics? You play with jackstraws, balls, bowls, horse and gun, estates and politics; but there are finer games before you. Is not time a pretty toy? Life will show you masks that are worth all your carnivals. Yonder mountain must migrate into your mind. The fine stardust and nebulous blur in Orion, "the portentous year of Mizar and Alcor," must come down and be dealt with in your household thought. What if you shall come to discern that the play and playground of all this pompous history are radiations from yourself, and that the sun borrows his beams? What terrible questions we are learning to ask! The former men believed in magic, by which temples, cities, and men were swallowed up, and all trace of them gone. We are coming on the secret of a magic which sweeps out of men's minds all vestige of theism and beliefs which they and their fathers held and were framed upon.

There are deceptions of the senses, deceptions of the passions, and the structural, beneficent illusions of sentiment and of the intellect. There is the illusion of love, which attributes to the beloved person all which that person shares with his or her family, sex, age, or condition, nay, with the human mind itself. 'Tis these which the lover loves, and Anna Matilda gets the credit of them. As if one shut up always in a tower, with one window through which the face of heaven and earth could be seen, should fancy that all the marvels he beheld belonged to that window. There is the illusion of time, which is very deep; who has disposed of it?—or come to the conviction that what seems the *succession* of thought is only the distribution of wholes into causal series? The intellect sees that every atom carries the whole of nature; that the mind opens to omnipotence; that, in the endless striving and ascents, the metamorphosis is entire, so that the soul doth not know itself in its own act when the act is perfected. There is illusion that shall deceive even the elect. There is illusion that shall deceive even the performer of the miracle. Though he make his body, he denies that he makes it. Though the world exist from thought, thought is daunted in presence of the world. One after the other we accept the mental laws, still resisting those which follow, which however must be accepted. But all our concessions only compel us to new profusion. And what avails it that science has come to treat space and time as simply forms of thought, and the material world as hypothetical, and withal our pretension of *property* and even of selfhood are fading with the rest, if, at last, even our thoughts are not finalities, but the incessant flowing and ascension reach these also, and each thought which yesterday was a finality, today is yielding to a larger generalization?

With such volatile elements to work in, it is no wonder if our estimates are loose and floating. We must work and affirm, but we have no guess of the value of what we say or do. The cloud is now as big as your hand, and now it covers a county. That story of Thor, who was set to drain the drinking-horn in Asgard and to wrestle with the old woman and to run with the runner Lok, and presently found that he had been drinking up the sea, and wrestling with Time, and racing with Thought, describes us, who are contending, amid these seeming trifles, with the supreme energies of nature. We fancy we have fallen into bad company and squalid condition, low debts, shoe-bills, broken glass to pay for, pots to buy, butcher's meat, sugar, milk, and coal. 'Set me some great task, ye gods! and I will show my spirit.' 'Not so,' says the good Heaven; 'plod and plough, vamp your old coats and hats, weave a shoestring; great affairs and the best wine by and by.' Well, 'tis all phantasm; and if we weave a yard of tape in all humility and as well as we can, long hereafter we shall see it was no cotton tape at all but some galaxy which we braided, and that the threads were Time and Nature.

We cannot write the order of the variable winds. How can we penetrate the law of our shifting moods and susceptibility? Yet they differ as all and nothing. Instead of the firmament of yesterday, which our eyes require, it is today an eggshell which coops us in; we cannot even see what or where our stars of destiny are. From day to day the capital facts of human life are hidden from our eyes. Suddenly the mist rolls up and reveals them, and we think how much good time is gone that might have been saved had any hint of these things been shown. A sudden rise in the road shows us the system of mountains, and all the summits, which have been just as near us all the year, but quite out of mind. But these alterations are not without their order, and we are parties to our various fortunes. If life seem a succession of dreams, yet poetic justice is done in dreams also. The visions of good men are good; it is the undisciplined will that is whipped with bad thoughts and bad fortunes. When we break the laws, we lose our hold on the central reality. Like sick men in hospitals, we change only from bed to bed, from one folly to another; and it cannot signify much what becomes of such castaways, wailing, stupid, comatose creatures, lifted from bed to bed, from the nothing of life to the nothing of death.

In this kingdom of illusions we grope eagerly for stays and foundations. There is none but a strict and faithful dealing at home and a severe barring out of all duplicity or illusion there. Whatever games are played with us, we must play no games with ourselves, but deal in our privacy with the last honesty and truth. I look upon the simple and childish virtues of veracity and honesty as the root of all that is sublime in character. Speak as you think, be what you are, pay your debts of all kinds. I prefer to be owned as sound and solvent, and my word as good as my bond, and to be what cannot be skipped, or dissipated, or undermined, to all the *éclat* in the universe. This reality is the foundation of friendship, religion, poetry, and art. At the top or at the bottom of all illusions, I set the cheat which still leads us to work and live for appearances; in spite of our conviction, in all sane hours, that it is what we really are that avails, with friends, with strangers, and with fate or fortune.

One would think from the talk of men that riches and poverty were a great matter; and our civilization mainly respects it. But the Indians say that they do not think the white man, with his brow of care, always toiling, afraid of heat and cold, and keeping within doors, has any advantage of them. The permanent interest of every man is never to be in a false position, but to have the weight of Nature to back him in all that he does.

Riches and poverty are a thick or thin costume; and our life—the life of all of us—identical. For we transcend the circumstance continually and taste the real quality of existence; as in our employments, which only differ in the manipulations but express the same laws; or in our thoughts, which wear no silks and taste no ice creams. We see God face to face every hour, and know the savor of nature.

The early Greek philosophers Heraclitus and Xenophanes measured their force on this problem of identity. Diogenes of Apollonia said that unless the atoms were made of one stuff, they could never blend and act with one another.[1] But the Hindoos, in their sacred writings, express the liveliest feeling, both of the essential identity and of that illusion which they conceive variety to be. "The notions, '*I am*,' and '*This is mine*,' which influence mankind, are but delusions of the mother of the world. Dispel, O Lord of all creatures! the conceit of knowledge which proceeds from ignorance." And the beatitude of man they hold to lie in being freed from fascination.

The intellect is stimulated by the statement of truth in a trope, and the will by clothing the laws of life in illusions. But the unities of Truth and of Right are not broken by the disguise. There need never be any confusion in these. In a crowded life of many parts and performers, on a stage of nations, or in the obscurest hamlet in Maine or California, the same elements offer the same choices to each new comer, and, according to his election, he fixes his fortune in absolute nature. It would be hard to put more mental and moral philosophy than the Persians have thrown into a sentence:

Fooled thou must be, though wisest of the wise:
Then be the fool of virtue, not of vice.

[1] These three philosophers lived in the fifth century B.C. Heraclitus maintained that everything originated in fire and was in a constant change or flux. Xenophanes asserted that there was one god who pervaded everything. Diogenes of Apollonia taught that air was the source of everything.

There is no chance and no anarchy in the universe. All is system and gradation. Every god is there sitting in his sphere. The young mortal enters the hall of the firmament; there is he alone with them alone, they pouring on him benedictions and gifts, and beckoning him up to their thrones. On the instant, and incessantly, fall snowstorms of illusions. He fancies himself in a vast crowd which sways this way and that and whose movement and doings he must obey: he fancies himself poor, orphaned, insignificant. The mad crowd drives hither and thither, now furiously commanding this thing to be done, now that. What is he that he should resist their will, and think or act for himself? Every moment new changes and new showers of deceptions to baffle and distract him. And when, by and by, for an instant, the air clears and the cloud lifts a little, there are the gods still sitting around him on their thrones—they alone with him alone.

1860

Terminus[a]

It is time to be old,
To take in sail:
The god of bounds,
Who sets to seas a shore,
Came to me in his fatal rounds,
And said: "No more!
No farther shoot
Thy broad ambitious branches, and thy root.
Fancy departs: no more invent;
Contract thy firmament
To compass of a tent.
There's not enough for this and that,
Make thy option which of two;
Economize the failing river,
Not the less revere the Giver,
Leave the many and hold the few.
Timely wise accept the terms,
Soften the fall with wary foot;
A little while
Still plan and smile,
And—fault of novel germs—
Mature the unfallen fruit.
Curse, if thou wilt, thy sires,
Bad husbands of their fires,
Who, when they gave thee breath,

[a]The Roman god of boundaries.

Failed to bequeath
The needful sinew stark as once,
The Baresark [1] marrow of thy bones,
But left a legacy of ebbing veins,
Inconstant heat and nerveless reins,—
Amid the Muses, left thee deaf and dumb,
Amid the gladiators, halt and numb."

As the bird trims her to the gale,
I trim myself to the storm of time,
I man the rudder, reef the sail,
Obey the voice at eve obeyed at prime:
"Lowly faithful, banish fear,
Right onward drive unharmed;
The port, well worth the cruise, is near,
And every wave is charmed."

1867

[1] Berserks, Norse warriors, who fought with almost superhuman strength.